D0426740

"Ya cannot spend your whole life running, Willow," Duncan said softly.

"You're smart enough to know that no matter how fast ya are, it's only an illusion of safety. Love comes unbidden, lass, and is as unstoppable as the sunrise."

Willow pulled free, returning her gaze to the fire. "You don't think you're a bit arrogant to assume I love you?" she asked without accusation.

"Nay," he said, his chest rumbling in amusement. "You're the arrogant one, if ya think to continue denying your feelings."

He lifted her chin again, gave her a quick kiss on the lips, then tucked her head against him with a deep sigh. "I've the patience to out-wait ya, Willow, and the means to eventually capture and keep ya."

She popped her head up and frowned at him. "What means?"

"My body, of course," he said, arching one brow. "Ya can't seem to get enough of it."

N'APPARTIENT PLUS
À LA BIBLIOTHÈQUE
MUNICIPALE DE GATINEAU

The Dangerous Protector is also available as an eBook.

ALSO BY JANET CHAPMAN

Charming the Highlander
Loving the Highlander
Wedding the Highlander
The Seductive Impostor
Tempting the Highlander

Published by Pocket Books

BIBLIOTHÈQUE MUNICIPALE DE GATINEAU

JANET CHAPMAN

THE DANGEROUS PROTECTOR

POCKET STAR BOOKS

New York   London   Toronto   Sydney

The sale of this book without its cover is unauthorized. If you purchased this book without a cover, you should be aware that it was reported to the publisher as "unsold and destroyed." Neither the author nor the publisher has received payment for the sale of this "stripped book."

This book is a work of fiction. Names, characters, places and incidents are products of the author's imagination or are used fictitiously. Any resemblance to actual events or locales or persons, living or dead, is entirely coincidental.

An *Original* Publication of POCKET BOOKS

A Pocket Star Book published by
POCKET BOOKS, a division of Simon & Schuster, Inc.
1230 Avenue of the Americas, New York, NY 10020

Copyright © 2005 by Janet Chapman

All rights reserved, including the right to reproduce this book or portions thereof in any form whatsoever. For information address Pocket Books, 1230 Avenue of the Americas, New York, NY 10020

ISBN: 0-7434-8631-5

First Pocket Books printing May 2005

10 9 8 7 6 5 4 3 2 1

POCKET STAR BOOKS and colophon are registered trademarks of Simon & Schuster, Inc.

Cover image by Getty Images
Cover design by Min Choi

Manufactured in the United States of America

For information regarding special discounts for bulk purchases, please contact Simon & Schuster Special Sales at 1-800-456-6798 or business@simonandschuster.com

To the state of Maine,
and to all the people who
call this wonderful place home

Acknowledgments

❈

I would like to thank Dr. Robert Bayer, Professor of Animal and Veterinary Sciences, and Director of the Lobster Institute at the University of Maine, for sharing with me his knowledge of lobster and fishermen, and the chemicals that can threaten them both. Dr. Bayer and his colleagues do great work at the Lobster Institute, and are invaluable to those making their living from the sea, as well as those who enjoy feasting on its bounty. The Institute's mission is as simple as it is far-reaching: *The Lobster Institute, with guidance and involvement from fishermen and all constituents within the lobster industry, and with both a community and global perspective, conducts and provides for research and educational outreach focused on protecting, conserving, and enhancing lobsters and lobstering as an industry and as a way of life.*

Check out their website to see just a few of the reasons why I love living here in Maine: www.lobsterinstitute.org.

Chapter One

❋

"*I can't decide if you're* the most patient man I know or the dumbest."

Duncan Ross set his drink down on the bar and followed Keenan Oakes's gaze to the booth in the back corner of the pub. "I prefer *cunning* to *patient*," he said as they watched the two chatting women. "*Patience* implies that I'm waiting for something to happen, whereas *cunning* denotes a plan."

Kee turned narrowed eyes on Duncan. "And does this plan involve any actual dating, or are you saving all of your energy for the honeymoon?"

Duncan shot him a grin, picked up his drink, and looked back at the booth over the rim of his glass as he took a sip. Willow Foster and Rachel Oakes were both hunched forward, whispering to each other across the wide oak table. Rachel suddenly sat back in her seat with a laugh, and Willow just as suddenly leaned away, folded her arms under her breasts, and snorted loudly enough to be heard over the hum of the crowded pub.

Duncan quietly chuckled. "It's going to be one hell of a honeymoon."

Kee slid his empty glass toward Duncan, nodding for a refill. "Inviting half of Puffin Harbor to your wedding *before* you've secured a bride is not a good plan."

Duncan felt a dull flush creep up the back of his neck. If he ever found out who had started that rumor, he was going to kick some serious butt. Having his love life bantered about town was not only *not* part of his plan, it could very well be the death of him. Duncan picked up the bottle he'd opened just a few minutes ago and absently ran his thumb over the embossed crest on the cap. "Have ya ever known me to fail in an objective once I've made up my mind to go after something?" he asked softly.

"No," Kee said. "But then, wife hunting isn't exactly your usual objective. And Willow Foster isn't exactly . . . easy prey."

Duncan had started to refill Kee's glass, but instead he set the bottle down again. "Willow's just scared, is all. It's a holdover from what she thought had happened between her mom and dad and Thaddeus Lakeman. Unlike Rachel, who thought passion was the root of all evil, Willow still thinks commitment is a four-letter word. All I have to do," Duncan said softly, finally refilling Kee's glass, "is convince Willow that marrying me won't be the end of her life as she knows it, but the beginning."

"Yeah, that'll happen," Kee said with a snort, picking up his drink. "Just as soon as you stop acting like a caveman."

"*Troglodyte*," Duncan said, puffing his chest and

smoothing down the front of his shirt. "She calls me a troglodyte."

Kee stopped in mid-sip. "To your face?"

Ignoring Kee's question, Duncan looked back at the booth. Willow was glaring now, her snapping hazel eyes reflecting the firelight from the stone hearth as she leaned on the table again and whispered something to her sister.

Rachel still hadn't stopped laughing.

"Willow knows about the betting pool for when—or rather *if* the wedding will take place," Kee drawled. "Mikaela told her."

"That little rat fink," Duncan said, his smile betraying his affection for Kee's seven-year-old daughter. "She's supposed to be part of my plan, not the spoiler."

Kee shrugged, his own smile filled with equally fierce affection. "My daughter is as impatient with you as the rest of us are." He leaned closer. "She wants you to sweep Willow off her feet and live happily ever after."

"Someone's been reading fairy tales to our baby again," Duncan accused, shaking his head. "Is it Luke? I told that man a thousand times that he's only inviting disaster. Ya know how Mikaela gets when it comes to stories. She's always trying to bring them to life. Hell, it's why she changed our wolf's name to Mickey Mouse, and insisted we call Jonathan *Captain Ahab* after somebody read her *Moby Dick*."

Kee held up a hand. "Willow's the one inviting disaster. At least four nights a week, she spends almost an hour reading bedtime stories to Mikaela over the phone."

Duncan relaxed back on his hips and hid his grin by sipping his drink as he looked over at the booth. He wasn't surprised to hear that Willow ran up phone bills reading to Mikaela.

Nothing about Willow Foster surprised him.

Especially not his feelings for her.

Duncan had fallen under her spell nearly two years ago, from the first moment he'd laid eyes on the stunning woman. She had been as drunk as a sailor on leave at the time, gulping strawberry daiquiris while having a rock-throwing contest in the pitch dark with her sister, arguing and giggling and nearly falling down every time she sent another missile wobbling into the fog-shrouded sea.

She had instantly captured his interest. And by the next night, when he and Kee had helped the two sisters anonymously place a large Puffin statue in the town park, Willow Foster had somehow captured his heart.

She was a bossy, sassy-mouthed, impulsive little tyrant who didn't know the definition of *retreat*. She was also beautiful, intelligent, and utterly feminine, and when she walked into a room heads turned and male hearts started breaking.

She'd been a state assistant attorney general in Maine for just over two years now, and had slipped into her role as the people's defender just as smoothly as Duncan's drink slid down his throat.

And she thought he was a troglodyte.

Not that he'd done anything to dispel that notion.

"Aren't you afraid some rising politician in Augusta will go after her?" Kee asked.

Duncan turned back to his friend. "Not really," he quietly admitted. "Willow's in love with me."

Kee lifted a brow. "A rather arrogant assumption, don't you think?" he asked softly.

Duncan tamped down another flush edging up his neck. "Not arrogant. Confident. There's a difference."

Kee studied Duncan through narrowed eyes. "What makes you so sure she loves you?" he asked. "She's been going out of her way to avoid you for the last eighteen months." He snorted and started to take a sip of his drink, but stopped and said, "That doesn't sound like love to me."

Duncan grinned and shook his head. "No? Then why do ya think she's working so hard to stay away? Because Willow is scared of her feelings for me," Duncan answered before Kee could. "And why do ya suppose none of those three-piece suits in Augusta have caught her eye yet? She's looking, I know, but according to Rachel, Willow can't seem to settle on anyone." He turned serious and leaned closer to Kee. "I didn't imagine what happened between us eighteen months ago. Willow Foster was definitely a woman in love when she spent the night in my bed, and she's still in love. She just hasn't realized it yet."

"Dammit, Ross," Kee snapped, leaning on the bar. "Then quit playing games while waiting for her to come to her senses. Show her you're not really a caveman and sweep her off her damn feet!"

Duncan said nothing as he pulled a worn leather box from under the bar, opened the delicate silver clasp, lifted the small tulip-shaped glass out of its tattered velvet nest, then half filled it from the bottle they'd been drinking from. "It's *troglodyte*," he calmly corrected, stepping out from behind the bar. "And the game stops when Willow decides it does."

* * *

Willow kept waiting for her sister to quit laughing, but when that didn't seem likely to happen she leaned over the table and said, "I mean it, Rae. Every time I think the chemistry might finally start to happen with someone I'm dating, my libido suddenly heads south. I'm in a sexual drought," she quietly hissed, clenching her fists on the table. "And if it keeps up much longer, the statute of limitations will run out and I'll legally be declared a virgin again."

Rachel's eyes glistened as she tried to stifle her laughter behind her hands.

Willow leaned closer. "I'm so frustrated I'm ready to jump the first breathing male that crosses my path. I can't go—"

Willow snapped her mouth shut the moment she noticed the change in her sister. Rachel's eyes were no longer laughing, but dancing with mischief. "Then here's your chance, Willy," she said, looking past Willow's shoulder.

Willow dropped her head with a groan. "Tell me he's not coming over here," she muttered.

"He is breathing and he's definitely male."

"Dammit."

"And I doubt chemistry scares him."

"Damn."

"Actually," Rachel continued, canting her head. "I don't think anything scares him. Not even you. Hi, Duncan," Rachel said, her eyes still bright with mischief as she slid deeper into the booth to make room for Kee. "Where's Ahab? My sister is looking for a breathing male to attack, and I thought he might be interested."

"Ahab's sworn off women for at least another month,"

Duncan said, sliding in beside Willow and setting a small glass of pale amber liquid on the table in front of her. "I might be interested, though," he continued. "If she promises to be gentle with me."

Willow found herself trapped between a hard oak-paneled wall and an even harder male body. The air thickened with a heady masculine warmth, just as it always did whenever Duncan Ross got close, and Willow fought the urge to squirm.

The memory of their one night together immediately sprang forward with images of their naked bodies entwined, Duncan's broad, powerful hands moving over her heated skin with gentle urgency . . . his intense, forest green eyes gathering intimate knowledge with each response she made . . . the feel of his sleek-muscled body covering hers, building her to a fevered pitch time and again throughout their nightlong, hauntingly carnal dance.

Damn, this sexual drought was hell.

She was sorely tempted to take him up on his offer.

Instead Willow turned her own brilliant smile on the man responsible for every damn one of her salacious dreams of the last year and a half. "Thank you, Dunky, but I'm afraid my intentions aren't the least bit honorable, and I just can't bring myself to crush your . . . ah, delicate sensibilities."

The devil himself winked out from the sparkling green eyes locked on hers. "What a sweet woman ya are, Willow Foster," he said, placing an arm on the booth behind her and letting his hand drop to her shoulder, "to not take advantage of me."

His other hand slid the glass of amber liquor toward her.

Willow remembered the last time she'd shared a drink
with Duncan Ross. It had been eighteen months ago.
He'd just signed the papers to purchase the run-down
Drop Anchor Bar, and the ensuing celebration had
ended with her waking up the next day in an equally
run-down farmhouse—in Duncan's bed—wonderfully
satisfied and appropriately horrified.

Things had gone downhill rather abruptly from there.

Before she'd even been able to find her clothes, much
less scramble into them, Duncan had started making
plans for her to move in with him. Seemingly oblivious
to her shocked silence, he'd held a one-sided discussion
on how they would handle the logistics of her working a
two-hour commute away.

"I'm so glad you understand," Willow said, patting his
arm and then wrapping her fingers around the stem of
the iceless drink. "Because our friendship is very important." She lifted the glass, sniffed its contents, then
looked up at him. "Single malt," she guessed, "aged fifteen or twenty years."

"Thirty," he clarified softly, nudging the drink to her
mouth. "I've been waiting a long time for this bottle to
arrive. Tell me, counselor, if my patience paid off."

Willow took a small sip, and just as Duncan had
taught her, she let the rich, peat-flavored liquor bathe
her senses before letting it slide down her throat.

"Mmmm," she hummed, closing her eyes as the
whisky settled in her belly like summer sunshine. "It was
definitely worth the wait." She looked up at Duncan and
smiled. "So that's what thirty-year-old Scotch tastes
like."

He took the glass from her, repeated the same sipping

ritual as she had, then held the glass up to the light and gazed into the tawny liquid. "Aye. It's hard to believe I was a mere lad of five when this Scot's gold was casked." He handed it back and nudged the glass toward her mouth again. "And it's not just single malt," he continued as she sipped. "It's single-barrel Scotch, which means it was taken from only one cask rather than vatted with others from the same distillery."

Willow savored the second wave of heat washing through her, then turned in Duncan's casual embrace and lifted an inquiring brow. "You know an awful lot about expensive whisky for a troglodyte."

Willow heard Rachel gasp and Kee choke on his own drink.

Damn. She'd forgotten they had an audience.

Duncan's grip on her shoulder tightened, drawing her close enough to meet his stare of glittering amusement. "I know quite a bit about a lot of things, counselor," he whispered. "Including how to survive a full frontal attack." He leaned closer, until his mouth was only inches from hers. "And it'll take more than a sassy little brat like you to crush my delicate sensibilities."

"Oh, for the love of God," Kee growled from across the booth. "You're like two teenagers with more raging hormones than sense. Willow, put the man out of his misery and take him to bed."

Willow blinked across the booth, undecided if she was scandalized by Kee's command or shocked by his vehemence. Her brother-in-law was supposed to be her defender, not her pimp. She suddenly narrowed her eyes. "How much did you wager?"

Two flags of color darkened Kee's cheeks.

Willow nodded. "Well, I've placed five hundred on myself, and I intend to use my winnings for a nice vacation in Bermuda."

"Five hundred?" Rachel squeaked. "You dropped *five hundred dollars* into the pool?"

"Most of Puffin Harbor is placing wagers on this imaginary wedding," Willow said, lifting her chin. "Why shouldn't I get in on the action?"

"Maybe because you *are* the action?" Rachel asked, darting a quick glance at Duncan before looking back at her. "Isn't that unethical or something? Sort of like insider information?"

"Nay," Duncan said with a chuckle. "Willow is actually bettering the odds so we can use our winnings to go to Tahiti on our honeymoon instead of Bermuda."

If it had been anything other than thirty-year-old Scotch in that glass, Willow would have tossed the drink in his face.

Duncan obviously read her intent and pulled her against his broad, laughing chest. Raw, sizzling heat consumed Willow with the suddenness of a matchstick flaring to life, and she couldn't stop the shudder of awareness that shot through every drought-ridden nerve in her body.

Duncan's arms tightened at the telling movement, and Willow cursed her body's betrayal. Dammit, why this man?

Of all the pleasant, civilized men in this world, why did she have to be so attracted to, so *turned on* by, Duncan Ross? He was an adventurer turned barkeep—a tall and ruggedly masculine, green-eyed, blond-haired throwback to a time when brawn was more useful than brain when it came to wooing naïve, starry-eyed women.

Willow pulled free of his embrace, leaned back against the oak-paneled wall, and crossed her arms under her tingling breasts. Either there were several regressive genes rattling around in her own body or the drought was affecting her more than she realized.

It was definitely time for a rain dance. And she was getting just desperate enough to do it on the front steps of the Capitol Building in Augusta.

"So," she said a little too brightly, looking at her sister, "what do you have for mailboxes that we can put out?"

Rachel blinked at the change in subject. "I, ah, I have two that are finished," Rachel finally said, her smile turning crooked. "Mikaela decorated them."

Willow winced, imagining what the mailboxes looked like after the seven-year-old had finished *decorating* Rachel's beautiful creations.

Rachel and Willow had been anonymously gifting unsuspecting homeowners around Puffin Harbor with new mailboxes for almost five years now. They did their work under the cover of night, digging postholes at the ends of driveways and setting up the handcrafted boxes to be discovered in the morning. But the best fun was then watching the entire town try to figure out who the "Mailbox Santa Claus" really was.

Two years ago, they'd broadened their benevolence and set an eight-foot Puffin statue in the town park, causing an explosion of speculation that still hadn't died down.

And Mikaela, Kee's daughter and the child of Rachel and Willow's heart, insisted on helping, both with the decorating and the installation. And young Nicholas

Oakes, Rachel and Kee's fourteen-month-old son, was already showing signs of getting involved in their clandestine hobby—although the toddler was more interested in eating the sawdust than he was in helping.

"You're only in town for the weekend, so we should put one out tonight," Rachel suggested, reaching across the table to pick up Willow's drink.

Willow immediately snatched it away from her. "You can't have that. You might be pregnant."

The stunned silence lasted for several heartbeats before Keenan Oakes turned to his wife, his ocean blue eyes so intense that it was a wonder Rachel didn't burst into flames.

Her face darkening with a soft flush, Rachel glared at Willow and then turned and smiled up at her husband. "I . . . ah, it's just a possibility. I haven't said anything because I wasn't . . . it's not . . ."

Willow poked Duncan's side and pushed him out of the booth ahead of her. "I can't do the mailboxes tonight, sis," she said as she scrambled to her feet and faced her once again glaring sister. "I'm meeting someone in an hour. But don't expect me home until late tomorrow morning."

Another silence—so absolute that the hum of the pub faded to nothing—settled around the four of them, seemingly centered just behind Willow's left shoulder, right in the vicinity of Duncan Ross.

Willow felt like smacking herself on the forehead. She was igniting one fire after another tonight, and if she didn't get out of there quick she was the one about to be burned.

"I got to go," she muttered, spinning on her heel away

from Duncan, too much the coward—or rather too intelligent—to meet the piercing green stare boring into her back.

Willow marched past the cheerily burning hearth on the back wall of the pub, smiling and nodding at several friends as she held her breath, half expecting a large, powerful hand to close over her shoulder.

She was not marrying Duncan Ross, but she sure didn't want to provoke him, either. Tugging a troglodyte's tail was not a wise thing for a woman in a sexual drought to do.

She made it into the restroom without being stopped. Willow closed the solid oak door, leaned her back against it, and let out a loud groan of disgust. She finally gave in to the urge and smacked her forehead. "Dumb. Dumb," she hissed, closing her eyes on the realization that she should have *left* the pub instead of hiding behind the first available door.

She stood there berating herself for a good five minutes, knowing full well Duncan was waiting for her, all the time eyeing the narrow restroom window and gauging her chances of fitting through it. Finally, with a sigh of resignation, she forced open the stubborn window and climbed out into the crisp June night.

Chapter Two

❉

With the patience of a predator waiting for supper, Duncan leaned against the candy red SUV in the dimly lit parking lot, his arms folded over his chest and his feet crossed at the ankles in a pose that might appear almost languid to anyone who didn't know him.

He was soon rewarded by the sight of Willow climbing out the restroom window of his pub; one shapely jeans-clad leg appearing first, followed by a deliciously firm little butt, followed by another leg, until she was hanging suspended over the sill. Her sweater caught on a protruding nail as her waving feet searched for a toehold, and she suddenly tumbled down over the stack of firewood with a curse loud enough to be heard all the way across the parking lot.

Despite his dark mood, Duncan couldn't stifle a smile. It was a wonder she could even walk after putting first one foot in her mouth by spilling Rachel's secret, then cramming in her other foot when she'd blurted out that she wouldn't be home until late tomorrow morning.

That Rachel had told Duncan she'd heard Willow on the phone with an old high-school boyfriend earlier also didn't bode well for the sassy-mouthed little brat.

He was one second away from dragging Willow home—kicking and screaming, if that's what it took—and tying her to his bed and not letting her go until she agreed to marry him.

Duncan's smile widened at the image of her tied to his bed. He watched Willow creep toward freedom while looking over her shoulder at the front corner of the building. A cool ocean breeze was blowing her long, blunt-cut brown hair across her face, the hem of her heavy wool sweater was hiked up over one shapely breast, and there was a smudge of white paint on her left knee. She was also fishing in her pocket for her keys, obviously forgetting that she had the same bad habit as most of the citizens of Puffin Harbor and had left them on the floor of her truck.

Those keys were now tucked safely in Duncan's pocket.

Apparently satisfied that she had made her escape relatively unscathed, Willow started sprinting toward her truck only to finally spot him, swallow a gasp, and skid to a halt just four paces away.

Duncan continued to watch in fascination as her chin came up, her shoulders squared, and her large hazel eyes glittered with challenge. Still he didn't move from his insouciant pose, but simply stared back, not saying a word, and waited to see how inventive her lie would be.

Lord, he enjoyed her games.

She suddenly made a production of looking at her watch, holding her wrist toward the dim light of the streetlamp. "I'm going to be late, Dunky," she said with a hint of impatience, lifting one brow as her shimmering gaze returned to his. "Was there something you wanted?"

"Aye. You."

She smoothed her sweater back down into place, settled her hands on her hips, and shook her head. "We both know that's never going to happen."

"Never say never, counselor. It's a word that always comes back to haunt ya. Where are ya going tonight, Willow?"

"If it's any of your business, I'm going to visit an old friend I haven't seen since high school."

"All night?"

Her chin rose the slightest bit higher, and her hands on her hips balled into fists. "We'll probably have a few drinks, so I won't be able to drive home. And if I know his wife, she'll cook a breakfast so big I won't be able to walk away from the table, either."

"Ray and Patty Cobb separated three months ago."

Willow's hands fell from her hips. "They're separated?"

Her surprise wasn't fake, Duncan realized. She truly hadn't known. "Aye," he said quietly. "So tell me, did you call Cobb or did he call you?"

She took a cautious step back, though he hadn't moved so much as an inch, but then she stiffened. "How do you know I'm going to see Ray?" Her eyes narrowed. "And who told you he and Patty are separated?"

"Your sister just told me, while you were hiding in the restroom," he said with an indifferent shrug. "As payback, I suppose, for your so eloquently telling Kee she's pregnant."

Duncan saw her wince. "Rachel's not even sure yet," she muttered. She took another step, this one sideways instead of back, obviously hoping to work her way toward her truck door.

Duncan was on her before she could react. He caught her around the waist and lifted her up as he turned, dropped her down on the front fender of her truck, and settled himself between her knees so quickly that she had to grab his shoulders to steady herself.

He threaded his fingers through her hair and cupped the sides of her face firmly enough to warn her against struggling. She went perfectly still, her eyes widening in alarm.

Or was it awareness?

"Come home with me tonight."

"I can't, Duncan. And you know why." There was anger in her whispered response. And also regret.

"Then stay and help me finish my bottle of Scotch."

She slowly shook her head inside his hands. "I'll just find myself waking up in your bed again."

"Eighteen months is a long time to be celibate."

Her face under his hands flushed with heat, and her eyes shimmered defiantly. "What makes you think I've been celibate? I'll have you know I've had lots of dates in the last year and a half. Probably hundreds," she said, waving an angry hand over his shoulder.

"But not one of those dates ended in bed."

"How do—Dammit!" She squirmed to break free and pushed at his shoulders. "Let me go. I have to go kill my sister!"

He ignored her struggles and covered her mouth in a kiss that was long overdue, holding her firmly as he tasted peat-dried barley malt mingled with her own sweet flavor.

She stiffened on an indrawn breath, her hands on his shoulders digging into his leather jacket. Duncan dropped his own hand to her backside and slid Willow forward, pulling her pelvis firmly into his. He groaned into her mouth, and with an aggression born of need, deepened the kiss, not backing down until he felt her shudder in response.

"Sweet heaven," he growled, forcing himself to come up for air. "Dammit, Willow, don't do this to us. You want it as much as I do."

She set trembling, delicate hands on either side of his face, and smiled sadly through passion-bright eyes. "You blew any chance for us eighteen months ago, Duncan, when you took me home, made incredible love to me all night, and then turned into a chest-beating caveman the next morning."

"It's troglodyte," he whispered, flexing his fingers on her hips. "I'm a troglodyte."

"Yes, you are," she whispered back, her own hands tightening on his face. "You're possessive, protective, and wonderfully physical, and you haven't evolved into this century. If I ever let down my guard with you, for even a minute, I'd find myself in more trouble than I could handle."

Duncan took her hands from his face and held them securely against his thumping chest. "But that's the very thing we have going for us, lass. Your own strength matches mine in a way that promises us a lifetime of passion."

"I'm not capable of making that kind of commitment, Duncan. Can't you understand that?"

"Aye," he said on a sigh, leaning forward and giving her mouth a gentle kiss. He pulled back slightly. "I've understood that from the beginning. Cancel your date with Cobb."

"I can't." She also released a shuddering sigh. "It's not even a date, really. I'm meeting Ray tonight because he has something to show me."

Duncan just bet Cobb had something to show her. "Then let me come with you."

She shook her head. "I can't. This is business."

"Attorney general business?" He canted his head. "Your sister said Cobb is a lobsterman. What's he got that concerns your office?" Duncan tightened his grip on her hands. "And why did you have to come here to meet him, and at night? All night, for that matter."

She wiggled to get free, and Duncan allowed her to shove him away and slide down off the fender of her truck. She turned with a snort and finally opened the driver's door. "This is exactly why we can't be together. I can't even have a simple meeting without you getting all possessive and protective. I've been doing my job for over two years now, and I've been doing it damn well without your help. Go tend your bar."

"I have a staff for that. I'm taking tonight off."

"You can't come with—" She stopped in mid-sentence and reached inside her truck, picked up the bottle he'd set on the seat while waiting for her, and turned back with one brow raised in question. "Pretty damn sure of yourself, aren't you?" She returned her gaze to the bottle, lifting it toward the street light to read the label. "Rosach

Distillery," she read out loud, looking back up at him. "It's the same name as your bar—The Rosach Pub."

He took the bottle from her. "They're my silent partner."

"But I thought you bought and remodeled the bar with your share of the reward you and Kee and the others got when you recovered Thaddeus Lakeman's stolen art?"

"Aye, I did. But I also went into partnership with the Rosach Distillery."

After giving him an odd look, Willow reached into the truck again and reemerged with the small leather box that had been sitting next to the bottle. "What's this?" she asked, running a finger over the faded gold letters embossed into the top of it. "Who's Galen Ross?" she asked, opening the box.

Willow shot him a quick look of surprise, then lifted the tulip-shaped glass from the velvet and held it up to see the etching. "This is the glass I just used inside," she said, looking back at him. "It has the same crest as the label on the bottle. Who's Galen Ross?" she repeated.

"My father."

"You have a father?" she blurted out. She shook her head and smiled. "I mean, I know you didn't really crawl out of a cave, but I never thought of you as having a family. You never talk about them."

He tucked the bottle under his arm and took the box and glass from her, set the glass back in the velvet, and carefully closed the lid. "My father and I were supposed to share this Scotch when it came of age, but he died six years ago."

"I'm sorry, Duncan," she said softly.

He tucked the bottle and box under his arm. "Life happens" was all he could think to say.

"So that's why you know so much about whisky," she continued brightly. "Your father worked for the Rosach Distillery. Was he one of those . . . what do you call them? A noser?"

"Aye, Galen Ross had a legendary nose for blending whisky."

"And that's his nosing glass," she said, stepping forward and lifting up on her toes as she pulled on the sleeve of his jacket. "Thank you for sharing your special Scotch with me, Duncan," she whispered. "And for letting me drink from your father's glass."

She gave him a quick kiss on the cheek and then turned and climbed into her truck. Duncan watched her grope around on the floor for her keys, then bend over with a muttered curse and continue her search in front of the passenger's seat.

Duncan took her keys out of his pocket but said nothing, deciding to let the woman's frustration build—even though he knew it wouldn't even come close to his own. He smiled when she suddenly stilled, his grin widening when she bolted upright, glared at him, and held out her hand.

He dangled the keys just out of her reach. "Take me with ya and I promise to be as quiet as a church mouse and not interfere in your work."

She climbed back out of the truck, stood directly in front of him, and stared up with a fierceness that would have worried the devil himself. "Do you trust me, Duncan?"

He relaxed back on his hips and folded the hand holding the keys under his arm holding the Scotch. "I trust ya not to lie to me about the important things," he said softly. "And I trust that ya know what you're doing when it comes to yar work. But I don't trust an old boyfriend not to have an agenda."

"Ray and I dated three months," she snapped, clearly at the end of her patience—and seemingly not at all impressed that he trusted her. "I am not interested in Ray Cobb that way."

"Then ya shouldn't have any problem with my tagging along."

She shoved her hand out again. "You are not coming with me."

He held his own hand over hers, the keys locked in his fist. "Then agree to have dinner with me tomorrow night."

She actually stamped her foot, and Duncan realized she'd just barely restrained herself from kicking him. "I will not be seen on a date with you. It would only feed the rumors about us."

"Then we'll eat in. At my house."

She looked down at his leg, specifically at his shin, her mutinous eyes obviously judging her aim.

But she looked back up at the sound of her jangling keys as Duncan made them disappear behind the zipper of his jacket, to an inside pocket over his chest. And then her eyes widened when his hand returned not with her keys but with a pen. He stepped forward, the bottle and box tucked firmly under his arm, and took her still extended hand in his and started writing on her palm.

Just as he'd known it would, Willow's curiosity held her still as she tried to read what he was spelling out in small, bold blue letters.

"What does that say?" she demanded, pulling free the moment he finished. She held her hand flat, facing the light, and squinted down at it. "*Potes currere . . .*" She looked up and scowled at him. "Either you can't spell worth a damn, Dunky, or this isn't English." She looked back down and tried reading it phonetically. "*Potes currere sed te occulere non potes.*"

Duncan winced. "Ya're slaughtering it, lass."

"What language is it? French? Latin? *Stone Age* gibberish? And what does it mean?"

He placed the pen back in his pocket, his hand returning empty. "You're an educated woman, counselor. Do what I did when ya wrote *troglodyte* on my palm two years ago. Look it up."

Her eyes glittering in the street light, Willow balled her hand into a fist and spun back to her truck with a muttered curse. She climbed in, slammed the door shut behind her, and tripped the electric locks. Then she reached up, pulled down the visor, and took out a hidden key. She shot him a triumphant smile as she crammed the key into the ignition and started the engine.

Duncan stepped back with a long-suffering sigh and turned to avoid the parking lot dust and debris shooting out from her screeching tires as Willow exited the parking lot with all the poise of a spoiled brat.

He was going to have to do something about her recklessness, Duncan decided as he loped to his car. He climbed into the right-hand seat, tucked the Scotch and leather box safely under the left-hand seat, fished his own keys out of his pocket, and started the fifteen-year-old Jaguar.

The engine rumbled to life with the distinct purr of a

jungle beast, and Duncan slowly pulled out of the parking lot. But the moment he turned onto the road, he pushed the powerful engine through the gears, only easing back on the throttle when he caught sight of Willow's taillights.

Aye, he thought with another sigh. The game continued.

Not only was their game continuing, Duncan decided thirty minutes later, it was getting curiouser and curiouser.

He could have been watching a B movie for all the drama of the scene unfolding through his binoculars: the old fishing pier hugging the shore of the fog-obscured cove, the halo of one weak bulb from the scale house illuminating the two people standing hunched over a wooden crate, and the thick, desolate silence broken only by an occasional, distant foghorn.

He'd witnessed this sort of scene more times than he cared to remember, and Duncan's gut tightened at the thought of Willow being in the middle of this one. Cobb's personal interest in her was no longer a worry; it was the situation the man was getting her into that made Duncan break into a cold sweat. When state's assistant attorneys general met with men who wanted to show them something on a desolate pier at night, it usually meant trouble.

Big trouble.

Usually more trouble than one tiny woman could handle.

Duncan was back to rethinking his plan of dragging Willow home and tying her to his bed. He straightened from leaning over the roof of his car, tossed the binoculars onto the front seat, softly closed the door, and started down the steep hill toward the clandestine meeting.

He had no trouble keeping to the shadows as he carefully worked his way out onto the pier, his ears tuned to the silence around him and the soft voices ahead.

"How long has this been going on, Ray?" Duncan heard Willow whisper.

"They started turning up about seven weeks ago," Cobb answered just as softly. "Just a few at first, and only in my traps closest to the island. And it's not just the lobsters. Even the crabs look like this."

Duncan inched forward and peered around the end of the scale house, but he still couldn't see what Cobb was holding, since the man was standing with his back to him.

"Why call me?" Willow asked. "You should have contacted Marine Resources."

"I did. George White covers this part of the coast, and I told him exactly what I'm telling you. I even gave him some of my catch."

"And?"

"And he said he'd look into it, but that was six weeks ago. I called his office several times and they told me he's gone on vacation."

"That's a long vacation for a civil servant," Duncan heard Willow murmur as she looked back at what Cobb was holding. "What about the other lobstermen? Are they turning up the same thing?"

Cobb dropped what Duncan guessed was a lobster back into the crate and brushed his hands on his pants. "Yes," Cobb said, closing the crate and picking it up. "There's about seven other fishermen who usually set traps around the island. But we've all had to move them because we can't afford to keep throwing back our catch."

Cobb started walking farther out the pier, and Willow fell into step beside him. Duncan silently followed.

"And that means we've started crowding each other," Cobb continued, stopping beside the gently bobbing roof of a fishing boat. "We're on the verge of starting a trap war."

"A trap war?"

Cobb snorted. "You know how territorial fishing gets. And we can't afford to just pull our traps, so we have to move into other areas," he explained, setting down the crate. "After I called and asked you to come down, I set some traps around the island so you could see for yourself what I'm talking about."

"And the sick lobster are only coming from this one place?" Willow asked. "They're not turning up anywhere else?"

"No. Other than an expected mutation and the occasional blue or harlequin lobster, all's normal."

The tide was low, and Cobb stepped onto the ladder that ran down to his boat, slid the crate onto its deck, then turned and faced Willow at eye level. "I run almost nine hundred pots from June to October, and about three hundred in winter. I've been fishing for over ten years, and I've never seen anything like this."

Duncan could just make out Cobb's smile as the man held out his hand. "Come on, Willy. It'll be just like in high school, when I used to steal my old man's boat and a bunch of us would head out to one of the islands for a party."

Dammit, he was not letting Willow get on that boat. Duncan silently moved forward, preparing to rush her, when the beam of a powerful light suddenly cut through the fog, scanning shoreward from the water in a sweeping arc.

Duncan stepped back into the shadow of several stacked crates and listened to the muted chug of an engine approaching at idle speed. The searchlight stopped on Willow as she stood on the pier, its beam also catching Cobb in silhouette.

"Hey *The Corncobb Lady*," the man in the approaching boat hollered. "That you, Ray Cobb?"

Duncan watched as Cobb quickly helped Willow down to the deck of his boat and rushed her into its wheelhouse. Then he climbed back up the ladder and moved down the pier to intercept the boat coming in.

"You're out late tonight, Gramps," Cobb said, leaning over to catch the roof of the other boat as it gently edged up to the pier. He took the rope handed to him and tied it off on a large post. "You have engine trouble?" he continued, moving back to help the old man up the ladder.

"Naw. I anchored myself off Pregnant Island and had a nap," he said with a chuckle. "Next thing I knew, I woke up and it was dark. Already radioed the missus, so she ain't worried none." Gramps leaned around Cobb, eyeing the younger man's boat. "Who you got there, Ray? I thought I recognized her."

Cobb moved into his line of sight. "Just a friend."

The old man squinted up at him. "You should be working on winning Patty back, not fishing new waters." He suddenly stiffened. "Willow Foster," he said, starting toward Cobb's boat. "That's who I recognized, damned if it ain't."

"Go home, Gramps," Cobb said gently, crowding him away from his boat. "It's not Willow Foster."

"I sure hope to hell not," the old man said, stopping and looking up at Cobb.

Duncan slid deeper into the shadows, since the men were only ten feet away now.

"I hear that huge Scot over to Puffin Harbor already got a claim on her," Gramps continued. "He owns The Rosach Pub, and I hear he used to be a . . . what you call them? A fortune soldier or something. Ayuh," he said with a nod. "Word is he's trying to take up with that Foster girl, but she ain't making it easy for him," he finished with a cackle. He pointed at Cobb's chest. "You mind whose traps you're pulling from. That Scot ain't no one to mess with. Go back to Patty."

"I'm trying," Cobb growled. "But she's being stubborn. She says I take her for granted or something."

Gramps glanced toward Cobb's sleek-lined, crisply painted boat, then cocked his head at the young man. "Maybe you should spend more money on your house than you do your boat, boy. Homes are important to women." He puffed up his chest. "I've kept the same missus and the same boat for near forty-six years, 'cause I spent my earnings on whichever one was complaining the loudest at the time."

"Maybe I'll do that," Cobb said, urging the old man toward land. "And you should get home before Mildred locks you out."

That said, Cobb jogged back to his boat, untied the ropes with quick efficiency, jumped onto the deck, and had the engine started before Gramps even got moving.

Duncan gritted his teeth in frustration, inching around the crates as the old sea salt finally walked by muttering something about the foolishness of horny toads.

By the time Duncan was able to move down the pier, Cobb's boat was already disappearing into the fog—and Willow Foster was standing on deck, waving back at Duncan.

Chapter Three

❈

Willow sat on a large box under the wheel-house of *The Corncobb Lady*, hugging her knees to her chest as she watched the spray of frothing water disappear into the darkness behind.

"Are you warm enough?" Ray shouted over the roar of the diesel engine, slipping out of his heavy canvas jacket and tossing it to her before she could answer.

"You'll freeze."

"Naw. I'm used to being damp and cold," he said, returning his attention to the dark sea ahead.

Once they'd idled out of the shore-hugging fog, about twenty minutes ago, Ray had given the powerful boat full throttle. Willow wasn't worried they'd run into anything; she'd made enough trips in speeding boats in high school to know that visibility was actually quite good on the ocean at night. She was only mad at herself for not remembering how raw it could get on the open water. Unlike kayaking, where one worked up a sweat, cruising the Gulf of Maine at twenty-five knots in June was damn cold.

Willow slipped into Ray's jacket, and it was as she was pulling the sleeves up to find her hands that she saw the ink on her right palm, though it was too dark to read it.

She was pretty sure it was Latin.

And just how did Duncan Ross—the definition of a troglodyte if there ever was one—know enough Latin to write an entire sentence on her hand?

Willow lowered her chin to her bent knees and wrapped her arms around them again as she remembered two years ago. She'd stopped into the old Drop Anchor where Duncan had been sharing a drink with Kee and Ahab and Jason and Matt and Peter four days after rescuing Willow and Rachel from Raoul Vegas and his henchman. Luke had been in the hospital, recovering from gunshot wounds, and Willow had still had several fading bruises from the frightening ordeal.

But before heading back to her job in Augusta, she had sought out the men to formally thank them for rescuing her. Especially Duncan, because he'd been the one to burst into the house where she was being held captive—looking like Zeus himself—and save her from one of the bad guys.

So she had paid for a round of drinks and Duncan had walked her out to her car. But before she could *especially* thank him again, her hero had hauled her into his arms and kissed her quite passionately—right there in the parking lot, right in front of God and the rest of the world.

That she had kissed him back, not even realizing

what a slippery slope she might be heading down, onl
proved that intelligence had nothing to do with com
mon sense.

Because right after that heart-stopping kiss, Willow
had unknowingly fired the first salvo of their upcoming
war. More mad at herself than at Duncan, she had taken
out her pen and written *troglodyte* on his palm, telling
him she'd spelled it out so he could look it up in the dictionary. Then she'd gotten into her car, cursing the fact
that he was either too dense or too amused to realize the
insult, and driven away.

And so had started their two-year-long, passionate
battle of wills. Every time she would come home for a
visit, the maddening Scot somehow managed to get her
alone and kiss her until she couldn't even remember how
to spell *troglodyte*, much less *hero* for that matter.

There were a hundred ways to describe Duncan Ross,
and only one way Willow could describe her feelings for
him: dangerous. What she felt for Duncan was dangerous
not only for herself, but for him.

Men like Duncan had a tendency to think in simple
terms, and when something caught their interest they
usually went after it with the determination of a hungry
tiger.

Finding herself the prey of such a formidable beast was
both frightening and exhilarating. And at times, like
tonight, damn frustrating.

Eighteen months ago she'd made her biggest mistake.

Going to bed with Duncan had only encouraged his
pursuit. It didn't matter that it had been the most incredible night of her life; she'd awakened a sleeping tiger who
up until that point had seemed contented with stolen

kisses and kicked shins, laughter and insults, and a bit of mutually enjoyable necking.

But for the last eighteen months, Willow had felt positively hunted. So instead of coming home one or two weekends a month, she'd thrown herself into her work and simply avoided Puffin Harbor as much as possible.

Or she had been able to until Ray Cobb had called her office Monday, saying he didn't know who else to bring his problem to. He knew her personally, he knew she specialized in environmental crimes against the state—high-profile, newsworthy crimes—and he knew he could trust her to quietly discover what was happening in her childhood playground.

So here she was, spending a Friday night in June racing through the Gulf of Maine in a lobster boat and foolishly wishing she was in Duncan Ross's bed instead.

Willow smiled, remembering the picture of him standing on the dock as they'd idled away. His fists had been planted on his hips, his feet had been spread in predatory anger as he'd watched her escape, and the fog had swirled around him in waves of simmering frustration.

Yes, *possessive* and *protective* described Duncan very well; as did *passionate, utterly physical,* and *perfect in all ways but one.*

Duncan wasn't willing to have a quiet, flaming affair with her—he wanted marriage. A lifetime of passion, he'd told her tonight. And for that reason alone, Willow knew she couldn't afford to lose this war, simply because she couldn't make the kind of commitment he was demanding.

Which also proved that intelligence didn't have anything to do with irrational fear, either.

"We're here," Ray said, throttling the engine down to an idle and pushing several buttons on one of the navigational instruments over his head.

Willow stood up and looked at the colorful monitor. "How far are we from Thunder Island?" she asked, trying to orient herself in reference to the map on the screen.

"Two miles. There," Ray said, pointing over her shoulder.

Willow turned and looked toward the black horizon, letting her eyes go out of focus just enough to see the outline of the island as it rose into the starry night.

"Nobody lives on it?" she asked, turning back to Ray. "It's still just an abandoned granite quarry? If I remember correctly, it took more courage than brains to even land there, since it was so rocky and the tides were so rough."

"Nobody lives there," he said, shaking his head and smiling at the memories the island held for both of them. "We had some really fun times, didn't we, the whole gang swimming in that old quarry pond?"

"It was the only place we could swim," Willow said, looking back toward the island. "The sun warmed up the pond water enough to make it just barely tolerable. Have you and Patty been there lately?" she asked, still looking at the island.

"Naw. What for?"

She turned to him. "To go swimming."

She could just make out the dull flush of his cheeks in the light of the instruments. "Why would Patty want to go swimming in that old quarry?"

"Maybe to bring back memories," Willow asked softly, "of youthful passion and a time when nothing else mattered but living each day to the fullest?"

Ray snorted, turned back to his screen, and punched several buttons. "I guess you heard what Gramps said. Patty left me."

"Has she filed for divorce?"

"No," he said softly, pulling the boat out of gear to stop their forward movement. "Not yet."

"Have you thought that maybe she doesn't want a divorce, Ray?" Willow asked. "That she only wants her high school sweetheart back?" She took hold of his sleeve and turned him toward her. "Maybe the Patty I remember wants the carefree young man she remembers."

"I have three kids, two mortgages, a sky-high overhead, and not enough days in a fishing season," he said, waving at the boat they stood in. "I can't afford to take Patty on trips down memory lane."

"You can't afford not to, Ray. What good is working so hard if there's no one to come home to at the end of the day?"

"I don't see you rushing home to anyone," he snapped, shoving on a pair of gloves. He picked up a stick with a hook in the end and waved it at the air. "If I remember correctly, you didn't keep a boyfriend more than four months all through high school. And you're—what— twenty-eight? And you still haven't settled down."

"This isn't about me."

"No, it's about lobsters," he said, turning to watch the screen on his Global Positioning System. "And about whatever's in these waters that's damn near killing my livelihood."

He put the boat in gear and idled forward while watching the monitor. "Look for a blue and pink buoy," he told her, turning on a floodlight and directing its narrow beam over the water.

Willow saw nothing but black ocean gently swelling around them. Ray slowly idled *The Corncobb Lady* in large circles for several more minutes, then turned the wheel sharply, pulled back on the throttle, and took the engine out of gear. He leaned over the side, reached out with his pole, and in one fluid movement dropped the snagged buoy onto the deck and tossed the attached rope over the pulley above his head.

Willow stepped back as the electric winch whined with the strain of dragging the trap off the ocean floor.

Ray leaned over the side of the boat and hefted the green wire lobster pot up onto the gunnel. He reached up and turned on the wheelhouse light, then manhandled the cumbersome trap down to the deck as if it weighed no more than a sack of groceries.

Willow took another step back from the odor of stinky bait wafting into the air, and watched as Ray opened the door on the top of the trap, reached in with his gloved hand, and pulled out a lobster.

It sat listlessly in his hand but for an occasional spasm of twitches, acting just like the one he'd shown her on the pier. Ray set it beside the trap and reached in again and pulled out a crab. The crab was obviously dead. He threw it onto the deck of his boat, then reached in a third time and pulled out what looked like a healthy two-pound lobster, its claws snapping and its tail flapping frantically.

"This seems to be about as far as the contamination goes," Ray said, quickly picking up a plierslike tool and slipping a wide rubber band over first one waving claw and then the other. "I've set a couple more traps closer to the island, and a few farther out and to the south and east, so we can see how far the problem's progressed."

Willow looked down at the dead crab lying next to the blue and pink buoy only to realize something. "I thought your colors were orange and white," she said, pointing to the buoy displayed on the roof of his boat.

Ray waved at the expanse of ocean around them. "These waters are usually filled with hundreds of buoys, but now there's only the seven I set Tuesday, so they stand out like a sore thumb. I wasn't about to advertise my interest in this area, so I painted seven buoys with colors that aren't already taken along this part of the coast."

Willow knew that each fisherman had his own distinct colors and designs on the buoys that marked his pots so that when fishing close to others he could distinguish one from another.

The fact that Ray didn't want anyone to know these were his traps set off alarm bells in Willow's head. "Why did you insist we come out at night?" she asked. "And why did you warn me not to tell anyone I was meeting you?"

Ray tossed the now banded lobster into a plastic bin, and gathered up the dead crab and listless lobster and tossed them into the bin with it. Then he carried the trap to the wide transom at the back of his boat, tossed the stinky bait into the ocean, and started undoing the shackle that secured the long rope to the trap.

"There's been some strange happenings around here lately," he said as he worked in the shadow of the wheelhouse light, obviously well acquainted with his equipment. "Dozens of trap lines have been cut, sugar has been poured into a few boat and pickup truck gas tanks, and Frank Porter's boat was deliberately sunk on its mooring."

"A trap war?"

Ray tossed down the freed end of the rope, turned to her with his hands on his hips, and shook his head. "Trap wars start with harmless but clearly implied warnings: a lobsterman might pull a trap and find all the doors open, or he'll find his rigging half hitched, or it might escalate to finding his lines cut. But a man's boat is sacred, and messing with each other's equipment just doesn't happen unless our livelihoods are truly threatened." He shook his head again. "But things around here have gone straight to hell without any warning, which tells us this is the work of someone who doesn't want word spreading that something's wrong out here. Only those fishermen who have been vocal about what they've been catching have been targeted."

He stepped closer and stared down at Willow, his frustrated eyes searching hers. "I'm counting on you to keep this quiet, Willy. Keep my name out of it, and don't even let on that the rumor of sick lobster has reached your office."

Those alarm bells in her head grew louder. "You think someone will come after you?"

"They already have," he growled, his eyes hardening even more. "Not long after I contacted Marine Resources, I had to rebuild the engine in my pickup when someone poured sugar in the gas tank."

Willow could only gape at him.

"There's eight of us who have been meeting secretly out at sea for the last month, away from watching eyes," he continued. "And we've discussed our options and decided that you're the only one we can trust." His features suddenly softened and he shook his head and smiled. "Well, except for Frank Porter. He remembers how wild you were in high school, and some of the pranks you pulled."

Prickling heat rushed to Willow's cheeks. Frank Porter had been the brunt of one of those pranks when she and a classmate had changed the name on the transom of Frank's lobster boat from *Kiss the Lazy Sun* to *Kiss the Lady's Bum*, and made it out of Skunk Harbor instead of Trunk Harbor. Willow spun away from the light of the wheelhouse and silently stared out at Thunder Island.

Ray quietly laughed behind her. "Frank said he knew it was you and Jenny McGuire who rechristened his boat when you came strolling onto the pier that morning to see the results of your prank and you both had red paint on your fingers."

"It was Jenny's idea," Willow said with a small laugh of her own, turning back to Ray. "And we only did it because Frank had tattled to our dads about seeing us smoking a cigarette while out kayaking. So who else is in this secret group of yours?" she asked, turning serious again.

Ray reached behind the bib of his rubber fishing overalls into the chest pocket of his heavy wool overshirt and pulled out a piece of paper. "I've made you a list and included our phone numbers, so you know who you're dealing with. You'll recognize just about everyone," he said as Willow unfolded the paper. "We've all agreed to keep quiet about what's happening here and decided to let you earn your paycheck."

Willow stopped scanning the list and frowned up at him. "I work just as hard as you to make my living."

He chucked her under the chin. "I'm aware of that fact, Willy. We all are, and we're all damn proud of you. Even Frank admitted he always knew you'd amount to something," he added, turning and putting the quietly idling boat back into gear. "But he said to tell you he's not so old that he can't put you over his knee if he catches you near his boat again."

"I'll consider myself warned," she said, tucking the paper into her pants pocket. "Have you seen anything out of the ordinary going on in the last year or so, Ray? Any strange boat traffic?"

"Nothing," he said, slowly starting them toward the island. "And believe me, that's been the main topic of discussion at our little meetings."

"Thunder Island is—what—ten miles from the mainland?"

"Twelve," he corrected, checking the monitor for the exact coordinates of where he'd set his next trap. "And the four Pilot Islands are five miles beyond that."

Even over the chug of the engine, Willow realized she could hear the waves of the incoming tide break onto Thunder Island. The two-mile-long, one-mile-wide island was nothing more than a huge outcropping of granite, and had likely gotten its name from the sound of the waves crashing against its craggy shoreline.

In its heyday, Thunder Island had been one of many quarries supplying the beautiful granite that had helped build the city of Boston. Sailing schooners had sidled up to the massive pier jutting into the water and been loaded with heavy, square-hewn blocks for the trip south.

But a four-lane highway had replaced the ocean as the means of interstate commerce over half a century ago, and tractor-trailer trucks had quickly replaced the schooners. Steel had become the cheaper building material of choice, and many of the granite quarries along the coast of Maine were simply abandoned, only to become the playground of high school kids looking for someplace to gather away from their parents' watchful eyes.

"You called it contamination earlier," Willow said, moving to stand beside Ray at the wheel. "Is that what you think is causing the twitching? It couldn't be a disease?"

"We keep up on diseases that could have an impact on our industry," Ray said as he reached up and pushed a button that changed the screen on his monitor. "And there's nothing like this in any bulletins. It's contamination, Willy," he added with a growl. "And it's only around Thunder Island."

"Have you been on the island to look around?"

"Sure. Frank Porter and I searched it three times just this month, and we couldn't find anything." He looked over at her and frowned. "The quarry pond is a lot fuller than when we used to swim there, but nothing else has changed. It's just like any other island around here—covered with weather-beaten scrub pine, wild roses, and a few rotting buildings."

"The quarry filled up? How deep?"

"The exposed walls were—what—forty feet tall when we were in high school?" he said. "Now they're less than twenty. It's filled all the way up to sea level."

"That wouldn't be unusual, would it? Granite has cracks that the seawater would seep through. It was just a matter of time before the ocean invaded the quarry."

"Yeah. But now you can see tidal lines on the sides, which means those cracks are big enough to let a high volume of water in and out."

"Didn't we decide back in high school that the water was about thirty feet deep then? So it must be fifty now," Willow calculated out loud. "Are you thinking someone dumped something in the quarry, Ray?" she asked, tugging on his sleeve to get his attention when he leaned over the side of the boat to look for another buoy.

"Yeah," he said past his shoulder. "That's our guess."

"But that means they'd have to land on the island with a boat big enough to carry barrels or crates or something," she continued. "It would take a lot of toxic waste to spread that kind of damage two miles out from the island."

Ray shrugged and took the boat out of gear. "That's your area of expertise, Willy. I'm just the messenger."

He grabbed his hook and reached over the side and pulled up another buoy. Willow stepped out of the way again, watching Ray work as she listened to the waves crash onto Thunder Island.

The heavy, resonating sound of the surf sent chills down her spine, and Willow snuggled deeper into Ray's jacket. The lobster sickness had to be coming from toxic waste, but if the toxins weren't coming from the island, then where?

It was possible that someone had dumped barrels overboard near the island, which made more sense, considering how hard it was to land a large boat there. Usually dumpers just drove along and tossed their cargo over the side without even stopping. It wasn't unheard of that some company had contracted to legally dispose of waste only to take the easy way out.

Doing things the right way cost money—lots of money—and then only after years of petitioning to open a licensed and closely monitored site. Which meant that slow-moving bureaucracy might invite some unethical and greedy people to take shortcuts.

Tracing the origin of containers dumped at sea was not easy. They either rotted quickly, or if found intact, all traceable markings would have been removed, including serial numbers.

That was assuming containers were even involved. Sometimes the chemicals were just poured into the ocean.

Willow watched while Ray worked into the small hours of the night to find and pull all seven traps, and by 3:00 A.M. she was starting to feel light-headed from both fatigue and constant shivering.

"We've got to head back now," Ray said as he stashed the last trap on the transom of *The Corncobb Lady.* "I want you gone before the dock starts getting busy."

Willow was sitting on the box just inside the wheel-house again, her arms wrapped around her knees as she stared at the bin full of sick and dead lobsters and crabs. "I want to take several specimens with me," she said, looking up as Ray stepped back to the wheel. "Including the healthy ones. I'm going to send them to the lab."

"Can you do it anonymously? Or use an out-of-state lab?" he asked. "You don't need to draw attention to yourself, either."

Willow thought about that. She doubted there was any danger to her personally, even if someone did figure out what she was doing. The bad guys might go after a few loudly complaining lobstermen, but they probably wouldn't mess with anyone in the AG's office. Angering the wrong people was tantamount to corporate suicide, not to mention long jail sentences for anyone involved.

"I'll think about using an out-of-state lab," she offered. "But it'll take longer to get the results. Meanwhile, you guys should continue to stay quiet and wait until I know exactly what we're dealing with."

Ray looked over and nodded, snapped off the wheel-house light, and plunged them into darkness but for the tiny running lamp at the back of the boat. He gave *The Corncobb Lady* full throttle again and headed them back to Trunk Harbor.

Willow burrowed deeper into Ray's heavy jacket, thankful he'd given it to her and hoping he didn't catch a cold for his gallantry. She was chilled all the way down to her bones now, although she didn't know if her shivers were caused from the cold or from what she had learned tonight.

Not only were the waters near Thunder Island contaminated, but it appeared that whoever was responsible was still hanging around, trying to cover up the crime.

Chapter Four

✦

$\mathcal{T}$he stars were just beginning to fade with the first hint of dawn when they idled into Trunk Harbor. Willow could see a few fishermen already had their boats tied to the dock and were loading them with bait, traps, and spools of thick rope.

Ray had found her a smelly old cap in his toolbox, and Willow twined her hair in a knot, crammed the cap on her head, and turned up the collar of Ray's coat as they edged against the far side of the pier.

"Don't talk to anyone when we head to your truck," Ray said, setting the covered plastic bin on the pier. "And wait until you get to Puffin Harbor before you stop to buy ice."

Willow understood he didn't want her seen near Trunk Harbor, which was twelve miles east of Puffin Harbor, and that she needed to get the lobsters on ice if she wanted them to be alive when they reached the lab. She scrambled onto the dock, her hand covering her face at her collar, and fell into step beside Ray as he strode down the dimly lit pier.

They walked in silence up the steep lane that led to the parking lot, and Willow was thankful the other fishermen were too busy preparing for a hard and hopefully profitable day at sea to do more than wave a greeting to them. She freed her hand from the long sleeve of Ray's coat and fished in her pants pocket for her spare key only to realize she'd left it on the floor of her truck.

It amazed Willow how quickly her hometown habits returned. She never left her truck unlocked or the keys on the truck floor in Augusta.

Ray suddenly stopped, holding the heavy crate in front of him. "Where's your truck?" he asked, looking around the mostly deserted parking lot. "And who is that?"

Willow stopped beside him, pushed the oversized cap off her forehead, and followed Ray's gaze to the shiny maroon Jaguar parked under the only streetlamp.

Duncan was leaning against the rear fender, his arms crossed over his chest and his feet crossed at the ankles, looking for all the world like the patron saint of patience.

Willow started forward again, not the least bit surprised he was here. "It's just Duncan," she said, only to stop and turn when she realized Ray wasn't following her. "It's okay," she told him. "He's a friend of mine."

"I asked you not to tell anyone," Ray said, eyeing Duncan suspiciously.

Willow walked back and touched his arm. "His name is Duncan Ross, and you can trust him. He's not interested in our problem."

"Then what is he interested in?" Ray asked. He suddenly looked down at Willow with dawning awareness, his eyes crinkling with amusement.

"Me," she snapped, turning on her heel and walking over to Duncan. "You stole my truck."

"Nay," Duncan said with a shrug. "Luke drove it home for ya."

"That was kind of him," she said ever so sweetly through clenched teeth. "Why would he do such a thoughtful thing?"

"Probably because he didn't want it to be seen parked at the Trunk Harbor pier all night."

Ray came up beside Willow. "You the guy she's supposed to marry?" he asked, giving Duncan an assessing look.

Duncan shrugged, still not straightening from the fender. "I suppose I am," he said. "You the guy getting her in trouble?"

Willow heard the undertone of warning in Duncan's voice, and apparently so did Ray. He set down the crate and crossed his arms over his chest. "I'm just a friend asking a friend for a favor," Ray said. "Which I wouldn't do if I thought there was any danger to her. She has the power of her office protecting her."

Willow dropped her gaze to the pavement and shook her head, half expecting one or both of them to start beating their chests.

"I'm tired and freezing," she said, glaring at Duncan. "And I have to get my lobsters on ice."

He finally straightened away from the fender, but instead of turning to open the trunk of his car, he reached out, pulled the cap from her head, unzipped her jacket and peeled it off, and tossed both to Ray. Then he took off his own jacket, settled it over her shoulders, and zipped it up to her chin.

Willow wiggled her trapped arms inside the spacious leather jacket and slid her hands through the sleeves. "Thank you," she muttered, walking to the passenger's side of the car. She opened the door and looked back at Ray. "I'll be in touch later this week. Until then, stay out of trouble."

That said, Willow slid into the seat with a tired groan, only to stare at the dash in utter confusion as she listened to the trunk open, felt the car dip under the weight of the lobster crate, then close again.

"Why is there a steering wheel in front of me?" she asked when Duncan walked up beside her still open door.

"Because the Jag was built for Scotland, not America," he said, reaching in and tugging her out by the sleeve.

He silently led her around the back of the car, and Willow saw Ray already jogging back to his boat. Duncan opened the left-side door, handed her in, then gently closed it behind her.

Willow leaned her head back with a sigh and closed her eyes. She was so cold she was numb, and so tired she couldn't even work up the energy to scold Duncan for following her and stealing her truck.

"You got Luke out of bed just to come get my truck?" she asked, not bothering to open her eyes when Duncan slid behind the steering wheel.

"That's what friends are for" was all he said, starting the car.

Willow smiled at the sound of the purring engine, and still didn't open her eyes when Duncan reached across her, pulled the seat belt over her chest and waist, and snapped it into place.

Willow thought about Duncan's answer. Heck, Luke was a lot more than a good friend. He had taken two bullets and nearly drowned trying to stop Raoul Vegas from kidnaping Willow and Rachel when they'd been out kayaking.

It had been two years ago, when Keenan Oakes had come to Puffin Harbor pretending to be Thaddeus Lakeman's heir. Kee had brought five men with him: Duncan and Luke and Jason and Peter and Matthew. Rachel called them Kee's disciples, but they were really partners in the business of salvaging whatever property paid well at the moment. Two years ago it had been stolen art, and the insurance reward had been substantial enough for Duncan to buy the old Drop Anchor with his share and remodel it into The Rosach Pub.

Luke and Kee had decided to settle in Puffin Harbor—Kee with Rachel and Luke with the peace and quiet of the area—and together the two men had started restoring historical buildings in nearby coastal towns.

Jason, Matt, and Peter still continued their lucrative salvage business, and last Willow had heard they'd been trying to refloat a sunken yacht off one of the Carribean Islands.

Ahab, the captain of Kee's schooner, the *Seven-to-Two Odds*, often went with them. But he usually stayed only long enough to get some woman so mad at him that he had to run back to Puffin Harbor to hide. Willow had noticed the *Seven-to-Two Odds* moored in front of Rachel and Kee's house yesterday afternoon, which meant that Ahab was back in town.

"Have ya fallen asleep?" Duncan asked as he pulled

onto the main road and pushed the powerful car through its gears.

"Yes," she said, snuggling into his nice-smelling jacket.

She only opened her eyes when she felt his hand on her chin, turning her face toward him. She could see his features in the glow of the dash lights, reflecting his serious gaze.

"The next time ya need to meet someone on a deserted pier late at night, and head out ta sea with them, I'll be going with ya, counselor."

Willow didn't hear any undertone of warning in his voice this time, or even reprimand. No, the man was merely stating a fact. "Okay," she said, pulling her chin free and closing her eyes again. "How about next Friday?"

"Excuse me?" he said, clearly surprised by her capitulation.

Lord, it felt good to catch Duncan off guard. It didn't happen that often. "I need to have a look around Thunder Island, and you can take me," she told him, pulling her hands up through the roomy sleeves to hug herself for warmth. "Can you scrape us up a boat by Friday?" she finished with a yawn that she didn't even try to stifle.

She never did hear his answer, since she quickly drifted off to sleep, not waking again until the gentle purr of the engine suddenly stopped.

Willow blinked in the early dawn light at the parking lot they'd stopped in. "This isn't home," she said in sleepy confusion. "It's the pub."

Duncan opened his door and got out. He walked around the car and unfastened her seat belt, lifted her out of the low sports coupe, and carried her toward the street.

Willow patted his chest. "You get a gold star for bringing me here instead of your house," she said, laying her head on his shoulder. "I'm impressed by your restraint."

His only answer was a faint smile as he stopped at the front door of The Rosach Pub, lowered her to her feet, and pulled his keys from his pocket. A stiff breeze blew in off the ocean from across the street, and Willow involuntarily shivered. Duncan put his arm around her to block her body with his, unlocked the door, and quickly hustled her inside.

The warmth of the dark, silent pub enveloped Willow as Duncan led her around the long central bar. He slid an overstuffed leather couch closer to the hearth, gently pushed her onto it, and turned and started piling kindling and wood in the huge stone fireplace. Willow immediately propped her feet on the hearth and looked around with languid interest as Duncan silently headed into the kitchen the moment the fire snapped to life.

There was nothing left of the old Drop Anchor. Willow knew the entire building had been gutted and rebuilt by Luke and Kee's construction company, carefully following Rachel's architectural designs, which had been based on Duncan's vision.

The walls were paneled with honey-stained local red oak, and matching booths and tables lined the large room. The plaster above the panels was painted a rich green and decorated with signs advertising ales and whiskies, a few nautical items, and even a set of crossed swords draped with a colorful plaid. The ceiling was wood strips finished in the same stain as the panels, and the floor was thick planking that had quickly weathered from the heavy traffic over the last year.

A long working bar dominated the center of the pub, with seating on all four sides except where a giant oak barrel, looking older than time, sat on display at one end.

The Rosach Pub had become a popular gathering place for locals on weeknights, Rachel had told Willow, and had been near to bursting with tourists on weekends this past summer.

One could almost imagine they were sitting in a pub in Scotland, and Willow guessed that was exactly what Duncan had been aiming for. She tucked her chin inside his jacket and smiled as she pictured Duncan spending his early years in a pub just like this one.

The image of his father's nosing glass came to mind, and Willow realized that the legacy of Scotland's gold was firmly entrenched in Duncan's soul. It made sense to her now that he'd been teaching her the fine art of drinking aged whisky the first six months she'd known him.

Too bad the lessons had stopped when she woke up in his bed.

A good twenty minutes passed before Duncan emerged from the kitchen carrying a large mug. But instead of bringing it over to her, he went behind the bar, pulled a bottle from a lower shelf, and poured a healthy amount of what she assumed was whisky into the steaming mug. Then he came over and waited until she could free herself from his jacket before handing it to her.

"Is this what you call a hot toddy?" she asked, lifting the mug to let the steam tickle her nose. She was surprised to smell chocolate and not coffee.

"It's what my mama would make when I caught a chill," he said, sitting down on the couch beside her with a tired sigh.

"You actually have a mother, too?" she asked, her teasing eyes meeting his firelit gaze.

"And a brother and sister. Drink," he ordered. "It'll warm ya up from the inside out."

Since she was in such a complacent mood, Willow carefully sipped the heady concoction, moaning in pleasure when the potent chocolate coated her sea-parched throat like soft flannel. She took another sip, then another, and welcomed the delicious warmth spreading through her body.

"How come you didn't make one for yourself?" she asked after yet another sip, holding the mug out to him. "Here, you can have a taste of mine."

"I intend to," he said, curling his arm around her shoulders and covering her mouth with his.

The kiss was a gentle, unhurried assault that neither coaxed nor demanded a response, and Willow simply let him have his taste. It was all she could do, really, since the whisky had turned her muscles to jelly. So she simply breathed in the smell of him, revisiting the taste of chocolate as their mouths melded together, and parted her lips with a sigh when his tongue slowly caressed hers.

A deeper, bone-thawing heat washed through her, along with a sense of contentment. She loved Duncan's kisses, the feel of his body engulfing hers, and the way his mere presence made her heart thump.

She lifted a hand and cupped his face when he pulled back to smile into her eyes. "I'm a mind reader, you know," she whispered, returning his smile. "And I see you're wishing you'd taken me to your home instead of your pub."

He shook his head, his gaze locked on hers. "Nay, lass. I knew that if I did I wouldn't have let ya leave."

She stroked her thumb over his tanned cheekbone. "My offer for an affair still stands, Duncan. No strings, no commitments, no more talk of marriage."

He turned his head and kissed her palm, then straightened, took the mug from her, and set it on the hearth. And before she knew what he was about, he slid a hand under her knees and scooped her onto this lap, then leaned back on the couch and studied her with heavy-lidded, assessing eyes.

Willow felt a blush creep into her cheeks and quickly tucked her head against his shoulder and stared into the fire.

"Ya cannot spend your whole life running, Willow," he said softly, his broad hand cupping her hip. He used his free hand to lift her chin to look at him. "You're smart enough to know that no matter how fast ya are, it's only an illusion of safety. Love comes unbidden, lass, and is as unstoppable as the sunrise."

She pulled her chin free, returning her gaze to the fire. "You don't think you're a bit arrogant to assume I love you?" she asked without accusation.

"Nay," he said, his chest rumbling in amusement. "You're the arrogant one, if ya think to continue denying your feelings." He lifted her chin again, gave her a quick kiss on the lips, then tucked her head against his chest with a deep sigh. "I've the patience to outwait ya, Willow, and the means to eventually capture and keep ya."

She popped her head up and frowned at him. "What means?"

"My body, of course," he said, arching one brow. "Ya can't seem to get enough of it," he added with a quick laugh, his hand closing over her wrist when she tried to take a swing at him. "I'm going to use your passion against ya, counselor," he said softly, his voice threatening and his eyes dancing. "So consider yourself warned."

"Forewarned is forearmed," she snapped, trying to pull her hand free.

"Aye," he agreed, dragging her back against him and folding her in a fierce embrace. "But I thought it was only gentlemanly to warn ya."

She snorted into his chest.

His arms tightened. "Tell me what favor you're doing for Cobb. And explain those sick lobsters I just carried in from the car and put on ice."

Willow instantly relaxed against him, greatly relieved for the change of subject. "Something's contaminated the waters around Thunder Island," she said, quickly proceeding to tell him her tale, beginning with Ray's phone call Monday and ending with last night's boat ride into the Gulf of Maine.

She left nothing out, not even her own thoughts about what was happening, and Duncan listened with the patience she'd come to expect from him, not interrupting once and not saying anything for several minutes once she was done.

She'd almost drifted off to sleep when he finally said, "So I take it you're heading back to Augusta today."

"No," she answered against his shoulder, too damned tired to lift her head and look at him. "I'm going to Orono first. I know someone at the University of Maine who is an expert on lobsters, and I'm taking her my specimens. Then I'll go to Augusta and dig through my files on all the licensed waste sites operating in Maine for the last five years. Right after," she finished with a yawn, settling deeper against him, "I have a nap."

Duncan said nothing, instead twisting until he was stretched out on the couch with her on top of him. Willow decided she couldn't ask for a warmer, more comfortable, more secure bed, and with one last yawn, she snuggled down and promptly fell asleep.

Duncan stared up at the ceiling and examined Willow's story from a dozen different angles, and decided that each one sent a cold chill down his spine. Any way he looked at it, the woman was rushing headlong into trouble.

People willing to dump toxic waste in the ocean were also willing to commit even more crimes to cover their tracks. And Duncan knew Willow would go after them with the aggression of a lioness, not only because it was her job, but because it was her childhood playground they'd fouled.

He tightened his arms around the softly snoring woman on his chest and slid a hand down her back to cup her bottom. Willow Foster was pure passion personified; she lived every day to the fullest, right up to the edge sometimes, without hesitation or apology—right up to the granite wall protecting her heart.

She would go after the bad guys with the same passion she'd brought to his bed, and Duncan knew he couldn't stop her, no matter that his gut was telling him to do just that. If he even hinted she should pass this problem off to investigators, it could very well mean the end of their tenuous relationship.

And he was getting too close to risk acting like the throwback she accused him of being.

To the world he was an affable, easygoing barkeep, but

beneath his veneer of genial indifference Duncan had a core of solid steel that would stun most people if they looked closely enough. It was a side of himself he'd kept hidden from Willow up to this point, although he knew she suspected it existed. But he could *feel* her softening toward him, all but see the protective wall she'd built around her heart starting to crack as she slowly inched closer.

Duncan didn't take Willow's refusal to love him personally. She simply refused to fall in love with any man, afraid of being vulnerable in what she perceived as emotional dependency. She was like a moth dancing around a flame, passionately flirting right up to the edge, then soaring away when the heat got too intense.

It was all because of her parents.

And because of an experience she'd had when she was fifteen.

Rachel had explained this to Duncan, after Willow had left his bed and run back to Augusta, by telling him what had happened to her sister that long-ago summer. A boy Willow had been dating, and had started to like quite a bit, had gotten his foot tangled in a trap line while lobstering with his father, and been pulled overboard and dragged below the surface. The boy had drowned, as had his father while trying to save him.

Since then, Rachel had explained, Willow had been shying away from anything remotely resembling a commitment.

As for her parents' role, Willow had grown up seeing them so passionately in love that just the thought of living without each other was impossible. Which was why for three years Willow hadn't had any trouble believing her father had killed her mother and Thaddeus Lakeman in a jealous rage, and then killed himself. And even after they'd discovered Raoul Vegas, an art smuggler, had been the one to murder them, it was too late—the potentially destructive power of love was firmly entrenched in Willow's psyche.

And so to this day Willow continued to protect herself by keeping that final bastion of her heart locked safely away.

Duncan had been searching for the key for nearly two years, and his patience was growing thin. Sometimes, usually alone in his bed late at night, he wondered if loving Willow Foster was nothing more than an exercise in frustration.

He smiled derisively as he lifted her limp left hand and looked at the smudged words he'd written on her palm. When Luke had come to get her truck, Duncan had noticed a piece of paper sitting on the passenger's seat on which she'd quickly scribbled the sentence to look it up later.

Duncan tucked her hand over his heart and stared up at the ceiling again. *Potes currere sed te occulere non potes.* Oh, did he wish to be a fly on the wall when she finally translated his not-so-subtle warning.

He patted her bottom and sighed in fatigue. His worry over what she'd been doing at sea had made for an unusually long night, and he was in dire need of a nap himself. They had three hours, he figured, before the lunch crew showed up and started banging pots around.

Duncan kissed Willow's hair and closed his eyes, finally going to sleep on the decision that it was time he turned her own game back on the infuriatingly stubborn woman.

Chapter Five

✵

It was after midnight when Willow finally stepped through the door of her apartment in Augusta, and lacking even the energy to hang up her jacket, she let it slide to the floor when she set down her briefcase and kicked off her shoes. She padded through the living room without bothering to turn on the lights, headed directly to the fridge in her tiny kitchen, and grabbed an already opened bottle of wine. She wiggled the cork free and drank straight from the bottle only to snort at the realization that she didn't want wine, she wanted a large glass of thirty-year-old Scotch.

It was all Duncan's fault, damn him. She had awakened in The Rosach Pub with an acute awareness that the body beneath hers was fully aroused. Duncan's hand had been stroking her backside, his other hand toying with her hair, and the heat radiating from him could have powered Puffin Harbor. There'd been a controlled strength in his touch, an almost palpable restraint, as if he'd been trying not to wake her while indulging himself in his sensual play.

Willow's own arousal had been immediate; the fine hairs on her body had stirred as her skin tightened in response to his touch, and her hips had unconsciously shifted to bring his arousal more fully against her own blossoming need.

Realizing she was awake, Duncan had tilted her head and kissed her quite thoroughly, coaxing her to respond with more boldly intimate caresses, and Willow had wrapped her arms around his neck and returned his kiss with abandon.

He'd run his hands under her sweater, encircling her ribs and lifting her just enough so his thumbs could trace her budded nipples through the thin lace of her bra. Willow remembered making a noise then—half moan, half demand—and sitting up and grabbing the hem of her sweater to pull it off over her head.

Duncan's answering noise had been that of a wounded animal as he'd yanked the sweater back down to her waist. "The lunch crew's in the kitchen," he'd ground out, sitting up and turning until Willow had found herself staring in horror into fierce green eyes not inches from hers.

"You started it," she had snapped, scrambling off him and taking a step back, smiling tightly when he grunted and quickly cupped his groin for protection.

It was then the first hint of impending doom had reared its ugly head.

Duncan had stood, she'd taken another step back from the gleam in his eyes, and he'd stalked her retreat until she was backed against the warm stones of the hearth. Towering over her like a mountain of menace, he'd taken hold of her chin, leaned down, and said, very softly, "Aye, and I'm going to finish it, brat, by accepting your offer. As of today, we are in an exclusive affair, to be conducted in private, with no more talk of marriage."

Her surprise must have shown because he'd smiled then, in a rather alarming way, and straightened, crossing his arms over his chest. "If you have any addenda, counselor, now's your only chance to voice them."

She couldn't even work up enough spit to swallow, so she'd simply shaken her head, her eyes locked on his immobilizing gaze.

He'd stepped forward, cupped her bloodless face with both hands, and tilted her mouth up to meet his kiss. "It's begun then," he'd whispered before turning away, his hand manacled around her wrist as he led her past the bar and into the late-morning sunshine.

Willow took another long swig of the wine, and pondered the fact that she was barely twelve hours into an affair and all she could think about was the dangerous look in Duncan's eyes when he'd dropped her off at her truck in Kee and Rachel's driveway. He'd kissed her one last time—with only a hint of what she had to look forward to—and said she'd see him in a day or two.

Which meant he intended to come to Augusta so they could conduct their affair in private.

Which also meant that she had ultimately won the war.

Or had she?

Willow looked down at the faded remains of ink on her hand. She'd gone straight from seeing Jane Huntley at the University of Maine to her own office in Augusta, and clutching the paper she'd scribbled Duncan's words on, she had pawed through her legal library until she'd found a Latin dictionary.

It had taken her twenty minutes to finally translate the convoluted sentence, and as she had read it over and over, that feeling of impending doom had grown stronger and stronger.

Potes currere sed te occulere non potes.

You can run, but you can't hide.

At about the same time Willow was trying to drown her worries with wine, Duncan was sitting at the wide granite-topped island in his kitchen, explaining his own worries to Kee and Luke and Ahab. He'd already told them about Willow's nighttime ride out into the Gulf of Maine, what she had found, and what he suspected was happening. His late-night visitors listened in silence, ever-deepening frowns creasing their brows, until Duncan came to the part about what had been happening to the more vocal fishermen.

Kee's head snapped up. "Whoever dumped the waste is still around?" he asked.

Duncan shrugged. "It seems so."

"And Willow is going after them," Kee said as a statement of fact, not a question. "Alone."

Duncan shook his head. "Not exactly alone," he softly corrected. "The four of us will be shadowing her. And the operative word here is *shadow*," he emphasized. "I don't want her knowing we're involved," he finished, leaning back on his stool and letting his intentions hang between them.

Kee frowned at his glass of soda, and Duncan knew his friend was wishing it was something stronger. But when he'd arrived an hour ago, and Duncan had offered him a beer, Kee had muttered that he wouldn't be drinking for the next nine months. Kee hadn't had anything stronger than soda for Rachel's last pregnancy, either, supporting her by abstaining from alcohol, sharing nutritious meals, and taking long walks.

Ahab didn't feel the need to abstain from anything for Rachel's sake, and had immediately asked for whisky when he'd arrived. Duncan had poured him a tall, ice-filled glass of blended Scotch, not inclined to waste his good stuff on Ahab's unsophisticated palate. Luke preferred beer, and Duncan always kept a few bottles of domestic ale in the fridge for him, along with chilled glasses in the freezer.

"Why doesn't she turn this over to investigators?" Kee asked. "The AG's office must have several at their disposal."

"She likely will," Duncan said, "when the time comes to build her case. But Cobb asked her to keep things quiet, and Willow has agreed to for now, until she knows exactly what's happening."

"What is it you want us to do?" Luke asked.

"I think we should start by having our own look around Thunder Island," Duncan said, setting down his glass of ale. "Underwater."

"You're talking about special equipment," Kee said. "If the water is contaminated, we can't be swimming in it. And the minisub is in the Carribean."

Duncan shook his head. "I don't think we need the sub. From what I saw of those lobsters, I'm guessing it's not lethal enough to affect us. Besides, we'll be fully suited."

Ahab involuntarily shivered. "The water temperature is forty-five degrees," he said, taking a gulp of Scotch to ward off his imaginary chill.

"We have dry suits," Luke interjected, looking at Duncan. "When do we go?"

Duncan eyed the wall clock. It was after midnight on Sunday morning. "Monday," he said, nodding to Luke. "Can you have our gear ready by then?"

"Maybe we should call in Jason and Matt and Peter," Kee suggested.

Duncan shook his head. "Too many of us will only draw unwanted attention." He shifted on his stool, cupping his own glass of ale as he looked at the men. "Willow asked me to take her to Thunder Island on Friday, so I want to make sure it's safe before then." He stopped his gaze on Kee. "I thought we'd use the *Seven-to-Two Odds*, so we'll appear to be nothing more than tourists."

"The schooner's known in these parts," Kee pointed out.

"I'll make it look as if I'm taking Willow on a picnic," Duncan said with a grin. "We'll bring Mickey to round out the domestic scene." Even though Kee actually owned the schooner, Duncan turned to Ahab. "If I promise not to scratch her, will ya let me take the *Seven-to-Two Odds* out by myself Friday?"

Ahab narrowed his eyes. "You can't run up her sails. She's not a two-man ship."

"I'll use the engine." Duncan looked over at Kee. "Do ya think Mickey would enjoy a day on the water with Willow?"

Kee grinned as he shook his head. "That damn wolf hasn't quit sulking since Willow left to go back to Augusta. He hadn't seen her for two months, and she didn't spend any time with him this visit. He'd love to have a whole day with her." Kee turned serious again. "Do you trust Ray Cobb?"

"Willow does," Duncan said. "And I trust her judgment." He looked at Ahab again. "Can ya quietly ask around the docks and see who knows what?"

Ahab's grin was more sinister than genial. "I can find out more in the bars than down at the docks," he said. He cocked his head in thought. "I think The Gale Wind over in Trunk Harbor would be the best place to start."

Duncan hid his smile by draining the last of the now warm ale in his glass. The Gale Wind was a hardcore drinking bar rather than a couples' gathering spot like The Rosach Pub. Ahab would be right at home there.

Duncan stood up and headed toward his back door, letting his friends know this meeting was over. They followed, and Luke and Ahab stepped out into the crisp, starlit night with a muttered good-bye as they headed to Luke's truck.

Kee stopped on the porch and turned back to Duncan. "I prefer that Rachel not know anything about this," he said. "Not yet, anyway."

Duncan nodded agreement. "That will be Willow's decision, whether or not she wants to involve her sister."

Kee suddenly grinned. "Willow told Rachel you've agreed to an affair. Sounds like a full-scale retreat to me, Captain Ross."

"Really?" Duncan said, returning his grin. "And here I

thought it was a tactical move forward. I'm hoping Wil low will discover that getting her wish granted might b more than she's bargained for."

Kee shook his head. "God, you're arrogant, Ross."

"You're confusing arrogance with desperation," Dun can softly contradicted. "I don't want to lose her."

Kee looked him level in the eye for several beats, the suddenly laughed and slapped Duncan's shoulder. "The don't ever let her meet your mother. At least not unt after the wedding." He just as suddenly sobered. "Willow will eventually come around, my friend," he said softly "We're all pulling for you."

Duncan snorted and stepped back into the house "Thanks but no thanks." He stopped from closing th door and glared at Kee. "And you tell little miss mouth Mikaela for me that if I find out she's placed bets on thi wedding, she'll be sweeping the Rosach floor all summe for punishment."

With a chuckle and nod of agreement, Kee headed down the steps to his own truck. Duncan closed the door turned to face his quiet house, and sighed. Lord, h wished he knew what he was doing when it came t courting Willow.

Willow had spent all day Sunday at the office goin through files on licensed waste sites, and now it was late Monday afternoon and she still hadn't figured out exactly what she was looking for.

There were five major waste-disposal sites and over fif teen smaller ones operating in Maine, and each of thei licenses had every *t* crossed and every *i* dotted perfectly Their evaluation reports also showed that everyone wa:

in compliance with state regulations, except for a few minor violations.

Jane Huntley at the University of Maine had thought it might be pesticide poisoning when Willow had shown her the lobsters and crabs Saturday, but had reserved judgment until after she could run her tests. Armed with only Jane's guess, Willow had narrowed her search to sites licensed to accept agricultural waste as well as applications for sites that had been turned down.

That's when things had finally gotten interesting. One company, Kingston Corporation, had been denied licenses on three potential plots of land along the Down East Maine coast several years ago, before site number 4 had been approved just three years ago. Kingston's records for the approved site showed that they were operating in full compliance, but there was something unusual about the paper trail; it was nothing she could put her finger on or wrap her mind around, just something . . . not right.

Willow hit the intercom button on her desk. "Karen, could you sneak into the Department of Environmental Protection archives again and find the original applications Kingston Corporation submitted? Look for three denied applications from about four to six years ago."

Silence was her only answer, and Willow looked toward her office door and saw that the outer office was dark. She looked at her watch, then closed her eyes on a groan and scrubbed her face with both hands.

It was eight thirty. Willow then remembered her secretary peeking in the door three hours ago to tell her that anyone with a life was going home. Karen had also muttered something about not wanting to come in tomorrow and find her boss crushed to death under a mountain of files.

Willow pushed back her chair, stood up, set the heels of her palms on her lower back, and groaned as she stretched her frozen muscles. There was no help for it, she was going to have to venture into the bowels of the building and look for the Kingston applications herself.

She slipped her feet back into her sensible black shoes, walked out of the office and down the silent corridor, then headed down the stairs leading to the basement. She flipped on lights as she strode along the lower hall, her only company the muted echo of her shoes on the granite floor. She knew the cleaning crew didn't come in until after eleven because she'd been startled by them more times than she cared to remember.

Maybe Karen was right that she needed to get a life.

That brought Willow's thoughts to Duncan. What was he doing tonight? Would he call? Willow snorted as she flicked on the lights of the archive hall. It wouldn't do him any good to call if she wasn't even home to answer the phone. And she had forgotten to give him her cell phone number.

She started her search in the back right corner of the archives, familiar with DEP's section ever since her first big case almost two years ago. She'd spent a lot of time down here since then, unwittingly becoming the AG's resident expert on environmental issues when her predecessor had left to join a private practice.

Willow reached up and ran her fingers along the dusty boxes as she read the labels on each one. It took her nearly twenty minutes to find all three boxes containing the three Kingston applications because two of them had been filed out of sequence and the third one was hidden behind four boxes of transcripts from a five-year-old wrongly filed murder trial.

She carried the boxes over to a table on the back wall, pulled up a chair and sat down, and started digging through the box dated six years ago. She found that the site Kingston had applied for was less than ten miles from Trunk Harbor, but it had been turned down due to a sub-surface aquifer that would be in danger of contamination. Other than that she found nothing unusual in the paperwork, and she stuffed everything back in the box and went on to the next application.

The second application was for a site fifteen miles farther down the coast but inland a good twenty miles. Kingston had proposed to bring in the waste via cargo ships and truck it to the site, but had been turned down because of a geological survey stating the granite was too close to the surface and riddled with fissures.

Willow looked at her watch. It was already nine thirty, and her stomach was growling. She was just eyeing the third box, debating whether or not to take it back to her office to read the next day, when the lights suddenly went out.

"Hey!" she shouted. "I'm in here!"

"What?" came a man's reply as the lights flicked back on. "Who's there?"

"It's me. Willow."

Willow heard footsteps headed her way, and stood up and peeked around the floor-to-ceiling shelving. "Who's here?" she asked, quickly moving to look down another aisle.

"It's only me, Willow," Greg Myers said, stepping into

her line of sight. His smile was immediate, and a bit disapproving. "What are you still doing here?" he asked, walking toward her. "You shouldn't be down here this late all by yourself."

"Last I knew, bogeymen don't haunt dusty archive halls," she returned, stepping back to the table and stuffing papers in the box. She looked up at Greg when he stopped beside her. "And I might ask you the same question."

Greg scooped up a few of the papers that had fallen on the floor. "I'm preparing for the Briggs murder trial next week. I was just walking by when I noticed someone had left the lights on in here. What's this?" Greg asked, holding up one of the papers. "Kingston Corporation?" he read, lifting one brow at her. "Isn't Edward Simmons associated with them? Remember him? Simmons ran for governor two elections ago for the Green Party." He snorted. "And now he's part owner of a waste site. Talk about an anomaly. Is Kingston Corp. being bad?"

Willow took the paper from him and dropped it in the box and closed the cover. "Not that I know of," she said, stacking the boxes on top of each other. "I was just looking for an old geological survey that someone said had been done for them a while back. I'm working on a timber-cutting violation Down East and thought the survey might help me."

Greg picked up the boxes when she went to do so. "Did you find it?" he asked, following her down the aisle and setting the boxes on the shelf she pointed to.

"I found it, but it won't do me any good. The survey is fifty miles west of where the timber cutting is going on. It's in a completely different watershed."

He shrugged and gestured with his hand for her to precede him down the aisle toward the door. "Too bad," he said. "But since we're both so dedicated to our jobs as to still be here after nine at night, how about we grab something to eat at Gilly's Bar and Grill?"

Willow stopped at the door and flipped off the lights, turning to smile up at Greg. "That sounds heavenly, but I still have work to do. I'm expecting a call."

No sooner were the words out of her mouth when her cell phone rang. Willow jumped and Greg simply smiled at her. She pulled the phone off the clip on her belt, flipped it open, and said, "Willow Foster."

"Willy, it's Jane. I haven't been able to find anything conclusive. I need you to get some water samples for me."

Willow smiled at Greg in apology, then turned and started walking toward the stairs. "You couldn't find anything?" she whispered. "No trace of any toxins?"

"No, although that wouldn't be unusual for pesticide poisoning. But the symptoms all point to it. Water samples are the only thing that will confirm it, though, and even then we might not find enough residue. The half-life of most modern pesticides isn't really that long."

"What about DDT?" Willow whispered as she climbed the stairs, aware of Greg not three steps behind her. "That stuff will be hanging around for generations."

"But not the modern pesticides. They're short-lived."

"Ah, Jane, can I call you back in a few minutes? What's your home number?"

There was a moment's pause and then Jane laughed. "I'm still at my lab. I've been trying your home number for the last hour. I didn't catch you in the middle of a date, did I?"

Willow snorted into the phone. "I'm still at my office."

Jane sighed. "No wonder we're both still single," she muttered. "I'll hang around until you call back. You have the number."

"Okay, 'bye," Willow said, closing the phone and turning to Greg. "Thanks again for offering to feed me. Another time?"

"Sure," he said, his smile understanding. "You want me to wait and walk you to your car?"

"No. I have to clean up my office if I don't want another lecture from Karen in the morning. And I have a few more calls to make."

One of which would be to Duncan, she decided.

Greg gave her a nod and turned and headed toward the front door. Willow watched him stop and talk to the night guard at the front desk, and saw them both look back at her. She gave them a wave and turned toward her office with a smile. Knowing Greg, he'd just asked the guard to keep an eye on her and walk her out to her car when she finally left.

Greg had joined the AG's office just three months before Willow had, and being the new kids on the block, they'd quickly become friends. For two years Greg had been hinting at something more than friendship, but Willow had been reluctant to pursue that avenue. She liked Greg, but dating a coworker was a bit outside her comfort zone, considering her history of revolving boyfriends. It would be awkward having to see him every day after they parted company.

Willow sat down at her desk, behind the mountain of

files she'd accumulated, and absently ran her thumb over the keypad of her cell phone. Jane wanted water samples. Well, she could get them this Friday, when she and Duncan visited Thunder Island. She punched a few buttons on her cell phone, calling up the number to Jane's lab, and pushed SEND. The phone was answered after only two rings.

"You owe me big-time for this," Jane said without preamble. "Do you know how hard it is to hide sick lobsters in a lab I'm sharing with three curious colleagues?"

"Would a long weekend on Monhegan Island put me back in your good graces?" Willow asked, leaning back in her chair and swinging it to face the window. "With five-star cooking and a bedroom with a fireplace and whirlpool?"

There was a heartbeat of silence, and then, "It might, if a blond-haired, blue-eyed hunk comes with that bedroom, who's long on muscle but not too brainy. I've had it up to my armpits with brainy men."

Willow laughed, remembering Jane Huntley's blatant pursuit of every jock in high school. "But then what would you talk about?" she asked.

"Talk?" Jane chortled. "If he's a hunk, why would I want to talk to him? Grunts and groans are enough."

"My God, you're shameless," Willow growled. "And to think I used to envy you."

"You stole Ray Cobb from me," Jane said without malice. "That wasn't shameless?"

"I was a sophomore," Willow said, figuring that was explanation enough.

"Is it really true? Patty left Ray?"

"Not for long, I don't think," Willow said, using her

foot to rock her chair. "Ray loves her too much to lose her. About those water samples—how do I go about getting them?"

"Swing by here and I'll give you some bottles and show you how to take the samples without contaminating them." Jane hesitated. "Are you sure you want to pursue this on your own, Willy? We have the equipment and manpower to look into this."

"I promised Ray, and by default I've also promised the other fishermen," Willow told her. "And I likely will call you guys in once I know the *who* and the *how* of what's happened and I'm ready to go public. Until then, I appreciate the favor you're doing for me by keeping this quiet. I'll call just as soon as I know when I can get up there to get the test kits."

"Okay," Jane said. "Meanwhile, I'll keep researching. You know, there was something similar to this down off Long Island a few summers ago. The lobster industry was all but devastated, and they attributed it to pesticides used for mosquito spraying that washed into the ocean. There's even a class-action suit by the lobstermen pending."

"But this poisoning is contained to only Thunder Island," Willow pointed out.

"I know," Jane agreed. "I'm just relating a similar occurrence. The Long Island Sound lobsters were also listless and millions died."

"And that's why you suspect pesticides? It couldn't be heavy-metal poisoning or something like that? Or a parasite or a naturally occurring disease?"

"Not heavy metal. Lead or mercury poisoning is a long-term, cumulative problem. As for a natural disease, I can't rule that out. That's why I need those water samples."

"Okay, then," Willow said with a tired sigh, scrubbing her face with her free hand. "I'll call you in a day or two. And, Jane? Thanks."

"Not a problem, Willy. Remember, blue eyes and blond hair."

Willow closed the phone with a laugh and leaned back in her chair and thought about blond hair and *green* eyes. And she also thought she must never introduce Jane Huntley to Duncan Ross.

Willow snapped her cell phone back in the clip on her belt and picked up her office phone. She opened her day planner to her address book, to the "Ds" for Duncan, and decided she would call the pub before she tried his home.

Chapter Six

❖

It was after ten at night when Duncan dragged himself up his porch stairs; the only thing keeping him moving forward was the thought of spending the next hour in a hot sauna and then falling into a soft bed.

Cold-water diving was hard on a man's body, and seeing all those dead lobsters and crabs littering the ocean floor around Thunder Island was just as hard on a man's heart.

"I knew when I was building that sauna it was the best part of your remodel," Luke said as he plodded up the stairs beside Duncan. "The Swedes certainly know how to deal with bone-chilling cold."

Duncan unlocked the kitchen door and stepped aside for Luke to go in first. "I noticed ya built it bigger than the blueprints called for," Duncan said. "Perhaps on the misguided notion that I share my toys?"

"I was still recuperating from my nearly fatal swim in

the Gulf of Maine," Luke said without apology. "I swear that kind of cold stays with a man for months. I was only planning ahead for days like today."

"Go turn on the sauna and I'll get the Scotch," Duncan suggested, taking off his boots. "The towels are in the—"

"Duncan!"

Duncan spun on his socked heels only to quickly open his arms to catch the lithe, feminine body hurtling toward him. "Molly!" was all he got out, the impact of her body against his making her name emerge more as a plea than admonishment.

"Ewww," Molly squealed, wiggling free and stepping back. "Ya're freezing." She suddenly noticed Luke standing in the hallway, and her smile moved to him. "Hi, Luke," she said, her cheeks turning a soft pink. "Ya look cold, too."

"A hug would warm me up," Luke said, opening his arms.

Molly hesitated only the merest of seconds before stepping into Luke's embrace. But when Duncan realized Luke had no intention of ending the hug anytime soon, he pulled his sister out of his friend's clutches and turned her to face him. "What are ya doing here, Molly?" he asked. He stiffened and look toward the living room. "Where's Mother?"

Molly's smile disappeared. "Home," she said succinctly.

"Ya came by yourself? Does Mother know ya're here?"

Molly shook her head. "I've run away."

Duncan rolled his eyes. "It's not considered running away from home when ya're twenty-six years old."

Molly darted an embarrassed glance at Luke, who was watching them with unabashed curiosity, then inched closer to Duncan. "Mother's being impossible again," she whispered. "She's even threatened to call the queen and ask her to lock me in the Tower of London."

Duncan ruffled his baby sister's long, thick mane of strawberry blond hair. "Believe me, squirt," he said with a chuckle, "if she hadn't been so worried about saddling Her Highness with ya, she'd have done that years ago."

Molly patted down her mussed hair. "She's also threatening to disinherit me again."

"Now what did ya do?" Duncan asked, running a tired hand over his cold face.

"I told her I was going to New Zealand to marry Ben."

Duncan came completely awake. "Ben who?"

"Benjamin Zane. He's a sheep farmer in New Zealand, and I love him and I'm going to marry him."

The silence in the kitchen was so suddenly absolute, Duncan could hear the blood rushing to his throbbing temple. He stared into Molly's challenging green eyes, not knowing whether to curse or roar in frustration.

"I, ah, think I'll turn on the sauna," Luke said, quietly disappearing down the back hall.

"And just where did you meet this Benjamin Zane, and how long have you known him?" Duncan whispered.

"I haven't actually met him. Not in person," Molly whispered back. "We met on the Internet."

"And you've fallen in love over email, and are moving halfway around the world to marry a man you haven't *actually* met," Duncan said even more softly. "And you've run away from home because Mother won't go along with your plans. Have I got it right so far?"

A dull flush colored Molly's cheeks as she nodded, her huge green eyes—now more uncertain than defiant—locked on his. "I love him," she said so softly Duncan barely heard her. "And I need yar support."

Duncan involuntarily shivered, not from the cold but from the image of his baby sister being lured to New Zealand by Ben the sheep farmer—if that's what he really was.

"So, will ya help me with Mother?" Molly asked.

"No."

"Duncan!"

He pulled in a calming breath. "Not tonight, Molly," he said, taking her by the shoulders and smiling warmly down at her. "Ya can't hit me with this kind of news and expect me to rush to your rescue. We'll talk tomorrow. How did ya get here from the airport?" he asked, not having seen a car in the driveway.

"I took a taxi."

"From Bangor?"

Molly wrinkled her delicate, freckled nose. "I hate driving on the wrong side of the road. The taxi might cost a fortune but at least I made it here alive." Her feminine brows lowered in a frown. "And how come ya don't leave a key under the mat? I had ta crawl in through the mudroom window."

"For the same reason I lock the door," he said, turning to the cupboards and taking down a new bottle of twelve-year-old Rosach Scotch. "To keep the honest people out. Does Camden know you're here, at least?" he asked, reaching into another cupboard for glasses.

"Nay," Molly said, climbing onto a stool at the island. "I stole away like a thief in the night."

Duncan pointed at the phone on the wall. "Call them."

"If I do, Mother will be standing in this kitchen by noon tomorrow," Molly warned, her eyes bright with renewed challenge. "Are ya that anxious ta see her?"

"Dammit, Molly," Duncan snapped, setting the glasses down with a thunk. He opened the Scotch with a violent twist. "I swear you'd try the patience of a saint."

"I love ya, too, big brother."

It took all of his willpower not to drink straight from the bottle, but Duncan carefully poured the Scotch into the three glasses, slid one toward Molly, and picked up another. "To family dynamics," he said, tapping his glass to hers, then downing the Scotch in one swallow.

Molly slowly sipped hers.

Duncan refilled his glass, then slid Luke's toward him when he came back and sat at the island.

"Oh, I answered yar phone earlier," Molly said. "About twenty minutes ago." Her eyes brightened again and her mouth curved into a huge smile. "She said her name was Willow."

Duncan downed his second glass of Scotch in one gulp.

Molly canted her head. "She seemed a bit surprised when I answered. Is she a girlfriend? Or should I say, *was* she a girlfriend?"

Duncan closed his eyes, again undecided whether to curse or roar. "I don't suppose ya told her you're my sister?"

"Now what fun is there in that?" Molly asked with a laugh. "I only told her I expected ya home soon." She folded her hands on the counter and stared innocently up at him. "I asked if she wanted ya to ring her up when ya got in, but she only said ta tell ya ta crawl back in yar cave."

Luke choked on his drink.

Molly's eyes danced. "I swear I heard her mutter something about a troglodyte as she was hanging up the phone."

"Ya're reckless for someone wanting my help," Duncan growled, spinning away from the island and walking to the door. "Luke, you can sleep *downstairs* in my bed," he said, bending over and putting his boots back on. He straightened and gave him a threatening glare. "And I'm trusting ya to be in it alone."

Luke snorted. "It'd be kind of crowded with me and Molly and the sheep farmer," he muttered, downing the rest of his own drink, shuddering when the warmth hit his belly.

"Luke doesn't have ta stay. I don't need a babysitter," Molly said, her defiant eyes moving from Duncan to Luke, then back to Duncan. "And anyway, where are ya going? Ya just got home."

"To straighten out the mess ya've made of my love life," Duncan said, grabbing his jacket and pointing it at her. "I'll be back by noon tomorrow, so don't even think of running off to New Zealand." He took a warning step closer. "Because if I have to chase after ya, you'll be *begging* to be locked in the Tower of London."

That said, and not waiting for a reply from either of them, Duncan slammed out of the house and into the cold night. Damn it to hell. Willow thought he had another woman staying with him. Talk about compounding problems; at the rate things were spiraling out of control he'd be lucky if Willow didn't shoot him when he showed up on her doorstep tonight.

Duncan climbed in his truck and headed toward Augusta, then spent the next two hours trying to decide if he should politely knock on Willow's door—or just quietly pick the lock, let himself in, and crawl into bed with her before she knew what was happening.

But in the end, Duncan decided knocking might win him more points than scaring the hell out of her. It was long after midnight when he finally walked up the steps to the back apartment of the huge old house in the center of Augusta, softly clapped the brass knocker, and waited with the patience of a man standing on the trapdoor of a gallows.

The distinct sound of metal clanking on metal tickled her subconscious, slowly pulling Willow from the depths of a restless dream. She fluttered her eyes open to peek at the clock on her nightstand, groaned when she saw it was just after one in the morning, then suddenly twisted upright at the realization that someone— and she was pretty sure who—was knocking on her door.

"I'm coming," she called, not caring that she sounded testy as she slipped into her robe. She snapped on a lamp when she padded into her living room. "So help me God, you better be on your knees," she muttered as she threw open the door.

"She's my sister."

"Troglodytes don't have families. They crawl out from under rocks," Willow shot back, sidestepping when he crowded his way inside. She gently closed the door and leaned her back against it, crossing her arms under her breasts.

Duncan turned in the middle of her huge living room, his hands on his hips and his fierce gaze locked on hers. "She's my sister," he repeated, his eyes darkening. "And ya don't open your door without knowing who's on the other side. Not in the middle of the night, and not during the day."

"I saw your truck through the window."

"You're supposed to close your curtains at night."

"Thank you. I'll be sure to close them from now on."

"Molly showed up unannounced," he said, slipping out of his jacket and letting it fall to his feet. He started unbuttoning his shirt. "She's a brat with a perverted sense of humor," he added, shrugging out of his shirt and letting it fall next to his jacket. "I've had a hellish day, my eyelids feel like they're lined with sandpaper, and I'm so cold I'm numb," he finished, pulling his navy blue T-shirt over his head and tossing it down on the coffee table. Then he took off his boots and socks, straightened, and started unbuckling his belt.

Willow could only stand frozen in place and watch, neither appalled nor surprised when he dropped his pants, stepped out of them, and stood facing her wearing only a scowl and navy blue boxers.

"So you just walked out on your sister?" she asked, fighting to stifle the laughter bubbling inside her.

Lord, but Duncan appeared right at home standing in the middle of her eclectic assortment of old-world furniture; he was big and solid and weatherworn, quite wonderful to look at, and he definitely held the promise of comfort.

His eyes narrowed. "Are you laughing?"

Willow pushed away from the door and headed to her bedroom, taking hold of his hand as she walked by, pausing only long enough to shut off the living room light. "I wouldn't dream of laughing at you, Dunky," she said, leading him over to the bed and shrugging out of her robe. "I know a man at the end of his patience when I see one."

She slipped into bed, scooted to the far side, and patted the mattress. "Come here and let me warm you up."

Her offer appeared to surprise him; he stood rooted in place, staring down at her through the muted shadows. "I need a shower."

"You need me more."

"I'm dead on my feet, counselor."

"Then get off them," she said, patting the bed again.

Still he didn't move.

Willow ducked her head to hide her smile. "If I promise not to attack you, will you just come to bed and let me cuddle you?"

"Cuddle," he repeated, deadpan.

"Why are you so cold?" she asked, inching her way closer to him. "What were you doing today?"

"Luke and I went—" She reached out, grabbed the leg of his shorts, and pulled him down into bed—quickly scooting out of the way before he landed on her. "—diving," he finished with a whoosh, his momentum rolling him over until he had his arms wrapped tightly around her.

"Diving where?" she asked, her face only inches from his.

"Around Thunder Island."

She reared back. "But why? I told you we can't draw attention to the island."

Duncan pulled her back against him, tucked her head under his chin, and heaved a weary sigh. "Don't worry, nobody saw us. I just wanted to have a look around underwater."

"And?" she muttered into his chest.

"And there's plenty more lobsters and crabs like those you got Friday night, and hundreds of dead ones closer to the island shoreline." He kissed the top of her head, reached down, and pulled the blankets up over them. "But other than that, there's nothing. No containers or anything else out of the ordinary."

Willow was silent for several heartbeats, then she wrapped her arms around him and said, "You don't feel that cold."

"I had the truck heater on full blast all the way here. A bone-deep chill is all I'm feeling now."

Willow threw her leg over his and snuggled him closer—and found that his mind might not be up to making love, but his body sure was interested.

She settled her cheek against his wonderfully muscled chest, ignoring his hand that slipped down her back to cup her bottom. "Go to sleep, Dunky. We'll start our affair in the morning."

His lips brushed over her hair, the rough stubble of his jaw combing through it, and Duncan's arms tightened around her with a soft sigh of contentment. Within two minutes his breathing evened out in the rhythm of deep sleep, and within five minutes Willow also drifted back to sleep—thinking that as affairs went, this one was starting out with a bit less than a bang.

Chapter Seven

✿

"*Y*a slipped out of bed and snuck off without waking me."

Willow smiled across her desk at Duncan, painfully aware that they were not alone. Karen stood hovering in the doorway of the outer office, seemingly uncertain whether to call Security or simply continue to stare at the handsome giant scowling at her boss.

"I did not slip out of bed, I was crowded out," Willow whispered through her tight smile. "And I didn't wake you for fear of my life."

"Excuse me?"

Willow laid down her pen, folded her hands together, and kicked up her smile several notches. "I wasn't about to roust a sleeping tiger. I am well aware they wake up grumpy."

"A tiger?" he repeated, puffing out his chest.

Willow lifted one brow. "You certainly sounded like

one, snoring loud enough to wake the dead." She leaned to her left to see past him. "It's okay, Karen. Everything's under control."

"Your, ah, nine o'clock is here," Karen said, forcibly tearing her wide-eyed gaze from Duncan to look at Willow. "Do you want me to get Mrs. Poole a cup of coffee?"

"That would be good, Karen. Tell Mary I'll be with her in a few minutes. And could you find me the Johnson file?"

"It's on your desk . . . ah, somewhere," Karen said, waving at the mountain of files.

"Thanks," Willow muttered, standing up and rummaging through the files, sorting them into new stacks on her blotter.

"What time did ya sneak out?" Duncan asked, taking a seat across from her, making himself right at home.

Willow carried one stack of files over to an empty shelf on the far wall of bookcases. "I did not sneak out. I showered, had breakfast, and left around seven." She walked to the door, closed it, then walked back to Duncan to better glare down at him. "Why were you diving around Thunder Island?"

"To see what was there. Luke, Kee, and Ahab were with me."

"Even though you knew I didn't want any attention drawn to that area, the four of you spent yesterday diving there."

"Ahab and Kee dropped Luke and me in the water and kept going, then picked us up several hours later so we could look over the island as well. Nobody saw us."

"They just dropped you and Luke in the ocean and then left? Isn't that against some diving code or something?"

Duncan shrugged. "There were two of us, and the island was right there if we ran into trouble while underwater. And we were in communication with Kee." He suddenly took hold of her wrist, pulled her down onto his lap, and kissed her quite thoroughly. "Good morning," he whispered the moment he was done.

Willow felt her cheeks flush as she darted a quick look at her closed office door. "Good morning," she whispered back, cupping his face in her hand with a sigh. "You're heading back to Puffin Harbor this morning, aren't you?"

"Aye. I only saw Molly for a few minutes last night."

"She just showed up unannounced? Why?"

"Mother trouble, it seems," he said, standing up and setting Willow on her feet. He pulled some of her hair over her shoulder and gave it a gentle tug. "Molly thinks she's in love with a New Zealand sheep farmer. So she's run away from home and is hoping I'll run interference for her with Mother."

"How old is she?"

"Twenty-six."

That surprised Willow. "But you make it sound like she's eighteen or something."

"Sometimes she is eighteen," he said with a sigh. "And sometimes she's older than I am."

"Are you going to help her?"

"Help her marry some shepherd she met on the Internet? Not without meeting him first."

"You'll go with her to New Zealand, then?"

He shook his head. "If Benjamin Zane wants my sister, he can damn well make the trip here and ask for her hand in person."

"My, aren't you the patriarch," Willow whispered, patting his chest and shooting him a crooked smile as she walked back around her desk. "You said you have a brother. Why didn't Molly go to him for help?"

"Camden?" Duncan asked, picking up the files she was reaching for. He carried them over to the shelf and set them beside the others. "He has bigger problems to deal with right now. Molly's love life is my cross to bear."

"Are you the oldest?"

"Aye."

"And there's just you, your mother, brother, and sister?"

"And a small army of assorted relations. Willow," he said, walking back and taking hold of her shoulders. "I wish I could stay but I can't. And I don't know if I'll get back here before Friday." He traced a finger down the side of her face. "I'm sorry about last night."

She shot him a smile. "It was kind of nice just cuddling."

He used his finger under her chin to lift her face to his, and leaned down and kissed her again. "We'll have the *Seven-to-Two Odds* to ourselves Friday," he said. "Just you and me and Mickey. We can anchor out for the night, if you'd like."

"Mmmm, that sounds nice. I haven't spent time with Mickey in ages."

Duncan's brows lowered and his eyes darkened in response to her being more interested in the wolf than in him. "Are ya arriving Friday morning or Thursday night? They're predicting a storm to come up the coast later this week, and that might impact our plans."

Willow glanced at the mountain of work on her desk. Even without the waste site files it seemed overwhelming. "Actually," she said, looking back at Duncan, "I

don't think I'll get out of here before Friday noon, because three cases I'm working on are coming together
more quickly than I expected. And I have to drive to
Orono and pick up some water sample kits first, so I
won't get into Puffin Harbor until around suppertime.
Weather permitting, can we go out Saturday instead? Or
maybe Friday night, if I get in early enough?"

Duncan pulled her into his arms again. "We'll plan for
Friday night, then, if the storm's passed." He leaned away
and smiled down at her. "Bring that cute little bit of lace
you were wearing last night, will ya?"

"On the schooner? I'll freeze."

"I won't let ya freeze, counselor," he said gruffly, dropping his head and kissing her again.

Willow wrapped her arms around his neck and lifted
up on her toes to deepen the kiss just as the intercom
buzzed. "John's secretary just called," Karen said frantically. "He's on his way down here."

Willow jerked free as if she'd been stung. "That's my
boss," she said, stepping away and rubbing her thoroughly
kissed lips with the back of her hand. She pointed at
Duncan. "You behave yourself, Dunky."

His mouth turned down in a wounded look, but his
eyes sparkled bright with challenge.

Willow shot around her desk just as the buzzer beeped
three quick times, a knock sounded on her office door,
and John Pike, Maine's attorney general, walked in. He
stopped just inside the door, his sharp blue eyes landing
on Duncan standing behind her desk before his gaze slid
to her. "Excuse me for interrupting, Willow, but I need
that file on the Johnson case for my meeting with Ed
Johnson this morning."

"I have it right here. Somewhere," she said briskly, turning to search her desktop.

John stepped toward Duncan and held out his hand. "John Pike," he said.

Duncan stepped around the desk and extended his own hand. "Duncan Ross," he returned. "I'm a friend of Willow's from Puffin Harbor."

"Ross," John repeated, having to tilt his head up to study Duncan's face. "Why do I know that name?"

"Duncan was involved in the Raoul Vegas incident two years ago," Willow explained, handing John the Johnson file. "He's one of the men who helped build our case against Vegas."

"Ah," John murmured, eyeing Duncan with renewed interest. "Ross," he repeated again. "Aren't you the guy who rescued Willow?"

"It was a team effort" was all Duncan said. He looked at Willow. "I'll see you later this week, counselor. Pack light," he added, his eyes dancing.

"Pack?" John echoed, looking up from scanning the Johnson file to frown at Willow. "You're going on a trip?"

"We're taking a weekend sail Down East," Duncan said before she could answer. He headed to the door, stopped, and looked back at John. "Her sister's been worried that Willow rarely takes the time to come home for a much-needed visit. And I would think, Mr. Pike, that ya'd be worried about losing a good assistant AG to exhaustion. Willow only takes her vacations in fragments, one or two days scattered here and there, rather than one or two full weeks like she should. At the rate she's pushing herself, she'll burn out in another year."

John snapped his gaze to Willow and caught her glaring at Duncan. "Is that true?" he asked. "You haven't taken a real vacation since you started here?"

"It's not as bad as it sounds," she defended, darting a scathing look at Duncan before giving John her full attention. "I prefer taking long weekends."

John shook his head. "The man's right, Willow. It's not healthy to get so wrapped up in your work."

"I'll see ya this weekend, counselor," Duncan interjected, drawing her and John's attention again and smiling much too congenially. Why wasn't she surprised Duncan's idea of behaving himself was not exactly the same as hers? "Take care driving back Friday," he added, turning to walk out the door. "Remember they're predicting a storm."

Just for a minute, and not for the first time, Willow wished her eyes could shoot real daggers so she could hit Duncan Ross right between the shoulder blades.

"Willow," John said when Duncan was gone, "an overworked assistant attorney general is no good to me. Is it true you haven't had a vacation in three years?"

"Two. I've only been here two years, John."

He canted his head at her, his smile warm and a bit wistful. "It's only been two? I remember my first couple of years here; I had the same fire you do for this job. I was forty-six when I left corporate America and went to law school. I came out three years later ready to take on the world." He shook his head. "It took watching my wife battle breast cancer to make me quit worrying about the big picture long enough to see the small one."

"But it's our job to worry about the big picture."

He shook his head again. "Not at the expense of the small picture. We can't slay dragons unless we're in top fighting form, or be effective unless we balance work with our personal lives. You have from now until Friday to clear your desk and delegate what's left, because you're taking next week off."

"But I can't leave right now. I have three cases pending."

"Greg can—no, he's got the Briggs trial. Paul can take over the Poole case, and Rita can work on that class-action suit for water rights in western Maine. I'll babysit the mercury lawsuit until you get back."

"But Mrs. Poole—"

John stopped her by holding up his hand. "I know you're meeting with her this morning, so I'll send Paul in and you can introduce them. Well-water contamination is not rocket science, Willow. Paul can handle it for the week you'll be gone." His blue eyes glistened with a fatherly smile. "If I've learned one thing in the six years I've worked here, it's that no one is indispensable, Willow. If you were to—God forbid—break your leg this afternoon, this office would keep running and your cases would still move forward."

"You make it sound like a chimp could sit at my desk."

That fatherly smile turned describably sportive. "I'll be sure to tell Paul that when I send him in to meet Mrs. Poole."

Willow winced, tamping down the flush creeping up the back of her neck. Oh yeah, she definitely was going to get Duncan for opening this can of worms. Maybe she'd accidentally trip and knock him over the side of the schooner Saturday.

"What else are you working on?" John asked, tucking the Johnson file under his arm. "Office rumor is you've been digging into the DEP archives of the Kingston Corporation. Is there something going on with them I don't know about?"

"No, nothing that I know of. I was just looking for an old geological survey."

He turned toward the door but hesitated. "Mr. Ross seemed a bit, ah . . . proprietary toward you." He held up his hand. "I know it's none of my business, Willow, but just for the record, I like him."

"You just met him."

John's smile turned fatherly again. "The fact that he's the guy who rescued my assistant AG might be influencing me, but there's something about Duncan Ross that rings . . . solid. Or maybe *courageous* is the word I'm looking for," he said, waving at the air. "And I have a feeling a man would need buckets of both to hold your interest."

Willow was a bit alarmed. Apparently John Pike had been quietly watching her personal life. Well, he hadn't gotten to be Maine's AG by wearing blinders. And he hadn't kept the position for the last four years by not knowing what his underlings were up to.

"Duncan's a good man," she admitted, her smile rueful. "When he's not driving me crazy."

"Have fun next week," John said with a laugh. "I'll tell Karen to buzz Paul's office and have him come down for your meeting with Mrs. Poole." He stopped in the doorway and pointed the Johnson file at her. "And thank Mr. Ross for me. I'm going to look into everyone's vacation schedules from the last few years."

"And I'm going to look into buying some mace," Willow muttered to herself as John left, walking back to her desk. "And the next time you show up at one in the morning, Dunky, I'm going to open the door and let you have it."

"He can probably give back as good as he gets," Karen said, walking in with Mrs. Poole. Karen fanned her face with her hand. "Whew. Does the guy have any brothers?"

"One," Willow said, going to greet Mary Poole. "The thought of which gives me shivers—to think there's more like him walking around. Hi, Mary," Willow said, taking the older woman's hand and leading her to a chair by the bookcases, preferring an informal setting for their meeting. "Thank you for traveling all the way down from the County this morning. I'm sorry to keep you waiting."

Karen let herself out and quietly closed the door—and the rest of Willow's Tuesday went by in a blur of meetings, a court appearance, lunch at her desk, and supper standing at her kitchen counter at ten that night.

Willow made it home by seven o'clock on Wednesday, after another grueling day for which she had a paper cut, a run in her stockings, and a pounding headache to show for it.

She let herself into her apartment, kicked off her shoes, and set down her briefcase by the door as she thought about trying to find time to schedule a pedicure, deciding that every girl needed pretty toenails to start off an affair properly. And maybe she'd shop online at a few lingerie sites, too, and have something sexy—maybe hot red and naughty—overnighted to her before Friday.

Yeah, that's how she'd get even with Duncan; she'd make the man's eyes permanently cross.

Willow had just stepped into the kitchen, smiling at her plan, when the brass knocker on her door rapped softly. She leaned over the sink and looked out the window, but only saw her SUV in the driveway. The knocker sounded softly again, and Willow finally realized who her visitor was.

She went back into the living room and opened the door with a warm smile. "Hi, Mabel," she said, stepping aside to let her landlady in. "Don't tell me you've been sitting in your window all evening watching for me to come home."

"I was listening to a new book on tape," the eighty-one-year-old said as she held out a small plastic container. "I brought you some macaroni and cheese for supper."

Willow recognized the Meals-on-Wheels container, and her heart skipped at the gesture. She reached out and took the box, knowing that if she didn't Mabel's feelings would be hurt.

"You're supposed to eat the meals they bring you, Mabel, not hoard them to give to me. What did you have for lunch today?"

The elderly woman waved her hand in dismissal and made her way into the kitchen. "I don't like macaroni and cheese," she said, sitting down and patting the table across from her. "I just ate the roll and cole slaw. Stick it in the microwave and come sit down and tell me what's wrong with your cable. The man came to fix it today, but I told him you usually warn me if someone's coming to work on your apartment."

Willow turned from putting the container in the microwave. "A man came here today? But I didn't call the cable company. It's working fine."

Mabel blinked behind her thick glasses. "He said he had a work order. He showed it to me."

"Did you let him in?" Willow asked softly, sitting down across from her.

Mabel shook her head. "I didn't have to. He said you told him where you keep your spare key." She reached out and touched Willow's hand. "You shouldn't do that, kiddo. You shouldn't tell strangers where you hide your key."

"I don't have a key hidden," Willow told her, looking toward the living-room door. "Did he come inside?"

"Oh, dear," Mabel said, nodding. "Were you robbed?" she whispered, also looking around.

Willow got up, went into the living room, and found that nothing seemed out of place or appeared to be missing. Aware of Mabel following her, Willow walked into her bedroom, saw that everything was just as she'd left it this morning, and came back out past Mabel and stepped into the bathroom. Again, nothing looked out of place.

Her apartment had only one bedroom, but all the rooms—the kitchen, bedroom, living room, and even the bath—were comparatively large. The apartment sat on the back end of a huge old nineteenth-century townhouse, and Mabel Pinkham had been renting to Willow for the last two years in order to supplement her Social Security check.

Mabel's only family—an older sister and younger brother—lived in Rhode Island. But when Mabel had been widowed three years ago, she had refused to move closer to them, explaining that Maine was her home now. Mabel had plenty of friends and a strong community of services for the elderly here in Augusta, and had quickly developed a motherly affection for Willow from the day they'd signed the lease.

For Willow, the feeling was mutual. Mabel Pinkham was like a grandmother to her. Willow had even taken Mabel down to Puffin Harbor several times, for a change of scenery and bit of adventure. Mabel, Willow and Rachel had quickly discovered, loved eating lobster and could pack it away faster than a growing boy.

"Nothing looks disturbed," Mabel said, wringing her frail hands and scanning the living room. "I cleaned in here just yesterday. I had to remake your bed," she said, shaking her head. "You must have been in a hurry to leave, because it looked like a five-year-old had made it."

Mabel was also Willow's cleaning lady, although *clean* was a relative term to someone with poor eyesight. But Mabel needed to feel useful, and the extra money helped her out, and Willow didn't mind sharing her apartment with a few dust bunnies.

Duncan must have tried to make the bed yesterday morning. Willow was glad he hadn't still been in it when Mabel had let herself in to clean.

"Should we call the police?" Mabel asked.

Willow walked to the living room door. "I don't think we need to," she said, looping her arm through Mabel's as they stepped out onto the porch. "Nothing is missing. It's probably just a mix-up with the cable company."

"But how did he get in, then?" Mabel asked, opening her own door at the opposite end of the porch. "I watched him. He was blocking the knob with his body, but he opened it easily."

"I don't know," Willow admitted, walking into Mabel's parlor with her. "But I don't want you to worry about it. And from now on, I'll make sure I lock the deadbolt when I leave."

Mabel sat down in her chair by the window. "I should have called your office today when he showed up." She looked at Willow, her wide brown eyes suddenly brightening behind her thick glasses. "Are you working on any interesting cases?" she asked. "Maybe the man was a spy, and he was looking for information."

Willow smiled and patted her arm. "Excuse me, did you say your name was Miss Mabel or Miss Marple? Have you been listening to Agatha Christie tapes again?"

Mabel pursed her lips and frowned. "You're an assistant AG, Willow," she said in a motherly, scolding tone. "You prosecute people who wouldn't hesitate to break into a person's home."

"Contaminated wells don't bring criminals out of the woodwork," Willow said, walking to the parlor door. She stopped and looked back at her. "I don't want you worrying about this, understand? I'll call the cable company first thing in the morning and find out what happened. Are you okay for the night? Do you need anything?"

Mabel waved her away and picked up her small tape player. "I'm fine. I'm going to finish my book and then go to bed. You lock your deadbolt tonight."

Willow stepped into the hallway, tested the knob on the door between her apartment and Mabel's, then stepped back into the parlor doorway. "Our connecting door is unlocked. If you need anything, just come in. Don't bother being polite and using the porch door."

Mabel slipped the headphones over her ears. "You do the same," she said, nodding. "Good night."

Willow waved good night, stepped back into the hall, and locked Mabel's porch door, then went through the connecting door into her own living room. She walked between her couch and two overstuffed chairs, stopped, and looked around. What in hell was a man doing in her apartment today? Mabel's idea that he might have been spying sent chills down Willow's spine, but for the life of her, she couldn't think of any reason why.

She walked over to the desk in the back corner of the living room and turned on her computer only to have a message pop up saying she hadn't closed it down properly the last time. Willow frowned, trying to remember the last time she'd used the computer.

It had been last week, when she'd balanced her checkbook. Most of her work from the office was done on her laptop, since working on state files on home computers was not allowed. Yet somebody had turned on her computer to look for something. But what? Her personal finances? Her financial program was password protected, but Willow knew a simple password wouldn't stop a computer hacker from getting into it. Was she in danger of identity theft?

Willow sat down at her desk, opened her finance program, and quickly scanned through her bank accounts. She checked all the balances in her savings and checking accounts to see if there had been any online activity—such as transfers.

After ten minutes of searching all her accounts, Willow leaned back in her chair, crossed her arms under her breasts, and stared at the computer screen. Everything looked normal. Still, tomorrow she was calling her bank and putting a freeze on all her accounts, for at least until she got back from her little vacation and could sit down with the bank manager and decide what to do about them. Identity theft was one nightmare she was not up to dealing with right now.

Willow reached for the mouse and properly shut down her computer, then stood up and looked around her silent apartment. She hugged herself as another shiver raced through her. This couldn't possibly have anything to do with her sick lobster; only the lobstermen, Duncan, Jane Huntley, and Kee and Ahab and Luke knew what was happening. And she trusted all of them.

So what had her intruder been looking for?

Chapter Eight

✶

$\mathcal{T}$he last time Willow had been this distracted had been in her first year of law school, though she couldn't remember feeling quite this restless. The image of Duncan Ross wouldn't stop popping into her head, making it difficult to concentrate on the well-water tests she was supposed to be analyzing.

But instead of comparing road salt levels that had grown increasingly higher this past year, she kept seeing Duncan sprawled across her bed two mornings ago, his arms thrown wide and his powerfully muscled body tempting her to phone in sick and crawl back into bed with him. She kept seeing his usually amused, vibrant green eyes pinning her in place, just daring her to kiss him senseless. Or she would picture him leaning against his car in the Trunk Harbor parking lot Saturday morning, waiting for her to come back from the sea and knowing he'd spent the night worrying about her.

This had to stop. She couldn't let Duncan get under her skin so deeply that her heart became engaged. She had promised herself years ago that a bit of healthy passion was okay, but loving a man to the point that nothing else mattered was strictly forbidden.

She simply could not fall in love with Duncan Ross.

Willow realized she was tapping her pen on her desk rather violently and immediately set it down, buried her face in her hands, and groaned. Dammit, the guy was driving her crazy. He was disrupting her life to the point that she couldn't tell if she was sexually frustrated or just plain angered by her inability to put Duncan in a neat little box marked BOY TOY.

How hard could it be to have a simple no-strings affair?

Willow snorted and picked up her pen again. It was damn hard when the boy had the persistence of a salmon swimming upstream to spawn. Duncan was far from subtle in his claim that he wanted her, but that had been apparent from the day they'd met. He had spoken about love, but had never actually told Willow he loved her. And now there was a betting pool on their wedding, even though Duncan had never asked her to marry him.

Willow remembered how his face had reddened when she'd said she had placed her own wager on their wedding, which meant that Puffin Harbor's preoccupation with their love life disconcerted him—apparently more than it did her. But then, she had grown up in Puffin Harbor and knew the townspeople loved nothing more than to speculate and gossip about one of their own. It was harmless entertainment, usually, though being the brunt of that gossip certainly did have its drawbacks.

For one thing, she couldn't openly date Duncan now, which forced them to conduct their affair long distance. That was certainly possible, though Willow did worry about scandalizing her landlady. Mabel was nearly blind but she wasn't deaf, and Willow's bedroom shared a wall with Mabel's bedroom.

Her desk phone rang, and Willow tossed down her pen again and noticed it was an in-house call. "Hello," she answered.

"I'm missing some of the Kingston files," Karen said without preamble. "I'm in the archives, putting away all the files we . . . ah, borrowed, but some are missing. Are they on your desk?"

Willow started rummaging through the much more manageable stack of files beside her. "How do you know some are missing? I thought you snuck them out without signing for them."

"I kept my own list so that I would know what I took. And two are missing."

"They're not here," Willow told her, looking toward the bookcases. "I gave you everything this morning," she added, sliding her chair back and searching the floor under her desk.

"You didn't open your briefcase this morning," Karen pointed out. "Did you take any of them home?"

With the phone held to her ear by her shoulder, Willow leaned over again and started rifling through her briefcase after taking out her laptop and setting it on her desk. She found a few folders, but none of them were DEP files. "I kept everything together, Karen," Willow said, straightening and glancing around her office. "You took everything I had down with you."

"I have to go," Karen whispered. "Somebody just came in and I don't want them to catch me in this section."

"If they do, just tell them you're replacing a geological survey I borrowed."

"That you didn't sign out," Karen reminded her, only to let out a sigh. "We're going to start an interdepartmental war."

"Take no prisoners," Willow said with a laugh, hanging up the phone. She stood up and began a methodical search of her office for the missing files, starting at the bookcases and ending up at the credenza under the windows just as Karen burst through the door.

"It was Ronald Gibbs from DEP," Karen said breathlessly, her eyes shining with the excitement of sneaking around. "I was able to distract him by asking him out on a date."

"You did what?" Willow squeaked. "You actually asked him out?"

The color in Karen's cheeks deepened. "I, ah—he started to ask me what I was doing, and I just blurted out that we should go to Gilly's tomorrow night for a drink."

Karen Hobbs was a cute forty-six-year-old bundle of energy who had sworn off men last year after a nasty divorce. Willow imagined that Ronald Gibbs had been as surprised by Karen's offer as she was.

Karen covered her red cheeks with her hands and shook her head. "You owe me big-time for this," she whispered, apparently just realizing what she'd done. "At least an extra personal day, preferably in July, on the hottest beach day that comes along."

"Done," Willow said, sitting back down. She frowned

at her blushing secretary. "Where do you suppose those files are?"

Karen dropped her hands and looked around the office, then scrunched her shoulders. "I don't know. I checked everything I brought down to the archives, hoping they were tucked inside another folder, but they weren't."

"Do you know which ones are missing? You said you kept your own list."

Karen pulled a folded piece of paper from her pocket. "One was the Kingston site denial four years ago, and the other one was also from Kingston, but it was the site-approval file from three years ago."

"I'd like to know what's in those two files and why they're suddenly missing. Do you suppose they're on DEP's electronic database?" Willow asked, glancing at her blank computer screen. She gave Karen a crooked smile. "And do you think you can get into that database and print it out for me?"

The gleam suddenly returned to Karen's doe-brown eyes. "I can get in," she said with a confident nod. "And I won't so much as leave a mouse track behind."

Having a secretary who was fond of computers was a blessing, Willow decided, but having a secretary who was also fond of sneaking around in other departments was even more of a boon. When Willow had asked Karen to dig through DEP's archives on Monday, and to not let anyone know what she was doing, Karen had been positively enthused. Apparently, being secretary to a state's assistant AG could get a bit boring.

Karen came around Willow's desk and turned on the desk computer. "Willow," she moaned. "I've explained a hundred times that you shut down your computer by telling it to shut down," she scolded, shaking her head. "And not by turning off the button."

"I did shut it down properly when I left last night," Willow said, peering around Karen to see the message that had popped up on the computer screen. "Could there have been a power surge or something?"

"No," Karen said, crossing her arms and tapping her toe while she waited for the computer to check for corrupt files. "You have a battery backup that prevents that."

Willow wasn't computer illiterate, but neither was she a technogeek like Karen. "I'm sure I locked up the office when I left last night so even the cleaning crew wouldn't have to clean around my mess," Willow said, frowning at her door. She looked up at Karen. "Somebody must have been in here. And yesterday a man posing as a cable repairman was in my apartment," she added softly. "I called the company this morning, and they said they hadn't sent anyone out. But my landlady saw him go inside my apartment, and I'm pretty sure he searched my home computer."

"And two files are missing," Karen added, also in a whisper as she looked around the office before bringing her gaze back to Willow. "What's going on? What exactly are we investigating?"

"Sick lobster," Willow told her. "Jane Huntley at the Lobster Institute thinks it might be pesticide poisoning."

Karen gaped in surprise. "How have you kept this quiet? Lobstermen get vocal when their livelihoods are at stake. How come this isn't plastered all over the news?"

"The contamination is contained to a very small area, and the lobstermen being affected asked me to quietly check into it, since those who have said anything have had their equipment sabotaged."

The computer toned that it was ready for work, and Karen turned and started tapping keys on the keyboard. Willow got out of her chair, and Karen immediately sat down without taking her eyes off the screen.

"Would the guard station out front have a log of who was in the building last night?" Willow asked, turning to lean against her credenza to watch Karen work. "And would it say what time they left?"

"Probably," Karen said, looking up from the screen. "But you need a good reason to ask for it. Besides, there's all sorts of people roaming around here at night—like the cleaning crew for one thing, and those carpenters who started remodeling the bathrooms on this floor. They work at night, when they'll cause the least disturbance. There were at least four carpenters still here this morning when I came in."

"Can you tell what was looked at in my computer?"

Karen was watching the screen again. "I'm checking that now. It appears whoever gained access was just browsing through your files. Nothing's been deleted and none of the files was actually opened." She started typing again. "You have to tell John that someone's been in your office and apartment, and going through your computers."

"I will . . . eventually," Willow said, shaking her head. "We really don't have much to tell him yet, do we? It's possible I didn't bother to shut my computer down properly last night. I was tired and in a hurry."

"What about someone breaking into your apartment?"

"Nothing was touched other than my home computer,

and I never keep anything on it." Willow waved at her laptop. "I only keep work files on my portable." She canted her head. "Can you download those missing files directly onto my laptop from the DEP database?"

Karen looked up with a frown. "Is that wise? If someone is after those files, you shouldn't be carrying them around."

"We don't know that they are. This could all be nothing. We could have misplaced those files, it's possible I shut off my computers incorrectly, and we could be getting paranoid just because we're trying to keep a secret."

Karen slid Willow's laptop over to the center of the desk and turned it on. She pushed back her chair and reached under the desk, unplugged the network cable from the desktop computer, plugged it into the laptop, then started punching keys on the small keyboard.

"There," Karen said, "good old DEP is diligent about backing up their files. Both of the missing ones are there." She swiveled her chair to face Willow. "They're downloading now."

"My God, I'm going to get you three personal days off," Willow told her. "Thanks, Karen. You're the best co-conspirator a lawyer could hope to do business with."

Karen stood up with a snort. "I don't like the sound of that. The secretary is always the one to go to jail, while the boss usually gets off scot-free." She stepped around the desk and headed back to her own office, but stopped in the doorway and pointed at Willow. "I'm going to sing like a canary, and you're going to be in the cell right next to me."

"On what charge?" Willow asked, lifting one brow.

"Interoffice espionage."

Willow waved that away with a laugh and sat down at her desk. "I'm sure we can find a good lawyer around here somewhere who can get us off with only parole and a few hours of community service."

"My luck, my service will be picking up trash on the State House lawn," Karen muttered as she disappeared around the wall to her own desk.

Willow moved her laptop out of the way and found her well-test papers again. She glanced at them, then at her watch, and sighed. It was ten o'clock on Thursday morning. She had a little over twenty-four hours before she was out of here, and she had about two days' worth of work to finish before her impromptu vacation started.

Or should she say her *forced* vacation?

Well, it was a blessing, really, and would give her all of next week to snoop around Thunder Island. Karen would be here in the office, slaving away, and Willow could call if she needed any more information. Yeah, it was a good plan, actually.

And a great chance to start an affair.

The storm Duncan had said was coming hit just before midnight on Thursday, pelting Willow's apartment windows with wind-driven rain, making for an emotionally turbulent night's sleep. Visions of spies crawling like spiders around her living room danced through her dreams, and by 5:00 A.M. Friday, Willow finally quit tossing and turning and got up. By six thirty she was sitting at her office desk, and by nine o'clock she was beginning to realize she might actually be able to leave for Orono by noon.

Willow glanced down at her rain-splattered briefcase.

Her laptop was the only safe place to hide her expanding accumulation of research. She and Karen had copied various articles on pesticide poisoning in marine life they'd found on the Internet, the two missing files were safely in there as well, and late yesterday afternoon a fax from Jane Huntley on her preliminary findings had been sent directly to the laptop instead of the office fax machine.

Even though Karen had given all the research files weird names that had nothing to do with anything, she had still been worried the laptop might become their mysterious spy's next target. Karen had repeated her concern again last evening when she'd left the office for the day, but Willow had assured her that a moving target was hard to hit. As long as she kept the laptop with her, their secret was safe.

Karen finally walked into work at nine thirty, looking like a drowned rat. "What happened to you?" Willow asked, watching as her scowling secretary ran her fingers through her short, wet blond hair.

"The wind tore my umbrella out of my hands," Karen muttered, plopping down in one of the chairs across from Willow's desk. "And the buses are running late, so I had to stand in the rain with a newspaper over my head."

"So that's ink on your face and not mascara?" Willow asked, pointing at Karen's cheek.

Karen rubbed her face with the back of her hand. "I tried getting into the bathroom, but the carpenters are still there." She looked around the office, then brought her gaze back to Willow. "Any visitors last night?"

Willow shook her head. "My computer started up just fine, and the strand of my hair I left in my office door was still there this morning."

Karen's eyes widened. "You put a strand of hair in your door?" she asked, breaking into a broad smile. "How inventive."

"It's a trick I learned in my junior year of college," Willow told her. "We had a guy in our dorm who kept sneaking into women's rooms and stealing panties, and I wanted to make sure he hadn't pawed through mine."

"Wow. Did they catch him?"

"Eventually," Willow said with a nod. "Red-handed. Or should I say red-faced?"

Karen stood up, reached into her trouser pocket, and pulled out a small key chain that didn't have any keys on it. "Here," she said, handing it to Willow. "This is a jump drive that plugs directly into the USB port on your laptop. I backed up all the files we downloaded yesterday onto it, including Jane Huntley's fax."

"When did you do this?" Willow asked, taking the key chain and turning it over in her hand. She wiggled the cap off, saw where it plugged into a USB port, and put the cap back on.

"I did it yesterday before I left. But then I took it home, went on the Internet again, and found more articles to download. It seems one of the board members of Kingston Corporation made the news six or seven years back, before Kingston was even formed, and the *New York Times* ran an article on him. It's all in there," she said, nodding at Willow's hand. "Put it in your purse or someplace inconspicuous. Just don't keep it with your laptop. That way if your computer gets stolen, you'll still have your research."

"I've never seen anything like this," Willow said, turning it over in her hand again. She looked up at Karen. "This tiny thing has all those files in it?"

"And it's not even a quarter full," Karen assured her, turning to walk out of the office. She stopped in the doorway. "It's password protected. I used the month I was born in." She smiled. "You remember when my birthday is, don't you, boss?"

Willow narrowed her eyes at her. "I have twelve chances to get it right."

Karen laughed and disappeared around the wall to her desk. Willow stared at the device in her hand that was no bigger than a pack of chewing gum. A jump drive, Karen had called it. "Sweet," Willow said, leaning over and dropping the drive into her purse. "I'll hide you someplace safe later," she told it.

With that taken care of, Willow returned to reading the complaint on behalf of several citizens in a small northern town she needed to file with the courts before she left. Some wells had been contaminated by road salt that had been stored not in a salt shed, as it should have been, but in a huge outdoor pile that had allowed the salt to leach into the ground. All the affected people were asking for was to have the town provide them with safe drinking water. Willow checked the document to make sure she'd dotted every i and crossed every t, so Karen could run it over to the courthouse this afternoon.

She'd have to remember to leave Karen her umbrella.

It was half past noon when Willow finally stepped out of her office and stopped by Karen's desk. "I'm off," she told Karen, handing her the court document. "Get this in by three and then you might as well head home from the courthouse, so you'll have plenty of time to get ready for your big date tonight." She gave her secretary a crooked smile as Karen took the large envelope from her.

"And don't do anything tonight that I wouldn't do."

Karen snorted. "You mean, like, don't scare him off on the first date?" she asked as she reached into the top drawer of her desk. "Here," she said, handing Willow a coiled cord. "This will hook your laptop up to your cell phone so I can send you files while you're out on your boat."

"Schooner," Willow corrected, taking the cord and stuffing it in a pocket on her briefcase. "If you call it a boat, Ahab will throw you overboard."

"Ahab?" Karen choked, her eyes widening.

"He's the captain of the *Seven-to-Two Odds*. His real name is Jonathan French, but Mikaela renamed him Ahab after somebody read her *Moby Dick*."

"Speaking of Mikaela, how are the hellions, anyway?" Karen asked, smiling warmly. "Nicholas must be walking by now."

Rachel and the two hellions had visited Willow at the office more than once in the last couple of years, and Karen, whose own two kids were away at college, had doted on Mikaela and Nicholas as if they were God's gift to the world. "He's not only walking, he's running everywhere," Willow told her. "And Mickey is the only one who can keep up with him."

Karen shook her head. "I'd like to meet that wolf someday. Mikaela talks about him as if he's human."

"To her he is," Willow said. "Well, I'm off. If anything comes up, call my cell phone."

"Not unless it's about what you're working on now," she said, nodding toward Willow's briefcase. "Everything else can keep until you get back. You're on vacation, remember? Oh," she said when Willow turned to leave.

"This was just delivered." She handed Willow the package on her desk, label side up. "From Victoria Secret. It feels rather . . . skimpy," she added in a sultry voice that was ruined by her cheeky grin. "Please, do something next week that I wouldn't do," she pleaded, twisting Willow's earlier words. "And bring back pictures."

Willow tucked the package under her arm and lifted a brow. "Of Duncan?" she asked.

Karen blinked. "I was thinking of your sailing vacation, but you can include pictures of him if you want. And maybe of his brother, if he's around."

With a laugh and final wave, Willow finally headed down the hall to the side door of the building. She opened it, only to step back as a gust of wind pelted her trench coat with rain. She steeled herself and finally rushed into the storm—propelled forward by the thought of Duncan waiting for her in Puffin Harbor.

Chapter Nine

❖

Willow automatically turned left at the light in Ellsworth, following Route 1 farther down east toward Puffin Harbor. While staying focused on driving through the still raging storm, she replayed the more interesting parts of her conversation with Jane Huntley. When she had called Jane this morning, they had agreed to meet at Pat's Pizza in Orono rather than at the lab. And while eating pizza and sharing a few beers, Jane had given Willow instructions on how to take the water samples and use the remote underwater camera she was lending her.

They had also caught up on their friendship, and time had flown by faster than Willow realized. Between the two beers she'd had during the four-hour visit, and the droning, rhythmic swipes of the wiper blades trying to keep her windshield clear, Willow felt the fatigue of her work-packed week finally catching up with her. Her dashboard clock read seven thirty, and with the storm firmly entrenched overhead, it was already starting to get dark. But she should be home in half an hour, just as she'd told Rachel when she had phoned from Orono to say she was on her way.

Again, it appeared her affair with Duncan would have to wait. Even Mother Nature seemed determined to conspire against them, making it impossible for them to sail out tonight. The radio weatherman said the nor'easter was stalled in the Gulf of Maine, apparently in no hurry to head out to sea past Nova Scotia.

Great, Willow thought, turning off Route 1 and onto the narrow road that hugged the coastline to Puffin Harbor. They'd likely be stuck in port until Sunday now.

Which gave her two nights of being able to read bedtime stories to Mikaela and Nick in person, she realized. That was a plus. So was being able to spend some time with her sister. What with Rachel having two children, a husband, and a rather booming architectural career, and with Willow's own demanding work schedule, they hadn't had much of a chance to simply sit around and do nothing together.

Maybe Kee would babysit tonight, and Rachel and Willow could have a girls' night out at The Rosach. But she was drinking soda, Willow decided, not only in deference to Rachel's pregnancy, but because another beer would likely put her to sleep.

Her cell phone rang, and Willow pulled it out of her purse. "I'm almost home," she said in way of answering.

"That sounds promising," Duncan returned.

"Duncan. I thought you were Rachel."

"Aye, I gathered as much. So ya're nearly into town?"

"Just passing Walker Point. It doesn't look like we'll be sailing tonight, does it?"

"Aye. Nor tomorrow, unless the sea settles down by the afternoon. Rachel said ya have all of next week off."

"Thanks to you, Dunky. John Pike made me go on vacation."

Duncan's chuckle came over the phone. "Then my trip to Augusta was not in vain. Are ya coming to The Rosach tonight? Ya can meet Molly."

"She's still here?"

"Aye. And I'm praying I get out to sea before my mother shows up to drag her home. I'd rather not be present for that scene."

Willow smiled at the windshield. "Coward."

"It's not cowardly to avoid a hen fight. It's wise."

"What happened with the shepherd? Have you heard from him?"

"Not yet. I called and left a message on his machine, asking him to call me, but that was three days ago. Molly's claiming I used my big-brother voice and scared him off."

"Let me guess. You told Molly that if just your voice can scare him off, then it can't be true love."

There was a moment of silence. "Ya know me so well, lass," he finally said, his voice low with implied meaning. "Willow, I called ta ask if—"

Willow threw the cell phone down with a curse, and slammed on the brakes when the pickup passing her cut back in too quickly and clipped her front fender. The pickup also slammed on its brakes, its blinding taillights glaring through the rain-washed windshield as Willow's truck crashed into it. The steering wheel jerk in her hands, the momentum sending her SUV careening off the side of the road.

Her truck hit something solid, and Willow's world tilted with dizzying speed as it became airborne while twisting upside down. Her briefcase and purse on the seat beside her flew wildly about, the box of jars and suitcase housing the camera banging in back.

With a scream of surprise, Willow braced her hands on the steering wheel and instinctively shoved both feet against the brake as the SUV landed on its roof. Every window shattered on impact and the side-impact air bags exploded. She tumbled again and again, the noise of metal crumpling with each hit, and the engine hissing to a sputtering death. The rolling suddenly stopped when her bumper slammed into something solid, causing the front air bags to explode, tearing another scream of surprise from her throat.

Wind-driven rain blew in through the shattered windows just as the sensation of pain crept into Willow's still spinning consciousness. She was hanging suspended by her seat belt, the SUV sitting on its passenger side.

It suddenly slid forward. Willow slapped at the slowly deflating air bags, suddenly aware of the sound of the pounding surf very close by. The truck tilted in slow motion, dropping onto its tires with a shuddering bang that started it sliding downward again. The screech of metal dragging over rock was deafening, until it suddenly stopped when the SUV fetched up again, shoving Willow into her seat belt so violently that the air rushed from her lungs.

A large wave broke over the hood, spraying seawater in with the rain. Willow clawed at her seat belt, frantic to escape before the truck continued to slip into the angry surf.

The dark silhouette of a man appeared beside her, his features vague in the stingy glow of what was left of her truck's lights. "Help me," she shouted, groping for the door handle and pushing against the crumpled metal. "Before I slide into the sea."

A hand reached in through the broken window, grabbed her hair, and tilted her head back just as something hard was shoved against her mouth.

"What the—" The taste of liquor burned her lips. Willow jerked away, yelping when he tugged on her hair and tilted the bottle to pour more of the choking liquid down her throat. She slapped at his hands, utterly enraged and reeling in confusion, digging her fingernails into his wrist and trying to twist her head free.

The cuts on the inside of her mouth stung as he continued to force the liquid fire down her throat. She choked and gagged, frantically trying to break free.

He threw the bottle against the truck dash, the sound of shattering glass competing with the howl of the wind and storm-driven surf against the hood. She was suddenly released and the man disappeared into the darkness.

Willow wiped her stinging mouth with the back of her hand, using her other hand to shakily grope for the buckle on her seat belt, all the time fighting the urge to throw up. She finally got her belt released just as the passenger side door suddenly tore open. The dark figure of the man leaned inside, his own hands searching through the black interior.

With a whimper of alarm, Willow tried scrambling out her driver-side window only to gasp as pain shot through her left leg. The shadowed man pulled away, and Willow could just make out something thick and heavy in his hand.

Dammit, he had her briefcase!

Another angry wave slammed over the hood of the truck, splashing into the interior with enough force to throw Willow against her seat. The truck slid downward with the backwash, the metal undercarriage dragging over the granite with an ominous groan of warning.

Willow tugged on her leg, trying to free her left ankle from the twisted brake pedal. Driving rain blinded her, and she swiped at her face with a curse of frustration and tugged harder while trying to wiggle her foot loose.

The sound of an engine revving came from up on the road behind her, and she heard tires spinning on the wet pavement as it sped away.

Willow stopped struggling long enough to catch her breath and take stock of her situation, closing her eyes against the rain mingling with the icy waves that sent her body into convulsions of shivers. Okay, she thought as she hugged herself. She was trapped in her truck and clinging to the edge of the shoreline by an angel's wing and a prayer.

What in hell had happened? She hadn't noticed any car lights coming up behind her; she hadn't noticed anything until that black pickup had suddenly appeared beside her and cut her off. Come to think of it, the first time she had seen any lights at all had been his taillights, blinding her.

Had the guy run her off the road on purpose? Had he nearly killed her just to steal her laptop? And what was his pouring liquor down her throat all about?

Willow spit out the burning taste in her mouth and suddenly remembered her cell phone. She'd been talking to Duncan. She groped around the passenger seat, then leaned over and blindly searched the floor. She found her purse floating in the accumulating seawater, but no phone. She sat back, having to cover her face as another wave crested over the hood and into the truck.

Duncan would realize she'd been in an accident. He had already called for help, Willow assured herself, and was probably on the way here himself.

God bless troglodytes. They could always be counted on in a crisis.

Duncan shouted Willow's name into the phone, then listened in horror to the sound of her second scream, brakes squealing, metal crunching, and finally the chilling sound of glass shattering. And then the phone went dead.

Duncan ran an unsteady hand over his bloodless face, staring down at the phone. He hit the OFF button, hit the ON button, and dialed 911. "There's been an accident," he said the moment he connected. "On Route 321, someplace between Walker Point and Puffin Harbor."

He listened to the dispatcher tapping a keyboard. "Are there personal injuries, sir?" the woman asked. "How many people involved?"

"Only one that I know of," Duncan replied. "I'm not at the scene. I was talking to the driver on her cell phone when I heard the crash and the line went dead."

"So you're not sure exactly where the accident is," the dispatcher said.

"She mentioned she had just passed Walker Point," he repeated, running to the door and grabbing his jacket. "On the Puffin Harbor side. Just send the bloody ambulance!" he shouted, throwing down the phone and rushing to his truck. He was out the driveway and headed toward Walker Point before he pulled his own cell phone from his belt and punched in Kee's cell number.

"Where are ya?" he asked when Kee answered.

"Home."

"I think Willow's been in an accident just this side of Walker Point," Duncan said, holding the phone to his ear with his shoulder as he snapped his seat belt into place. "I was talking to her when I heard a crash and the phone went dead."

There was a heartbeat of silence on Kee's end before he said, "I'm on my way."

Duncan ended the call and punched in Luke's number. "Find Ahab and get him to Kee's house," he said when Luke answered. "Willow's been in an auto accident, and Ahab needs to babysit so you can drive Rachel to the hospital."

"How's Willow?" Luke asked.

"I don't know. I haven't gotten to the accident yet. It just happened. She's near Walker Point someplace. Find Ahab."

"I'm on it," Luke said, hanging up before Duncan did.

Duncan tossed his phone on the seat and let back on the accelerator as he neared the center of town. He noticed the doors of the fire station were open and that the ambulance, one fire truck, and the rescue pickup had already left. He slowly sped up as the town street turned to wooded road again, his gut churning with worry and self-reproach. Dammit, he shouldn't have called her cell phone.

In minutes that seemed like hours, Duncan spotted the red and white strobes of the fire trucks ahead. He slowed down and fell in behind them, watching as they scanned both sides of the road with powerful floodlights. They suddenly pulled over, and Duncan stopped and was running toward the skid marks before his own truck had quit rocking.

Nearly blinded by the floodlights and ignoring the shouts of the firemen, he scrambled over the bank and came to a sliding halt beside the driver's door of Willow's SUV. He ducked in through the broken window, his eyes trying to see in the beams of waving flashlights coming down the bank.

The truck was empty.

He was roughly pulled out of the way. "Get back," one of the firemen shouted. "Let us in."

In seconds Willow's SUV was surrounded by rescuers, all finding the same thing he had—nothing. Duncan grabbed one of the firefighters by the arm. "Train yar light down here," he said, stepping onto a boulder beside the truck. "She may have been thrown out. It's Willow Foster," he added, loudly enough for the others to hear above the pounding surf, hoping her name would get him—Hell, he didn't know what it would prove! Where the bloody hell was she?

All but two of the flashlight beams turned and started searching the area around, above, and below the mangled truck. "Listen," Duncan shouted over the howl of the wind, grabbing the closest man's arm. "Did ya hear that?"

"I'm here," came the weak voice again.

"There," Duncan said, pointing and then moving up and away from the truck. "She's up this way."

The beam of a flashlight moved ahead of him, landing on Willow's tiny shivering body balled up against the trunk of a pine tree. Duncan tore off his jacket as he made his way up the steep bank, going down on his knees the moment he got to her. "Where are ya hurt?" he asked as the others approached, several beams of light falling on her. "Willow, you're okay now. We've got ya."

Instead of answering him, she reached out and grabbed his jacket, making a sound of distress when she couldn't slide it over her wet, shivering shoulders.

But before Duncan could help her, one of the paramedics did. "You're Ross, aren't you? From The Rosach?" he said, glancing quickly at Duncan. "You'll have to move back while we check her out."

Duncan stood up and stepped back, but not very far, and watched as the paramedics went to work checking Willow for broken bones, pupil response, and bleeding.

"Have you been drinking, Willow?" one of them asked.

With the penlight shining in her eyes, she nodded, stopped and shook her head, then nodded again. "T-two beers, hours ago," she whispered, blinking against the bright light.

"That's a bit more than beer I'm smelling," the guy said. "What's my name, Willy? Do you recognize me?"

She smiled past pale blue, shivering lips, and waggled her fingers at him, the movement causing her to sway slightly. "Hi, Danny."

"How many fingers am I holding up?" Danny asked, turning his light so the beam hit his hand.

"Two. No three. Stop moving them," she muttered, hugging her belly. "Oh, God, I'm going to be sick again."

The men quickly scrambled out of the way just in time for Willow to lean over and empty her stomach onto the ground, her pitiful gags carried away on the wind.

Duncan went to step forward when a strong hand landed on his shoulder. "Let them work," Kee said. "She's talking and puking; she's going to be okay."

"They think she's drunk," Duncan growled softly.

"It certainly looks like she is," Kee said.

"The inside of her truck smelled like bourbon," Duncan told him. "But Willow hates bourbon."

"Nor does she drink and drive," Kee added as they both watched the paramedics finally ease her onto a rescue litter and strap her in, Duncan noticing they were being careful of her right arm and left leg.

"She said she had some beer this afternoon," Duncan said.

"That's what she told Rachel when she called," Kee agreed. "But that was over a four-hour dinner at least two hours ago. She's not drunk, Duncan. She's just disoriented from the crash."

Duncan looked over at the tangled remains of her SUV, seeing four firemen milling around it, tying a rope under the rear axle to anchor it from sliding into the sea. The entire area was flooded with light now, and Duncan's own gut twisted.

It was at least a forty-foot drop from the road to where her truck had landed, and the vegetation was untouched for a good twenty feet, which meant she'd been airborne at least that far. Duncan guessed the landing had been rather violent, and that he'd probably be acting drunk himself if he'd been in that truck.

"Come on," Kee said, pulling on Duncan's arm. "We'll

follow the ambulance to Ellsworth. Luke called me to say he'll bring Rachel once he gets Ahab. Willow is going to be okay," Kee assured him when Duncan didn't move. "That's all that matters right now."

"Aye," Duncan said, rubbing a hand over his face. The rain had let up but the wind was still fierce. He took one last look at the SUV, specifically at its front bumper sitting in the churning surf, and shuddered when another wave broke over the hood and washed through the interior all the way to the back seat. He finally followed Kee up the steep, boulder-strewn bank, and was waiting at the back of the ambulance when they carried Willow over and set the litter on the waiting gurney.

Kee said something to the paramedic Willow had called Danny, then turned and nodded to Duncan. Duncan stepped forward and smiled down at Willow, running a trembling finger along the side of her bloodless cheek as he leaned close and whispered, "Ya picked a hell of a way to get out of our date, lady."

"There—there was a man," she whispered in broken shivers. "He ran me off the road and . . . and stole my briefcase. And he . . . he poured liquor down my throat."

Duncan showed no reaction to her news other than his free hand balling into a fist. He kissed her cold forehead. "Just be a good patient for them, counselor," he whispered. "I'll be at the hospital right behind you."

The paramedics shouldered Duncan out of the way and lifted Willow into the ambulance. One of the firemen closed the doors and pounded on them, and the ambulance took off toward Ellsworth, its sirens blaring and its strobes flashing through the darkness.

Duncan headed to his truck. Kee followed.

"What did she tell you?" Kee asked. "How bad is she hurt?"

Duncan stopped by his truck door. "I don't think she's hurt that badly. Her new truck had front and side air bags, and they seem to have done their job. She said a man ran her off the road and stole her briefcase, and that he poured liquor down her throat."

Kee stiffened, the harsh planes of his face visible in the strobes of the fire trucks. "This was deliberate?" he growled. "And she said a man showed up, but instead of helping her, he poured liquor down her throat and then left her for dead?"

Duncan opened his truck door and climbed in. "Aye," he said, looking back at Kee. "After he stole her briefcase."

He shut the door, started his truck, then pulled onto the road around the fire truck when Kee headed to his own pickup. It was another eighteen miles to Ellsworth, and Duncan made it in twenty minutes, thanks to the fact that few people were on the road in the storm.

Kee pulled into the hospital parking lot right behind him. They entered through the emergency room doors together, and were immediately stopped by Deputy Larry Jenkins, though he wasn't in his sheriff's uniform.

"I was just headed home when I heard the call," Larry told Kee. "They're checking her now. I got here just as they were bringing her in, and Danny doesn't think any bones are broken or that she even has a concussion." He darted a glance at Duncan, scowled, and looked back at Kee. "They're doing a blood alcohol test. She appears to be drunk."

"Willow doesn't drink and drive," Duncan snapped, drawing Larry's attention. "She said a man was at the scene, and that he poured liquor down her throat and stole her briefcase. After he'd run her off the road."

Larry just stared at Duncan.

"She wasn't driving drunk, Jenkins," Kee growled, adding his own endorsement. "You know that as well as we do."

Larry shook his head. "If that blood alcohol test comes back over the legal limit, and we don't find anything to corroborate her story, then our knowing Willow won't mean a hill of beans."

Rachel came through the automatic doors just then, pushing at them to open quicker, and rushed to Kee. "Where is she?" she asked, her face ashen white. "How bad is she hurt?"

Kee wrapped an arm around her shoulders. "She's going to be okay, honey," he told her. "They're checking her now, but she was conscious and talking at the scene."

Rachel buried her face in her husband's chest with a quiet sob of relief, and Luke came through the door and stopped beside the men. His face was also as pale as snow.

"She's going to be okay," Duncan assured Luke. He turned to Jenkins, nodding for the man to step away with him. "Willow told me she'd been run off the road," he told Larry once they were a safe distance away from the others. "The inside of her truck smelled like bourbon, and Willow can't stand the taste of it. And her briefcase was stolen. Surely there will be evidence of another vehicle's involvement. Maybe paint on the fender or fingerprints on her truck."

Larry frowned, shaking his head. "Not if he was wearing gloves. But if another vehicle made contact with hers, we'll be able to tell that." He eyed Duncan speculatively. "Why would someone run Willow off the road and pour liquor down her throat?"

"She's an assistant AG," Duncan reminded him. "Who knows who she's pissed off."

Larry thought about that and slowly nodded agreement. "I'll call the deputy who's at the scene now, and have him look around for evidence of a second vehicle. But don't hope for much. Everything's likely been trampled by firemen and equipment."

"And if that blood test comes back over the limit, can ya keep it quiet?" Duncan asked.

Again, Larry thought about that, then shrugged. "I can try." He looked Duncan straight in the eye. "I don't know whether to hate you or thank you for catching Willow's interest. Trying to date Willow was an exercise in frustration for me."

"I haven't caught her yet," Duncan growled, looking toward the examining rooms, then back at Jenkins. "And I'm feeling some of that frustration myself."

Larry shoved his hands in his pockets. "Still, I placed my money on you," he muttered, turning and walking out the automatic doors.

Duncan had just rejoined the others when a doctor appeared, stopped at the desk, then walked over to Rachel. "Are you Willow Foster's sister?" he asked.

Rachel stepped away from Kee and nodded. "How is she?"

"Remarkably, she's in pretty good shape," the doctor said. "Some cuts and bruises, a banged knee, and her right wrist has a hairline fracture, but there's no concussion or anything serious. In fact, you can take her home tonight if you want."

Rachel leaned to see past him. "Can I see her now?"

He nodded. "Sure. Your sister's a lucky woman. According to the paramedics, her truck was totaled." He frowned. "She's still a bit drunk, so I didn't dare give her anything for the pain. I'll send something home with you for later."

"Drunk?" Rachel said in surprise, only to quickly shake her head. "She can't be drunk. I just talked to her an hour before the accident and she was completely sober. She'd had a couple of beers, but she'd switched to soda long before she'd left the restaurant."

"Her blood alcohol was point-two-three," the doctor said. "That's high enough to make an elephant stagger."

Rachel gasped. "There's been a mistake. Do the test again."

"We did repeat it," the doctor assured her. "I'm sorry, but I have to report my findings to the sheriff. She was involved in an automobile accident, and she's almost three times over the legal limit."

Rachel spun toward Kee, her eyes snapping in outrage. Kee silently shook his head at her, looked at the doctor, and nodded. "Thank you," he said. "Can we see her now?"

"Just two of you," the doctor said, frowning at Duncan and Luke before looking back at Rachel. "And check with the nurse for instructions before you take her home."

Rachel took hold of Duncan's hand and led him through the examining room door with her, leaving Kee behind. They arrived to find Willow sitting up on a gurney, staring at her splinted right hand and wrist.

The nurse beside her patted Willow's arm. "This must be your sister," she said with a warm smile. She stepped out of the way when they walked to the gurney. "She's going to be just fine," the nurse assured Rachel in a whisper, darting a worried look at Duncan. She stepped closer to Rachel. "She's still a bit drunk, but when that wears off she's going to be sore all over."

Duncan ignored the conversation, trying to decide where he could touch Willow. Her hair was still damp, there was a bruise on her temple and left jaw, her right wrist was in a plastic splint, and her left knee looked big under the blanket covering her legs.

Willow blinked up at him, her huge hazel eyes glazed and teary, and smiled tremulously as she reached out with her good hand and touched his chest. "I'm okay, Dunky," she whispered, wincing and quickly touching the cut on her swollen lip. "Please don't look like you're going to faint."

He carefully took hold of her left hand and gently held it against his chest. "I can see that, lass," he said softly, his own wince of sympathy ruining his attempt to glare at her. "And troglodytes don't faint."

"No, they come to a girl's rescue," she said, curling her fingers into his damp shirt. "I knew you'd find me, Duncan. I waited for you."

"Oh, Willy, now what have you done to yourself?" Rachel said, her scolding ruined by her tear-washed smile as she moved to the other side of the gurney and brushed the hair back from Willow's face. "You wrecked your brand-new truck."

"I was checking out its air bags," Willow answered, laying her cast-covered hand on Rachel's arm. "It appears they work just fine."

Rachel swiped at a tear rolling down her cheek and

choked on a laugh. She quickly sobered. "Why are they saying you're drunk, Willy?"

Willow darted a look at Duncan, and reached out and took hold of Rachel's hand. "Because I guess I am. Duncan," she said, looking at him. "Will you give me a moment with Rachel?"

"Aye," he said, leaning over to give her a quick, gentle kiss on her wet hair. "I'll be right outside."

With that, Duncan turned and followed the nurse out of the exam room, and walked over to Kee and Luke in the waiting area. "About what happens now," he said to Kee. "I want Willow to come home with me."

"Rachel's not going to allow that, and you know it," Kee said. "She damn near lost her sister tonight."

Duncan nodded agreement and blew out a tired sigh. "I know. But if what Willow told me is true, she might still be in danger, and I don't think we need to put your family in the middle of it. Especially not Mikaela and Nick."

Kee shook his head. "It doesn't matter. Willow is part of my family. Between you, me, Luke, and Ahab, we can keep everyone safe until we know what we're dealing with."

"We can do that just as well at my house," Duncan rebutted. "Without involving the kids."

"Rachel won't allow it," Kee repeated, shaking his head again. He set his hand on Duncan's shoulder. "I know how you're feeling, my friend. We'll ask Rachel, but understand that you're going to have a fight on your hands."

"When I picked up Ahab, he told me he found out something at that bar in Trunk Harbor," Luke interjected. "Seems there's two men who have been hanging out there for the last couple of weeks. They were asking about Willow. Said they'd heard she'd been in town last weekend and wondered if she was coming back soon. They claimed to be friends of hers from Augusta."

Both Duncan and Kee turned to Luke.

"Ahab said they looked more like guys Willow might have prosecuted than friends," Luke continued.

"When was this?" Duncan asked.

"Just last night," Luke said. "Ahab was going to tell us tonight, when he came to The Rosach. He might have more, but I didn't hang around long enough to hear it. I just dropped him off and brought Rachel here." Luke shook his head. "Rachel saw them pulling Willow's truck over the bank when we drove by. She's not going to let her sister out of her sight for a long time, I'm afraid. Seeing that twisted chunk of metal really shook her up."

Rachel came through the exam room door just then, saw the men, and walked toward them. Duncan steeled himself for the battle ahead, wondering how to persuade Rachel it was best for Willow to come home with him and how not to end up in a fistfight with Kee when the man took his wife's side.

Which would be nothing, Duncan realized, compared to the fight he was about to have when he told Willow she was going home with him.

"Come on," Rachel said to her husband. "I have to pack some things for Willow."

"They're keeping her?" Duncan asked.

"No, she's going home with you," Rachel said.

"She is?" Duncan asked, clearly nonplussed. "And you agree?"

Rachel patted his chest, smiling at his surprise. "No,

but I don't have a choice. Willow insists. She told me about the man who ran her off the road and stole her briefcase, and she's afraid to put Mikaela and Nick in danger." She frowned over at Kee. "She thinks what happened might be linked to the sick lobster."

"You know about the lobster?" Duncan asked, drawing her attention again.

Rachel nodded. "Sisters talk to each other, Duncan," she said, turning and walking to the door. "Come on, I want to get home and assure Mikaela that Willy's okay. She can come with us when we go to Duncan's house, to see for herself that her aunt is fine," she finished as she stepped through the automatic doors.

With a shrug indicating his own surprise, and a smile that said he never would understand women, Kee turned and also disappeared out the door. Luke hung back.

"I think I'll follow you home," Luke said. "And maybe spend the night."

"Thanks," Duncan said, nodding. "But I also need ya to find out where they took Willow's truck, and see if ya can get her purse and other stuff and bring it to the house. And while ya're at it, try to find out what the authorities think caused the accident. Maybe have a look at the vehicle yourself."

"I can do that," Luke said. "What about Molly? She's at The Rosach, isn't she? I'll bring her home."

"Aye. She's tending bar." Duncan broke into a smile. "Business is up since she started three nights ago. And she's been making a small fortune in tips."

Luke also broke into a smile. "We know it's not her accent, considering you sound a lot like her," he drawled. "Must be the package that accent comes in."

"Ya never mind my sister's package," Duncan growled. "Ya're too old for her."

Completely undeterred by the warning in Duncan's voice, Luke's smile widened. "We have the same age difference as there is between you and Willow," he pointed out. He canted his head. "Or are you getting used to the idea of your sister marrying a sheep farmer?"

"I'm beginning to prefer my mother's idea of locking her in the Tower of London," Duncan shot back. He handed his keys to Luke and turned and headed to the exam room. "Start my truck, will ya, so it'll be warm when I bring Willow out?"

Duncan knocked on the exam room door, then stepped through it to find Willow sitting in a wheelchair dressed in a hospital gown and bathrobe, and with a blanket tucked around her shoulders.

The nurse handed him a small brown bag and a piece of paper. "Here are the instructions for what she has to do for the next week, and some pain medicine. She needs to go see her own doctor within the next few days, once she's feeling up to it."

"What about the clothes she was wearing?" Duncan asked.

"She told us to toss them. Oh, here's your jacket," the nurse said, picking it up from a chair and handing it to him. "There's a bit of blood on it, but it should wash out."

Duncan tucked the jacket under his arm and quickly scanned the instructions. They seemed easy enough, so he looked at Willow and found her smiling up at him— either still a bit drunk or downright pleased with herself.

"So ya've appointed me your nursemaid for the next week?" he asked.

Her eyes lit up. "I've always had a thing for playing doctor and patient," she told him. She turned serious. "I can't go to Rachel's, Duncan. It wouldn't be right."

"Aye," he said. "And just as soon as it calms down, we'll head out to sea for a long, relaxing sail."

"That sounds like a wonderful idea," the nurse said, her cheeks a bit pink from Willow and Duncan's not-so-subtle word play. She started pushing Willow out of the exam room. "There's nothing like fresh air and sunshine to heal a person."

Duncan tagged along behind them, all but whistling at the thought of Willow being completely dependent on him for the next week. The fact that it was her idea was only icing on the cake, he decided, wondering where he could buy one of those white doctor coats and maybe a stethoscope.

Chapter Ten

❧

*W*ith her head tucked in the crook of Duncan's shoulder and her arm lying across his broad chest, Willow smiled into the darkness as she remembered falling asleep with a deep sense of contentment. Duncan had brought her home last night, carefully installed her in his bed, and then patiently stood back while a parade of people had come to see for themselves that she had survived the crash whole and relatively hearty.

The visitations had started with Rachel, Kee, Mikaela, and Mickey. Mikaela had climbed up on the bed, her baby blue eyes fraught with concern, and proceeded to take stock of Willow's every cut and bruise and bandage. The seven-year-old had then read Willow a bedtime story from one of the books she'd brought with her, finishing by announcing that Mickey was so worried about Willow that he wanted to spend the night.

Mickey was now snuggled against Willow's back with

his nose resting on her thigh, making Willow feel like a well-guarded sandwich.

Luke had also come in last night, declared that Willow looked like hell, and told her he'd gotten her things from her truck. A box of Mason jars had been broken, the underwater camera housed in a metal case appeared to have survived the crash intact, everything in her purse was wet but likely salvageable, and her suitcase had soaked through and Rachel would have to deal with her clothes before she could wear them.

Willow had finally met Molly, but she hadn't been able to comprehend how such a stunningly beautiful, vivacious, and obviously civilized woman could be related to Duncan. Whereas Duncan was tall and powerful and roughly masculine, Molly Ross was utterly feminine— from her elegantly dressed model's body to her baby-doll face and shining green eyes, all the way to her sexy mane of red-blond curls.

Duncan had put up with the intrusions with commendable patience before finally shooing everyone out by declaring that Willow needed her rest. But Willow had worried *rest* might be a relative term when Duncan had come back into the bedroom, stripped down to his boxer shorts, and crawled into bed beside her. He had then tried for ten minutes to get Mickey to sleep on the floor, but when the wolf had finally resorted to growling and closed his eyes with a lupine sigh of finality, Duncan had taken Willow in his arms with an answering sigh of his own and gone directly to sleep. Deciding she couldn't feel more protected and secure, Willow hadn't even finished a yawn before she'd fallen asleep herself.

"Are you awake, Doctor Dunky?" she whispered.

Duncan's arm gently tightened around her. "I'm awake. Are ya sore, lass? Do ya need one of your pills?"

"No. I am sore, but it's kind of a cozy I-don't-want-to-move soreness. You're all the medicine I need right now."

Duncan lazily rubbed her arm, the movement making Willow cuddle more closely against him as she curled her fingers into the springy soft hair of his chest. She couldn't see the clock by the bed, and was too comfortable to lift her head to look, but Willow guessed it was early morning. The storm was still raging outside, the wind blowing a heavy rain against the windows of the nineteenth-century farmhouse.

Duncan had bought the seventy-three-acre, saltwater farm just before he'd purchased his pub. The stately but rundown house sat on a shallow bluff that jutted into the ocean east of Puffin Harbor, about three miles from the center of town.

"Are ya thirsty? Would ya like a glass of water?"

"No," Willow murmured, turning her head just enough to kiss his chest. "I only need to cuddle and talk."

"Then we'll talk, counselor. Tell me why you were run off the road."

"Only if you promise not to get angry," she said, tickling his chest hair when she felt him tense. "And not get all chest-beating protective on me."

"Ya told Rachel ya thought it had to do with the sick lobsters," he said, neither agreeing with nor arguing against her edict. "What makes ya think that? What else has happened?"

"A guy was in my apartment Wednesday and snooped through my home computer," she said, moving her bandaged hand to trail her fingers over his clenched jaw.

"And somebody was in my office that same night, and went through my files and office computer. He stole some papers."

"And did ya tell your boss?"

"No."

"Why not?"

"Because I couldn't prove any of it."

"And now your laptop was stolen."

"Yes. It had copies of the files that were stolen, articles on pesticide poisoning from the Internet, and a fax from Jane Huntley. Jane," Willow said on a gasp, lifting her head toward Duncan. "What if she's in danger, too? They might even break into her lab."

Duncan gently pulled her head back down and ran his fingers soothingly through her hair. "We'll call her and warn her this morning," he said. "And we'll suggest she take a little vacation. What do ya think is going on, Willow? What have ya discovered about the lobsters?"

"Jane is pretty sure it's pesticide poisoning, and that there must be a lot of it draining into the waters around Thunder Island for it to be killing lobsters over half a mile out."

"And ya're thinking someone dumped this pesticide near the island," Duncan softly surmised. "But we saw no containers. Could they have just poured it into the sea?"

Willow moved her head against his chest. "No. Jane said if it had been poured out, it would have been dispersed by the ocean currents. For it to still be affecting the lobster, the source is still intact and leaching the poison with each tide. That's why she wants the water samples." She lifted her head and tried to see through the darkness. "That's what we were supposed to do this weekend. Take samples and look in the quarry with the underwater camera she loaned me."

Duncan gently urged her head back down again. "We still can. Just as soon as the storm plays out, we'll head to sea."

Willow popped her head up again, digging her bandaged fingers into his chest. "We could bring Jane with us. That way she can help, and we'll know she's safe."

Even though it was dark, there was enough light coming from the crack under the hall door for Willow to see Duncan's scowl. "This is supposed to be our time together," he said. "Just you, me, and Mickey."

"But I'll be useless for several days. Jane can crew for us. She comes from Fisherman's Reach and knows her way around boats. And she can help you take the water samples."

"No."

"But it's perfect," Willow continued, warming up to her plan. "Hey, what about Luke? He could come with us. Luke has blues eyes, doesn't he? And his hair is sort of blond."

Duncan carefully untangled himself from around her, got out of bed, and turned to tower over her, a dark silhouette against the dim light from the hall. "What in hell does the color of Luke's eyes have to do with anything?" he growled.

Willow lay back on the pillow, reaching over and running her fingers through Mickey's fur. "Jane's got a thing for blond-haired, blue-eyed hunks. If I tell her about Luke, she not only won't argue about coming with us, she'll probably run all the way down here."

"Luke's busy distracting Molly."

Willow gasped in surprise. "You've got your best friend distracting your sister away from the sheep farmer?" She snorted. "My God, Dunky, you really are a caveman."

Duncan crouched down by the side of the bed and took Willow's chin in his fingers. "You're calling me names, when you're suggesting we use Luke to lure your scientist friend down here?" he whispered. Willow could just make out the slash of his grin as he shook his head. "We both should be ashamed of ourselves."

"But they'd be perfect for each other, Duncan. Jane lives for adventure. And she's really cute."

Duncan leaned over and softly kissed her lips. "So are you, counselor. Especially when you're lying in my bed."

Willow relaxed back onto the pillow with a sigh. "We're never going to get this affair going," she muttered. "The gods are against us."

"I've warned ya about never saying never," Duncan said, standing up and heading to the master bath. He snapped on the light, then turned to face her. "You'll get your affair, woman. I only hope ya can deal with the consequences when ya do."

With that cryptic remark, he disappeared into the bathroom and shut the door. Willow heard the shower start, and she rolled toward Mickey. "So, Mr. Mouse, what do you suppose he meant by that?" she asked, ruffling his fur.

Mickey's answer was a yawn that ended when he jumped off the bed and trotted to the hallway door. Willow threw back the covers, sat up on the edge of the bed, and snapped on the bedside light. She pulled up the hem of Duncan's T-shirt she'd worn to bed, and looked down at her left knee. The doctor hadn't bandaged it, and she could see a bruise darkening the lower outside of the joint. She must have banged it against the truck door during the crash.

Willow stood up, keeping her weight on her good right leg, then slowly settled her weight onto her left leg. She didn't feel more than a warning twinge, and decided the doctor was right, that it wasn't sprained, only bruised. She'd be mobile, at least, though definitely slow. Every muscle in her body felt as if she'd gone a few cycles in a tumble dryer—which Willow supposed she had when she'd rolled down that embankment.

She limped to the door and opened it, allowing Mickey to go trotting down the hall toward the kitchen. Willow followed more slowly, frowning at what she was seeing, suddenly gasping when she stepped into the kitchen.

This was not Duncan's house. There was no sign of the warped white cupboards, scarred countertop, chipped enamel sink, cracked linoleum floor, or rusted tin ceiling. The old appliances—avocado green, if she remembered correctly—were gone, as was the battered table that used to sit in the center of the room and the ancient relic of a wood cookstove that used to be at the end of the counter.

No, instead Willow found herself standing in a kitchen that could have come straight from the pages of *Better Homes and Gardens*. She wouldn't have been surprised if Emeril Lagasse walked in and started cooking breakfast.

This new kitchen had counters of granite, cupboards of solid cherry, red oak planked floors, and the ceiling was definitely newly installed painted tin. The appliances were stainless steel, the six-burner range looking like it belonged in a five-star restaurant. Old-world charm was everywhere she turned, but with a carefully detailed sense of modern efficiency.

It was stunningly sophisticated. An epicure's kitchen.

What it definitely wasn't was a kitchen that belonged to a troglodyte. Heck, Willow realized, *she* wouldn't know how to cook in this kitchen.

She really must have been drunk last night, because she hadn't noticed any of this when Duncan had brought her home. Though he'd carried her straight into the bedroom, he had carried her through the kitchen, but she couldn't remember if the lights had been on or not.

Mickey whined from somewhere to her left, and still gawking around in wonder, Willow limped into what she discovered was the mudroom. She opened the porch door, let Mickey out into the wind-driven rain, and turned and shuffled back through the kitchen, continuing on to where the old parlor used to be.

The narrow doorway separating the two rooms had been replaced by a wide arch trimmed with intricate, painted molding that opened into a completely remodeled living area. The old double-hung windows were gone, replaced by a bank of solid glass facing the ocean. The fireplace, which had been held together with more soot than mortar, was now a river-stone hearth that took up the entire end wall. And in the center of the polished hardwood floor, surrounded by leather couches and chairs, was a thick, richly colored Persian rug that was nearly as large as her apartment in Augusta.

Willow walked over to the hearth when she noticed there was wood laid out in it, just waiting to be lit. She pulled a match from the silver-plated matchbox standing on the mantel, struck it, and set the flame to the bottom of the kindling. Once she was satisfied the fire was going, she pulled the cotton throw off the back of a nearby leather chair, sat down on the couch, and carefully tucked her legs up to cuddle under the blanket. She rested her chin on the arm of the couch and stared into the fire with a heavy sigh, listening to the storm and feeling safe and contented for the first time in what seemed like years.

"For as lovely as ya were in my bed, lass, ya've never looked more beautiful than ya do right now."

Willow turned at the sound of his voice, self-consciously running her fingers through her tangled hair. Duncan was standing in the archway, fully dressed but barefooted, holding a glass of water in one hand and what looked like a prescription bottle in his other hand.

"When did you do all this, Duncan?" she asked, pulling her fingers from her hair to wave them at the room. "It's beautiful."

He walked around the opposite couch and came to stand in front of her, the corner of his mouth turned up in a tiger's grin. "Ya like it, counselor? It's not too masculine for you?"

"It's perfect. It's . . ." She frowned up at him. "It's a true gentleman's home."

Duncan looked around the large living room, then back at her. "I suppose it is a far cry from the cave I crawled out of," he said, his eyes dancing in the crackling firelight.

Willow canted her head, her own eyes narrowing. "Who are you, Duncan Ross?"

He sat down on the couch beside her, put the glass and pills on the coffee table, then took her legs and lifted them over his so that she was sitting with her back against the arm of the couch and her knees cradled in his lap. He resettled the blanket over her legs, then tucked a strand of her hair behind her ear.

"I'm the man it's safe for you to love, Willow. I know better than anyone, except maybe Rachel, how delicate yar heart really is, lass. But I can hold it securely, because I'm the one man who loves ya more than life itself."

"Oh, Duncan," Willow whispered, cupping his face in her hands, looking directly into his piercing green eyes. "I don't want you to love me."

"Too late, counselor. I've loved ya since our first kiss in the town square, when ya kissed me back and then poked my ribs and started scolding me."

"That was lust, Dunky."

"Aye," he admitted, his nod moving her hands. "There's always been lust between us." He removed her hands and held them against his heart. "And when we're sitting in rocking chairs on the porch, watching our grandchildren flying kites in the front field, I'll still be lusting after ya."

"You . . . you want children?" she whispered, not knowing if the sudden pounding in her heart was excitement or horror—or downright fear. "I hadn't thought about having babies."

"Never?" he asked, clearly surprised. "Ya never pictured yourself as a mama? Not even when you were a child?"

"Of course I did. But then I grew up and realized that to have babies I had to have a husband."

"Is that when yar dream died? When ya decided a husband was more . . . what is it, Willow? Have ya ever put into words what ya fear?"

"Getting my heart broken."

"Aye," Duncan agreed, nodding. "That's the risk we take when we open ourselves up to loving someone. But where I've jumped in with both feet, you can't even seem to get your toes wet."

"You're calling me a coward?" she asked, digging her fingers into his shirt.

He shook his head, pulling her hands away and holding them safely tucked inside his, down on her thighs. "You're probably the bravest woman I know, Willow Foster. In all things but one," he clarified. "Ya've decided that if ya let yourself fall madly in love with—oh, let's say me, for instance—that ya wouldn't survive if something happened to me."

"That's a bit melodramatic," she snapped, trying to tug her hands free.

Apparently afraid she'd further hurt her wrist, Duncan let her go and captured her chin instead, making her look at him. "But it's dead-on, Willow. When ya do decide to love, you'll do it with complete abandon. But ya're afraid to cross that line because ya're afraid to lose part of yourself."

She pulled her chin free and glared at him.

Duncan merely brought her good hand up to his lips, kissed its palm, and shook his head. "I've been trying to warn ya, lass, that ya can't hold back the forces of nature. You're wanting an affair, but do ya really think ya can share my bed and not get emotionally involved?"

"I do."

"Ahhh. Right words, wrong context," he said with a chuckle. "Keep telling yourself that, counselor, and I'll keep loving ya despite yourself. Are ya ready for some of your pain pills?"

Willow blinked at the maddening man. He was so damned sure of himself. So sure of her! Dammit, she was not falling in love with Duncan Ross.

"My, but isn't this a wonderfully domestic scene," Luke said as he padded down the stairs. He reached the bottom step, yawned, and ran a hand through his tousled, sort-of-blond hair.

Willow suddenly remembered her earlier idea. "Luke, can you get away from your construction company for a few days?" she asked, ignoring Duncan's hand tightening on her thigh. "And crew for us on the *Seven-to-Two Odds*? We need to take some water samples, and you'd get to use that fancy underwater camera," she added for good measure, deciding she probably shouldn't mention Jane Huntley just yet.

Luke's gaze shot to Duncan. "I thought you didn't want a crew," he said. "That you want it to appear as if you and Willow are . . ." He waved a hand at the air and looked at Willow. "I thought you were going to use the cover of Duncan trying to court you so that you could snoop around Thunder Island. Having me along would kind of blow your cover, wouldn't it?"

"Not if we bring another woman with us," Willow said. "Then people will think the *Seven-to-Two Odds* is really just a floating bordello."

Luke instantly perked up. "Molly?" he asked, looking at Duncan again. "Is she coming with us?"

Duncan stood up, tucked the blanket back around Willow's legs, and turned to the coffee table and picked up the bottle of pain pills. "Molly is going to stay right here and run The Rosach," he said as he gave the cap a twist. He pointed the open bottle at Willow but looked at Luke. "She's trying to set you up with her scientist friend from the Lobster Institute. Apparently, Jane Huntley likes men."

"You make her sound like a hussy," Willow said, first glaring at Duncan and then turning to smile at Luke. "Jane's an intelligent, dedicated marine biologist who also happens to be my good friend."

Luke snorted. "Intelligent. Dedicated. Good friend," he repeated. "Which means she wears glasses thicker than Coke bottles, and she can't carry a conversation that doesn't involve words containing less than twelve letters." He shook his head and lazily scratched his belly through his shirt. "I'm already booked, Willow. I'm distracting Molly for Duncan."

"You *know* Duncan's using you?"

Luke's grin slashed in the firelight. "Of course. Buddies watch each other's backs." He stepped down the last stair and walked over to the hearth, turning away from the blaze as he clasped his hands behind his back and eyed Willow speculatively. "Jason's flying in today. Why don't you ask him to crew for you? An intelligent, dedicated scientist is right up his ally."

"Jason's coming in?" Duncan asked, drawing Luke's attention. "How come?"

"Kee called the guys, but Matt and Peter are busy delivering the yacht they raised to its owner. Jason said he'd come up, though, and help out however he could."

"I can't remember," Willow said. "What color are Jason's eyes?"

Luke gave her a quizzical frown. "Hell, I never noticed. Blue, I think."

"They're gray," Duncan snapped, finally shaking a pill from the bottle. "Just one," he growled, handing it to her. "I need ya sober this morning, before ya forget yourself and try and hook *me* up with your friend."

With a smile that said she wasn't the least bit intimidated, Willow popped the pill in her mouth, took the glass from him, and washed her medicine down with a large gulp of water. She snuggled back under her blanket, resting against the arm of the couch, and stared past Luke into the fire. "I like my bacon cooked crispy," she said to whichever one of them seemed inclined to start breakfast. "And do you have a television in here, Dunky? I want to watch Saturday morning cartoons. Oh, and Mickey's outside."

Apparently realizing they'd been dismissed, the two men quietly disappeared into the kitchen. Willow smiled at the fire, deciding that gray eyes were damn close to blue, and that Jason was a much better match for Jane, now that she thought about it.

By noon, Duncan's house was full of people, not the least of which was little Nicholas Oakes, commanding the center of everyone's attention. The fourteen-month-old had already pulled all the pots from three of Duncan's bottom cupboards, and was now working on a drawer of plastic bowls and lids. Mickey was supervising, occasionally chasing one of the lids that rolled toward the living room.

Molly was busy putting together a lasagna for tonight's dinner, and the men—Duncan, Kee, Luke, and Ahab—

were in Duncan's study doing men stuff. Willow was sitting at the island counter with Mikaela and Rachel, eating ants on a log, chocolate-coated eyes of newt, and snake egg sandwiches.

Despite their dubious names, Willow had been eagerly devouring the treats, now that her pain pill had finally worn off enough to no longer upset her stomach. Mikaela had come up with the names for the rather odd combinations of food—not without plenty of help from her five and a half uncles. The "uncles" were Duncan, Luke, Jason, Peter, and Matt—five men who had been working as salvagers with Kee when Mikaela's birth had made her a very integral part of their lives. (Ahab still refused to officially be associated with Mikaela, but the young girl kept insisting he was at least half hers. Anybody seeing Mikaela and the schooner captain together, however, would immediately know that Ahab's salty old heart was *fully* engaged.)

Ants on a log were celery sticks slathered in peanut butter and lined with raisins; eyes of newt were frozen grapes dipped in melted chocolate; and snake egg sandwiches were raw peas slipped between two slices of banana. Peanut butter was the spread of choice to keep the peas from falling out.

There was a knock on the door. Rachel popped an eye of newt in her mouth and slid off her stool to go answer it. Mickey, apparently deciding no one was entering the house without his approval, quickly bounded past her into the mudroom.

"Jane!" Willow heard her sister say. "You made it through the storm okay. It's great to see you again."

"That's your friend, the lady scientist?" Mikaela asked around a mouthful of celery.

Willow nodded as she wiped some peanut butter off Mikaela's chin. "You're going to love her, kiddo," Willow said after swallowing her own snake egg sandwich. "Jane is smart and funny and she isn't afraid of anything."

Mikaela's eyes rounded. "Not even spiders?"

"Especially not spiders," Willow confirmed. "Jane says spiders are a lot like lobsters, only they don't taste as good."

Mikaela narrowed her eyes. "She didn't eat a spider."

"She did," Willow said with another nod. "When we were in high school, we got stranded on one of the Pilot Islands overnight while kayaking, and Jane thought we needed to eat bugs to survive. So she swallowed a spider and then tried to get me to do the same."

Mikaela's eyes widened again. "And did you?" she asked in a whisper, her expression more horrified than curious.

Willow laughed and ruffled Mikaela's blond curls. "I refuse to answer on the grounds it might incriminate me," Willow said, slowly lowering herself from her stool to go greet Jane.

She had to wait, though, until Jane finished hugging Mickey. The tall, athletic, beautiful scientist finally stood up with a laugh and smiled at Willow. "I've always wanted to hug a wolf," she said, wiping her cheek with her hand. "But being kissed by one is even better. Ohmygod, look at you."

Willow lifted her hand and touched the bruise on her jaw. "I know," she said, returning Jane's smile. "I saw myself in the mirror this morning and screamed."

Jane shook her head. "I stopped to have a look at where you went off the road last night. You're damn lucky you didn't drown. The trees were broken all the way down to the tide."

Willow took hold of Jane's arm and led her into the kitchen. "I'm just glad my new truck had all those airbags. Jane, this is Molly Ross, Duncan's sister. Molly, this is Jane Huntley, my friend I told you about."

Molly wiped her hands on the towel she was using for an apron and shook Jane's hand. "It's nice ta meet ya, Jane Huntley." Molly's sexy green eyes sparkled. "You've been the main topic of discussion around here this morning."

Jane seemed neither surprised nor appalled at being talked about. "It's great to meet you, Molly. Is that spaghetti sauce I smell?" she asked, looking toward the range.

"Willow told us lasagna is yar favorite," Molly said, going back to the sink to finish washing a pan. "So I decided ta try out this fancy kitchen my brother thought he was needing," she continued over her shoulder.

"Jane, I'd like you to meet my niece, Mikaela," Willow said next, moving behind Mikaela to take hold of her shoulders. "Mikaela is learning to kayak so she can paddle in the Crane Island Kayak Race this Fourth of July."

Jane came over and held out her hand. "So you're the hel—the girl wonder I've been hearing about. I have a niece paddling in the peewee race," she said, shaking Mikaela's hand while making a production of looking her over. "You better build those muscles up if you hope to win. My Jasmine's determined to get the trophy this year."

Mikaela blinked up at Jane, her hellion's smile firmly in place, and handed Jane a stalk of peanut-buttered celery lined with raisins. "You want some ants on a log?" she asked, her expression sweetly expectant.

Jane was just reaching for the gooey treat when she suddenly changed direction. She bent over, peeled Nick's tiny fists off her pant legs, and lifted him into her arms with a laugh. "You must be Nick," she said.

"Boo," Nick said, pointing at Willow.

"Yes, Aunt Willy's got a boo-boo," Jane confirmed, holding still while Nick touched her own jaw.

"Boo," he repeated, only this time shaking his head.

"No, I don't have a boo-boo," Jane told him, handing him to Rachel when she reached for her son. "He's gorgeous, Rae."

"Thank you," Rachel murmured, settling up on a stool with Nick in her lap and handing him the stalk of celery Mikaela was holding. But instead of eating it, Nick simply sucked off the peanut butter and started playing with the raisins.

"So," Jane said, clapping her hands and then rubbing them together. "Where are all these gorgeous men I get to choose from?"

Willow smiled. Molly stopped washing and turned to gape at Jane. Rachel didn't so much as bat an eyelash, having known Jane for years, and Mikaela simply answered for everyone. "Daddy and Dunky and Lunky and Ahab are in the study," she said as she lined up more raisins on another celery stick. "Junky's going to be here by noon, and . . ." She canted her head at Jane. "I'd choose Junky, if I were you. He's almost a scientist and he's not afraid to eat a bug, either."

Jane blinked in confusion. "Junky?" she repeated.

"His name's really Jason, but when I was a baby I

couldn't say 'Uncle Jason' very good, so I renamed him Junky," Mikaela explained. She handed her finished celery to Jane. "Here. It's a lot better than spiders."

Jane took the treat, popped it in her mouth, and chewed vigorously while nodding to Mikaela. There was a noise on the porch and Jason stamped into the house, quickly rushing in ahead of the driving rain. Mickey let out a woof and bounded over to him, reared up, planted his paws on Jason's chest, and licked his chin.

"Hello, mutt," Jason said with a laugh, pushing him away. "I've missed you, too."

"And me!" Mikaela yelped, jumping down from her stool and hurtling herself at Jason. "You been gone forever, Junky!"

Jason caught Mikaela, tossing her in the air then catching her against his chest so he could give her a noisy kiss on the cheek. "I've missed you, too, baby," he said, burying his face in her hair.

"Oohhh, you're wet," Mikaela squealed, wiggling to get down.

"And you're sticky," Jason countered, setting her on the floor and walking into the kitchen. He stepped over to Rachel, kissed a sticky Nicholas on his head, then kissed Rachel's cheek before straightening. He turned with a smile to Willow, but stiffened and scowled. "You look like hell."

Willow was getting used to everyone's opinion on how she looked, and simply grinned at Jason, taking in his deeply tanned skin, rather compelling gray eyes—and damn if his hair didn't have sun-bleached highlights running through it. "It's great to see you, too," she told him, turning toward Jane to introduce her just as the men came walking down the hall from Duncan's study.

The greetings continued for another few minutes, Willow learning that Jason and Matt and Peter had been away for almost two months. Molly walked into the fray of men, pushed them aside, and stepped in front of Jason. "Hiya, Jase," she said.

"Molly?" Jason breathed, his expression shocked. He suddenly pulled her into his arms. "When did you grow up?"

"Just recently," Molly said with a laugh, hugging him back. "I woke up one morning, looked in the mirror, and stopped braiding my hair." She leaned away and frowned up at him. "If ya'd come ta Scotland with Duncan once in a while, ya'd have known that."

Jason tapped the end of her nose. "You haven't out-grown being a brat," he said. He turned to Willow, lifted one brow, and gave a slight nod toward Jane.

Willow started to introduce Jane to Jason again, but instead she snapped her mouth shut in amazement. If she didn't know better, Willow would think Jane was about to faint. Her friend's sapphire blue eyes were huge, her face pale, and her mouth was hanging open as she stared at the large, gorgeous, very manly men filling Duncan's kitchen.

"I'm Jason," Jason said, having to walk around the is-land to hold out his hand to her.

Jane actually took a step back, still gaping, still mute.

Willow couldn't believe it. Jane Huntley had just been *outmanned* by four hunks. Or rather five, if she included Ahab. It was as if Jane couldn't believe so much testos-terone could be in one room without something explod-ing—or maybe *she* was the one about to explode.

"This is my good friend, Jane Huntley," Willow said, walking over and lifting Jane's hand to place it in Jason's. "She's a marine biologist at the University of Maine, and she's going to sail with us tomorrow."

"A fish doctor?" Jason asked.

Willow poked Jane in the back.

"Ah, lobsters, actually," Jane stammered, her pale face suddenly flushing pink when she tried to get her hand back, only to find that Jason wasn't quite ready to let it go.

Jason canted his head. "Lobsters, huh? Baked or boiled?"

"A-alive," Jane said, staring into his smiling gray eyes.

"I'm Luke," Luke interjected, pushing Jason aside and taking Jane's hand from him. "Your underwater camera survived the crash okay, but we'll have to buy another case of Mason jars to take the water samples."

Willow took pity on her obviously overwhelmed friend and pulled Jane free, led her to a stool at the island, sat her down, and handed her a snake egg sandwich. "Is that the only luggage you brought?" she asked, nodding toward the mudroom.

"I have a suitcase in the car," Jane said, then gasped and jumped off the stool. "Oh, I brought you today's *Bangor Daily News*," she said, rushing into the mudroom and walking back with her briefcase. She pulled out the newspaper and slapped it down on the counter in front of Willow. "You made the front page, I'm afraid."

Willow just stared at the newspaper. There was a picture of her totaled SUV, a small headline on the bottom of the front page that said "Maine Assistant Attorney General Cited for OUI," and an article long enough that it continued on page 3. The kitchen went suddenly silent as Rachel and Duncan and Kee crowded close to look over Willow's shoulder. Willow softly started reading the article out loud.

"State's assistant attorney general Willow Foster was involved in a vehicle accident Saturday night in Walker Point that totaled her late-model SUV. There were no other vehicles involved, and Foster was transported to an Ellsworth hospital where she was later released with only minor injuries. Foster's blood alcohol level was reported to be point-two-three.

"Foster couldn't be found for comment, and deputy sheriff Larry Jenkins told reporters that his department is looking into circumstances surrounding the accident. When contacted, attorney general John Pike said he had no comment at this time."

Willow stopped reading, not bothering to turn to page 3, since the article went on to summerize her two-year career with the attorney general's office. She looked up at the sea of faces watching her, their expressions guarded. Willow set her elbows on the counter and buried her face in her hands.

"You were not drunk," Rachel said, putting her arm around Willow's shoulder.

"Yes, I was," Willow said, lifting her head to look at her sister. "My blood alcohol level had spiked by the time they got me to the hospital and I was tested. Which is exactly what that guy wanted." She looked over at Duncan and tapped the newspaper. "This is exactly why he poured that liquor down my throat. He wasn't only after my laptop—he wanted me to have to deal with this instead of the case I'm working on."

Duncan said nothing, just nodded agreement.

"I have to call my boss. Can I use your study?" Willow asked, standing up and turning toward the hall without waiting for Duncan's answer. She stopped and looked at Rachel. "Where's my suitcase? I need my bag of toiletries from it."

"I brought everything but the few clothes I hadn't had time to deal with," Rachel said, running into the mudroom and returning with her own suitcase. "There's still a load in the dryer at home."

"I only need my toiletry bag," Willow said, waiting while Rachel dug it out and handed it to her. Willow searched through the bag until she found the jump drive Karen had given her, glad now that she'd put it in a watertight wrapper in case some of her cosmetics leaked. "Jane," she said, palming the jump drive and looking at her friend. "When I'm done talking to John, may I use your laptop? My secretary downloaded an article and some files that I should probably read."

"What's blood alcohol?" Mikaela asked, looking from Willow to her dad, then to her mom. "Is it red stuff that Dunky serves at The Rosach?"

"No, sweetie," Willow answered before either of them could. "It's a measure of how drunk a person is, of how much alcohol is in their blood."

Mikaela shook her head. "You ain't supposed to drink and drive, Aunt Willy," she said, her frown disapproving. "They told us at school that you get in accidents when you do. That's why you went off the road and smashed your truck."

Willow closed her eyes on a deep breath, then walked back to the island counter and took Mikaela's frowning little face in her hands. "I wasn't drinking and driving, sweetie," she told her. "But I did have some alcohol after the accident, and that's why the test said I was drunk. I promise you, baby, I would never put myself or anyone else in danger by driving after drinking."

"Okay," Mikaela whispered, her immediate smile moving Willow's hands. "I promise not to drive when I drink, either. When I'm old enough to drive," she clarified. "And I won't even ride my bike when I have some beer."

Willow choked on a laugh and hugged Mikaela, looking over the young girl's shoulder at Kee and Rachel. Shocked speechless, Rachel vigorously shook her head. Kee just looked dumbfounded.

"Ya can't drink until your twenty-first birthday," Duncan said, glaring at Mikaela.

Mikaela looked at him with wide, innocent eyes. "Not even a beer from the fridge? Even when it's really, really hot, and I'm really thirsty, and there's no soda in the fridge?"

Rachel smacked Kee in the stomach, making him grunt. "I'm dumping out that beer," she told him. "You want a drink, you go to The Rosach."

"This is Matt's fault," Luke said. "He would give Mikaela sips of beer when she was a baby so she'd go to sleep."

"Munky still gives me sips," Mikaela informed them, though it was obvious she thought that was a good thing. "And he gives Nick beer, too, when he babysits. Munky says it's good for our . . . constit . . . for our guts. That kids drink wine and stuff all the time in other countries."

"But not here, baby doll," Jason said, stepping over and sweeping Mikaela into his arms. "You have to be twenty-one. But don't you worry about it—I'll explain everything to your Uncle Matt when I see him again."

Satisfied that Matt would be duly chastised by more than just the females in the room, Willow turned and headed down the hall to Duncan's study, mentally preparing herself for what was sure to be an unpleasant conversation with her boss.

John wasn't going to like that one of his assistants had made the front page of a statewide newspaper, any more than he was going to like the fact that she hadn't told him what she was working on.

Maybe she should think about extending her vacation to two weeks. Or maybe three.

Chapter Eleven

❖

*W*illow woke up with a muttered curse and swatted at whatever was shaking her, finally opening her eyes when she heard Duncan chuckle.

"Hush, now. I need ya to be quiet," he said, gently rolling her onto her back and sitting her up. "I don't want to wake the others."

Willow blinked at him in the soft light coming from the master bath doorway. "What time is it?" she asked, pushing the hair off her face, nearly poking herself in the eye because she forgot her hand was bandaged. She glanced at the nightstand. "Four?" she said, turning to scowl at Duncan. "You got me up in the middle of the night to give me a pill?"

"Are ya always this cranky when ya wake up?" Duncan asked with another chuckle, handing her not a pain pill, but a pair of her jeans, a T-shirt, and one of her sweaters. "Get dressed. I want to catch the outgoing tide."

Willow came completely awake, just noticing Duncan was fully dressed, including his jacket. "We're leaving? Right now? Are Jane and Jason awake?"

"Nay," he said, walking to the bureau. "They'll catch up with us later."

"But why are we leaving so early?"

Duncan tossed a pair of wool socks on the bed, leaned down, and captured her chin. "Because if I don't get ya all to myself for at least half of today, I'm liable to do something I'll regret."

Willow blinked up at him, a warmth of awareness suddenly washing through the pit of her stomach. It appeared Duncan had finally reached the end of his patience, and their affair was starting this morning come hell or high water or outgoing tide.

Willow cupped his hand holding her chin and beamed a smile up at him. "You could have had me all to yourself last night, but you never even came to bed."

"I'm not wanting an audience of ears around when we finally get this affair started. Especially with my innocent baby sister sleeping in the bedroom right above us."

Willow snorted and pushed him away, swinging her feet over the edge of the bed. "If Molly's an innocent baby, then I really am a virgin again," she muttered.

"Ya take that back," Duncan said, facing her with his hands on his hips. "My mother's sole purpose in life for the last ten years has been to keep starry-eyed men away from Molly."

"Which is why your sister resorted to cruising the Internet to find a boyfriend," Willow countered, also putting her hands on her hips. "What is it with you and apparently also your mother? You act like this is the Stone Age instead of the twenty-first century. Molly is twenty-six, not sixteen. And you're her big brother, not the ordained patriarch of the Ross clan."

"Ah, but I am, counselor. I inherited the position six years ago when my father died."

Willow snorted. "You take yourself way too seriously, Dunky. Molly is an intelligent young woman who is more than capable of taking care of herself."

"Might I remind you that she came running to me?"

"Which only proves her intelligence. Molly knew better than to head off to New Zealand by herself, but she apparently needed to get away from her mother. So she came to you."

"So I could deal with the sheep farmer," Duncan snapped.

"No, so you could deal with your mother. For all you know, the sheep farmer doesn't even exist. Molly's just tired of being treated like a child and being told what to do."

"You've figured this out by spending one day with her?"

"No, because I *was* her," Willow told him. "Because my father was just as overprotective and as bossy as you are. Why do you think I was such a brat all through high school?"

"Then why isn't your sister like you?"

"She is," Willow said with a sudden smile. "Rachel is just as headstrong and determined to get her way as I am, only she's much more subtle about it. Where I kick and scream and bluster, Rachel just quietly goes about getting what she wants."

Duncan crossed his arms over his chest, lowering his brows in a frown. "We can't always get what we want, counselor."

"And why not?"

"Because sometimes life intervenes. Or sometimes what we want is not what's best for us."

Willow canted her head. "A philosophical troglodyte," she whispered, mimicking his stance by crossing her own arms under her breasts. "You've decided you want me," she said, her tone nonaccusing. "But what if getting me is not what's best for you? What if it's the worst thing that could happen?"

He dropped his hands to his sides, nonplussed. "How could loving you possibly be bad for me?"

"I could break your heart."

He immediately shook his head. "Ya wouldn't. Once ya give your heart, lass, you'll give it for keeps."

"I could die. I could have died two nights ago."

Duncan strode over to her, his eyes all but glowing in the dim light. He took hold of her shoulders, and despite his obviously foul mood, pulled her gently against him. "Aye. Ya would have broken my heart then," he whispered against her hair. "Which is why you'll be more careful in the future."

"Careful?" she muttered into his chest. "I was run off the road."

He stepped back, holding her by the shoulders, and scowled at her. "Ya should have told someone what had been happening to you. Ya could have told me if ya didn't want to tell your boss. I would have gone to Augusta and driven ya here."

"Then we both would have been run off the road."

He shrugged. "Maybe. But at least we'd have been together."

Willow reached up with one hand and cupped the side of his face. "Duncan, you're proving my point instead of your own. Giving your heart so completely only means it will be impossible to bear when something happens."

"Not *when* something happens, lass, but if. And not giving your heart means being only half alive."

Willow sighed and picked up her clothes. She headed to the bathroom, stopped in the doorway, and turned back to Duncan. "I had this same conversation with Rachel two years ago, when she was trying not to fall in love with Kee. Now you're the one trying to convince me that it's better to have loved and lost than never to have loved at all," she said softly. "What you wrote on my hand the other day, that I can run but that I can't hide—you weren't saying I couldn't hide from you, you were telling me I couldn't hide from love."

"Aye."

"Having an affair isn't hiding. It's jumping in with my eyes wide open."

"Passion is no substitute for love, Willow."

She canted her head. "Then maybe we should call off the affair, if you don't think it will go anywhere."

"Not on your life, woman," he growled. "Ya've made the offer, I've accepted, and two seconds after we drop anchor off Thunder Island, it begins."

Willow went utterly still, a shiver of awareness coursing through her at the realization that Duncan was deadly serious. Unable to respond, Willow quietly turned and entered the bathroom, softly shut the door, and closed her eyes on a deep sigh. For the first time since meeting Duncan Ross, she was afraid she really was in danger of getting what she wished for.

Duncan stood at the wheel of the *Seven-to-Two Odds*, his attention divided between the silent woman beside him sipping hot chocolate and the rough sea ahead as he guided the schooner toward Thunder Island. Since leaving the house two hours ago, Willow had been unusually quiet, and Duncan was starting to worry.

He was pushing her, he knew, but he couldn't seem to help himself. He still hadn't recovered from the scare she'd given him two nights ago; nor would he likely recover until he got Willow naked beneath him again and could feel her come alive in his arms.

The truth of her words this morning, that she could have died in the crash, had made it appallingly clear just how scared she was of loving him—because Duncan had gotten a good taste of that fear himself. But he loved her, dammit. And even though she'd deny it with the tenacity of a true lawyer, she was in love with him.

Hell, they acted like an old married couple most of the time; they trusted each other, were there for each other when they needed a shoulder to lean on, and could all but read each other's minds most of the time. Like now, for instance. Duncan knew Willow was rethinking her offer of an affair—not because she suddenly didn't want him, but because she was finally beginning to realize that she might be wanting him too much.

Duncan silently watched as Willow set the cup of cocoa next to the thermos he'd made her before they'd left the house. She stood up and walked toward the bow of the ship with drunkenlike steps, the deck pitching and rolling on the rough sea, Mickey padding along behind her.

The storm had finally moved out to sea, leaving crystal-clear skies and a stiff northwesterly breeze that continued to raise four- and five-foot swells ahead of them. The sails were furled tightly closed, and the *Seven-to-Two-Odds*'s powerful diesel engine cut through the waves with ease.

The sun was a full hour above the horizon by the time they pulled into calmer waters on the lee side of Thunder Island. Duncan noticed that the sound of the wind-driven, crashing surf was growing fainter as they moved down the eastern shoreline of the island. He brought the engine to an idle, tied off the wheel, and also walked forward.

"How's this?" he asked as he came up beside Willow. "Shall we anchor here for the day?"

She turned from staring at the island and gave him a tentative smile. "This is the best place for now," she said softly. "But we'll have to move to the Pilot Islands for the night. It gets too rough here when the tide's coming in."

"Can ya take the wheel while I set the anchor?" he asked, pulling the pin that locked the heavy anchor in place.

Her smile suddenly turned crooked. "What would Ahab do if he found out you let me steer his precious ship?"

Bolstered by that tiny spark of mischief, and feeling like a schoolboy who had just caught the eye of the class beauty, Duncan returned her smile. "He'd likely beat me to a pulp. That is, if someone were to tell him."

She canted her head. "Because you wouldn't defend

yourself, would you," she said as a statement of fact.

"Aye. Not against a man half again my age."

"Nobility is important to you, isn't it, Duncan?"

He shrugged, wondering where this conversation was going. "No more than it is to you, counselor." He waved at the island. "Ya're steaming mad that someone is fouling the waters around here, and ya won't quit until whoever is responsible is behind bars."

"We're too much alike, Duncan."

"Aye," he agreed, nodding. "That's why it's going to work for us, Willow."

"It also might be the one thing that makes us not work."

He shook his head, pulling her into his arms and kissing the tip of her nose. "But just think of the children we could have," he whispered. "They'd be remarkable people."

"They'd be hellions," she said on a sudden laugh as she wrapped her arms around him and laid her face on his chest. "We wouldn't know a moment's peace."

"Aye," he said with a sigh, hugging her to him, again bolstered by their easy banter. "But it would be fun." He set her away, afraid to give her a chance to get serious again, and turned her toward the stern of the ship. "Take the wheel, woman. I'm not wanting to have to paddle home and explain to Ahab why his ship is sitting on the rocks."

Her journey back was much easier, now that they were in fairly calm water. Mickey looked up at Duncan, cocking his broad head much the way Willow had, and whined.

"Don't look at me," Duncan said with a shrug. "You go try talking some sense into her."

Mickey rumbled deep in his chest, turned, and trotted down the deck to Willow.

"Engage the engine and turn to port," Duncan shouted to Willow as he stood next to the anchor release. He waited until he thought they were in a good position, then flipped the release. The anchor hit the surface with a muted splash and dropped into the depths. Duncan waited until the heavy line stopped. "Now put the engine in reverse and turn starboard," he shouted, waving backward at Willow.

Again he waited while the line played out another hundred or so feet before he brought the spool to a stop, steadying himself against the sudden jolt when the anchor fetched up on the bottom.

He waved his hand again. "Try to drag it back," he shouted. "Then turn the wheel to port and see if it's set."

Satisfied they weren't going to drift either out to sea or in to shore, Duncan walked the length of the schooner, unable to stifle a grin at the picture Willow made. She was standing at the wheel, which was nearly as tall as she was, completely focused on her task, her brows lowered in a frown as she disengaged the engine, spun the wheel to a neutral position, and tied it off.

She looked up as he approached, her smile brilliant. "You can call me Captain Foster," she said as she puffed out her lovely bosom and saluted him. "And you can be my first mate."

"I'd rather be your cabin boy," he said, taking her in his arms again.

She leaned into him and wrapped her hands around his neck. "I like the sound of that," she whispered, toying with the back of his hair. "What do cabin boys do?"

"They serve their captain's every need," he whispered back.

"Every need?"

"Aye."

"Even . . . personal needs?"

"Especially personal needs," he told her, leaning down to cover her mouth with his.

She rose to meet him halfway, parting her lips with a soft sound of anticipation. Duncan took advantage of her sweet invitation and deepened the kiss, savoring the taste of salt air and hot cocoa that mingled with her own delightful freshness. Her response was immediate, her tongue sweeping against his and her hands tightening on his neck.

Duncan's own response was to groan as he pulled her hips forward, lifting her into his groin. She stretched herself up, wrapping her legs around his waist and breaking their kiss to bury her face in his neck.

"Make love to me, Duncan," she whispered. "I want to feel you inside me."

A shudder of desire ran through him. Lifting her up, Duncan strode to the ladderlike stairs that led below, but stopped when he realized he couldn't carry her down the steep steps. He lowered Willow to her feet and cupped her face. "Go below," he growled. "I'll make sure all is set up here, and I'll be right behind ya."

She stood on tiptoe and gave him a quick kiss. "Which bunk is ours?" she asked, her eyes filled with passion and her smile with promise.

"The one up front on the port side," he told her, opening the half door and helping her down to the first step.

She stopped, turned, and looked up at him. "Can you give me five minutes?"

"Two," he said through clenched teeth. "Don't bother to put on that cute bit of lace, lass. It'll only get ruined."

Duncan watched in fascination as her eyes widened and her face flushed pink. She said nothing else, but climbed backward down the ladder and disappeared below.

Duncan turned and looked at the island, tugging on the pant leg of his tight jeans. The little witch. She couldn't help herself any more than he could.

He strode to the bow, checked the anchor line, then scanned out to sea and then back along the island's shoreline. They were alone—finally. He had warned Jason not to show up before noon. He walked back to the aft stairs, but stopped when Mickey tried to go down ahead of him. Duncan pulled on the wolf's mane and stepped on the stairs to block his path.

Mickey sat down and cocked his head in question.

Duncan ruffled his fur. "You stay up here and keep watch for boat traffic," he told the wolf. "I'm not needing your help below."

With that he closed the half door and climbed down, deciding that he'd have Willow all to himself for at least the next five hours. Enough time, he hoped, to start capturing her elusive heart.

Chapter Twelve

✦

She was suddenly frightened. Not shy. Not exactly nervous. Just suddenly scared to take off her clothes, crawl under the covers, and spend the rest of the morning being the sole focus of Duncan's attention.

Something had changed between them. If she had to guess, Willow would say it had happened the night of her accident. When Duncan had walked into that hospital exam room and silently stood there staring at her, Willow had realized she no longer felt hunted—she'd felt . . . well, she had felt loved.

Not that Duncan had kept his feelings for her a secret, but those feelings had always been tempered by the safety of lust. Lust was a much more definable emotion, and definitely more manageable. But for the last two days, Willow had been aware of an underlying tension between them. She'd sensed a new determination on Duncan's part that she stop running long enough to take him seriously. He wanted her to love him comletely, to take that frightening leap of faith into his arms.

So why couldn't she? What flaw was there in her that topped her from taking that last step off the precipice nto total commitment?

Her sister had certainly jumped in with both feet. Rachel loved Kee with all her being, and she appeared to e not only surviving, but thriving. Rachel had a dream usband and family, and she didn't seemed at all worried vhat the future might hold.

But then, Rachel had always been the brave one. For s long as Willow could remember, Rachel had quietly one after whatever she wanted without seeming to vorry about the consequences.

Unlike herself, Willow thought as she stared at the arrow bunk built into the port side of the ship's bow. The more frightened she became, the more she blustered, oping the world would never realize what a coward she eally was.

Duncan would realize, though. He would soon understand that he had fallen in love with a scared young girl vho would rather dance in the fires of passion than lose erself to love. Dammit, didn't he realize she was going o break his noble heart?

"Ya needn't glower so. There's no bedbugs, I promise," Juncan said softly from right behind her.

Willow leaned back until she could feel the heat of his ody, and continued to stare at the bed. "I don't want to ove you, Duncan."

"Then don't," he whispered, cupping her shoulders nd slowly turning her around. He lifted her chin to look t him. "It's never been my intention to upset ya, lass. I ave enough love for the both of us."

"But it's not fair to you."

"Ah, Willow, life's not fair," he said on a sigh, pulling her into his arms. "And that's the challenge," he finished as he leaned down and covered her mouth with his.

Willow wrapped her own arms around his neck and kissed him back with the urgency of eighteen months of wanting him. To heck with her worrying; she was going to throw caution to the wind and make love to this wonderful, beautiful man.

Without breaking the kiss, and pulling Duncan with her, Willow scuffed off her shoes and crawled up onto the high bunk until she was kneeling level with him. She unwrapped her hands from his neck and started unbuttoning his shirt, leaning away only enough to give him access to her own buttons.

They undressed each other with more passion than grace, occasionally stopping just long enough to appreciate each new patch of revealed skin. Duncan kissed her bare shoulder while he unfastened her jeans; Willow slid off his shirt and ran her lips across his naked chest while she unbuckled his belt.

The fever inside her grew to the point where time stopped and the world narrowed to only vivid sensation; he smelled wonderful, tasted divine, and felt powerfully warm and virile. Willow's anticipation heightened as desire washed through her with the force of a surging tide.

Duncan nudged her back until she was lying on the bunk, slipped off her pants—lace panties included—and tossed them away. He then stepped out of his own pants—boxers included—and crawled up beside her to pull her back in his arms.

The contact sent ripples of fire coursing through her. "Yes," she whispered, burying her face in his chest and running her hands over the quivering muscles of his back.

"Aye," he breathed, lifting her head up for his kiss. "Ya feel so wonderful, lass. So alive."

Willow pulled his mouth down to hers, parting her lips to get the full taste of him. Her legs moved restlessly against him as she explored every inch of him she could reach.

He captured her hands, gently pinning them over her head as he leaned back and looked down at her so fiercely, Willow stopped breathing. His dark emerald gaze moved with slow deliberation over her face and down her neck to her bra-covered breasts, his free hand tracing the same path with a feather-light touch. He slid one finger under the clasp of her bra, snapped it open, and brushed the thin material aside.

Willow felt a self-conscious blush tinge her face as he carefully ran his finger along the dark bruise from her seat belt that started at her left shoulder, crossed her chest between her breasts, and ended just above her waist.

"I'm glad ya bought yar new truck," he whispered, leaning down to kiss the bruise between her breasts. "It saved yar life."

His sweet attention was killing her. Willow shifted, moving one of her breasts under his lips, whimpering when his mouth finally closed over her budded nipple and he gently suckled. But he still didn't release her hands, heightening her frustration as he moved on to the other breast, pulling another faint cry from her. She settled one leg over his thigh, using her heel to pull him against her, then growled in response to his deeply rumbled chuckle.

"We have the whole morning," he said, his mouth moving up from her chest to kiss her chin. His dancing eyes gleamed into hers. "I'd forgotten how impatient ya get."

Willow glared up at him. "It's been *eighteen months*, Duncan. I want to feel you inside me. Now," she finished with a growl, using her heel to pull him over her, then wrapping both legs around him so tightly that he reared up at the shoulders.

His smile vanished. "Unless ya're wanting to start a family, lass, ya need ta give me a minute," he said, reaching under the pillow with his free hand.

Willow immediately unlocked her legs, allowing him to roll off her so he could open the small foil packet. She noticed the packet was one of three, and her own smile quickly returned.

He had to free her hands, and Willow quickly began exploring his beautiful body again, running her fingers over the taut muscles of his chest and across his broad shoulders. She could feel the tension in him, the hum of his own desire and impatience, and her smile widened.

"You only brought three?" she asked.

He finished slipping on the condom and just stared at her, completely nonplussed.

"And I thought you were a practical man," she continued, ignoring the warning in his eyes. "It's a good thing my sister knows me well. She put two dozen in my suitcase."

Still saying nothing, his eyes gleaming again, Duncan slowly peeled her hands off his body, held them back over her head, and carefully lowered himself between her thighs. Willow snapped her mouth shut, her eyes widening as the tip of his shaft probed against her.

He gently brushed the hair from her face and kissed her. Willow's response was immediate. She wrapped her legs around him again and wiggled just enough to feel him start to enter her. "Now, Duncan," she whispered into his mouth. "I need to feel you inside me now."

Either his patience was finally played out, or Willow revealing she had two dozen more condoms at their disposal gave him permission to hurry things along this time. Duncan at last released her hands, braced himself above her, and gently—with maddening care—entered her.

Willow had to remember to breathe and make herself relax—which was hard, considering her heart was pounding with the force of storm-driven waves crashing on Thunder Island. She couldn't tell which inflamed her more, the feel of Duncan moving so deeply inside her or the intensity of his dark green eyes locked on hers.

For Willow, it was over before it even began. She quickly spiraled out of control, cresting around him with a cry of utter abandon that echoed off the walls of the tiny berth. Duncan continued to move, carrying each pulse of her fulfillment to new heights, washing her in a storm of never-ending pleasure.

And still he didn't stop, instead slowing to a gentle rhythm that allowed her to ebb the merest of seconds before the storm started to build again. His eyes mirrored her response, all but sparking with energy as he watched her peak with another mindless explosion of sensation.

He joined her this time, throwing back his head as his

shout of joy hummed through the air and melded with hers. He stilled, buried deep inside her, his eyes locked on hers, and Willow felt her insides throb with the rhythm of their pounding hearts.

He closed his eyes on a sigh and lowered himself beside her, keeping his hips between her thighs to catch the last lingering pulses of their pleasure.

Willow stared up at the ceiling and realized she was smiling. The drought was over, and the deluge of passion had certainly been worth the wait.

"Aye," Duncan muttered beside her ear. "Droughts are definitely hard on a body."

Willow realized she'd spoken her thoughts out loud. She looked over at Duncan and lifted an inquiring brow. "Are you implying you've been celibate for the last year and a half?"

He frowned back. "Are you implying I live by a double standard?" he asked instead of answering her. "That I expect ya to stay out of men's beds while I dance from one woman to another?"

"You're a—"

He covered her mouth with his hand. "No name calling."

She wiggled free. "I was going to say you're a guy," she told him ever so sweetly, patting his cheek. "And the only guys I know who are celibate are dead."

"Or so crazy in love we've gone insane," he muttered, rolling completely off her and pulling the blanket over them. "You get a thirty-minute nap, counselor," he said, wrapping her tightly against him so that her face was buried in his neck. He patted her bottom through the blanket. "Maybe only ten minutes. I intend to put a big dent in your thoughtful sister's supply of packets before Jason and Jane get here."

They spent the rest of the morning making love with the laziness of a gentle rain rather than a raging storm, effectively putting an end to their mutual droughts. They dozed to the gentle rocking of the ship, woke to explore each other's bodies, and simply cuddled in silence for long periods of time. Duncan found he couldn't get enough of Willow—that he couldn't hold her closely enough to erase the memory of nearly losing her two nights ago.

And neither, it seemed, could she.

She was snuggled so tightly against him right now, Duncan didn't know where he ended and Willow began. She was softly snoring, her warm breath wafting over his chest, her bandaged hand tucked in his armpit, and her right leg thrown over his as if she were afraid he might escape.

Duncan stared up at the ceiling and silently sighed. Escape hadn't even been part of his vocabulary for nearly two years.

Mickey gave a soft "Woof" overhead, and Duncan heard him padding toward the stern of the ship. It seemed the honeymoon was over. Jason and Jane were likely approaching in the launch, and it was time they turned their attention to Willow's mystery. Until it was solved, Duncan knew he wouldn't be able to stop worrying about her, much less be free to concentrate on winning her heart. He gently shook her awake. "It's time to get dressed, counselor. Company's coming."

"Make them go away," she muttered into his chest,

snuggling even closer. "You killed me, Dunky. I can't move."

He sat up, bringing her with him and smiling as he brushed the hair off her scowling face. "We're going to have to work on your waking up in a better mood."

"We, ah, could practice right now," she said, lazily running her fingers down the length of his ribs.

Duncan stopped her before she reached her potential target. He scooted off the bunk, again pulling her with him, and stood her on her feet. "The shower's just big enough for a squirrel to bathe in," he told her, turning Willow toward the head. "I'll have yar suitcase sitting open on the bunk when ya get done. Leave it there so I can stow it later. I still don't want ya lifting anything heavier than a coffee mug," he finished, giving her a pat on the backside to get her moving.

She wrapped the blanket around herself and sashayed down the length of the rocking ship with the poise of a drunken sailor. "I'm going to like being waited on hand and foot for the rest of the week." She stopped at the door to the shower, her chin lifted so she was looking down her nose at him. "I didn't get any breakfast this morning."

Duncan slipped into his pants, found his shirt, and shrugged it on. "Can Jane cook?" he asked.

Willow shook her head with a crooked smile. "She can't even butter toast. I guess it's up to you men to feed us."

He stopped from tucking his shirt in his pants. "Remind me again why we brought you women along?"

"You mean, why *we* brought *you guys* along," she shot back, her smile widening even more. "We women are the brains of this little operation. And Jason and you," she said, pointing an imperial finger at him, "are the brawn."

That said, she hiked her blanket up with a flourish and disappeared into the shower. Duncan was left scowling at her when something bumped into the side of the ship.

"Ahoy the boat!" Jason shouted. "We could use some help out here."

Duncan scooped up his shoes and used the forward ladder to climb on deck just in time to see Jane Huntley come shooting over the rail with a startled shriek. She immediately spun around, rubbing her backside, and scowled down at Jason.

"I am perfectly capable of boarding without your help," she told him, only to turn her scowl on Duncan when she heard him chuckle. "I was born on a boat."

Jason crawled over the rail next, and Duncan noticed that his friend's clothes were wet, his hair was windblown as if it had dried on the ride out, his eyes were bloodshot, and his lips were blue.

"Born on a boat?" Jason growled, shrugging his shivering body. "More likely you were spewed from the sea."

Duncan sat down and put on his shoes. Jane turned with a harrumph and headed aft to go below, stopping only long enough to give Mickey a pat and urge him to follow her.

"Decide to bathe in the ocean this morning?" Duncan asked, lifting an inquiring brow.

Jason unzipped his wet jacket, peeled it off, and pointed at the stern of the ship. "That witch bumped me off the pier on purpose."

"The nerve of her, blindsiding you without provocation," Duncan said, shaking his head in utter disgust.

Jason's frozen-pale face darkened. "All I did was make a perfectly innocent comment, and the next thing I know I'm swimming in forty-degree water." He peeled off his shirt and threw it onto the deck. "I just wondered out loud if a Mae West life vest might be redundant for her."

Duncan just stared at his shivering friend.

Jason unlaced his boots, emptied out the water, then undid his pants and struggled to peel them off. He had to sit down beside Duncan so as not to fall down, and bent and pulled the wet jeans off over his feet. He straightened and glared at Duncan, his teeth chattering and his eyes narrowed. "The woman is built like an Amazon," Jason said. "She's got to know that. And she's got to be used to men giving her compliments."

"So telling her she's got a chest like a Mae West life vest is a compliment?" Duncan asked. He shook his head. "You've been at sea too long, my friend."

Jason stood up—wearing nothing but wet boxers, socks, and goose bumps—and looked over the rail. "I need my duffle bag." He turned back to Duncan. "And I'm so numb now, I'll likely take another swim while trying to get it."

Duncan heaved himself up with a sigh and climbed over the rail and down to the inflatable launch. One by one, he threw up Jason's bag and the many bags and metal cases that apparently Jane Huntley couldn't live without.

It looked as if they were in for an interesting few days.

Chapter Thirteen

❈

"*It's nice to see that* some things never change."

Willow mimicked Jane's stance, her feet spread and her hands on her hips, as they both stared down at the old quarry pond. "Other than that tidal line showing, this place is exactly the same," Willow agreed. "The water is awful muddy, though. Do you suppose the storm riled it up?"

Jane lifted her hands in question. "I can't imagine why, since it's protected in here, unless more than just a crack in the granite is letting the ocean in. Maybe there's actually a cave. That would be enough to churn up the bottom and make it this murky."

"But we covered every inch of this island in high school and never came across any caves. They don't just suddenly appear," Willow said, squinting through the sunlight at her friend. "They're either dug by man or formed by eons-old eruptions, aren't they?"

Jane slowly moved along the edge of the twenty-foot cliff while looking down the sheer wall of the quarry. "After you told me about the pond suddenly having a tidal line, I checked geological records for seismic activity along the coast in the last ten years." She spoke over her shoulder to Willow. "There were several tremors last winter, some of them big enough to open some good-size cracks."

"Maine doesn't have earthquakes," Willow said, surprised.

Jane stopped walking and turned to smile at her. "Sure we do. One theory is that a glacier from the last ice age, over a mile thick in places, depressed the land with its massive weight to the point that the ground is still rebounding. They're not quakes in the sense that plates are sliding past each other, but simply the earth shrugging out the kinks."

Willow angled her head. "And there were several of these tremors near here last winter?"

"That's what my research said. In both December and January."

"And if they were strong enough to open up cracks in this quarry, and there really is something down there," Willow surmised, pointing at the murky water, "it makes sense that it's being washed into the sea with every tide. And the timing is right. The sick lobster just started showing up this spring."

"They would have shown up this winter," Jane clarified, "but fishermen don't set traps around here then, because lobster head out to deeper water in the winter."

Willow also started walking along the cliff, but in the opposite direction of Jane. She scanned the craggy sides

f the quarry while trying to see into the usually clear but
low murky water.

"If ya fall, I'm not jumping in to save ya," Duncan said
s he stepped through the thick pines and set down the
wo metal cases he'd carried up from the launch.

"You'd let me drown?" Willow asked, turning to grin
t him.

"I might throw ya a rope."

"Which I'd use to pull you in with me," she coun-
ered.

"My entire diving suit, tanks included, doesn't weigh as
nuch as this stuff," Jason said, also breaking through the
ines and dumping his load on the moss-covered ground.

"Be careful with that," Jane hissed, rushing over to
ick up one of the metal cases. "These are very delicate
nstruments."

"In well-padded cases," Jason reminded her. He
unched down and watched as Jane started to set up her
quipment. "Your precious camera survived Willow's
rash—I think it can survive my handling. Not that it's
;oing to be helpful. The water's too muddy to see any-
hing."

The rest of their conversation was lost on Willow as
he limped farther along the quarry edge, ducking under
ranches and being careful she didn't slip. The quarry
vas as long as two football fields and half again as wide.
t sat at the west end of Thunder Island, on the highest
ection of ground, and was just a stone's throw away from
he shoreline. The center of the island was littered with
otting buildings, broken blocks of granite and tailings,
nd a rusty old rail line that ran from the quarry down to
granite pier that jutted a good fifty yards into the sea.

The east end of Thunder Island sharply tapered off to a series of ledges, where the tide frothed in powerfully breaking waves that kept the rocks washed clean of even the most tenacious sea life. Rugosa roses, scrub pine, low-growing blueberry bushes, and a lush carpet of thick moss and saw grass provided a parklike feel to the island. There were also plenty of rather noisy seagulls flittering about, apparently as happy as Willow to see the storm gone.

"Didn't ya say Ray Cobb and his friend already searched this island?" Duncan asked, moving up behind her.

Willow kept walking along the perimeter of the quarry. "Ray said they searched it three times." She suddenly stopped. "But I doubt if they saw this," she said, pointing at the ground. "What does that look like to you?"

Duncan stepped up beside her and studied the ground she was pointing at. "Those are drag marks," he said, moving closer and hunching down to touch the disturbed moss. "Something heavy was dragged across here. In that direction," he added, pointing toward the shoreline. He stood, looked at the marks that came from the edge of the quarry, then visually followed their path into the trees. Finally, he walked to the pond rim, hunched down again, and touched the scraped edge of the cliff.

"This is recent," he said, looking back and pointing at the marks moving past Willow. "They were made during the storm, is my guess. See how the granite is all muddy from the chewed up moss? Something was hauled out of the quarry and dragged away."

He stood and came back to Willow, taking hold of her hand as he walked past, and led her through the trees, following the now obvious path. They walked for several yards and came out on the rocky shoreline. "Whatever it was, they loaded it onto a waiting boat."

"During the storm? But that would be all but impossible. The surf would have been too rough."

"The winds were out of the northeast," he said, looking around. "This side of the island was in the lee." He pointed at a tiny cove the size of his house, where the incoming tide was breaking in spewing waves. "There. See how the moss is disturbed all the way down to the high-water mark? They landed right there and loaded their cargo."

"But during the storm?"

He looked at her. "What better time, counselor, if ya're not wanting anyone to see you? No one in their right mind goes to sea during a nor'easter."

"Except criminals with enough to lose that it's worth risking their lives," she growled, turning to start back through the trees.

But Duncan stopped her by pulling her into his arms. "And desperate enough to run you off the road," he added. "It looks like yar hunch was right, Willow. And it also looks like they're trying to get rid of the evidence."

She leaned back in his embrace and smiled. "I'm going to get them. I'm going to build a case against them that a spider won't be able to slip through."

"Can we call in yar investigators now?"

Her smile disappeared. "Not yet. Not until I can give them a direction to look in. Drag marks are not a smoking gun. We have to know what they took out of that quarry, so we know who we're after."

Duncan sighed and tucked her head in the crook of his neck. "Three days, counselor, and then I'm visiting your boss and telling him what you're doing."

"Too late," she mumbled. "I told John everything on the phone yesterday." She leaned back and smiled up at him. "He gave me the rest of the week to look into things down here."

Duncan tapped the end of her nose. "But I'm only giving ya three days," he repeated. "And I'm sticking to your side like a Siamese twin."

"Oh, I like the sound of that," she whispered, pulling his face down as she stretched up to kiss him.

He was very obliging, and bent to meet her mouth, tightening his arms around her and tilting her head so he could deepen their kiss. Every riotous sensation she'd felt this morning welled up inside her, and Willow responded with the same passionate urgency that consumed her every time Duncan touched her. Hell, who was she kidding? She got hot and mushy if he even stepped into her field of vision.

"I've decided to be a marine biologist when I grow up," Jason said. "They get to play with really neat toys."

Duncan broke the kiss with a sigh and tucked Willow's head back under his chin, not letting her turn to Jason. "Ya already have a master's in computer science," Duncan said. "And ya would have had your doctorate if ya hadn't run off with the dean's wife."

Willow popped her head up and twisted in Duncan's arms. "You have your master's degree, Jason?" She suddenly frowned. "And you had an affair with a married woman?"

"I didn't sleep with her," Jason said, glaring at Duncan before looking at Willow and shrugging. "She was unhappy, and I only helped her out of a bad situation." Apparently wishing to drop the subject, Jason pointed through the trees. "I've figured out why the pond is muddy. Divers riled it up."

"How do you know that?" Willow asked.

Jason held up his hand, and she noticed for the first time that he was holding something the size of a football. "This rock has lead scrapings on it. I found it about eight feet from the quarry, right beside the path."

"They pulled lead out of the water?" Willow asked.

"I doubt it," Jason said, shaking his head. "This rock also has yellow paint on it, which probably came from diving weights. And I found a footprint in the mud that was definitely made by a diving boot. My guess is they used dry gear and bell helmets. If the water is contaminated, that's the safest way to go in."

"Has Jane set up the underwater camera?" Willow asked.

"Yes. But it's murky straight to the bottom. She's taking water samples now." He looked at Duncan. "We can go down. We have the equipment."

"No," Willow said, turning back to Duncan. "It's too dangerous."

"Dangerous how, lass? It's only a quarry pond."

"If your suit springs a leak, you could get sick just like the lobsters and crabs."

"If our suit gets a leak, we'll be the first to know it and we'll surface."

"No," she said, stepping back and crossing her arms under her breasts. "Until I know what is—or was—down there, you're not going in."

"If we don't dive, we may never know," Jason pointed out.

Willow spun to face him. "I'll call in the state's dive team, then. They can search the quarry."

"Why is it okay for them to dive and not us?" Duncan asked, causing Willow to spin back to him. "We're just as capable as they are."

Yes. Why was she willing to risk men she didn't know? "Because it's their job," she snapped.

Duncan suddenly smiled—not at all nicely—and crossed his own arms over his chest. "Careful, counselor," he said softly. "I might think ya're starting to care for me, and it just might go to my head."

"Dammit, Duncan!" She stomped her foot in frustration, knowing damn well he wasn't going to listen to her. "This is my operation, and you are not diving."

He stared at her in silence for several heartbeats, his eyes dark and unreadable, then suddenly looked past her to Jason. "Go tell Jane we're diving, then I'll help ya get our equipment off the *Seven-to-Two Odds*."

"No!"

Duncan took hold of her shoulders when she shouted at Jason, and turned her back to face him. "We'll be perfectly safe," he told her. "We won't be down more than half an hour."

Willow gathered the front of his heavy sweater in her good fist. "Don't do this, Duncan. You don't have to prove anything to me."

He kissed her forehead. "Maybe I have to prove something to myself, lass." He wrapped his arms around her again and gently held her against him as he spoke into her hair. "Haven't ya noticed that I've never asked ya to marry me, Willow?"

She frowned into his shoulder. She knew he was changing the subject with the intent to distract her, but he had certainly gone about it quite effectively. "I—I've noticed," she said just as softly, leaning back to look up at him.

"And have ya not wondered why?"

Her frown deepened. "Because you'd rather get the whole town to ask for you."

He shook his head, his face reddening slightly. "I swear I don't know how that rumor got started. I can only promise you that it wasn't from me. I'm never going to ask ya to marry me, Willow."

"You're not? Never?" She cocked her head, eying him suspiciously. "Never say never, Dunky."

He suddenly smiled. "You're learning, counselor."

"So you don't want to marry me? Then what was all that talk about children and grandchildren?"

"Just talk. Giving ya something to think about."

"But shouldn't these children be born in wedlock?"

"Aye," he said, nodding. "But there can't be a wedding unless one of us proposes."

Willow leaned as far back in his embrace as he would let her. "Me?" she gasped, realization dawning. "You expect *me* to propose to *you?*"

He nodded, the devil himself smiling from his eyes. "With romance, and an engagement token befitting a true gentleman."

She was utterly and completely shocked. He expected her to propose to him? "Are you crazy?"

His smile never wavering and his eyes all but dancing, Duncan slowly shook his head. "A man needs to be needed, Willow. And I," he said, squeezing her shoulders, "need ya to ask for my hand in marriage."

She didn't know whether to kick him or burst out laughing, so she reached up and patted his cheek. "Oh, Duncan. You really are a troglodyte."

"And you, counselor, are a brat."

He kissed her again, this time on the mouth, but so quickly Willow didn't have time to react before she was suddenly let loose and he was gone. She turned and watched him jog up the path and disappear through the trees.

"You are not diving!" she shouted after him.

"Quit pacing, Willy. You're wearing a rut in the rocks."

Willow stopped and glared at Jane, then turned her glare on the tiny bubbles breaking the surface of the muddy pond. Dammit, when had she lost control of this operation?

When she had asked Duncan to come along, that's when. She should have known he'd take over, what with his maddening need to protect her. Oh yes, she understood he was diving despite her objections because he wanted this mystery solved *now*.

And since the crash, Willow had to admit that she truly might be in danger. Apparently, whatever this crime was, it had far-reaching ramifications if those involved were willing to go after someone in the AG's office.

Willow sat down on a large rock near the rim of the quarry, propped her elbows on her knees, and cupped her chin in her palms to stare down at the rising bubbles. What stupid little piece of the puzzle was she missing? This wasn't merely an illegal dumping of toxic chemicals; this had to be more than a random, single occurrence. "That's it," she said, jumping back to her feet.

Jane looked up from her camera screen. "That's what?"

"This isn't an isolated incident."

Jane's face paled as she looked around. "You think there's more waste dumped around here?"

"Not necessarily here," Willow said. "It could be on some of the other islands, too. Why else are they trying so hard to stop my investigation? There have to be other dumps."

"But this coast is covered from Canada to New Hampshire by lobstermen this time of year. And nobody has come forward with any more sick lobster."

Willow turned and frowned down at the bubbles again. Jane was right. "Unless the other dumps aren't leaking." She looked back at Jane. "We have to check the other islands."

"That's going to take a whole lot of manpower," Jane said. "There are over two thousand islands off the Maine coast. And most of them are uninhabited."

A dark shadow rose to the surface of the pond and a masked face appeared in a flurry of bubbles. Willow scooted to the edge, lay down on her stomach, and peered over the rim of the quarry.

Jason slid his face mask up on his hooded forehead and spit out his mouthpiece. "It's a veritable dump down there," he said. "We found several bicycles, two lawn chairs, a mattress, and enough beer cans to build a boat. Who the hell lugs that kind of stuff out to an island?"

"Teenagers," Jane said succinctly, also lying on her belly to peer over the edge. "Did you find anything else, Jason? Any barrels? Wooden crates? Large bags or sheets of plastic?"

Jason looked surprised. "We did see some large plastic sheets. Why? Is it important? I thought we were looking for barrels or crates."

"Wooden crates would have been lined with plastic if the chemicals were in powder form."

Treading water, Jason slipped his mask back over his face and reached for his mouthpiece.

"Wait!" Jane shouted, motioning for Jason to lift his mask again. "Don't put that back in your mouth. It could be contaminated. Here," she said, scooting over to grab a water bottle. She tossed it down to him. "Rinse it off first."

"Why, Einstein, you really do care," he said, pouring the water over his mouthpiece. He popped it in his mouth, capped the bottle, and floated over to the wall of the quarry and set the bottle on a tiny ledge.

"Where's Duncan?" Willow called down to him.

Jason took out his mouthpiece, holding it above the water, and grinned up at her. "He found a wide ledge on the west wall that had several scrape marks on it. He's checking it out."

"You guys have been down there over twenty minutes," Willow informed him. "It's time you came out."

"Soon," he said, replacing his mouthpiece and sliding his mask back down, smartly dismissing her by simply sinking below the surface again.

"They're fine, Willy," Jane said softly, looking along the rim toward her. "I've explored a lot of quarries. It's almost like diving in a swimming pool."

Willow scanned her gaze across the pond. "This place is going to be overrun with teenagers in another few weeks. We're going to have to find a way to keep them out."

Jane snorted and returned to her equipment. "That'll be like trying to hold back the tide." She took control of the underwater robot and started guiding the camera again. Despite the murky water, she'd been able to skim the bottom with the powerful lights on the camera. So far, they'd only seen one of the bicycles Jason had told them about and several beer cans.

"We used to have some great times here, didn't we?" Jane said as she watched the screen.

Willow went back to watching the bubbles, noticing that Jason's bubbles were heading toward the west end of the quarry, to where Duncan's bubbles were rising. "Yeah, we did," Willow agreed, looking over to her friend. "How come you aren't married?"

There was a moment's silence, then Jane chuckled. "I came close once. But just in the nick of time, I realized he might like me, but he didn't have a clue what to do with my brain. It was his loss," Jane continued with a shrug. "I just can't seem to find a guy who . . . who fits. You know what I mean?" She glanced toward the bubbles, then looked back at Willow with a crooked smile. "Maybe I'll give that gray-eyed devil a whirl, and see if he knows what to do with my brain." She lifted a brow. "What about you, Willy? Duncan seems like a really good fit. He's gorgeous as all get-out, intelligent, and he obviously loves you."

"He's bossy, overprotective, and he's got it in his head that I'm supposed to love him back."

Jane just stared at her, open-mouthed. "Oh, Willy," she said softly, her eyes darkening with concern. "Brad died over ten years ago. You can't keep letting your parents' and his deaths affect the rest of your life. Not falling in love isn't going to keep you immune to tragedies."

"It can avoid a good many of them."

"No," Jane said, shaking her head. "It only makes for a lonely life."

"I'm not lonely. I have Rachel and Mikaela and Nick. And they're enough for me to worry about without adding Duncan Ross." Willow sat up and faced Jane. "I just know that if I go to sleep in Duncan's arms every night, sit across the table from him every morning and evening, and have his babies, I'll be so consumed by him that I will lose myself."

"Or you'll find yourself," Jane softly suggested. "Being part of a couple isn't a weakness, Willy—it's empowering."

Willow snorted. "Said one spinster to the other."

"I've never deeply loved a man, but I damn well know that I intend to one day. And when I find him, he's not going to know what hit him." She pointed at Willow. "And if you would just use that intelligence God gave you, you'd pounce on Duncan before he realizes what a brat you really are."

"Too late," Willow said with a heavy sigh. "He already knows."

Jane smiled back. "And he still wants you?"

"What he wants is for me to propose to him. Down on my knees, I imagine, with candlelight and roses and wine."

Jane lifted her hand to cover her laughter. "Oh, Willy. How can you not—"

Mickey let out a sharp "Woof" from across the quarry. Willow looked over to see him standing on the opposite side, staring down at the water. Both Jane and Willow scrambled to their feet.

"Where do you suppose he's been all this time?" Jane asked, quickly reeling in the line attached to her remote camera.

"Exploring, most likely," Willow said, moving down

the rim to where Duncan and Jason were surfacing. "Hey, I think they found something."

"Grab a rope, Willow," Duncan shouted.

Willow ran back, grabbed a coil of rope, and rushed back along the rim until she was standing over the two men.

"Toss me down one end," he told her, treading his way to the wall. He grinned up at her. "See, counselor, I survived."

"I'm still writing you up for insubordination, and putting it in your file."

"I have a file?"

She held her thumb and index finger two inches apart and nodded. "It's really thick, Dunky. And it's getting thicker all the time."

"Then maybe you'll want to start a new file. One for my more outstanding accomplishments."

She made a production of rolling her eyes. "Just get out of the water," she said, tossing down one end of the rope.

"Tie your end to one of the pines," Jason instructed, holding his mouthpiece safely above the water. He popped it back in and sank below the surface again.

Jane came up beside Willow. "Don't put that back in your mouth," Jane said to Duncan as he reached for his own mouthpiece. "It's contaminated. Let Jason tie off what you found."

Apparently, Duncan was willing to take orders from Jane. He dropped the mouthpiece and started swimming toward the old access road that ran down into the quarry at the opposite end. Willow tied off her end of the rope on a pine tree and ran to meet him.

"I'll wait until Jason surfaces," Jane hollered to her.

"Have Duncan take off his flippers, but make him keep his suit on. Take him to the ocean and have him get in and wash off his equipment."

Without stopping, Willow waved her hand that she'd heard, and rounded the edge of the quarry in time to meet up with Mickey. They both walked down the access road just as Duncan came walking out of the water.

Willow didn't know how he could even stand upright with all that heavy equipment on, much less walk. He looked like an alien from another world, ten feet tall and bulletproof. He also looked damn good to her—every stubborn, exasperating inch.

"Jane said you have to go jump in the ocean to rinse off," she told him, trying to take his flippers.

"Don't touch them, then," he said, moving them out of her reach. "I found a ledge that looked like it had crates stored on it at one time," he told her as they started walking up the road. "It's high tide now, so that means the ledge would have been above the normal waterline before the sea invaded the quarry."

Willow stopped walking. "You're saying the crates weren't just dumped, but stored on a ledge above the water?"

He nodded and continued walking. "Aye. It's possible whoever put them there thought they'd be safe and dry, and pose no danger." He shrugged his shoulders to straighten his tanks over his back. "Maybe the dump was just temporary, but the quarry flooded before they could move them."

Willow ran ahead and held back the branches of a scrub pine so Duncan could step through. "What is Jason hauling up?"

They stopped on the narrow strip of beach and Duncan dropped his flippers into the softly ebbing high tide. "I found some slats of wood on the bottom of the quarry, just below the ledge. One of the crates must have fallen. Jason found a large sheet of camouflage material and some plastic, and I found this," he said, pulling something from his belt. "It was with the wood on the bottom."

She reached for it, but he turned and stepped into the water, bent down and swirled it around to rinse it off, then held it out to her. "It looks like a bill of lading from one of the crates. The paper inside is wet, but the plastic sleeve has kept it intact."

Willow took the packet and tried to make out what it said through the plastic sleeve. Duncan turned again and walked into the ocean until he was thigh deep, then simply sat down and started splashing himself with seawater.

Willow set the packet beside a rock and turned to watch him unbuckle his heavy tanks and let them slip off his broad shoulders. He swirled the tanks through the water while running his hand over them, then sat them on a seaweed-covered rock. His weight belt quickly followed, then his mask, gloves, and the knife holster he had strapped to his thigh, until he was down to only his suit. He turned and dove under the water with a powerful kick, then stood up with just his head and shoulders above the surface, and smiled at her. "Ya want to come in for a swim?" he asked, wiggling his fingers at her. "It'll wash away yar black mood."

"My mood is just fine," she said, setting her hands on her hips. "And I intend to stay mad at you for a long time."

He walked back to shore in silence, continuing out of the water until he was standing right in front of her, and ran one cold, wet finger down her cheek, his fierce green eyes locked on hers. "Aye, Willow. Anger is yar only defense," he said softly. "So hold on to it for as long as ya need to, lass, while I do what I need to do to keep ya safe. If it means diving in a quarry, then you're just going to have to deal with it. But I promise, I will never take foolish risks. Not when I know you're waiting for me to come back."

Dammit, he was a master at disarming her. She was so mad at him she could spit, and so damn grateful he was okay she wanted to kiss him senseless. "You're making me nuts," she snapped, stepping back and turning to pick up the packet. She pointed it at him. "And the only engagement token you're ever getting from me, Duncan Ross, is a ticket back to Scotland."

He broke into a sudden grin and scratched his chest through his dry suit. "That's a great engagement gift, lass. Scotland would be a perfect place for our honeymoon," he said. "I can't wait to show ya around."

Willow just gaped at him. Either the guy was denser than dirt or he was determined to push her anger over the edge. "Ooohhh!" she hissed, spinning on her heel and stomping through the dense pine, his soft laughter propelling her into a run.

Chapter Fourteen

❖

$\mathcal{W}$illow *sat quietly at the* small table in the belly of the *Seven-to-Two Odds* and watched as Jane tried to separate the wet bill of lading from its plastic sleeve.

"So where'd the name *Seven-to-Two-Odds* come from?" Jane asked as she used the tweezers to slowly peel back the sleeve without damaging the fragile paper inside.

Willow leaned closer, watching Jane's meticulous progress. "Rachel and Kee, Duncan, Jason, Matt, Peter, and Luke are the *seven*," she explained. "And Mikaela and Nick are the *two*. The schooner used to be called the *Six-to-One Odds* before Rae and Nick came along and Kee had to rename her."

"So who's winning?" Jane asked, darting Willow a quick grin before returning to her task.

"The kids," Willow said with a laugh just as the paper finally came free.

"It's not a shipping label," Jane said, using the tweezers

to carefully unfold the soaked paper. "It's a warning insert."

They suddenly both had to grab the edge of the table to steady themselves when the schooner rose on a wave and dropped into a deep trough. Willow caught Jane's PDA as it slid by her elbow, and Mickey slid across the floor and into her foot with a disgruntled growl, sighed, and went back to sleep.

"Are you sure they know what they're doing?" Jane asked. "Maybe I should go up and help them before we sail right past the Pilot Islands."

"They know what they're doing," Willow assured her. "They used to live on the *Seven-to-Two Odds*. What do you mean, it's a warning insert?"

Jane turned her attention back to the paper. "Just that. You know, like the insert that comes with medication, listing its chemical makeup, affects, and what to do if ingested." She then began to silently study the paper.

"Well, does it say what we're dealing with?"

"A pesticide," Jane said, still scanning the fine print. She finally looked at Willow, tapping the paper. "It's in a concentrated form, and I'm pretty sure this particular pesticide was banned about five or six years ago. I think it was found to be detrimental to livestock who ate the feed it had been used on. I'll have to go online to be sure."

"It's agricultural, then?" Willow asked.

"Most pesticides are. But yes, this one was used mainly by U.S. corn growers until it was banned, if I remember correctly. They probably hired Kingston Corp to dispose of all their remaining stock."

"Does the insert have a manufacturer and lot number that would pinpoint its origin?"

Jane went back to examining the insert, turning it over with the tweezers again and scanning the other side. "It did," she said, shaking her head. "But only two of the numbers and one letter are still visible. The rest were ruined by the water." She pointed at the frayed top right corner. "It's eroded away."

Willow heaved a weary sigh. "Damn. Of all the bad luck."

"No, this is good luck, Willy. At least now we know what we're dealing with. And because the guys went diving, we also know there's none of it left in the quarry. The half-life of these pesticides is rather short, and now that we know the source is gone, the tides and mother nature will clean up after herself. The lobster will recover."

"But we still don't know how it got here in the first place," Willow pointed out. "If I could just find where it came from I could follow the paper trail. If it was banned, then its disposal must have been contracted to a licensed site. But I need to know who manufactured it."

"You can follow a paper trail even if it comes from overseas?"

"What?" Willow asked, alarmed. "Is that likely?"

"Sure. A lot of fertilizer and pesticides used in the U.S. are manufactured overseas, because environmental restrictions are lighter for the companies. And labor's cheap."

"Damn." Willow set her elbows on the table, cupped her hands over her face, and scrubbed her forehead in frustration. The schooner took another dive into a deep trough, and Willow ended up in Jane's lap, the paper, PDA, and tweezers ended up on the floor, and Mickey slid into the cupboards with a surprised yelp.

"That does it," Jane snapped, scrambling out from behind the table. "I'm throwing them overboard and taking the wheel."

"But that's mutiny," Willow said, quickly scrambling behind her so she wouldn't miss any of the fun.

Mickey was obviously in total agreement, and reached the deck of the schooner before them, growling wolf curses at Jason as the unsuspecting crewman stood at the wheel. Jane stepped onto the deck and Willow poked her head into the bright sunlight just as the seventy-foot ship took another dive. The schooner rolled starboard, carrying a large wave over the rail that hit Jane with enough force to send her flying toward Jason.

Grinning like a pirate, Jason reached out, swept Jane into his arms, and stood her between himself and the wheel before she could finish screaming. "Am I going to have to tie you to the mast, Einstein?" he asked. "Or do I just save us the trouble and throw you overboard now?"

"You should be keelhauled, you moron," Jane shouted back, trying to wiggle out of his steel embrace. "It's not near as rough as you're making it. You want thrills, go to Disney World."

One minute Willow was standing on the ladder, grinning like an idiot, and the next thing she knew, hard hands had picked her up and she was flying through the air. Her scream of surprise was answered by deep male laughter as Duncan carried her to the schooner's doghouse, sat down, and held her securely on his lap.

"Now, doesn't this beat sitting in a stuffy office all day?" he asked, brushing the hair from her face so she could see his smile. "Ya should do this more often, counselor, to recharge your batteries."

"Are those the Pilot Islands behind us?" she asked, lifting a brow. "Did you . . . ah, not see them?"

His grin broadened. "Jason and I haven't been sailing together in ages, so we thought we'd give the *Seven-to-Two-Odds* a run into the Gulf before we bring her to anchor. We have two or three hours of sunlight left." His arms tightened when another wave washed over the rail and splashed at their legs. "Tell me ya don't love this, Willow."

Willow sighed and snuggled against him, mesmerized by the cresting whitecaps breaking in the stiff breeze ahead of them. "Of course I love this," she said, tilting her head up to look at him. "So much that I'm tempted to just keep sailing until we run out of ocean."

He kissed the tip of her nose. "You have no idea how tempted I am, lass. Tell me what ya found with that bill of lading."

"It's a warning insert," Willow told him, resting her head in the crook of his shoulder so she could keep looking up at him. "And it is a pesticide, but Jane said the quarry and lobster will be okay, if it's all been removed. But I'm still going to have our state divers give it another check next week, and take several water tests before the kids get out of school and start coming around."

"Did the insert say where the pesticide originated?"

"Nope. The lot number was washed away."

"So what's your next step, counselor? Like ya said, a few broken boards, some drag marks, and a slip of paper aren't exactly evidence."

"Now I call in the Coast Guard and Marine Resources and have them search for any unusual boat traffic. And I call in my investigators and the Department of Environmental Protection, and they can start checking every waste site in this state. We go over every record, every bill of lading, and see what's arrived as of three days ago. Those crates had to be taken somewhere."

"Maybe out to sea," Duncan said softly, cupping her cheek to hold her hair out of her face. "They may have just dumped the entire mess overboard."

"I've thought of that."

"So how can I help ya, Willow? What's *your* next step?"

She tucked her hair behind her ear, patted his hand back in place over her cheek, and grinned up at him. "I go public. I let it leak out that I'm closing in on them, that I've found evidence left behind in the quarry, and that I'm already building my case."

"No."

"People do really dumb things when they feel someone breathing down their necks," she continued, ignoring his glare. "They'll slip up, maybe go after another dump site on some other island. And every law enforcement official at my disposal will be watching, and we'll catch them."

"No."

She reached up and patted his hand on her face again. "I'll live with a whole platoon of state police officers until this case is solved, Duncan. I won't be in any danger, because I'm going to sit at my desk and follow a paper trail right to their doorstep." She shot him a feral grin. "I do intend to be the one to knock on their door and read them their rights, though. But I'll have that army of officers standing behind me. And you can come, too, but if you punch out the guy who ran me off the road, I am not posting your bail."

"I agree with your plan right up to the point of your going public," he growled, his hand on her cheek moving to encircle her neck. "You are not setting yourself up as bait."

"Not me personally," she explained. "My office. They're not going to risk open warfare with the AG's office, Duncan."

"No."

Willow straightened on his lap and looked him directly in the eye. "Then come up with a better plan."

"I agree with your original plan, only without leaking word that you know who they are. Find your paper trail, but do it quietly."

"But I can't. I have to involve all the departments. Too many people will know, so a leak is inevitable."

"Then misdirect the leak. Come up with another reason for your investigation."

Willow had to think about that. She turned in his arms and stared out at the sea again, only absently aware of Duncan's heat engulfing her and his lips brushing over the top of her hair. Another rogue wave washed over the bow, and she would have been drenched if Duncan hadn't twisted just in time to catch the brunt of it himself. She laughed and slid her arms around his soaked back, and turned see Jane and Jason, both at the wheel, both laughing as Jane tried to wrestle for control of the wheel.

"What's for supper?" Willow asked, turning to look up at Duncan.

"I left the menu up to Jason," he told her, his eyes dancing in the sunlight and his hair blowing around his tanned face as he looked over at Jane and Jason and then back at Willow. "So I suspect we're having lobster."

* * *

They did, indeed, have boiled lobsters for dinner, and salad and some very fine wine. Jason had completely forgotten about dessert, but had found an old bag of Mikaela's gummy bears in the cupboard. He'd arranged them on a plate and drizzled them with chocolate syrup—also found in the cupboard, and only God knew how old it was.

So the four of them sat down at the tiny table, moored in a calm cove in the shadow of the second Pilot Island, and ate lobster with their fingers and gummy bears with their forks. The men, complaining of having put in a hard day diving, went to bed around ten, each to opposite ends of the ship. Mickey also went to sleep up on the deck, supposedly as lookout.

"Ah, where do I sleep?" Jane whispered as she emptied the last of the wine into her glass.

"Anywhere you want to," Willow told her after sipping from her can of soda, not yet inclined to drink anything alcoholic since her accident. "Pick a bunk." She wiggled her eyebrows at her slightly drunk friend. "Occupied or empty, it's your choice. Except that one," she clarified, pointing toward the port bow. "I've already called dibs on Duncan."

Jane snorted and stood up, downed the rest of her wine, and headed toward the stern of the boat. Willow smiled, not at all surprised when her friend climbed into the berth on the opposite side of the boat from where Jason was sleeping. Jane might adore tall, gorgeous, and wonderfully physical men, but she had never been accused of being easy. Willow suspected it was the thrill of the hunt Jane enjoyed the most—that titillating, I-think-you're-cute-but-can-you-handle-me phase of courtship.

Willow sat listening to the silence of the evening that was broken only by the gentle lapping of the sea against the hull and the muted creaks of the wooden schooner as it recovered from its brisk run through the Gulf of Maine. She imagined the talk in town right about now, from the fishermen who'd passed them today during their sail. They were likely spreading the rumor that Duncan Ross had Willow Foster trapped with him at sea, and by morning, when everyone realized the *Seven-to-Two Odds* hadn't returned, the betting pool was likely going to swing in Duncan's favor.

Willow worried she might have placed her own bet on the wrong side. Because even though she might be running for her life, there truly wasn't any place for her to hide.

Not from Duncan.

Not from love.

With a sigh that ended in a rather deep yawn, Willow got up and padded through the narrow center of the ship toward the front berth. She would take her cue from Duncan, she decided, and deal with one thing at a time. First she would solve the mystery of the sick lobster and bring the culprits to justice. And only then would she be free to confront her personal demons once and for all—and either break through that final, seemingly impenetrable barrier, or turn tail and run so deep into the darkness that even Duncan wouldn't be able to find her.

Duncan woke up but didn't move when Willow quietly crawled into bed beside him. He did notice she was naked, though, and that she felt soft and warm and smelled nice.

He was so damned thankful she hadn't been killed or even badly hurt in the accident, and so damned grateful she hadn't shut him out of the case she was working on, that he didn't care if Willow fought him tooth and nail for the next fifty years. He loved her. He had her in his bed. And when she was with him, the rest of the world didn't exist—for either of them.

The trick was in getting her to *stay* with him.

Not that she needed encouraging now. Duncan captured her roaming hand, pulled it away from his groin, and tucked it over his chest and held it there.

She kissed his nipple and squirmed closer. "What's the matter, Dunky?" she whispered. "Too much sun today? Have a headache? Or are you worn out from this morning?" she asked with a note of feminine pride.

Fine beads of sweat broke out on Duncan's forehead. "We're not alone, lass. It was your idea we bring Jason and Jane along, so behave yourself and go to sleep."

She popped her head up and stared at him in the faint moonlight shining through the overhead deck prism. "They're way down at the other end of the boat." He could just make out the slash of her smile and teasing eyes. "I promise not to scream or moan, no matter how wild you make me," she huskily added, curling her fingers into his chest hairs.

Since holding her hand wasn't working, Duncan rolled over to trap her in his embrace. "Go to sleep," he growled, throwing a leg over hers to stop her from rubbing intimately against him. "We're only cuddling tonight. Maybe next time you'll think twice before inviting an audience to our affair."

"You're serious," she muttered into his chest. She wiggled her head free and looked into his eyes, her own eyes wide with dawning awareness. "That's why you didn't come to bed last night, or why you didn't make love to me the night before. Not because your innocent baby sister was there, but because we weren't alone in the house." She leaned even farther away, her eyes shining in the diffused moonlight. "You can't . . . ah, do it when other people are around?" she whispered in awe.

Duncan tucked her back against him. "Aye," he said with a deep sigh. "It's been a bit of a problem most of my life."

She tilted her head just enough to see him. "So you've never even made out with a girl in the backseat of a car when you double-dated?"

He shook his head. "Go to sleep, Willow."

"Now? After learning your little secret?" she squeaked, squirming until he let her go enough that she could prop her head on her hand. "I am wide awake, Duncan, and probably won't feel the least bit sleepy until I know why you can't make love within earshot of anyone. Come on, tell me, and I promise," she said, crossing her hand over her heart, "that I'll take your secret to my grave."

Duncan watched her through narrowed eyes. "You're not going to let this go, are ya?" When she shook her head at him, he turned and propped his own head up on his hand, realizing she was in her lawyer mood, and that neither of them would get any sleep until he came clean.

"When I was about eight, my family rented a cottage on the Isle of Skye for the summer," he told her. "There were just the four of us—my parents and me and Camden—because Molly wasn't born yet. Hell, she wasn't even conceived yet." He shook his head. "But she certainly existed by the time we returned home that September."

Duncan turned onto his back, folded his hands behind his head again, and stared up at the deck prism as he continued. "It was a small cottage, and Camden and I slept in the loft, directly over my parents' bedroom."

He turned his head just enough to watch Willow's reaction. "I heard them," he said softly. "Nearly every night for three months, I could hear them making love. At first, I hadn't a clue what was going on down there. I got worried and tried sneaking in, but their bedroom door was locked."

"Are you saying that ever since you heard your parents . . . ah, doing it . . . you haven't been able to . . . to . . ." She reached out and touched his chest with one delicate finger. "Duncan, they obviously loved each other and wanted another baby."

"I was eight," he softly snapped. "And eight-year-old boys do not want to know that their parents do it. Making love is private. Intimate. It damn well isn't a spectator sport."

She smiled crookedly. "So what about all those children you want? Once the first baby is born, you won't be able to make another one because it might hear you."

"We'll wait until it's in school. Then we'll work on a second kid."

Her smile suddenly outshone the moon as she leaned forward and gave him a quick, quiet kiss on the mouth. "Poor baby," she crooned just inches from him, her eyes locked on his. "You've been scarred for life by the most natural act in the world."

"Are you saying ya never heard your own parents, or if you did that it didn't affect you at all?" he asked.

"Of course I heard them," she said, mimicking his pose by lying back and folding her hands behind her head, her elbow overlapping his on the narrow bunk. "I don't ever remember *not* hearing them." She turned her head toward him. "So I think it was a natural thing for me. I did feel kind of funny, though, when Dad used to take Mom in his arms and carry her upstairs." She snorted. "I was thirteen and Rachel was sixteen, and Daddy was still telling us they were just going upstairs to have a little afternoon nap."

Duncan turned toward her, laying his hand on her stomach just below her very lovely breasts. "So did ya ever make out in the backseat of a car on a double date?" he asked.

She eyed him suspiciously. "Is this one of those trick questions, like when a woman asks a guy if her pants make her hips look fat? If I say yes, you'll get all huffy to think I made out in the backseats of cars with guys. And if I say no, you'll think that I'm lying because I don't trust you."

"I'm not asking ya to kiss and tell, counselor. I'm only trying to picture you as a teenager."

"I was a brat."

"Ya still are."

"But that's what you love about me."

"Aye," he said, leaning over and kissing the soft peak of her breast. Keeping his head down, but turning to look at her, he smiled. "So ya're thinking I should get rid of this trauma I've been carrying all these years? And that you might be able to help me do it?"

She glided her fingers through his hair, nodding as she smiled back at him. "This is the perfect place to start. There's no bedsprings to squeak, and we'll both practice being really, really quiet," she whispered.

Duncan rolled onto his back, taking Willow with him so that she was sitting straddling his waist. "I firmly believe that one is never too old ta learn new things," he said, folding his hands behind his head again with a deep sigh. "Teach me, counselor."

He should have known better than to give Willow such an open-ended invitation, because teach him she did, until Duncan thought he'd die of delight. She worked him into such a frenzy, he was certain they'd hear his shout all the way to the mainland. And the wonder of it was, as he lost himself in her magic, he couldn't seem to care.

It was a very long and rather enchanting night, and by morning Duncan decided that if Willow's stubbornness not to love him didn't kill him, having an affair with her certainly would.

Chapter Fifteen

❉

*T*he men seemed to think it was important they take the *Seven-to-Two Odds* for another run out on the gulf before settling down to their day's work. Apparently, Jason had decided—likely sometime during the long night alone in his bed—that he would fair better by buttering Jane up, since riling her didn't seem to be working for him. He began by trying to impress her, not with his skill as a sailor, but with his willingness to let her think she was in charge.

Jane certainly wasn't shy about taking command, keeping both Duncan and Jason running to hoist sails and then scrambling to reset them whenever she changed tack. Poor Ahab would likely have had a cursing fit if he had seen his beloved schooner being put through her paces. Either that, or he'd have asked Jane to marry him.

It was noon before they moored off Thunder Island

again and went ashore to study the tarp and wood and plastic they'd found in the quarry and had stowed on the island last night. But they weren't there twenty minutes when Ray Cobb and Frank Porter came walking through the pine trees toward them.

Jane was the first to react, throwing herself into Ray's arms and giving him a big, noisy kiss on the cheek. Willow leaned over and informed Jason that Ray Cobb was Jane's old high school flame. Jason's reaction was to saunter over and glare at Ray so hard it was a wonder the lobsterman didn't turn to stone.

Frank Porter came up to Willow, looked her straight in the eye for several heartbeats, then pulled her into his aging but still powerful embrace. "Sweet Jesus, girl," he growled. "You ain't changed a bit." He leaned away and smiled down at her, his hazel eyes shining with delight. "You still got that look of mischief about you. I can only thank God you're plaguing them bandits in Augusta now instead of us."

"It's great to see you, too, Frank," Willow said, patting his whiskered cheek with a laugh. "How's Linda?"

The weathered old fisherman frowned, still not releasing her. "She's got some fool notion we should retire to Florida. What in hell am I gonna do in a place that ain't got no seasons? A man could work himself to death fishing year-round."

"I think retirement means that you don't fish at all, Frank. You lie on the beach and watch all the crazy people."

"I'm too young to retire," he grumbled, finally releasing her and turning to Duncan. He held out his hand. "Frank Porter. You're the Scot who owns The Rosach, ain't you?" He darted a glance at Willow, then looked back at Duncan. "I put twenty bucks on my girl here," he said, nodding toward her. "Ain't never seen no one able to pin her down long enough to reason with her."

"Duncan Ross," Duncan said, shaking his hand. "And I've found that ya don't try to reason with an ocean current, but simply travel with it."

Frank cocked his head and studied Duncan in silence through narrowed eyes, then suddenly nodded and turned away, muttering something about changing his bet when he got home.

"We've got some bad news, I'm afraid," Ray said, coming over to Willow. "Gramps is missing, and we haven't been able to raise him on the radio. Mildred said the last she heard from him, he was eight miles past Thunder Island, following some boat he thought looked suspicious. We've been out helping search for him, and saw the schooner and thought we should stop and tell you."

Duncan stepped behind Willow and took hold of her shoulders, obviously realizing how Ray's news affected her. "How long has he been out?" Duncan asked, drawing Ray's attention.

"He's been gone since early yesterday morning. He left port just as soon as the storm had blown itself out."

At around the same time they had, Willow realized. But Gramps would have left from Trunk Harbor—and they had left from Puffin Harbor—a good twelve miles apart.

"Did he say what sort of boat he was following?" Jason asked. "And why he thought it was suspicious?"

Ray nodded. "He said it was a fishing trawler, but that

he hadn't seen it around here before. He also said it wasn't rigged for any fish found in these waters." Ray looked at Willow. "Gramps knows just about every fishing boat that runs this coast from Blue Hill to Winter Harbor. And if he's suspicious, and he caught it coming away from this island, that's enough to make me suspicious, too."

"And me," Willow agreed. She turned to Duncan. "We have to help search for him."

"Aye," he said, turning and rolling up the camouflage tarp to stash it away again. Jane and Jason started helping him.

"What's that?" Frank asked.

"We found it in the quarry," Willow told him. "Along with evidence that crates of pesticides had been stored there." She looked at Ray. "Remember that ledge we used to dive off?" she asked, pointing at the west end of the pond. "We think the crates were stored on it and covered with that tarp so they wouldn't be seen from a plane. But when cracks opened in the granite and the sea invaded, the ledge flooded, and that's why the lobster got sick. They were being systematically poisoned with each tide."

Both Ray and Frank looked shocked. And quite angry. "What kind of bastard would store pesticide out here?" Frank asked.

Willow shrugged. "That's what we're trying to find out. It seems whoever put the crates here came and got them sometime during the storm."

"That would be suicide," Ray said.

"But it would also be the best time to move them without being seen by anyone," Willow pointed out. "No one else would be on the water during the storm. Gramps must have caught them leaving yesterday morning and decided to follow them. Duncan and I would have just missed them. We were out here a couple of hours after sunrise."

"Gramps called Mildred around six yesterday morning," Ray told her. "But when he didn't come home last night, and she couldn't raise him on the radio, she started calling us. Every boat in five harbors and the Coast Guard have been searching all of last night and this morning. Gramps did tell Mildred that the boat he was following was headed east."

"East?" Willow repeated, frowning. "There's a waste site forty miles east, about fifty miles inland. If that's where they're headed, they'll have to transfer the crates to a truck." She took hold of Duncan's arm. "Does the schooner have a radio? Or did you bring your cell phone? My phone got ruined in the crash."

"We have a marine radio. And my cell phone is on board."

"Then how come we didn't hear about Gramps on the radio?" she asked, just now realizing how quiet and isolated they'd been.

Duncan's face reddened. "I shut everything off, lass," he said softly. "So you could rest undisturbed."

"And I shut off my own cell phone," Jane admitted, shooting Willow a sheepish smile. "Jason asked me to turn it off when we came out in the launch yesterday. And I agreed that you could use some peace and quiet." She held up her hand when Willow started to speak. "There's nothing wrong with being unreachable once in a while, Willy. The world will survive without you for a few days."

Willow snapped her mouth shut, undecided whether she was mad at the three of them or deeply touched by their obvious concern. Had she really appeared that fragile to them?

Maybe the better question was, *was* she that fragile?

She wasn't used to anyone looking out for her welfare. Well, except for Rachel. But sisters took care of each other; that was a given. "Was Rachel in on this?" she asked, looking from Jane to Jason to Duncan.

All three of them silently nodded.

Damn. She hadn't been paying attention. She'd blindly gone along for the ride, suspecting nothing. Maybe she *had* been more shaken by the accident than she'd been willing to admit.

"That boat would have made landfall and off-loaded by last night, if it was only going forty miles down the coast," Ray said. "And the boat likely headed to Canadian waters after that." He shifted uneasily. "We've got to call the Coast Guard and tell them to extend the search for Gramps farther east, all the way to the border if need be. We've been concentrating on the waters around Winter Harbor."

"I'll call the Coast Guard," Willow said, turning to head to the launch. "And I'm calling my boss." She stopped and looked back at Duncan. "He'll make up an excuse to search the waste site. I'll have him say they're looking for a load of heavy metal, not pesticides."

Duncan studied her for several seconds, obviously remembering their conversation yesterday on the schooner. Finally, he nodded, and Willow turned and walked through the trees. By the time she had the launch untied, Jane and Mickey had boarded and Jason and Duncan pushed it off the tiny beach. Ray and Frank quickly climbed into their own tiny raft and headed out to *The Corncobb Lady*, anchored safely away from the rocks.

"Ray, I want you to call me at Duncan's house," Willow shouted just before Jason started the launch engine. "The minute you hear anything about Gramps."

Ray waved his hand in agreement, pulled the starter rope on his engine, and backed up and turned and headed out to his boat. Jason turned their launch and headed toward the *Seven-to-Two Odds*.

Willow sat in silence, staring back at Thunder Island, and hoped with all her heart that Gramps was okay. What could be wrong that he hadn't called home again after six A.M. yesterday morning? Were the men who had moved the crates so desperate that they'd actually harm an old man? Willow quietly made a sound of disgust. They'd been desperate enough to risk their own lives in the storm.

Duncan reached over and covered her hands, and Willow realized she had nervously undone the Velcro laces that held her splint in place. He carefully removed it, resettled it over her wrist and around her thumb, and smoothed it snugly closed again. "They'll find him," he told her, wrapping his arm around her shoulders and leaning down to smile into her eyes. "That old salt hasn't made his living on the water this long to be taken out by a few crooks."

"You don't even know Gramps."

"Aye, but I do. I was there on the pier that night you went out with Cobb, when Gramps caught ya. Remember? Ya waved good-bye to me."

She leaned into Duncan's warm strength. "I remember. You looked mad enough to spit nails."

"Not mad, Willow. Scared. You were heading out to only God knew where, into only God knew what kind of trouble, and I was helpless to protect ya."

She tilted her head up and smiled at him. "You appeared remarkably calm when I returned."

"Aye," he said, giving her shoulders a squeeze. "Ya might want to keep that in mind in the future, counselor. The more furious I am, the calmer I get."

Willow blinked up at him. He'd been angry? She had only seen Duncan mad once, and that had been when he'd barged into the house where she was being held, to rescue her two years ago, when she'd been kidnapped. And even then his anger had been tempered with an ominously lethal control that, perversely, had made Willow feel sorry for the guy who'd been holding her hostage.

Willow realized she had never been afraid of Duncan, not once in the two years she'd known him. Which was probably why she'd gotten in his car that morning on the Trunk Harbor pier, and easily fallen asleep, secure in the knowledge that she couldn't be in better hands.

Talk about blind trust. She had never *not* trusted Duncan with her body, her well-being, and—damn it all to hell—with her heart as well.

But the scariest part was that Duncan was trusting *his* heart to *her*. He was either the bravest man she knew or the most reckless.

"They'll find Gramps safe and sound, lass," Duncan reassured her as Jason edged the launch against the *Seven-to-Two Odds*. "He obviously has the heart of a warrior, to go after that boat the way he did. He'll be okay. Please don't look so worried."

Willow couldn't bring herself to tell Duncan that it was his warrior's heart she was worried about. So she simply let him hand her up to Jason, who was now leaning over the rail of the schooner to pull her up, since she couldn't climb the rope ladder because of her wrist. Jane quickly scrambled up the ladder behind her, and Duncan lifted Mickey over the rail.

Willow immediately headed toward the aft ladder. "Where's the radio?" she asked. "And your cell phone, Duncan. I need to call John Pike."

"My phone is in my duffle bag," he called to her as he walked toward the anchor line. "And as soon as we set sail, I'll get on the radio with you to the Coast Guard."

"Jane, I'm going to use your laptop to find that article on my jump drive, okay? There was something in it . . . a name or something . . . that's bugging me," Willow said over her shoulder just as she started down the ladder. "Jason, set a course for Puffin Harbor."

"We're not going to look for Gramps?" he asked. Jane and Duncan also stopped to wait for her answer.

Willow stood on the top step and shook her head. "Every available boat on this coast is out searching. We won't be missed if we don't join them. I need to get home to your office, Duncan. I want to go on the Internet."

After two seconds of stunned silence, her three shipmates scrambled to pull anchor and get the *Seven-to-Two Odds* under way. Willow headed below, turned on Jane's computer as she walked by the table, then went in search of Duncan's cell phone while the laptop booted up.

That article was the key to this crazy mess. It mentioned a name that had sounded familiar to her, but she hadn't thought much of it at the time. She'd read that name again just recently . . . maybe in the stolen files that Karen had downloaded for her.

Willow rifled through Duncan's duffle bag, only to suddenly stop in mid-search and hold up a box of condoms. Good lord, between Rachel's supply and Duncan's stash, they could have sailed to Europe and back without having to stop for birth control. Willow wondered if everyone was trying to send her a message that she was simply too dense to get.

"What was the file name of that article?" Jane called from the galley. "I'll find it for you."

Willow tossed the condoms back in the bag. "I think Karen named it Interesting or something silly like that," she called back, once again rummaging through Duncan's bag for his cell phone. She finally found it and headed back to the galley, where she found Jane already reading the computer screen.

"It's an article about a guy named Brent Graham. It says that the attorney general of New York convicted Graham of bribery when he bought off two state officials." Jane snorted and shook her head. "Of all the . . . The guy was trying to get a trash incinerator plant built in the Adirondacks."

"Graham. Graham," Willow repeated, sliding into the booth beside Jane. She pointed at the screen. "Open the file named Lost Lamb One and see what it is."

Jane clicked a few buttons, and an application for a waste disposal site dated four years ago popped up on the screen. "There he is," Willow said, tapping the bottom of the screen. "Brent Graham is the one who applied for the license."

Jane scrolled down the document. "It says he was denied."

Willow nodded. "Something about an underwater aquifer. Open the file named Lost Lamb Two and see what it is."

Jane did, and together they read the new document as Jane scrolled down. It was an approval for the Kingston Corporation to open a waste disposal site in eastern Maine. The same site, Willow realized, that was just forty miles down the coast and fifty miles inland.

"Keep scrolling," she told Jane. "There. Stop." She pointed at the screen. "Brent Graham is listed as one of the corporate officers. That's it. His name was muddied from the New York conviction, so they buried him deep in the paperwork."

"So?" Jane asked, looking at Willow. "It's not a crime to be tenacious. The guy is obviously in the trash business, and he simply stepped aside so the new application could go through. You told me that the Kingston waste site is reported to be in complete compliance."

"Yeah, but Kingston's silent partner, Brent Graham, has already proven himself to be a crook. *Tenacious* is probably the right word," Willow agreed with a nod. "Graham changed states, and changed from incineration to landfill, but that doesn't mean he's suddenly found religion. He's already tried taking the easy way by bribing officials; what's to stop him from shuffling a few crates of pesticides around until he can get his site approved?"

"But wouldn't it have been easier to just dump them

out at sea? Why go through all that trouble of storing them and then moving them later?"

Willow pointed at the screen again. "Three of those names listed as Kingston officers are upstanding citizens of Maine. Hell, one of them—this guy," she said, tapping the screen, "ran for governor under the Green Party ticket two elections ago."

Jane leaned forward and squinted at the screen. "My God, you're right. I remember him. Hell, I voted for him. Now he's on the board of a trash dump?"

"He might be the best thing that happened to the Kingston Corporation," Willow pointed out. "He's going to see that they police themselves better than our field inspectors could. I know Edward Simmons personally, and he's a good man."

"Who just happens to be in bed with a crook," Jane reminded her. She nodded at the cell phone Willow had set on the table. "What are you going to tell your boss?"

"Everything I know or suspect to this point."

"So now you'll officially call in the Lobster Institute and let us monitor the water around Thunder Island? We need to study them for any lasting effects."

"Consider yourself officially called in."

"So my exile is over? I can return to work?"

Willow immediately shook her head. "It ain't over until the fat lady sings, Jane. Until everyone is rounded up, none of us is safe."

"Including Gramps," Jane whispered, her eyes darkening with concern. "I used to haunt the docks as a kid, and Gramps would bring me odd specimens he caught in his traps so I could study them. He gave me a four-legged starfish one day, and told me to watch it grow back its lost limb. That damn starfish lived in my saltwater aquarium for six months, but Gramps talked me into returning it to the sea when it was whole again."

Willow reached out and hugged Jane. "They'll find him," she whispered. "Safe and sound. Duncan said old salts don't get taken down by crooks. Gramps is a wily one. He'll come floating home on his own once he's had his adventure."

"God, I hope so," Jane returned with a sob, hugging her back. "I can't imagine this coast without him. He's been a fixture in the community forever."

"And that's why everyone is out looking for him," Willow said, pulling away and patting Jane's shoulder. She picked up the cell phone. "I've got to call my boss. He's got to get someone out to that site before they bury those crates."

Jane got up and started rummaging around in the cupboards for something to eat. The *Seven-to-Two Odds* gave a creaking moan and listed to port as the sails snapped, catching the full force of the wind. Willow punched in John Pike's number just as the schooner turned and started plowing northwest through the sea.

Twenty-two miles as the seagull flew, from Thunder Island to Puffin Harbor, and Willow sighed as she listened to her boss's phone ring, realizing that it would probably take the entire trip to persuade John to let her remain in charge of this case.

It wouldn't be an easy sell, considering their last conversation, when John had pointed out that Willow was now known across the state as a drunk driver. She had been publicly disgraced and her credibility as an assistant AG was shot.

John finally answered, and the ensuing conversation was surprisingly short and rather shocking. Willow softly closed the phone and stared across the ship at nothing.

"What did he say?" Jane asked, setting crackers and cheese on the table beside the laptop. "You listened more than you talked, and you barely got out the information on the crates."

Willow looked up at Jane, seeing her through a surreal fog of detachment.

"Willy? What did John say?"

"That I've been dismissed."

"Dismissed from what? This case?"

"My job," Willow whispered. She looked down at the table, frowning. "I've been put on leave pending an investigation into my finances."

"What!" Jane leaned over to make Willow look directly at her. "What do you mean, your finances? You don't have any. You inherited five million dollars from Thaddeus Lakeman, but you gave it away two years ago. Other than your parents' trust fund, you're broke."

Willow rubbed her forehead and stared down at the table. "It now appears that I also have half a million dollars in an overseas bank account."

There were several heartbeats of silence, then Jane made a noise of disgust, turned on her heel, and walked to the stairs. "Duncan!" she hollered. "Get down here!"

Willow was vaguely aware of footsteps overhead, and suddenly both Duncan and Jane were standing in front of her, and Mickey had his paws up on the seat and was licking her face.

"What's going on?" Duncan asked softly, pulling Mickey away and studying Willow. "What's happened?"

"Tell him," Jane said. "Tell us both exactly why your boss is investigating your finances."

"Yar finances?" Duncan repeated. He leaned back against the counter, crossed his arms over his chest, and continued to study her. "What did Pike say?" he asked.

"He said that he received an official document, anonymously, that showed that I have half a million dollars in an overseas account, and that it was deposited there just three weeks ago."

"And," Jane prodded. "Are you saying John believes this anonymously sent document?"

Willow answered Jane but looked directly at Duncan. "He does now. There was also a note with the document, saying that the money was a payoff for throwing a case I lost six weeks ago. John couldn't just ignore such an accusation, so he got a search warrant for my apartment Sunday afternoon. They found the overseas account on my personal computer, right there in my finance program, and they also found the password to it on a piece of paper in my bureau drawer. It shows that I accessed the account just last week, for a balance check."

Jane snorted and shook her head as she looked at Duncan. "Can somebody do that? Can they open an account in another person's name, and make deposits and stuff?"

Duncan said nothing, merely nodded, and Willow realized he was furiously thinking—about the motivation, the ramifications, and the next course of action for them.

Them. That's why she wasn't panicking, why she wasn't sobbing in hysterics or cursing out John Pike for even thinking she was guilty—because she was one half of a *them.*

"Duncan. Say something!" Jane snapped. "Willow did not take a bribe."

"That's it," Willow said, sitting up and looking from Jane to Duncan. "I've been set up to look like I took a bribe." She turned to Jane. "And who do we know who's well acquainted with bribes?"

Jane gasped. "Brent Graham," she whispered, clutching her throat. Her eyes narrowed. "Did he run you off the road, too?"

Willow shrugged. "Probably. That's why alcohol got poured down my throat. Again, to discredit me."

"But why?" Jane asked. "Over some stupid pesticide that wasn't stored legally?"

Willow nodded her head at Jane, though still aware that Duncan hadn't said anything yet. "Do you have any idea how much money is involved in the Kingston waste site long term? Setting up an assistant AG who's investigating you isn't so much of a stretch. And half a million dollars is pocket change. Graham, if it is him, is only buying himself time to clean up his mess and cover his tracks. He's just making sure my case disappears before I have a chance to build it."

"But how did he learn you were even building a case?" Jane asked.

"According to Ray Cobb, all the fishermen were being watched once word got out that the lobster around Thunder Island were dying. Someone must have seen me go out with Ray. And that's why my apartment was broken into last Wednesday, and why my files were stolen from my office that same night."

"The whole thing sounds like a thriller," Jane muttered, shaking her head. "It doesn't sound like the kind of stuff that goes on around here."

"But that's exactly why it's happening here," Willow said. "Because the rest of the world thinks of Maine as a territory, not a state, run by a bunch of woodsmen who wouldn't know a crime if it came up and bit us on the butt."

Duncan suddenly smiled. Jane just looked confounded, with her hands balled into fists at her sides and her face red with building anger.

Willow couldn't help but smile herself, and she suddenly relaxed with a deep sigh. Everything was going to be okay. She was going to be okay, because an angry and very calm troglodyte was the other half of her *them*.

Chapter Sixteen

❈

They pulled into an eerily silent harbor, idling past mostly empty moorings that gave testament to the fact that just about every seaworthy boat was out searching for Gramps. Willow knew from past experience that the Fox home, which sat just up Main Street, was the center of an age-old vigil where the women were gathered around Mildred Fox to wait for word on her husband.

Willow could even picture the scene in vivid detail, because she had been part of such a vigil during her sophomore year of high school. She had sat all night and into the next morning with Bradley Grant's mother, and been there when the Coast Guard and the harbormaster had come in and told Mrs. Grant they'd found her husband's body about two hundred yards from his idling boat. And then they'd explained what they thought had happened, and that her son had likely been pulled under in five hundred feet of water. In time, they'd told her, the sea might give Bradley up, but they could only offer sincere condolences for her loss.

"Ah, lass," Duncan said, hugging her to his side as they stood at the rail. "Have faith, woman," he continued. "Gramps is going to come home to be the star witness of your case."

Willow turned and buried her face in Duncan's strong, warm chest. "He had no business sticking his nose where it didn't belong."

He hugged her securely, using his chin to hold her head against him, and rocked her gently back and forth. "Aye, counselor, but he did. These are his waters, and he has every right to get involved in whatever is threatening them."

When she popped her head up to argue his point, Duncan used his thumb to wipe a tear off her cheek. "Ya cannot deny a man his convictions, Willow. Nor can ya control his actions."

"I can still give him hell when he gets back."

His soft chuckle vibrated against her. "Aye, ya can try. But he'll likely give ya hell right back."

Jane guided the *Seven-to-Two-Odds* against the Puffin Harbor pier, and Jason jumped off and secured the ropes. Willow stepped out of Duncan's arms and nodded. "I'll stand for a lecture from Gramps, as long as he's giving it to me in person. Preferably today, before nightfall."

Kee's truck drove all the way out onto the pier, and before he could even shut it off, Rachel got out and came running toward them. "We saw you sailing in and came right down. John Pike's been trying to get hold of you since Sunday morning," she told Willow. "He sounded serious, but he wouldn't tell me what he wanted."

Willow stepped onto the pier and hugged her sister. "I just spoke to John. He was calling to tell me I'm in big trouble," she told Rachel, taking hold of her sister's shoulders to brace her against the news. "It seems I'm being set up to take a fall. Somebody opened an overseas account in my name, deposited half a million dollars in it, and said it was for throwing one of my cases six weeks ago."

Rachel gasped, her face reddening with anger. "John doesn't believe that, does he?"

Willow shook her head. "He said he doesn't believe any of it, but the evidence is solid and the damage to my reputation is already done." Willow gasped. "Mabel," she said, squeezing Rachel's shoulders. "We have to go get her."

"Your landlady? But why?"

Willow turned to include Duncan and Kee in the conversation. "John mentioned that the press had also been sent the documents, so he couldn't keep it contained. I would bet there's several news vans camped out at my apartment. We have to get Mabel out of there. She's going to be outraged by the accusations, and she'll likely go outside and tell them off."

"Mikaela and Nick and I will go get her," Rachel said. "She knows us, and she'll be comfortable at our house. Ah, Gramps is missing," she softly continued, touching Willow's arm. "He's been gone since yesterday morning."

"We know," Willow told her. "I'm going to Mildred's house now."

"Sorry, counselor," Duncan said, turning her to face him. "The best thing ya can do for the Foxes is solve this case. Let the townsfolk take care of Mildred and look for

Gramps, and we'll approach the problem from our own direction. We find those crates, they'll lead us to the boat, and the boat crew just might lead us to Gramps . . . with a bit of persuasion."

Willow had to think about that. Duncan was right; sitting around waiting, holding Mildred's hand and feeling somehow responsible, was not going to accomplish anything. "Okay," she said, turning to Rachel. "You go get Mabel in Augusta, and I'm going back to Duncan's house and see if I can't put all these pieces of the puzzle together."

"Ah, about Duncan's house," Kee said, looking from her to Duncan. "You've got company."

Duncan went utterly still. "Who?"

Kee grinned. "Your mother and Camden."

Willow watched, fascinated, as Duncan paled and muttered something nasty under his breath.

"Grammy Ross brought me a tea set," Mikaela said through the open window of the truck. "And she brought Nick a stuffed pony. And Uncle Camden brought us both bottles of whisky."

Willow stared at Mikaela, then at Rachel, then turned and glared at Duncan. Duncan finally came out of his stupor and shrugged. "It's for their twenty-first birthday celebrations," he explained, grabbing Willow's hand and turning on his heel to lead her up the pier to the parking lot. "We broke a pulley," he told Ahab as the captain came rushing down the pier toward them. "It was likely needing replacing anyway."

Ahab didn't bother to stop, but mouthed a curse and broke into a run toward his beloved schooner. Willow looked back as Duncan continued leading her to his car, and saw Ahab shaking his fist at Jason and scolding anyone within earshot.

"So it looks like I'm going to meet your family," Willow said, turning her attention back to the silent, serious man beside her. "I can't wait."

Duncan stopped beside the left door of his Jag and took hold of her shoulders. "I need to warn ya about my mother," he said. "She can be a bit . . . well . . . intimidating."

"I imagine she must be," Willow said, reaching up and tracing a finger over his tense jaw. "She raised you and obviously lived to tell about it. She must be quite a lady."

"Aye," Duncan whispered, his face flushing. "She is a lady. Her Grace, Margaret Went Ross, to be exact, Duchess of Spierhenge."

Willow paled. "Duchess," she repeated in a whisper. "As in . . . in lords and ladies and that kind of stuff?"

He nodded.

"And you're the oldest son, so that makes—" She swallowed and tried again. "A duke," she croaked.

He nodded again and finally smiled. "Not bad for a troglodyte, huh, lass?"

Willow went so weak in the knees, Duncan had to hold her up. He turned with a laugh, opened the car door, and carefully sat her inside. Willow's head spun as she stared straight ahead while Duncan fastened her seat belt, only vaguely aware when he shut the door, walked around the car, and got behind the wheel.

His Grace, Duncan Ross. Her Grace, Margaret Ross. And that would make Molly what? Lady Ross. Aw, hell. She'd been calling a peer of the realm a troglodyte. She'd even written it out on his palm so he could look it up.

No wonder he'd returned the favor in Latin! He was likely more educated than she was.

Without even thinking, Willow reached out and smacked Duncan in the belly with the back of her hand, making him grunt and making her sore wrist throb. "You jerk. You've been laughing at me all this time."

"I don't use the title, Willow. I didn't ask for it, don't want it, and ran off on my twentieth birthday and joined the navy in order to avoid it."

"Why didn't you tell me?"

He started the car, looked over, and smiled. "Because I wanted ya to fall in love with me, not my title."

"I think I was just insulted. I am not mercenary, Ross."

"Aye," he said quickly, covering her still-throbbing hand and rubbing her fingers. "I know ya're not. But it was rather fun being a troglodyte instead of a duke, even for a little while." He leaned over to peer into her eyes, his own eyes serious again. "I never once played myself down to ya, Willow. The man you've known for the last two years is the real me." He shrugged and put his hand on the gear shift, pushed in the clutch, and started out of the parking lot. "That ya decided I was a caveman was your way of keeping me at a distance."

And again Willow had to think about that. Is that what she'd been doing? Snobbishly calling Duncan a troglodyte as an excuse to avoid falling in love with him?

It certainly looked that way. "Why did you walk away from your heritage?" she asked softly.

He darted a glance at her, then gave his attention back to the road. "Over a stupid falling-out with my father when I was just twenty. He wanted me to step up and take his place as head of The Rosach Distillery. I saw my whole life mapped out for me, and it wasn't the life I was wanting."

"You're an adventurer."

"I was," he said, darting her another glance, this time with a quick smile. "But I've gotten it out of my system now. I'm wanting to settle down."

"So you'll go back to Scotland and run the distillery and take up your title?"

"Nay. Camden's heart is in the business, not mine. I have a wish to own a quaint little pub on the coast of Maine."

"Are you . . . are you rich?"

"I suppose I am." He shot her another quick smile. "Most of my money is in the distillery or tied up in family lands, though. That's why we had to take out a loan to pay off Mikaela's mother when Mikaela was born. I wanted to cash in some of my stock then, but I couldn't do that to Camden. Why, is being rich as bad as being a troglodyte?"

Willow finally found her own smile. "Almost."

"That's right, you gave away your inheritance from Lakeman a couple of years ago. Five million dollars is a lot of money to throw away."

"For three years I considered it blood money. And by the time I found out different, I still couldn't bring myself to keep it. So I gave it away, anonymously, to various charities. Did you make up with your father before he died?"

He seemed startled by her question, and nodded curtly. "Mostly. We were no longer estranged, but I'm thinking he was disappointed I never came home to stay."

"We can't always please our parents," Willow said, looking down at her hands and fidgeting with the Velcro on her splint. "Lord knows I tried to live up to my father's dream. He was so determined I'd be governor of Maine one day."

"But aren't ya? That's what Rachel is thinking."

Willow shook her head. "I know. And I don't have the heart to disappoint her, either."

Duncan pulled the car off the side of the road just a quarter mile from his home and shut off the engine. He turned to her, his deep green eyes intense. "If ya're not really wanting a career in politics, then what do ya want?"

She gave him a tremulous smile. "I want to hang out a shingle for a private law practice down here on the coast, and help individuals solve what seem to them like huge problems."

"But I thought ya loved your AG job."

"I do, some of the time. But most of the time I'm defending faceless entities with class-action suits and 'the state versus the bad guys.' I know the citizens are my true clients, but I want to get to know them on a first-name basis and not be hampered by bureaucracy. As an AG, I have to play exactly by the rules, and those rules get in my way sometimes. Can you understand that, Duncan? Sometimes I just want to fight dirty, and holding public office doesn't allow that."

The smile he gave her was crooked, and his eyes danced with warmth. "Oh, I understand. But only because I know there's really a brat's heart beating inside ya. And that's the heart I fell in love with."

"Oh, Duncan," she whispered, throwing herself at

him, only to be brought up short by her seat belt, making her next words come out as nothing more than a yelp.

"Behave yourself," he said with a laugh, patting her knee. "I tried making out in this car when I got it, and I still have the scar to prove it can't be done. Save yar kisses for after we see my mother. I'm definitely going to need them then."

Willow tamped down her blush and started fidgeting with the Velcro laces on her splint again. "Oh, how bad can she be if she raised you and Molly?"

Having no choice, considering the death grip he had on her good wrist, Willow trailed into Duncan's kitchen behind him, only to find herself walking into a silence that could have been cut with a knife. The first thought that popped into her head, when she first spotted Her Grace, Margaret Went Ross, was *dragon lady*; the woman only lacked wings and a bit of smoke puffing from her imperially raised nose.

Duncan had heard this . . . this person making love to his father almost every night for an entire summer? Either Margaret Ross had changed rather drastically in the last twenty-six years or Willow was glad she would never have to meet Galen Ross. Duncan's father must have been a dragon himself—or a really brave man.

Willow finally pulled her gaze from Margaret Ross, looked past Luke standing by the fridge, past Molly doing dishes at the sink, and stopped when she came to a man who could be Duncan's identical twin minus a few years. Camden Ross was breathtakingly gorgeous, Willow decided. He was nearly as tall and just as muscular as Duncan, had the same piercing green eyes—which were studying her back with unabashed interest and a bit of male appreciation—and overlong, wavy hair that was blonder than Molly's. There had to be Viking blood somewhere in the Ross ancestry.

The tension in the kitchen kicked up several notches when Duncan quietly led Willow to the island counter, pulled out a stool for her, and waited until she sat down. Then he walked over to his mother sitting at the other end of the island—also studying Willow with unabashed interest but with a bit more critical regard—and gave her a familial kiss on the cheek.

"Hello, Mother," he said quietly. "How nice of ya to come for a visit. If you'd have given me some notice, I would have dusted a bit and cooked a special dinner."

"You knew perfectly well I would be coming after Molly," Margaret said in a decidedly more British than Scottish accent, tilting her head to glare up at Duncan.

But that was when Willow saw it, right there in Margaret Ross's eyes, the unmistakable hunger of a mother feasting on the sight of her son again. For one unguarded moment, Willow saw pride, tenderness, and unconditional love as Margaret's beautiful, vivid green stare remained locked on Duncan's utterly calm face.

Willow relaxed back in her seat with a silent sigh. The woman was a sham. She might wear a mantle of rigid nobility, but beneath that seemingly impervious cloak beat the heart of a marshmallow. Duchess Margaret Went Ross was nothing more than a love-struck mama who obviously didn't have a clue how to deal with her independent, overwhelming children.

"Hello, Mrs. Ross," Willow said with a warm smile. "I'm Mikaela's aunt, Willow Foster," she told her, figuring that was the best way to explain who she was. "Is this your first visit to Maine?"

Margaret tore her gaze away from her eldest son, and the marshmallow was suddenly gone, replaced by assessing eyes the exact mirror image of Duncan's. "Yes, Miss Foster, this is my first time in Maine. And it's 'Your Grace,' not Mrs."

Willow waved that away. "Oh, we don't stand on ceremony here, because it gets much too complicated. You can call me Willy." Willow ignored the stunned silence from Luke and Molly and Duncan, and especially from "Her Grace." She instead turned her attention to Camden. "Mikaela said you brought her a bottle of whisky. What an unusual gift for a seven-year-old. Just the other day, we were discussing children having alcohol. You must be Camden. I've heard a little bit about you from Duncan."

Camden nodded from where he was leaning against the counter beside Molly, his smile sincerely warm and maybe in league with the devil. "I've been hearing quite a lot about you, counselor," he said, using Duncan's endearment to let her know he talked with his brother often. "And don't worry, I told Mikaela the whisky was for her twenty-first birthday. It came out of the cask the year she was born."

"It's our tradition, Miss Foster," Margaret interjected, "to gift children in our family with a bottle of whisky from a cask tapped during their birth year."

"How sweet that you consider Mikaela family, just as I do," Willow returned to Margaret before looking back at Camden—simply because he was such a pleasure to look at. "And that was nice of you to think of Nick, too. So," she said, clasping her hands together and leaning on the island. "This is a wonderful family reunion. I know Duncan's been looking forward to all of you coming to Puffin Harbor to see him. We should have a proper celebration tonight at The Rosach Pub."

Her suggestion was met with more silence, until finally Duncan sighed loud enough to make his mother flinch. "Ya said ya wanted to use my computer?" he reminded Willow, nodding toward his office.

"Oh, that can wait, Dunky. I'd rather have tea with your mother," she said, nodding toward the teacup sitting in front of Margaret.

Duncan's glare should have knocked her off her stool, but Willow simply propped her elbows on the island, dropped her chin onto the back of her good hand, and smiled at his mother. "Do you have tea every afternoon in Scotland, Margaret? With scones? We have a lot in common, you and I—did you know that?"

"We do?" Margaret asked softly, sounding as if her throat were too constricted to speak.

Willow nodded in her hands. "There are times we'd both love to smack Duncan with our shoe." She canted her head, still keeping her chin on her hands. "I'm sure you know what I mean."

"I would never . . . smack one of my children, especially not with my shoe. What happened to your face, Miss Foster? Is that a bruise? And what did you do to your hand?"

Willow hopped off the stool, walked past a gaping Molly, and took the lovely china teapot off the warming plate on the stove. "I totaled my truck when I got run off the road by a criminal I'm investigating." She waved her hand. "My wrist is only cracked, so I'll get the splint off in another week. You've never even been tempted to kick Duncan? Not even when he was a teenager?"

"Of course not. I thought you were a lawyer. How come you're investigating criminals? Don't you have detectives to do that?"

"So Duncan has told you about me," Willow said, refilling Margaret's teacup. "I wasn't officially investigating anyone—I was just looking into a problem for a friend. Molly, aren't you going to join us? And Duncan, don't you and Luke and Camden have some catching up to do?" Willow asked, looking at the wall clock. "We'll head to The Rosach around seven. And we'll invite Rachel and Kee and the kids. Oh, and Mabel. She'll likely have the lobster roll."

"Who's Mabel?" Margaret asked, folding her hands in her lap.

"She's my landlady in Augusta. Rachel went to get her because the media is likely camped out in front of my apartment, and I don't want them to harass Mabel."

"Why is the media there?"

"Because I'm about to be indicted on bribery charges, not to mention drunk-driving charges," Willow told her with a smile, pouring tea into the two cups Molly set on the island. "This is beautiful china." She looked at Duncan. "You have amazingly girly tastes, Dunky."

"I sent him the china," Margaret said, now holding the tiny cup in front of her. "For a housewarming present. It's part of my mother's set that he will inherit. The rest is in storage for when Duncan gets married."

Willow lifted a brow. "The rest?" she asked, glancing at the hutch on the far wall, then back at Margaret.

Margaret nodded. "It's service for one hundred and twenty. I didn't want to overwhelm him, so I sent him enough for a dinner for twelve."

Willow frowned at Duncan. "Do you have eleven friends?"

The poor man looked like he wanted to kick her. Either that or kick himself for bringing her home to meet his mother. Willow shooed him ahead of her as she made her way back to her stool. "You three go put your heads together and come up with a way to sneak into that waste site tonight. We have to find those crates."

"That would be the singular 'we,' counselor," Duncan said over his shoulder as she pushed him from the kitchen. "You are not sneaking into anything, except maybe the network at your office."

"Oh, my secretary's going to love that," she said, motioning for Luke to escape with Duncan. She stopped Camden by taking hold of his sleeve. "You make really fine whisky, Camden. I never have a headache the next day."

Camden leaned down and kissed her cheek. "It's our aim ta please, lass. Go easy on my mother," he whispered, still leaning close. "She's not liking that her children are getting scattered ta the four winds."

"Do people call her Maggie?" Willow whispered back.

That devil came dancing in Camden's eyes again. "Only her cousin, the queen," he said softly, straightening to saunter down the hall after his brother and Luke.

Willow was left staring after him, utterly immobilized. Her cousin, the queen? Of England? Oh, she was going to take off her shoe and beat Duncan to a pulp the minute she got him alone. The man really was a troglodyte, and he had the sense of humor to prove it, too.

Willow finally turned around with a pleasant smile plastered on her face, and returned to her stool at the island. Molly set down a plate of thick, gooey-looking brownies, and Willow could have kissed the young woman. Willow immediately grabbed three brownies and set them on a napkin she pulled from the holder, licked her fingers, and turned to Duncan's mother. "So, Mrs. Ross, you must be excited that your baby girl is getting married. Have you spoken to the sheep farmer's mom yet, to start the wedding plans?"

Chapter Seventeen

✶

It was a somber celebration at The Rosach that evening, considering the varied moods of those in attendance. Only Mabel was oblivious to the underlying currents running through the private room on the second floor of Duncan's pub. Willow's landlady was instead involved with eating the famous Rosach lobster roll and discovering that she also had a taste for fine Scotch.

Margaret Ross was still recovering from this afternoon's girl chat in Duncan's kitchen, but at least the woman was speaking to her daughter again—albeit stiffly—now that Molly had admitted Ben Zane was nothing more than her attempt to be taken seriously. Mother and daughter were huddled next to the crackling hearth that was an exact replica of the one downstairs.

The men—Duncan, Kee, Luke, Jason, Camden, and Ahab—were sitting at one end of the long trestle table that dominated the banquet room, drinking Scotch and talking about only God knew what. Willow thought they might be discussing the pesticide and Gramps's disappearance, since all the men had serious faces.

Rachel, Jane, Mikaela, and Nick were sitting at the opposite end of the table with Willow, all of them drinking soda and picking at their food. They weren't talking about much of anything, what with Gramps being foremost on their minds, though they were careful not to worry Mikaela about him. Nick was blissfully stuffing his face with french fries, getting more ketchup in his hair than on his food.

The steps leading up from downstairs gave an ominous creak, and everyone looked over to see a tall, strapping man open the door and step into the room. "Ah be looking for a lass named Molly Ross," he said, slipping his hat off and tucking it under the package he had tucked under his arm. "Ah bin told she's up here. Ma name's Benjamin Zane, an Ah've come from New Zealand ta fetch ma bride."

The declaration was delivered with bold conviction.

The ensuing silence was absolute.

And Benjamin Zane looked like he was seventeen years old.

Five men immediately stood and turned toward him. Ahab remained seated, apparently figuring Molly's impending nuptials were none of his business.

Molly also stood with a squeak, her eyes the size of dinner plates as she looked around for a crack to crawl into. Her mother, apparently, was planning on joining her. But then Molly suddenly turned and straightened her shoulders. "I'm Molly," she said.

The wall of men stepped in front of Ben Zane when

he started toward her. The young man stopped. "Are ye all her brothers?" he asked without even flinching. "Which one of ye left the message on ma machine?"

Willow was having a hard time understanding Ben, his accent was so strong. She couldn't misunderstand the male posturing, however, especially from Duncan and Camden. Luke didn't look very pleased, either.

"I'm Duncan Ross, Molly's oldest brother and the one who left the message." Duncan raised an eyebrow at Ben. "I asked ya to call me, not come here."

Ben shifted his package and hat to his left arm and held out his newly freed right hand. "Yar message reminded me of ma manners, Mr. Ross, and had me realizing ma poor mum is likely rolling in her grave for my not coming to ask fer Molly's hand proper like."

Duncan shook the boy's hand, then tucked his own hands behind his back and straightened to his full height. "Exactly how old are ya, Mr. Zane?" he asked.

"Eighteen this last March," Ben imparted, leaning to the side to see Molly, apparently missing—or not at all worried by—the body language of all the men. Ben grinned at Molly, his eyes shining with male delight as he soaked in the sight of the woman he'd traveled halfway around the world to meet.

Camden stepped between. "I'm Molly's other brother, Camden Ross. Are ya expecting us ta turn over our sister simply because ya got on a plane and came ta 'fetch' her?"

Ben didn't have far to look up to see into Camden's eyes. "Ah'm a landowner of good standing back home," he began, only to turn to speak to Duncan. "Ah run a flock of four thousand sheep and two hundred cattle with ma brother. We inherited our ranch when our parents died last summer, and it's debt free. Ah don't drink ta excess, smoke, or brawl. Ah attend church when Ah can, ah don't beat women, and there's no bairns running in town with ma eyes."

Ben moved directly in front of Duncan. "With a wife by ma side, Ah can branch out our ranch and double ma herd of cattle and increase ma flock to make us a good living. Ah give ya ma word, Mr. Ross, Ah'll take good care of yar sister."

The entire room held its collective breath while Duncan crossed his arms over his chest and silently studied Ben Zane. Finally, he reached out and slapped Ben on the shoulder. "Ya have my blessing, son," he said, using his hand on Ben's shoulder to push him toward Molly.

A collective gasp ran through the room. Margaret Ross actually yelped. Molly, her face as pale as new-fallen snow, took several steps back until she was pressed against the wall.

"Duncan!" Margaret snapped.

Duncan held up his hand. "Last I knew, I was still head of this household. Ya have a problem with that, have your cousin rescind my title." That said, Duncan calmly sat back down at the table and picked up his glass of Scotch.

Everyone, including Mabel, turned to stare at the young couple in the corner, and watched as Ben Zane thrust his brown paper package out to an utterly frozen Molly. He finally had to lift her hand and place the package in it.

"Ah remembered from yar emails that ya like lace." He then had to start unwrapping it for her, since Molly still couldn't seem to move. "This was ma mum's, that she carefully spun from our own wool and tatted herself. It's ma bride's gift to ye, Molly."

"I—I didn't . . . ya asked me but I . . . I didn't say yes, Ben," Molly whispered so softly that everyone had to lean in to hear her. Even Mikaela and Nick seemed to realize something important was happening, and were being as quiet as church mice.

"Oh, Ah know ye haven't said yes," Ben agreed. "Which is why Ah've come ta court ye in person."

Willow could see Molly's hand shaking as she picked the delicate wool lace out of the paper and held it up. She turned to her mother, her deep green eyes pleading for help.

"Mr. Zane," Margaret said. "I am Molly's mother, Her Grace, Margaret Went Ross."

Ben's gaze, which had turned to Margaret, quickly snapped back to Molly. "Ya're a *lady?*" he whispered, his composure slipping for the first time. He backed up a step. "Ya didn't say that in yar emails."

"I—I didn't think it was important," Molly whispered.

"It's not," Duncan said from the table, not bothering to look at them. "Love knows nothing of titles. Is that not right, Mother?" he asked, finally turning to look at Margaret, one of his very dukeish-looking brows raised in question.

Margaret Ross blushed to the roots of her natural blond hair, and began studying the tiny diamond on her left ring finger.

Duncan turned in his seat to face Ben. "Our father was a commoner, Zane. He was brewing whisky when he met my mother on a stormy road in Spierhenge. So don't worry, ya've fallen in love with a lady whose family doesn't bow to tradition, but instead bends it to suit ourselves. Ya do love Molly, don't ya, Ben?"

"I—ah, Ah've only just met her, sir," Ben stammered, fine beads of sweat breaking out on his deeply tanned forehead. "We've only been corresponding six weeks."

Poor Ben looked like he was wishing he'd never bought a computer, much less gotten on the Internet. Willow's heart went out to the man. Boy. Young man. Apparently her title wasn't the only thing Molly had forgotten to mention to Ben. It seemed neither of them had thought to ask each other's age.

Willow wondered if Margaret might finally be ready to take off her shoe and smack Duncan. The duchess was sitting in her overstuffed chair by the hearth again, still studying her ring, her face flushed with . . . Willow didn't know if Margaret was embarrassed or simply thinking about her commoner husband.

The stairs creaked again, this time with running footsteps. Everyone turned to the door, and a young woman came rushing in, her eyes wide with distress.

She ran directly to Duncan. "There's two state police detectives downstairs," she said in a winded whisper. "They're asking for Willow Foster."

Duncan stared into his drink as silence returned to the room. Willow closed her eyes and dropped her head into her hands. Damn. She had known this was coming. John had warned her that it would only be a matter of time before they put together enough evidence to actually arrest her.

"Ya can play by your attorney general rules, counselor, or ya can break them," Duncan said softly, causing Willow to look down the table at him. He was deadly serious and ominously calm.

Did that mean he was angry? With her? With John Pike?

"It's a formality," she told him. "They have to book me, but then I'll get out on bail."

"How long will it take? Can I get ya back out tonight?"

Willow thought about that, and also considered the option Duncan was offering. If she let them arrest her, she could be in jail twenty-four to forty-eight hours, unless they had decided to bring her in for questioning—which wasn't unheard of if they wanted more time to build their case. But would John do that to her? And could she afford to let that happen right now?

"I could be tied up for days. So, Your Grace, which window opens onto the fire escape?" she asked, ignoring Rachel's gasp and shooting Duncan a wide grin. "This appears to be one of those rules I might like to break." She shrugged. "Although I'm not really doing anything wrong. I haven't seen any state detectives."

Duncan turned to the woman who had run upstairs with the news. "Tell them Willow Foster already left about half an hour ago, would ya, Colleen? Say ya think she mentioned she was heading back to her apartment in Augusta."

Colleen, whom Willow used to babysit for at least ten years ago, nodded at Duncan and then looked over at Willow. "You always made me go to bed by nine," she said, smiling crookedly. "So I'm only doing this because I've bet all of last week's tips on Duncan. And I really want a new MP3 player."

"I put you to bed but you never stayed there," Willow said, getting up and walking to one of the back windows. "Thanks, Colleen. If you lose your tips, I'll buy you that MP3 player."

"Careful, counselor," Duncan said as he joined her at the window and opened it. "That's coming close to actually obstructing justice."

"I'm not buying you an MP3 player," Willow quickly told Colleen. "Just stay up here a few minutes. You can have my supper. I haven't touched it," she offered, waving at her plate beside Rachel.

"Luke, go out and see if they're watching the back of the pub," Duncan said, waving him over to the window. He looked at Kee. "We'll meet in two hours."

"Willy," Rachel interjected. "You can't do this."

"Sure I can, sis. I haven't been handed a warrant for my arrest by anyone." She ran back, hugged Rachel, and kissed her cheek. "I'll turn myself in once I figure everything out. Please don't worry about me. You know I'm in good hands."

"Why are you going out the window, Aunty?" Mikaela asked. "Because you don't want to get caught driving drunk again? You only had soda."

Willow sighed and hung her head.

"I'll explain to her what's happening," Rachel promised, giving Willow a push. "Just get out of here."

"All's clear," Luke told Duncan, sticking his head back in the window. "I'll let the air out of their tires just as soon as you get out of here. Take my truck." Luke handed Duncan his keys, then waited while Duncan dug in his pocket for his keys and gave them to Luke.

Duncan put one leg over the sill, but stopped and

looked back at the room. "Kee, could ya take Ben to a hotel for tonight? And, Mother, I expect ya to stay right here in Puffin Harbor until I get this settled."

Margaret sniffed. "You are not *my* guardian, Duncan Ross."

"Nay, but I am in possession of yar passport," he said with a pirate's grin. "Jane, ya're not to get more than ten feet from Jason, understand? We don't need to be hunting for you, too."

"Yessir!" Jane said with a snappy salute. She turned and smiled at Jason. "I'll be all over him like hot butter."

Willow watched Duncan look around the room, as if checking to see if he'd missed giving orders to anyone. "They'll survive without you, Dunky," she said, shoving him out the window. But then she stopped and turned to smile at their gaping audience. "Sorry to break up this exciting party. But please, continue without—"

Duncan reached in, grabbed Willow by the shoulders, and pulled her out the window.

They made their escape to Luke's house in Luke's truck, and Willow couldn't remember ever being on such a surreal adventure—not even in high school. She was running on nothing but adrenaline and riddled with guilt at the realization that this was really serious business. Gramps and the crates were still missing, she was hiding from both sides of the law, and Duncan was sticking his neck out to aid and abet a now wanted criminal. And they still weren't any closer to understanding what was going on.

"Is there a reason you and Kee live in beautiful homes and Luke lives in a shack?" Willow asked, flopping down on the tattered couch in the living room of the gently collapsing old farmhouse.

Duncan walked through the darkness to the window, and peered outside. "Because Luke thinks this is a mansion," he said, turning to face her. She could just make out the slash of Duncan's grin. "And he doesn't know how to go about setting down roots. He grew up on the streets of New York, and is content if the roof doesn't leak and the toilets flush."

"He's not *that* uncivilized," Willow said with a laugh. "He acts more sophisticated than you do most of the time."

"Because he attended the school of hard knocks. That, and he sat through four years of classes at Columbia University." Duncan shrugged. "Though ya don't get a diploma unless ya pay tuition."

"He stole his education?"

"More than that—he made his living doing term papers for the real students."

Willow just stared in awe at Duncan, until she realized something was poking her thigh. She reached under herself and pulled out a sneaker. "It appears he doesn't entertain much, either," she said with another laugh, only to finally sober and get back to their serious business. "Why do you suppose they stored those crates in the quarry? That pesticide was banned four years ago."

"Banned in this country," Duncan said. He came over and sat down in a chair facing her. "It's possible Kingston Corporation contracted to legally dispose of the pesticide, but instead of putting it in their landfill, they stashed it to sell to another country where it isn't banned."

"But four years? Kids swim in that quarry every summer. How come they didn't find it? Jane thinks the pond flooded early last winter, so the crates would have been visible before then."

Duncan thought for a minute, then tilted his head at her. "What if this was just one of many shipments? What if they put those particular crates there last fall, and were planning on moving them this spring before the kids got out of school? I'm sure nobody goes out to that island in the winter. It would be nothing but a frozen rock."

Willow thought about what he was suggesting, and suddenly sat up straighter. "Then Kingston Corporation's records would show they've been taking in that particular pesticide on a regular basis for the last four years. But if we don't find any of it actually buried at the waste site, that would mean they've been selling it all along."

"Are ya planning on working the shovel, or are ya leaving that job to me? How in hell are ya going to find out if there's pesticides buried there or not?"

"It's a hazardous waste site. Surely they have to keep a log or map or something of where they bury everything. They can't risk putting two incompatible chemicals beside each other, or they could blow a good chunk of Maine off the map."

Duncan stood up, paced back to the window, and turned to her. "So ya're wanting us to break into Kingston's office, rifle through their files, and then start digging where we *think* the pesticide is?"

"No," she said, waving that away. "We'll break in, rifle through their files, and see if they have a record of taking in that pesticide. If they do, then we'll sneak back out and call my boss and let *him* do the digging."

"The moment he hears yar voice, Pike's going to demand ya turn yourself in. Or have ya forgotten your half-million dollars sitting in an overseas bank account?"

She waved that away, too. "I know lots of good lawyers. I didn't throw that case, and I can prove it."

"How?"

"I keep meticulous records."

"I imagine ya would, especially if you're planning on losing a case, counselor. A good prosecutor will blow your records out of the water."

Willow hung her head. He was right. It's what she would do if she were prosecuting someone in her position. "That overseas account has got to be connected to this Kingston thing." She looked up at Duncan. "Why else would it have suddenly appeared with my name on it, along with an anonymous letter to John and the news media? I bet it's an account they've had for some time, a sort of insurance policy that they could put anyone's name on to set them up."

"Aye. But proving that is going to take some doing."

Willow shook her head. "All we need is one credible witness," she said, leaning back on the couch and crossing her arms under her breasts. "This entire operation takes manpower. It's not just a few executives shuffling paperwork; it's several men willing to risk their lives to move crates, a broker who sets up their foreign sales, and someone on the clerical staff at Kingston who's willing to look the other way when the bills of lading show up without the crates."

"Okay," Duncan said, crossing his own arms over his chest. "Let's assume we do find that they've been selling illegal pesticides for the last four years. That would mean the boat that left Thunder Island yesterday morning did not go just forty miles down the coast, it likely went out to sea."

"And if Gramps was following them . . ." Willow whispered, unable to finish the sentence.

Duncan came over, sat down beside her on the couch, and took her hand in his. "Ya need to prepare yourself for the worst, lass. Gramps would have followed them until he had only enough fuel left to bring him back home. And he would have been in radio contact with someone."

"You think he's dead, don't you?"

"I think it's a very good possibility, Willow. Unless he had mechanical trouble that caused an electrical failure, we would have heard from him by now. And the Gulf of Maine is a very busy place this time of year. If Gramps's boat were simply floating on the currents, someone would have crossed his path by now."

Willow turned and buried her face in Duncan's chest, heaving a shuddering sigh when he enclosed her in his warm, comforting embrace. "That would change everything," she said into his shirt. "It would escalate this crime to murder."

He tilted her chin up to look at him in the dim light. "Aye, but only if we find Gramps's boat and can prove there's something foul about his disappearance." He smiled down at her. "Then again, the old bastard may come rowing home on his own. I saw his boat that night on the pier. It's fully equipped with survival gear. So what I'm saying, lass, is that ya should be prepared for the worst, but don't write Gramps off just yet."

Willow stretched upward until her lips came into contact with his. Duncan tightened his arms around her with a grunt of approval, and canted his head, urging her to open her mouth.

Need blossomed inside her like the static charge of an impending storm. Willow wiggled around until she was sitting astraddle his lap, not once losing contact with Duncan's deliciously provocative lips. How could this man—this protective, possessive, dangerously passionate man—make her forget her resolve every time he touched her?

"We have to stop," he growled, breaking the kiss and running his lips over her cheek. "They're here."

"They?" she whispered, trailing her mouth across his jaw to nuzzle his ear.

He took hold of her shoulders and held her away. "Our partners in crime just drove up."

No sooner had he said that, when Willow heard a vehicle door slam. She tried scooting off Duncan's lap, but he pulled her back against him and tucked her head under his chin. "Shhh. Let them think we've been making out. I love watching Jane's reaction when we remind her ya're getting some action and she isn't."

Willow poked him in the side. "You pervert. Jane's my friend, and it's not nice to enjoy her frustration."

"She could end her frustration any time she wants. Jason is ready, willing, and able."

"But does he respect her mind?"

Duncan drew his head back. "Her mind?" he repeated, rolling his eyes. "For Jason, the mind is the most sensual organ."

Willow beamed at him. "And for you?" she asked quickly, hearing the kitchen door open. "What turns you on, Duke Duncan?"

"Having a woman write *troglodyte* on my hand," he said with a laugh, leaning down and kissing her with all the drama of a stage farce.

The living room light snapped on and a snort came from the kitchen doorway. "You two are worse than a pair of lovesick rabbits," Jane said. "Come on, we have an office to break into."

Duncan still didn't release Willow.

"They found Gramps's boat," Kee said solemnly. "Or rather, they found what's left of it floating at sea. It appears to have burned down to the waterline."

Willow gasped, and Duncan pulled her tightly against him, one of his large hands holding her head to his chest, as if he could protect her from the heartache of the news. "And Gramps?" he asked.

"They didn't find any sign of him," Kee said. "Only his empty life raft, opened and floating near the wreckage, and his cold-water survival suit."

"I have to go to Mildred," Willow said, struggling to get free.

Duncan held her tight. "Nay, lass. Ya have to finish this. We have to figure out where that boat is going so it can be intercepted while still in possession of its cargo."

"They found the wreckage seventy nautical miles east of here," Kee said. "Draw a straight line, and it looks like Gramps was heading to the southern or southeastern tip of Nova Scotia."

"There's nothing on the eastern side of Nova Scotia but sparsely populated fishing villages," Jason added, stepping over and putting his arm around a softly weeping Jane. "It is, however, the most direct route to St.

John's, Newfoundland, which is a good jumping-off point for air cargo."

"It's an awful roundabout way to go just to ship cargo," Duncan said, still holding Willow and still keeping his hand over her head. "But they may be using one of those fishing villages or a deserted old cannery or something on the eastern shore of Nova Scotia."

Willow was shaking—not just with grief, but with anger. There had been no need for those men to kill a defenseless old man. And so help her God, if she ever caught up with the bastards, she'd throw them overboard and let the sea claim their soulless bodies the same way they had let it claim Gramps.

Willow knew it was very un–attorney general of her to think that way, but then, she was sorely tired of being politically correct when it came to dealing with criminals. Sometimes she wished society would smarten up and bring back public floggings.

Duncan finally took hold of her shoulders and leaned her away just enough that he could see into her eyes. "We'll find them, Willow," he said gently. "And then ya can get your revenge in court."

"I have no intention of prosecuting them," she said. "I'm going to make sure they have an accident at sea."

He clasped her chin, his smile tender and his eyes dancing. "Aye, that's what I'm needing to hear, counselor. So are ya ready to drive the getaway car?"

"I want to go inside with you."

"Nay," he said, his hand on her chin tightening. "You and Jane will be our lookouts. We'll do the breaking and entering." His grin slashed sinister. "We're good at it, ya see."

"You don't know what you're looking for."

"I know as much as you do," he countered. "Jason and I go in, you and Jane keep watch, and then we play whatever cards we find. Maybe we'll find some sort of paperwork that will give us a ship's name, or a contact."

"Edward Simmons can't be part of this," Willow said, glancing at Jane. "It must be going on without his knowledge."

Duncan used her chin to make her look back at him. "Who is Edward Simmons?"

"He's one of the owners of Kingston Corporation. And he's a prominent lawyer here in the state. He ran for governor two elections ago. He's a good man. Maybe we can get him to help us."

Duncan immediately shook his head. "If Simmons doesn't know what's going on, then he's off the hook. But until we know all the players and their roles, we trust no one. Understood?"

Jane stepped away from Jason. "I get to drive the getaway car."

"Why you?" Willow asked, finally crawling off Duncan's lap when he turned to glare at Jane.

"Because I didn't just total my truck."

Willow shot her a scathing glare, then walked up to Kee. "You're not coming with us," she told him. "I will not be responsible for worrying my sister sick. Go home."

Kee looked like he was trying very hard not to laugh in her face. Duncan sighed and stood up, walked over, and turned Willow to face him. "If ya need to go to the bathroom, go now," he told her, also glancing at Jane to include her. "Ya can't be visiting the woods when you're a getaway driver. Ya got to be ready to drive."

"Kee is not going with us."

"He's got something else he's doing for us."

"What?"

Duncan just smiled and pushed her toward the hallway. "We'll meet ya in the truck. Ya have three minutes, then we're leaving without ya."

Willow stopped in the doorway of the bathroom and looked past Jane, who had followed her. "You don't even know where you're going."

"I can read a map," Duncan told her. "And Jane *is* driving."

Chapter Eighteen

❧

"*He doesn't kiss like a caveman,*" Jane whispered.

Willow turned from staring out the window at the woods where Duncan and Jason had disappeared thirty minutes ago, and looked at her friend. "Duncan kissed you?"

Jane looked momentarily startled, then snorted and shook her head. "Not Duncan. Jason," she whispered, fidgeting with the key chain dangling from the ignition of Luke's truck. "On the *Seven-to-Two Odds,* right after you and Duncan left, and Ahab got done bawling us out for breaking that pulley. I was down below, getting our gear, when Jason came down and . . . and kissed me."

Willow blinked at her friend in amazement. "Are you blushing?" she asked, squinting through the moonlit cab of the truck. Who the hell had ever heard of breaking and entering on a moonlit night? "Jane Huntley is blushing like a schoolgirl because a guy kissed her?"

Jane lifted her chin. "It's not just the fact that he kissed me, but *how* he kissed me. And . . . and what he said afterward."

Willow didn't know what she wanted to address first—the *how* he'd kissed her or *what* he'd said. "What did he say?"

"He said it was okay for me to be afraid. That if I wasn't, we might as well just walk away from each other right then."

Willow turned to fully face Jane. "What did he mean by that? You're not afraid of Jason, are you?"

"Of course I am," Jane said, rolling her eyes. "And Jason knows it, and he also knows that being afraid means I'm smart enough to realize I've met my match."

"My God, you really like him, don't you?" Willow said in wonder. "Not just for a fun time, but for . . . you only just met him two days ago. You can't feel that strongly for him."

Jane nodded, the moonlight slashing across her blushed cheeks. "Something sparked between us the moment he walked into Duncan's kitchen. Why do you think I took leave of my senses?"

"Okay," Willow said, also nodding. "*How* did he kiss you?"

"Like he was kissing *me*, not my mouth," Jane whispered, her blush furiously dark now. "He was taking a taste of all of me."

Willow could only stare at her friend.

"And that scared me to death," Jane softly admitted. "And Jason knows I'm scared, and he's going to grab onto that like a dog onto a bone."

"Because he had the same reaction when he walked

into Duncan's kitchen and spotted you?" Willow asked.

Jane nodded again, then quickly looked down at her watch. "Haven't they been gone long enough?" she asked, obviously wanting to change the subject. "It's been half an hour."

"Duncan said to give them a full hour. He's got a cell phone, and said he'd call if they ran into any trouble."

"They can't call if that trouble happens to be at the wrong end of a gun barrel," Jane pointed out. "And what if they don't come back in an hour, and they don't call? Then what do we do?"

"Duncan said for me to call Kee on his cell phone."

" 'Duncan said,' " Jane repeated. "My God, you sound like a mindless parrot."

"I'm just telling you what he told me. I didn't say I was going to mindlessly listen to him."

"Is he really a duke?" Jane asked, apparently wanting to change the conversation again.

Willow nodded. "It seems so. Duncan explained that the title came down through his mother, not his father. Apparently Margaret was an only child. And Camden told me she's a cousin to the queen."

"Of England?" Jane squeaked. Her eyes suddenly rounded as she looked past Willow's shoulder, her previously blushing face turning a stark pale white.

Willow spun around, and came nose to tip with the barrel of a shotgun pointing at her through the window. The guy at the other end of the gun, the one with his finger on the trigger, looked like he might be enjoying the fact that he was scaring her witless. And the guy standing beside him, pointing a handgun at the truck, had an even nastier grin.

"What do we do?" Jane whispered.

"Whatever they tell us to do," Willow whispered back, not taking her eyes off the first man.

He waved the barrel of his shotgun, motioning for them to put their hands in the air. Willow immediately complied, and prayed to God Jane did, also.

"Do you suppose the guys got caught?" Jane whispered.

"Shut up and get out," the second guy said. "One at a time. Both of you use this door," he ordered, motioning to Willow's passenger door.

Slowly, using only one hand while keeping the other hand in sight, Willow opened the door. The first man backed up, then quickly moved the barrel of the shotgun so that there wasn't any glass between them anymore. He then grabbed her by the arm, dragged her the rest of the way out, and shoved her against the side fender of the truck.

Jane was also pulled out and shoved into the side of the truck so hard she grunted sharply, and Willow worried she might have bruised a rib.

"You don't have to manhandle us," Willow said calmly, putting her arm around Jane as her friend clutched her side and tried to catch her breath back. "We're cooperating with you."

"What are you doing here?" the second man asked. "This is posted land. You're trespassing on the Kingston Corporation waste site."

Willow rounded her eyes. "This is a waste site?" she asked, looking around in surprise. "We didn't see any signs. We just drove down this dirt road, looking for a place to go . . . ah, well, to get some privacy."

Ugly Face with the shotgun appeared surprised. "Priacy?" he echoed, looking from Willow to Jane, then back to Willow. His eyes narrowed to two black slits in the bright moonlight. "Privacy for what?"

Willow cuddled closer to Jane, lowering her head and giving the guy a sheepish smile. "Well, my mother's come to visit, and she's been here over a week, and we haven't had a moment's privacy in our own home. And Mom can't get used to my choice of lifestyle, and we don't want to flaunt it in front of her, so we were just . . . you know . . . looking for a quiet place to be . . . ah, alone."

Jane looked over at Willow with incredulous eyes. Willow cupped Jane's face and kissed her cheek. "It's okay, sweetie. If these guys bruised your ribs, we're going to sue whoever runs this waste site."

Willow looked back at her jailers. The first man had his mouth hanging open and his shotgun dangling at his side, trying to comprehend the fact that two women might be looking for a lover's lane on a moonlit night. The second man, however, the one with the handgun, still appeared more suspicious than intrigued.

"I want you to write the name of the company that owns this waste site and your two names on a piece of paper for us," Willow continued, pressing her advantage. "You guys are going to pay for my friend's doctor visit to see if you hurt her." Willow cupped Jane's face again and looked deeply into her eyes. "Can you breathe, sweetie? Where does it hurt?"

Jane bent forward even more, and started panting. "My—my left side," she croaked. "I think a rib might be cracked."

Willow cuddled her closer and turned and glared at the men. "She's very delicate," she told them. "Ever since she finished chemotherapy last year, she bruises easily."

The shotgun guy paled, and the suspicious guy finally slipped his handgun into his holster. "Hey, we're sorry," he said, walking to the truck door and holding it open as he waved them inside. "We've had some trouble from teenagers around here lately."

Willow carefully handed Jane into the truck, then turned and faced the men, holding out her hand. "Your names, please," she said. "And put down the name of the gentleman who runs this place."

"Aw, hell, lady—" he started, digging into his shirt pocket only to suddenly stop. "Hey, what's that noise?"

It was Duncan's cell phone is what it was. The damn thing was vibrating her thigh hard enough to make the three quarters and two nickels in her pocket rattle.

The man looked at her pants, specifically at her left hip pocket. "That's a cell phone or beeper," he said, stepping back and drawing his gun again.

Willow also stepped back until she was pressed against the fender of the truck, and held her throat in shock. "What are you going to do, shoot my cell phone? I told you my mother hasn't given us a moment's privacy."

"Ain't you going to answer it?" the other guy asked.

Willow shook her head. "It's my mother," she repeated through gritted teeth, sending a scathing glare toward Jane. "Sweetie, here," she continued tightly, nodding toward the truck, "gave Mother my number, even after I warned her not to."

Handgun Guy held out his hand. "Give it to me," he said, suddenly suspicious again. "I'll answer it, and if it's your mother, I'll tell her I'm your new boyfriend."

Willow shook her head.

The guy stepped forward, and before she knew what was happening, shoved his hand in her pants pocket and pulled out the still vibrating phone. Willow swatted at him, trying to knock that damn phone to the ground as she stepped away with a startled yelp.

The guy flipped open the phone and held it up to his ear, but said nothing.

Willow winced when she heard Duncan's voice all the way from where she was standing. "We struck out tonight, counselor. The office is full of men, and we may have been seen. Get out of there," Duncan commanded. "We'll meet you down on the main road."

"That's not possible, mister," the guy said into the phone. "Your lady friends have guns pointed at them right now."

Willow closed her eyes and hung her head, listening to the silence coming from the other end of the phone. Dammit, they'd almost gotten away. She looked back up to find Shotgun Guy pointing that lethal barrel at her again.

So close. She had been so close to persuading these guys to let them go. Willow could tell Duncan was saying something else to the man, though now his voice was lowered to a calm softness. But she could tell that whatever Duncan was saying, it was having an effect; the listening man's eyes got wide and his grip on the phone tightened.

"No, I suggest you come to your truck." He looked from Willow to Jane. "Both of you. I know there's two of you out there."

He paused, listened, then shook his head. "You have five minutes, mister, or one of these ladies is going to have more than a cracked rib." He suddenly reached out and grabbed Willow by the hair, pulling her against him so roughly that she yelped.

"Did you hear that? That was the woman with the cast on her hand. Her hair seems a might sensitive."

Willow twisted, trying to get free, when the man suddenly released her. "Five minutes," he growled into the phone just before snapping it shut and stuffing it in his pocket. He pulled his gun back out of its holster with one hand, and reached back on his belt and pulled his walkie-talkie free with his other hand. "There's two men and two women out here snooping around. What do you want me to do with them?"

"We'll send Joe and Mike out," came a voice over the walkie-talkie. "And then bring them all to the office. Where are you?"

"We're on the west road, just behind the tire dump. Tell Joe and Mike to watch for the two men. They're inside the fence—near the office, I think. I told them to come to me."

"Okay. I'll tell them."

"Ask the women for their names," another voice said over the walkie-talkie.

Handgun Guy nodded at Willow. "What's your name, sweetcakes?"

"Mary Bingham," Willow said.

"Paula Wright," Jane said when he looked at her.

"Mary Bingham and Paula Wright," he repeated into the radio. "But one of the guys called one of the women 'counselor.' "

There was a moment's hesitation on the other end. "Check their IDs," that same voice demanded.

Handgun Guy looked to make sure his partner had

both women covered, then walked around the truck, opened the driver's door, and search around inside. "Where're your purses?" he asked Jane.

"We don't have any. We're liberated women."

He gave Jane a good glare in the overhead light of the cab, then reached up, flipped down the visor, and pulled out the registration. "They don't have IDs, but the truck is registered to Luke Skywalker," he said into the radio, his voice trailing off as he finished reading the name.

Willow kept her face expressionless. Luke *Skywalker*? Jane, however, couldn't stifle her snort of surprised laughter.

And again the radio remained silent for several heartbeats before the voice said, "Just bring them in!"

Handgun Guy tossed the registration down on the seat and pushed Jane out of the truck. "Let's go," he snapped, palming his gun again and rushing back around to their side. He took Willow by the arm and started dragging her down the dimly lit road. "We were expecting you," he said proudly. "We doubled the guards."

"Congratulations," Willow shot back, rushing to keep up with the bruising grip on her arm. "You've captured two defenseless, unarmed women. They'll probably put a bonus in your check this week."

"They did say they'd make it worth our while," he admitted, the insult zipping right over his head.

"Do *they* have a name?"

"The general manager is Al Heron, but it's Mr. Simmons and Mr. Graham who showed up three days ago and told us to expect you. They're the ones who offered the bonus to anyone who caught you."

Willow stopped walking, despite the pain she felt

when she also jerked him to a stop. Jane bumped into her back only to yelp when Ugly Face rammed his shotgun into her already sore ribs.

"Edward Simmons is with Brent Graham? Here, in the office?" She narrowed her eyes at him. "And you said 'caught you.' Who exactly were you expecting?"

Handgun Guy shrugged. "Mr. Graham said to expect a woman and a big Scottish guy to come snooping around here. And the guy on the phone did have a bit of an accent, so you must be 'you,'" he finished sarcastically, dragging her along again.

Edward Simmons was part of this? Talk about being disillusioned. Willow knew Edward from several dinner parties they'd both attended in Augusta, and she had always found him to be a civilized, intelligent man with a pretty wife and a promising future.

They continued on in silence, leaving the road and stepping onto a dark path. They walked through a gate in the fence and quickly arrived at the office. Handgun Guy shoved Willow in through the door ahead of him, and she came face to face with a very worried-looking Edward Simmons.

"Miss Foster," he said rather sadly. "I was so hoping it wasn't you."

"Mr. Simmons," she acknowledged, nodding to him as she rubbed her sore arm. "Not as much as I was hoping I wasn't going to find you here."

"And you must be Dr. Jane Huntley," another man said, standing up from a desk and walking up to them, looking at Jane. He shook his head. "Such a waste. I don't know why you women didn't stay in your offices and push papers and do experiments."

"Brent Graham, I assume?" Willow said, giving him a nasty smile when he nodded. "How many bribes did it take to get your little dump opened here in Maine?"

Instead of answering her, Brent turned scathing eyes on Edward. "I told you not to underestimate her. Now do you see why we have to move quickly? No telling who she's told."

"Everyone," Willow said, drawing his attention again. "From John Pike to every local fisherman. I even sent a packet to the media."

"She's lying," Edward said. "I just spoke with Pike this afternoon, and he's not even pursuing her claims." He looked at Willow. "It seems she's on the run from her boss, who has issued a warrant for her arrest." He looked back at Graham. "The drunk driving and that payoff scheme you set up seems to have worked. Her credibility is shot."

"Where's Ross?" Graham asked, looking from Willow to Handgun Guy. "Stokes, you said he was inside the fence."

"I spoke with him on her cell phone," Stokes said. "I told him that if he didn't turn himself in, we were going to rough up his girlfriend."

Graham held out his hand. "Give me the cell phone."

Stokes handed it to him, and Graham turned and handed it to Willow. "Call him, Miss Foster. Tell him where you are and that I want him in here in five minutes or we shoot Dr. Huntley."

"Graham!" Edward snapped.

Graham waved him away, his attention focused on Willow. "Call him," he repeated.

Willow looked down at the phone in her hand, realizing she didn't have much choice. She flipped it open, then just stared at the tiny screen. "I, ah, I don't know the number," she whispered, looking back at Brent Graham. "I don't know whose phone he's got. This one is his," she explained, lifting it up.

"Check the caller ID for the last call," he said impatiently.

"Oh yeah," Willow muttered, punching a few buttons, trying to keep her hands from shaking as she worked the unfamiliar phone. She finally found the right menu, the number appeared on the screen, and she pushed SEND.

The phone rang once, twice, three times before Duncan finally answered but said nothing. "Duncan," Willow whispered. "I . . . Jane and I are in the office. We're here with Edward Simmons and Brent—"

Graham jerked the phone out of her hand. "Dr. Huntley gets shot in the leg if you don't show up in five minutes, Mr. Ross."

Willow could just make out the mumble of a voice on the other end of the phone. Brent Graham snapped it shut and tossed the phone on the desk. He stepped behind the desk and sat back down, lacing his fingers together and setting his hands on the back of his neck as he rocked in his chair, studying her.

"So, Miss Foster, just how much have you figured out?"

"Most of it," she said with a shrug. "I've figured you have records of receiving a banned pesticide here for proper disposal, but if we dig for it, we're not going to find it, are we? Instead, its slowly killing the population of some Third World country the same way it was killing our lobster and crabs."

"Miss Foster," Edward said, taking a step toward her.

"Willow, it's not really a lethal pesticide when used properly. The FDA's ban was more political than anything. It wasn't manufactured here, so our own manufacturers wanted it outlawed."

"That's your justification, Edward?" she asked, lifting one brow. "It's not 'really lethal' so we can make a few extra bucks off other countries?" She turned to fully face him and crossed her arms under her breasts. "So you've been rounding up the stockpiled pesticides for the last four years, getting paid a goodly sum for disposal, then getting paid a second time when you sell them. And you really don't see anything wrong with this, Edward? No moral or ethical questions?"

She waved at Brent Graham. "Hopping into bed with a tried and convicted crook doesn't keep you awake nights?" She balled her hands into fists at her sides and stepped closer. "What about killing an old man, Edward?" she asked softly. "Does that sound like nobody is being harmed by your greed?"

Edward stepped back, clearly surprised. "We didn't kill anyone," he said. He darted a nervous glance at Graham, then looked back at Willow. "The deal was, nobody got hurt. We just needed to keep you from putting everything together for two more days."

"Tell that to Cecil Fox. They just found his boat ninety miles east of here, burned to the waterline, and no sign of him."

"What makes you think we had anything to do with that?" Edward asked, paling.

"Gramps was following the boat you sent to Thunder Island to pick up your latest—*leaking*—shipment of poison. What happens in two days, Edward?" she asked, studying his eyes. She'd never noticed before, but Edward Simmons had beady little eyes.

"It's none of your business," Graham said.

"We're selling Kingston Corporation," Edward told her, despite Graham's warning. "We sign the papers and then I'm on a plane out of this backwoods state. I intend to disappear."

"Duncan Ross will hunt you down," Willow said calmly. "There isn't a corner of this world where you can hide from him."

"Ross will be in no position to hunt anyone down," Graham said, standing up and walking from behind the desk.

Willow turned to him. "Then there are five more men right behind him," she told Graham. "They make their living hunting crooks like you."

"They won't come after us as long as no one gets hurt," Edward said to Brent Graham. "We just have to make this little problem go away for two more days. You promised, no killing. Selling contraband is one thing, Graham, but I draw the line at murder."

The two men who had caught Willow and Jane, who had remained quiet up until now, suddenly started moving restlessly. "We didn't sign on for no killing," Stokes said, his face pale. "We're just security guards."

"We aren't killing anyone," Graham snapped, waving a hand in dismissal. "We're only holding them for two or three days."

The door opened and Shotgun Guy turned, pointing his gun at Duncan and Jason as they sauntered into the office. Both men looked unusually calm to Willow, and reassuringly big.

"We're here," Duncan drawled, taking in everyone in the crowded room, his gaze finally landing on Willow. "Are ya hurt, lass?" he asked.

"No. Just mad. Duncan, this is Edward Simmons. And this," she said, waving toward Graham, "is Brent Graham. They've been selling the pesticide for four years, and they killed Gramps."

"We did not," Edward growled, darting a worried look at Duncan. "I don't know what happened to him, but we are not murderers."

"Just common thieves," Duncan said softly, stepping over to Willow and taking hold of the back of her neck as he trained his gaze on Graham, apparently deciding he was the real threat. Duncan then started to gently massage her, and Willow guessed she must look a bit tense. "So, gentlemen, what now?"

"Now you go for a little ride," Graham said, picking up the walkie-talkie. "I do hope none of you gets seasick. Joe. Mike," he said into the radio. "Bring the truck down to the office and pick up your cargo."

"We're not going to hurt any of you, Willow," Edward assured her, glancing at Duncan and taking a step back before continuing. "In a few days this will all be over. Kingston Corp will have been sold to a perfectly legitimate company from Utah, all the pesticide will be gone and the lobster will recover, and Graham and I will fall off everyone's radar screen."

"And Cecil Fox will still be dead," Willow whispered.

Chapter Nineteen

❈

They endured a bruising ride in the back of a cargo truck, were dragged onto a lobster boat at an isolated dock down the coast, and sped through the Gulf of Maine until they met up with a fishing trawler in the middle of nowhere and were shoved down into its stinking hold.

The four of them had had their pockets emptied back at the office, and had been tied up like Christmas turkeys readied for roasting. Jason had a swollen cheek and a black eye from when he'd gone after the guy called Mike, when Mike had made Jane's knots too tight and she had hissed in pain.

Other than that, both Jason and Duncan were so damnably calm, it was starting to grate on Willow's nerves. They couldn't possibly believe they wouldn't be killed, despite Edward's repeated assurances. The only probable motive for going through so much trouble to take them so far out to sea was so they could be dumped overboard and their bodies never found.

Just like Gramps.

Graham probably figured it had worked once, he might as well do it again. Besides, he had seemed in a rush to get them off Kingston Corporation property as well as away from Edward.

Edward Simmons, despite his actions to the contrary, did not have the disposition to be a career criminal. The guy was way too nervous and he talked too much, especially when Willow subtly plied him with questions couched in the form of a discussion on obvious loopholes in the laws.

She got Edward to explain how they had used five different islands over the years to stash their contraband, and it was only bad luck that the quarry had flooded last winter, otherwise no one ever would have known about their harmless operation. Yes, Edward was still maintaining the illusion that no one was being harmed. He'd also let it slip, while he'd nervously watched Mike tie Willow's hands in front of her in deference to her splinted right wrist, that pesticides weren't the only commodity with an overseas market.

That was when Graham had lost his patience and gotten them hustled out of the office, sending them on the harrowing journey that had ended in this cold, damp, smelly hold.

"How are ya doing, lass?" Duncan asked through the darkness from someplace off to her right. This was the first time they'd been left alone and were able to talk, though they were competing with the noise of the droning diesel engine. "Did they tie the rope on your cracked wrist too tight?"

"No," Willow said, wiggling her hand inside the

splint. At least they had bound her hands together in front of her, but then Mike had run the rope around her waist so she couldn't use her teeth to untie the knots.

"Can ya slip out of the splint, Willow," Duncan asked, "and get yourself free?"

Finally, they were going to take some sort of action to save themselves. "It's about time you came up with a plan," she snapped, wiggling her fingers to peel back the Velcro closures. "You *do* have a plan, don't you, Dunky?"

His soft chuckle echoed through the darkness. "Aye. I'm calling it plan B, since ya went and got yourself caught and blew our plan A."

"We were almost home free," she growled, ignoring the pain as she slowly wiggled her hand out of the splint. "We had them convinced Jane and I were lovers out parking on a moonlit night. But then your stupid cell phone started vibrating, and the guy named Stokes heard it. What's plan B?"

A loud masculine snort came from someplace off to her left. "Lovers?" Jason echoed, only to suddenly grunt when it sounded to Willow as if Jane had kicked him with her bound feet.

"It was an excellent ruse," Willow continued. "It caught them totally off guard, and when I threatened to sue them for bruising my girlfriend's ribs, they were helping us leave as fast as we could. My hands are free," she said, giving a soft cry as her hand slipped out of the splint with one final, painful tug. "Does plan B involve kicking and biting and scratching? Because I'm game for that," she said, twisting her right arm around to reach the knot at the back of her waist. "Don't you keep a knife in your boot or something, Dunky? Or does your belt buckle turn into some sort of lethal weapon?"

There was another soft chuckle from her right. "Nay, lass. I have only my bare hands."

She stopped struggling with the knot, panting with the pain of working fingers that hadn't moved for nearly a week. "What kind of hero are you? You need to carry backup, Dunky."

"Hands can be lethal weapons, counselor," he said in an even, deadly tone. "And they also have the advantage of being silent."

Willow felt a chill run through her, knowing firsthand that Duncan wasn't boasting. She remembered when he had come into the house where the guy had been holding her two years ago. Duncan hadn't had a weapon then, either, that she had seen. Only his bare hands. And her jailer had silently crumpled to the floor before he'd even known Duncan was there.

"How are those knots coming?" Duncan asked, his tone now decidedly gentle.

And calm. He was so damnably calm, they might as well have been on a Caribbean cruise. Willow held on to her patience and went back to work on the knots, trusting that the calmer Duncan seemed, the better off they were. "I'm almost free," she told him.

"As soon as ya are, put your splint back on before ya crawl over and untie me. I don't want ya to finish breaking your wrist. Ya might need both hands for the swim home."

She stopped again, blinking in his direction through the darkness, trying to decide if he was kidding or not. Jane squeaked in horror.

"It's okay," Jason said, his voice sounding as if he were straining against something. "My belt buckle is really a homing device. And my secret decoder ring just got a message that help is on the way." He suddenly grunted again. "Will you cut that out," he growled at Jane when she apparently kicked him again. "I'm trying to explain that plan B is already up and running."

"I'm free," Willow said, reaching down and untying her ankles.

"Put the splint back on," Duncan reminded her. "And watch out for those barrels when ya crawl over here. I think one of them is leaking, and it smells foul."

"Actually, it smells like solvent," Jane said.

Willow snorted. "Graham never wanted to run a site to dispose of waste, he wanted a steady supply of chemicals that he could market around the world," she muttered, feeling her way over to Duncan. "Say something nice and sweet to me, Dunky, so I know where you are."

"Have I mentioned how impressed I am with your composure?"

"My composure? Nothing about my cute butt? Or my lovely breasts?"

"I'm impressed with *your* lovely breasts," she heard Jason tell Jane. She also heard him grunt again.

"So what is plan B?" Willow asked, groping her way past the barrels, wondering why Jason and Jane got to be near each other but they had put Duncan clear across the hold.

"Plan B is Kee and Luke and Camden," Duncan told her.

Willow stopped crawling. "Kee is home with Rachel, making sure she doesn't worry herself sick."

"Aye, that was your suggestion," Duncan said with a soft laugh. "Kee didn't care for it, though. He and Luke actually came to the waste site from the other direction to cover our backs. Camden and Ahab were standing by with your friends Ray Cobb and Frank Porter at Cobb's boat at the Trunk Harbor pier."

While all the womenfolk stayed home and worried themselves sick, Willow thought. She started crawling again, only to finally bump into Duncan's legs. "They're all part of this?" she asked in amazement, working on the knots around his ankles. "Ray and Frank, too?"

"We needed someone with a fast boat for a little insurance, just in case we ended up at sea. Cobb was more than willing to get involved, and Porter wasn't about to be left out. He told Luke he had a score to settle with whoever scuttled his boat."

Willow got Duncan's ankles untied and pushed on his hip to get him to turn so she could untie his hands.

"I'm free," Jason suddenly said.

"How?" Jane asked.

"Unlike my foolish partner, I always carry a knife in the heel of my boot," he told her. Willow heard a loud smacking sound, somewhat like a wet kiss on a cheek. "Am I your hero, Einstein?" he asked.

Jane made a noise, and Willow couldn't decide if she had snorted or muttered an expletive. "We might be untied, but we're still on a boat at sea with several armed men," Jane pointed out. "And it's a big ocean. I don't care how fast Ray's boat is, they won't have a snowball's chance in Hades of finding us."

"Ah, but you're forgetting my belt buckle. It really *is* a transponder," Jason said. Willow could tell by the sound of his voice that he was untying Jane. "Kee's been tracking us since the waste site," Jason continued. "He and

Luke likely left for Trunk Harbor just as soon as they heard Graham ask if we got seasick. Did I mention my watch is also a wireless mike?"

Duncan stood up the moment Willow pulled the last knot free. He hauled her to her feet beside him, his arm around her and his other hand lifting her chin through the darkness. "Did ya hurt yar wrist again?" he asked, his lips inches from hers. "I'm sorry I got ya into this mess, lass."

"I'm not. I'd rather be here with you than sitting at home worried sick," she whispered back, stretching up and kissing him softly on the mouth, being much quieter than Jason had been. "Now what?"

"Now we wait for the navy to arrive, and be ready to help them any way we can."

"I don't suppose you have a light in your other shoe, do you, 007?" Jane asked.

There was the sound of rustling, then suddenly the interior of the hold lit with the dim glow of a disposable lighter.

"Oh," Jane said, reaching up and cupping Jason's face, turning his head to see his left eye. "You poor baby. That coward sucker-punched you while your hands were tied."

"But he was limping when he put us in the truck," Jason pointed out, his eyes—even the bloodshot one—dancing in the faint light as he looked down at Jane.

"Bring the light over here," Duncan instructed. "See if ya can read what's in these barrels."

Both Jane and Jason walked over, and the four of them crouched down by one of the barrels. "It's industrial cleaning fluid," Jane said, reading the label. "And this is fertilizer," she added, moving Jason's hand to a crate beside it. "My God, they've got them stacked almost touching each other. If they were to mix, the toxic fumes could be deadly. And volatile. They could blow this boat into oblivion."

The two men straightened and started exploring their prison, Jason lifting his tiny lighter up in front of them. Willow could see that the hold was nearly as big as Duncan's kitchen, and was half filled with barrels and crates.

"They've got a chemical cocktail down here that's just waiting to reek havoc," Jane said, scooting over to the other side, away from the cargo, dragging Willow with her and sitting down. "Don't these guys realize that if they get into rough seas and some of this spills, they won't be collecting whatever money Graham is paying them?"

"Apparently, they don't care," Willow said, rubbing the fingers on her sore hand. "I'm sorry I got you involved in this mess, Jane," she added, repeating Duncan's earlier words.

Jane threw her arm over Willow's shoulder. "This is my old playground, too. And Gramps was my friend. And we're not in a mess, we're on an adventure. Jason and Duncan will take care of us."

Willow shook her head, staring down at her hand. "They're not supermen. Luke was nearly killed two years ago trying to save Rachel and me from being kidnapped."

"I remember your telling me the story. And Luke Skywalker is right back at it, isn't he, doing the exact same thing," Jane pointed out.

Willow couldn't stifle a smile. "That can't possibly be his real name," she said, looking over at Jane, though it was too dark to really see her. "Duncan told me Luke grew up on the streets of New York. He must have picked that name as a joke."

"And then used it to register his truck?" Jane said, chuckling. "Jason, what's Luke's last name?" she asked loudly, as the men had wandered all the way down to the narrow bow.

Jason turned, then cursed. The lighter went out, suddenly plunging them back into absolute darkness. "Damn that gets hot," he muttered. "It's Skywalker. Why?"

"But what's his real name?" Willow asked.

"Skywalker," Duncan confirmed. "Why?"

"You, ah, don't see anything . . . odd about that?"

The incessant drone of the diesel engine suddenly eased to an idle, and the momentum of the trawler noticeably slowed. Footsteps scurried overhead. With his lighter glowing again, Jason walked back and sat down beside Jane, and Duncan came over, took Willow's hand, and led her back to where she'd been sitting.

"Make it look like ya're still tied up," he whispered, the noisy engine no longer protecting their conversation.

He then disappeared behind the barrels, and Willow found the rope and twined it back around her ankles and then her wrists. A deafening noise suddenly sounded, making the entire boat shudder.

"They've dropped anchor," Jason said. "And we're not in very deep water, since it couldn't have dropped more than a couple hundred feet."

The engine revved again and the trawler started backing up. Willow realized they were setting the anchor, which meant they were planning on being here for a while. "Do you suppose they have another pickup to make?" she asked, just loud enough to be heard over the laboring engine as it tried to drag the anchor.

"What can we do with these chemicals, Einstein?"

Jason asked. "Can we start a fire or make some smoke to create a distraction?"

"Sure, if we don't mind blowing ourselves up," Jane shot back. "Or choking to death. They're toxic."

"Combined," Jason reminded her. "But what about alone? What can we do with them individually?"

Jane was silent for several heartbeats. "Well, the cleaning fluid is highly combustible. You could soak your shirt in it, light it, and throw it up on deck. You know, like one of those Molotov cocktails, only without the bottle."

Willow heard another loud smacking sound. "What do you think, Duncan?" Jason asked, ignoring Jane's hissed warning to quit kissing her like that. "Do we burn their boat just like they did Gramps's, and swim to the island?"

"That's assuming we're by an island and not pulled up near a large cargo ship," Duncan returned.

Willow wasn't caring for Jason's plan, and decided she should probably let him know that. "The water temperature is barely fifty degrees," she reminded him. "I'm all for doing something, but couldn't we adjust the plan to sneak off in a raft instead of swim?"

"Or we could wait for Ray and Frank and your friends," Jane suggested.

But Willow could hear Jason already trying to open one of the barrels of cleaning fluid. "I'll just soak my shirt for a bit of insurance. Whew, that smells strong."

"You're going to burn your hands," Jane scolded. "Just dip a corner in it, then wrap the soaked corner inside the rest of the shirt. Try not to touch the fluid."

The overhead doors suddenly opened toward the back

of the boat, flooding the hold with light, and Willow realized it was already after sunrise. Jason quickly scrambled back and sat down, rolling his shirt into a ball and tucking his hands behind his back as if they were tied.

The guys Graham had referred to as Joe and Mike climbed down into the hold. Mike the jerk really was limping from where Jason had lashed out and kicked him in the office. "End of the line, folks," he said, walking past Willow toward Duncan. "Time for you to join that crazy old codger who followed this trawler two days ago."

Willow couldn't help herself. "You bastard," she snarled, stretching her legs out and tripping the jerk, sending him careening face-first into one of the barrels. "He was a defenseless old man!"

"He wasn't defenseless when we boarded his boat," Joe said, kicking her feet back out of the way. "The bastard had a shotgun and put up one hell of a fight."

Willow couldn't imagine why a lobsterman carried a shotgun. "I hope he gut-shot some of you," she hissed.

Joe looked down at her with narrowed eyes. "You're a bloodthirsty thing, ain't you?" he muttered, stepping around her to help Mike back to his feet.

Jason and Duncan suddenly exploded into action. Jason wrapped his shirt around Joe's face, tying it off before the man could do more than yelp, then followed through with a powerful punch to Joe's unguarded belly. At the same time, Duncan went after Mike in a blur of motion, kicking him in his already sore knee, then following through with an uppercut to Mike's jaw that hit so hard Willow was sure she heard something break. She only hoped it was the jerk's face and not Duncan's knuckles.

"Come on," Duncan said, standing Willow on her feet

and pulling her toward the bow of the boat. She looked behind her in bewildered awe at Mike and Joe, both lying motionless on the floor. A bare-chested Jason dragged Jane to her feet, but stopped and undid his shirt from around Joe's face. "Why are we going to the front?" Willow asked, finally giving her attention back to Duncan.

"There's a hatch in the bow we can climb through," he said, stopping at the narrow ladder. "It's slimy, so be careful. Can ya climb with yar splint?"

"I'll make it," she assured him, grabbing a rung, only to recoil at the feel of fish slime.

"Nay, I go first," Duncan said, moving her out of the way. "Jason next, then you. Jane, make sure she makes it up. Push her if ya have to."

"I'll make it," Willow muttered, watching Duncan climb the ladder until he could reach up and slowly twist the latch. He opened the tiny door just a crack and looked outside.

"Joe! Come on, man, you're wasting time!" someone hollered down through the aft cargo doors. "Captain says we got two hours to load, before we lose the tide. Joe! Mike!"

"Go," Jason said to Jane and Willow as he rushed back to the main part of the hold. He grabbed one of the stacked crates and pulled it down so that it smashed on the floor. It broke open on impact, pluming the powered fertilizer into a noxious cloud that filled the hold, dusted Joe and Mike, and obscured Jason. "There's been an accident down here!" Jason hollered toward the aft hatch. "One of the crates fell!"

That said, he turned and ran forward to Jane and Willow. "Get up the ladder," he growled, grabbing Willow by the waist and lifting her up past several rungs.

Duncan was already topside, and he reached down and took hold of Willow's good hand the moment she reached the top. He pulled her out and immediately pushed her toward the large winch that held the anchor line, shoving her down behind it. "Stay put," he said, looking around and then going back to the hatch.

He pulled Jane out and pushed her toward Willow, then started creeping to the wheelhouse, crouched low and watching toward the rear of the boat. Willow could see four men, all shouting, as two of them scrambled down into the belly of the boat, past the softly billowing white dust.

Jason still hadn't emerged from the hold yet.

"Einstein!" he called from below.

Jane and Willow ran over and peered down the small hatch.

"Are we by an island?" he asked, looking up through the white haze he'd created. "How far away?"

Jane looked starboard, then back down at him. "Maybe two hundred fifty, three hundred yards," she told him.

He suddenly grinned up at her. "Get ready to jump."

"No!" Jane shouted as he disappeared back into the cloud.

Duncan pulled them both away from the hatch. "It's now or never, ladies," he said, dragging them toward the rail of the boat. He shoved a life vest into Jane's hands. "I only found one. Share it."

"This is suicide," Jane told him. "They'll come to the island and kill us there."

"They'll be too busy saving their own necks," he said. "Wait for us. We jump together."

A sudden, violent *whoosh!* came from the back of the boat. The shouting stopped for the merest of seconds, then suddenly started again with a new sense of urgency as flames shot out of the back cargo hold.

Jason still hadn't appeared.

"Look. It's *The Corncobb Lady!*" Jane shouted, pointing off the port stern. "They're coming for us!"

Willow looked at where she was pointing and almost wept in relief. The beautiful lobster boat was plowing through the water at full throttle, close enough now that she could see Kee and Luke and Camden leaning past the wheelhouse on one side and Frank Porter and Ahab standing toward the back of the boat, doing something with what looked like a life raft capsule.

"We have to jump now," Duncan said, suddenly right beside her. "This tub is going to blow."

"But Jason."

"I'm here!" he said, running to join them, having to snag Jane on the way by, because she had been shouting down the hatch for him to hurry up. "I had to wait until they hauled Mike and Joe topside before I started the fire toward the back." His grin slashed white inside his blackened face. "You were right, Einstein. It's highly combustible."

Willow noticed Jason was missing part of one eyebrow, and one side of his hair was considerably shorter than the other. Jane punched him in the arm. "You idiot," she snapped.

In response, Jason swept Jane into his arms, walked to the side of the boat, and threw her off—grinning down until her shout of outrage ended abruptly with a splash. Then he very gallantly jumped in after her.

Willow looked to the stern and saw the crew suddenly realize they should probably abandon ship as well. She looked back at *The Corncobb Lady* just in time to see Frank and Ahab toss the raft capsule overboard as they neared the furiously swimming crew. Ray cut the throttle and came to an idle, the momentum carrying them closer to Jane and Jason.

There was a muted explosion below that shuddered the boat.

"Are ya thinking that if ya wait long enough, the water will warm up?" Duncan asked, nudging Willow to the rail. "We need to go now, counselor."

"I—I haven't been in the water since my kayak was rammed two years ago."

"Ah, lass. It's just like riding a bike," he said, lifting her legs over the side so that she was perched on the railing. She clung to it in a death grip and stared down into the water. "I promise not to push ya off," he said, climbing over the rail until he was perched beside her. "But ya must take a leap of faith with me, lass, and trust I'll be right here beside ya. Tuck yar splint up to yar chest and protect it with yar good hand. On three, we jump together, okay?"

She could feel the heat of the fire at her back, the stormy inferno roaring acrid smoke around them as she watched Jane and Jason being pulled aboard *The Corncobb Lady*. She looked over at Duncan and smiled. "I'll jump with you, Dunky. All the way. Forever."

He stared at her for several heartbeats, apparently trying to assess her sudden smile, then nodded and started counting. "One. Two. Three!"

Without hesitation, Willow pushed off, clutching her hand to her chest and screaming curses the whole way down.

Even though she knew it was going to be cold, the shock of hitting the frigid water felt like a million tiny needles piercing her skin. She sank farther than she was expecting to, but strong hands grabbed her waist and pushed her back up. She broke the surface with another scream, this one directed at the sea itself.

Duncan surfaced with her, laughing through his own shout of shock. He took hold of her good hand and started towing her toward *The Corncobb Lady*. "Just turn on yar back and kick," he instructed. "And keep cursing so I know ya're still breathing."

There was a sudden, violent explosion deep in the belly of the trawler. Duncan dove, pulling Willow with him to avoid the initial percussion. They surfaced seconds later, and he turned her toward him. "Again," he said as the billowing fireball rose above them. "Ya have to stay under the whole time the debris falls. Understand?" he shouted over the roaring inferno, taking a deep breath and pulling her down before she had time barely to fill her own lungs, much less answer him.

Hot twisted metal, some of the chunks the size of furniture, bombarded the water just over their heads, sizzling on impact and sounding like muted cannons going off around them. Duncan pulled her deeper, until Willow thought her eardrums would burst. She clawed and twisted toward the surface, but he wrapped his arms tightly around her and held her utterly still, clinging to her like a second leaden skin.

The man seemed determined to save her life, so Willow decided she should probably let him. She stopped struggling, and together they slowly sank into the cold depths, the firestorm of deadly missiles continuing to rain over their heads and around them.

The barrage finally subsided, and Duncan kicked furiously, jetting them upward until they broke the surface, this time with Willow directing her sputtering curses at him.

And again he laughed as he filled his lungs with air. "Aye, ya can't be too drowned if ya can still cuss like a sailor," he said as he continued pulling her toward *The Corncobb Lady*.

Frank and Ahab were furiously putting out tiny fires from the fallen debris. Kee and Luke were reaching over the side, waiting to pull them aboard, and Camden was wrapping a half-naked Jane in his coat, then taking off his sweater and giving it to Jason. Willow's teeth were chattering hard enough to crack by the time they reached the boat. Kee stretched down to take hold of her under the arms, and Duncan lifted her out of the water to him. Luke caught her thighs and finished pulling her over the side. Willow plopped down on the deck like a beached whale, gasping for breath while cussing at Jason at the same time.

But Jane beat her to it. "Did the fumes rot your brain?" Jane shouted at Jason, her chattering ruining her anger. "Why in hell did you ignite that cargo?"

"To create a diversion," Jason said, turning to smile at Duncan as he came over the side and fell beside Willow. Jason leaned over and wrapped his arm around Jane. "We decided we needed something big enough to panic the crew and create lots of chaos. And we decided we'd rather deal with flames than dodge bullets." He then gave Jane a big, noisy kiss on her pale white forehead, quickly capturing her hand when she took a swing at his midsection. "It worked, Einstein. I didn't hear one gunshot."

"Only because the explosion deafened us," she growled back, tugging her hand free. "You came close to killing us."

"Close only counts in horseshoes and hand grenades," he said, turning her until her face was buried in his chest. He covered her head with his broad hand and cuddled her shivering body close, his lips moving across her wet hair. "You did good, Einstein. You can cover my back anytime."

Willow turned away from watching them, only to find Duncan had already stripped down to his boxer shorts and was putting on Kee's jacket. "Strip off, counselor," he said, taking the blanket Kee handed him and coming over to her. "You'll warm up as soon as ya get out of those wet clothes."

Ray was idling *The Corncobb Lady* away from the burning wreckage while carefully dodging floating debris. Willow pulled off her own sweater, and Duncan held up the blanket to give her privacy while she finished stripping down to her bra and panties. He then wrapped her up in the blanket, sat down, and cuddled her on his lap.

"Hey, wait!" Frank shouted from the bow. "What's that?"

Everyone looked in the direction Frank was pointing. Willow saw the island, but nothing else.

"There, on the beach," Frank said. "Ray, hand me the binoculars."

Ray took the boat out of gear, found the binoculars on the shelf by the wheel, handed them to Camden, who then handed them to Frank over the roof of the wheel-house. Frank stood with his feet spread for balance on the front bow and focused the glasses on the island. "My God," Frank shouted. "It's Gramps!"

"What?" Willow said with a gasp, scrambling off Duncan's lap. "Are you sure?"

"The old bastard's waving at us," Frank said, his voice choked with emotion. "It's Cecil. He's alive!"

Ray turned the wheel, heading *The Corncobb Lady* toward the island, sounding his horn to let Gramps know they'd spotted him. Frank climbed down to the deck, handed the binoculars back to Camden, and came over and hugged Willow. "He's alive," he whispered, reaching out to include Jane in his hug when she ran over. "That crazy old bastard is alive."

Willow couldn't bring herself to point out to Frank that he was only maybe seven or eight years younger than Gramps.

Frank turned to Ray, still keeping his arms around Willow and Jane, who were both busy keeping their blankets around themselves. "This is Pink Rock Island. There's a steep-sloping bank of gravel on the east side where you can beach her," he told Ray. "Just watch out for the ledge on the right."

Ray throttled forward and headed alongside the small pink granite island covered with pines. Willow looked back at the burning trawler, wondering if everyone else got off the boat okay. "What happened to the crew?" she asked, ducking out from under Frank's arm and going over to Duncan. "Are they swimming to the island?"

"Nay, they're in the life raft Frank threw them," he said, pointing about three hundred yards past the trawler.

Willow could see the fluorescent orange life raft bobbing on the waves, part of it singed black and another part half deflated, obviously burned by the debris. She could also see several men with their arms hanging over the side, furiously paddling toward the island.

They weren't making much headway against the outgoing tide.

"We contacted the Coast Guard when we left Trunk Harbor," Kee said, also watching the raft. "We'll call them again and explain what happened. They can pick up the trawler crew." He turned back and watched Gramps making his way along the shore to where they were going to beach the boat. "Maybe we'll let them drift a day or two before we let the Coast Guard know their exact location. We'll see what Gramps thinks of that idea."

"Ah . . . how come they didn't just let him go down with his boat?" Willow asked in a whisper. "Wouldn't he have been a witness?"

Duncan held her close. "Murderers are a different breed from common criminals, counselor. And murder by committee is a hard thing to get a unanimous vote on, especially if there's an alternative. Simmons said he was only trying to buy a few more days, until he could sign those papers of sale." He shrugged, shrugging her with him. "It was easier to just stash Gramps on the island and call in his location later."

"A gang of crooks with a conscience?" Willow asked, smiling up at Duncan.

"Aye," he said, kissing the tip of her still shivering

nose. "Thank ya for trusting me enough to jump. And for not fighting me underwater."

She turned inside his embrace, wrapped her arms around his waist, and kissed his sweater right over his heart. She looked up with another brilliant smile. "Thank you for trusting me to trust you," she told him back, squeezing him tightly when he gave her a confused look. "How come you gave Ben Zane your blessing to court Molly?"

If possible, Duncan looked even more confounded. "What brought this up?" he asked.

Willow shrugged. "Oh, I don't know. Just something that's been bugging me. We left right after you gave Ben your blessing with Molly. How come you did that?"

"Because he came all this way with the best of intentions, and he deserves the right to try courting a lass he thinks he might fancy. He's obviously too young for Molly; she'll have him wrapped around her little finger within a month. But then, I'd give my blessing to anyone brave enough to saddle themselves with my sister. I gave it to Luke, too."

"You what?"

Duncan nodded. "He asked just before Mother arrived if I would mind if he fell in love with my sister."

The boat jerked to a sudden stop, and Duncan held Willow steady as Frank powered *The Corncobb Lady* onto the gravel bar in the tiny cove of the small island, Ray having given over the wheel to the man of experience.

"Jumped-up Jehosaphat! I was afraid you'd think I was one of them and drive off without me," Gramps said, scrambling over the last boulder and all but tripping onto the narrow beach. "Am I glad to see you!"

Ray ran across the bow and jumped down to the beach, running up to meet Gramps, catching him in a big hug when the old man stumbled. Frank was right behind Ray, but Duncan held Willow back from following them.

"You're not dressed for going ashore, counselor. You can hug him all the way home."

She was jumping in place, she was so excited, watching as Frank and Ray lifted Gramps up to Luke and Camden. Within seconds, the huge deck of *The Corncobb Lady* looked like a Grange social, what with Jane and Willow dancing around for their turns to hug him. By the time they were done, Gramps's dirty old shirt was wet with their tears, and his dirty old face was grinning from ear to ear.

"They said they was taking me with them to Central America," Gramps finally said, once he was done wiping his own misting eyes. "They sunk my boat. Made me watch while she burned." He looked over at the still blazing trawler and shook his head. "I still don't consider us even. That ugly old tub should have been scrapped years ago, while my *Pretty Woman* was one of a kind."

"We'll help you replace her, Gramps," Willow vowed. "We promise—even if we have to have a fund-raiser."

He looked over at her in surprise. "I'm old, girl, not foolish. I had her insured for full retail value. She was my retirement fund."

Willow blushed, only to realize the warmth felt good on her cheeks. "We have to call Mildred," she rushed to say, urging Gramps toward the radio. "Right now. She thinks you're dead."

Jane and Willow started bawling again the moment Mildred's tear-soaked voice crackled over the radio as she whispered her disbelief. And they smiled through their tears when she shouted in relief and then started scolding her husband of forty-two years for scaring her that way.

Ray gave the wheel of *The Corncobb Lady* to Frank again, to get them off the gravel beach and back into deep water. Willow and Jane and Duncan and Jason snuggled together in the tiny wheelhouse, covered to their ears with whatever clothing each man could spare, and rode home in tired, contemplative silence.

Willow used the time to formulate her own plan, and decided she was calling it plan LOF.

Chapter Twenty

By the time they pulled into Trunk Harbor, it looked like the entire town and most of Puffin Harbor was standing on the pier and overflowing into the parking lot. There were lights flashing, and Willow realized a fire truck and an ambulance were standing by as well as a sheriff's car and a state police cruiser. She also would have bet there was a state detective's car hidden someplace in the crowd.

Willow could almost picture what had happened the moment Mildred Fox had gotten off the radio with her husband. Everyone who'd been sitting at the house with her would have gotten on their cell phones and into their cars and spread the joyous news. Trunk Harbor was welcoming back one of its own they'd prematurely given up for dead. It wasn't very often the sea gave back a soul, alive and well, that had been missing for three days.

Though obviously not surprised, having witnessed a

few homecomings over the years, Gramps was looking a bit overwhelmed by it all. Frank was having to steady the trembling old man as Ray nudged *The Corncobb Lady* against the pier. Eager hands helped Gramps onto terra firma as the crowd magically parted to reveal Mildred, who was weeping uncontrollably and holding her arms out to Cecil. The crowd closed back in, and Willow lost sight of the couple, though the tears filling her own eyes might have had something to do with it.

"Oh, Willy," Rachel cried, jumping into the boat and throwing herself at Willow. "I've never been so scared. I've been sitting by the radio all night." She shot a glare at her husband, then looked back at Willow. "All Kee would tell me is that you were taken out to sea and that Ray Cobb was helping him go get you guys. Then the call this morning saying he was on his way back with you, all safe and sound."

Willow hugged her tightly back. "I'm fine, Rae. Not a scratch. We're all fine, and we even found Gramps."

"Miss Foster, I'm afraid you're going to have to come with us," a man said from the pier.

Willow looked up to see two plainclothes detectives. Or rather she could see them before Duncan stepped in front of her.

"She needs to shower and dress first, and have something to eat," Duncan said.

Both detectives shook their heads. "Someone can bring her some clothes, but the only way she's leaving this pier is in our custody."

Willow grabbed the back of Duncan's jacket and tugged. "It's okay," she told him, stepping around to face him. "I might as well get this over with." She gave him a brilliant smile. "I know it's hard to go from being protective to passive, but I need you to trust that I can handle things from here. I'll speak with John and make sure everyone is rounded up."

"Ya've had a rough night, lass. Let me drive ya in this afternoon. Call your boss and explain things."

"I can't, Duncan. I have to go with them now. They're only doing their jobs, so don't force them to arrest you." She leaned up and gave him a kiss on his cheek. "I need you to drive Mabel home for me. You can stay at my apartment and come visit me in jail." She toyed with the button on his jacket. "Will you post my bail? I promise not to skip town on you."

He sighed hard enough to move her still damp hair. "Aye," he said, wrapping his arms around her and kissing the top of her head. "Ya won't disappear on me."

"I brought you and Jane some clothes," Rachel interjected, jumping back onto the pier, stopping only long enough to glare at the two detectives before she ran to her truck.

"Detective Plum, isn't it?" Willow asked, addressing the detective who had spoken. "I believe you worked on a case for me last year."

His cheeks tinging a deep red, Plum nodded and shifted his feet. "Look, I'm sorry, Miss Foster. I'm just following orders."

"I know," she said, stepping out of Duncan's arms and reaching out for the clothes Rachel handed her. She looked around at the massive audience, now all focused on the scene taking place aboard *The Corncobb Lady*. "I—ah—I'm just going to step into the wheelhouse and change," she told Officer Plum, turning and ducking into the tiny wheelhouse without waiting for his approval.

"Ya need to stop in Ellsworth and let them look at her wrist," she heard Duncan tell Plum. "She may have injured it again. And get her some breakfast."

"We can do that," she heard Plum say as she hooked several pieces of clothes over the windows.

Jane stepped inside with her, also holding clothes that Rachel had brought her. Rachel positioned herself as guard at the door.

"What do you want me to do?" Jane asked as they both started slipping into the warm, dry clothes. "How can I help?"

"Maybe you should continue to stick close to Jason," Willow suggested. "At least until we know everyone is rounded up. Then I'm going to need you as a witness."

"They—This isn't going to go to trial, is it?" Jane asked, sitting down to put on her socks and sneakers. "I mean your case with the overseas account. You can get out of that, can't you?"

"If Graham left any sort of paper trail to that account, I can. Or if Edward Simmons turns state's evidence for us, the charges against me, including the drunk-driving charge, will get dropped."

Willow finished tying her own sneakers, stood up, and faced her sister. "It's over, Rae," she told her. "Please try to stop worrying, okay?"

"No. I'm going to worry as long as you live and breathe," Rachel said with a smile, reaching out and pulling Willow into her arms again. "Even when you're living in the governor's mansion, and have tons of body guards."

"Ah . . . about that," Willow said, leaning away and

returning her smile. "Just as soon as this is over, you and I are going to sit down and have a nice little talk. 'Bye, Jane. Try not to kill Jason while I'm gone," she continued, pulling free of Rachel's embrace and stepping out of the wheelhouse.

Willow stopped in front of Ray and Frank. "Thank you, guys, for coming to our rescue. A Coast Guard cutter wouldn't have any more effective. You're both heros," she finished, giving each of them a kiss on their blushing cheeks.

She stopped in front of Kee, Luke, Camden, and Ahab next. "You guys are amazing. Thank you," she said simply, giving each of them a hug and kiss before turning to Duncan. "I'll call you at my apartment just as soon as I know what's happening." She stretched up while pulling down on his jacket, so she could whisper in his ear. "You've got really nice legs, Dunky. If we didn't have an audience, I'd show you just how much I like them."

That said, she gave him a quick kiss on the cheek and turned and held out her good hand to Detective Plum, so he could help her over the rail and onto the pier. But Duncan simply lifted her by the waist and set her down in front of Plum.

Willow turned back and pointed at Jason, who was also bare-legged. "I am not going on any adventures with you again, Jason. You might carry lots of neat stuff around, but you get a bit overzealous when it comes to foiling the bad guys."

Jason merely nodded, and threw his arm around Jane when she moved to stand beside him. "Ah, but Einstein here will come with me, won't ya?" he asked, finishing his declaration with a wet, noisy kiss on her forehead, and then a laugh when she punched him in the ribs.

Willow turned and walked between the two detectives; the crowd of onlookers, most of whom she knew, parting like the Red Sea, forming an aisle all the way into the parking lot. She stopped when she spotted Margaret and Molly standing beside Rachel's SUV. Molly was holding Nick in her arms, and Margaret had Mikaela by the hand. Mickey was sitting beside them, his tongue hanging out and his tail wagging.

"Can I please say good-bye to my niece and nephew?" she asked Detective Plum. "They've been so worried. I want them to see that I'm okay."

Plum nodded, and Willow walked over, kissed Nick on his sticky cheek, then crouched down and hugged Mikaela. "I've got to go back to Augusta for a few days. But then I'm coming back and I'm going to be your coach for the Crane Island Kayak Race."

"It's only two weeks away," Mikaela whispered, clinging to her in a tight hug. "And . . . and you haven't been kayaking for two years."

Willow leaned away so that Mikaela could see her smile. "Ah, but I'm going to start again. While waiting for me to get back, you put a couple coats of wax on your kayak and do lots of stretching exercises. Okay?"

Mikaela nodded and then hugged her so tightly again that they both squeaked. Willow finally stood up, nodded to Molly, and then said to Margaret, "Could I speak with you a moment?"

Willow nodded to the side, indicating that she wanted them to speak in private. Molly took hold of Mikaela's hand, and Margaret stepped to the front of the truck with Willow.

They spoke for quite a long time. Or rather Willow did most of the talking and Margaret mostly listened.

Her posture guarded and her face serious, Margaret finally nodded. "Very well, Miss . . . Willow. Willy. I will stay until the Fourth of July."

"Thank you, Maggie," Willow said, reaching out and giving her a big hug. "Thank you. It means a lot to me."

And so, with phase one of plan LOF already taken care of, Willow turned, smiled at the detectives, and motioned for them to lead the way to their car.

Chapter Twenty-one

✦

$\mathcal{T}$*wo weeks can seem like* forever if a person is waiting for their exciting and wonderful new life to begin. Then again, two weeks can zip by in a blur when a person is busy upsetting everyone else's lives in the process. Willow was experiencing both quirks of time as she cleaned up the remnants of her old life and painstakingly created her new one.

And yes, she was definitely upsetting a few people.

She started with Edward Simmons and Brent Graham. As she had suspected, Edward folded like a cheap suit when faced with a list of crimes that stretched from fraud to kidnapping. He quickly turned state's evidence and was instrumental not only in putting Brent Graham in prison for a very long time, but in clearing up Willow's little matter of being wrongly accused of accepting a pay-off for throwing a case. Willow's charges were dropped, Edward's charges were reduced considerably, and Brent

Graham would likely be celebrating his seventieth birthday behind bars. Any leftover waste still stashed on remote islands was being cleaned up, the Lobster Institute was monitoring the slowly returning health of the marine life around Thunder Island, and the crew from the fishing trawler were being deported back to whatever country they had snuck in from. Mike and Joe were sitting in jail, awaiting trial for running Willow off the road, sinking Frank Porter's boat, and putting sugar in Ray Cobb's gas tank.

Oh, and John Pike was in a rage.

John didn't care to learn he was losing his best (his word) assistant attorney general. But then Willow only added insult to injury when she told him she was taking her secretary with her to start her own private practice in Puffin Harbor.

Willow managed that feat by offering Karen complete autonomy in running the office, then sweetened the deal by promising a blank check for buying office computers. She also informed Karen that there were plenty of lonely, honorable, manly men down on the coast, and that most of them owned fast boats. She did not, however, mention that those boats usually cost more than their houses.

The only touchy matter to clean up in Augusta was Mabel. But what Willow had thought was going to be a hard sell turned out to be almost too easy. Willow had begun by claiming Mabel was like a mother to her, and that Mikaela and Nick could get used to having a grandmother around. Mabel had waved that away before Willow had even finished her prepared speech, claiming she hadn't realized the coast of Maine was such an exciting place to live. The octogenarian pointed out that there were plenty of women her age to hang out with, who surely knew a hundred different ways to cook lobster. The FOR SALE sign had gone up in front of Mabel's house within the first week, and she had already started packing. No, she didn't want to move in with Willow, though it was kind of her to offer, but preferred to get her own little apartment right in the middle of town—within walking distance of The Rosach Pub.

With all the loose ends in Augusta finally tied up, and a termination date for her job set for August 31, Willow was able to take her first breath of new-life air on July 3. She arrived at her sister's house with one day to spare before the annual Crane Island Kayak Race and the Fourth of July celebrations.

It wasn't really a party Rachel was having that Saturday afternoon, but more of a family reunion, what with Matt and Peter showing up unexpectedly late last night. What people didn't fit into Rachel's kitchen spilled over onto the porch and down across the lawn.

Willow was surprised to see that Ben Zane was still here. She was even more surprised to see that he didn't seem too brokenhearted over the fact that Molly Ross and Luke Skywalker appeared to be attached at the hip.

Margaret had stuck around as promised, but Camden had gone back to Scotland a week ago claiming he had a distillery to run. Ray Cobb showed up with Patty on his arm, and Frank and his wife also stopped by. Cecil and Mildred Fox were there, and Gramps announced to everyone that he was going into partnership with Ray Cobb, figuring someone had to show the young pup how to properly haul traps.

Ahab was sitting in the corner of the kitchen eating a

bowl half-filled with strawberries. The other half was filled with sugar. Nick was kneeling on a chair beside him, a spoon in his hand and pink sugar plastered all over his face, trying very hard to baby-talk Ahab into sharing. Mickey was sitting with his nose pressed up to the edge of the table, hoping Nick's penchant for making a mess might send some of the strawberries rolling his way. Willow had never stopped to think that wolves might like fruit.

Mikaela was running around in her neoprene wet suit and life vest, trying to talk Munky and Punky into taking her kayaking, explaining that she needed to practice for tomorrow's race and that everyone else was already practiced out.

"We're all set for tonight," Rachel whispered to Willow as they stood at the sink washing glasses. "Are you sure this is a good idea? It's not too late to back out. I can remodel it and we can set it someplace else."

Glancing at Duncan standing by the island counter, Willow whispered back, "I haven't changed my mind. You did a beautiful job. Thank you." She looked at her sister. "How did you manage to work on it without Kee finding out, and without Miss Big Mouth telling everyone?"

"I made it at Duncan's house. Margaret helped."

"At Duncan's?" Willow hissed in a whisper. "Are you crazy?"

Rachel waved that away. "He never goes in his workshop. It was the safest place for me to work without getting caught."

"Let's leave at midnight tonight, then," Willow said, glancing at Duncan again to make sure he was staying put. "You'll have to tell Kee that Nick is being fussy, and that he'll have to sleep with him tonight. Otherwise you won't be able to sneak out. And bring Mickey," Willow suggested, quickly drying her hand, setting it on Rachel's shoulder, and squeezing. "It'll be just like old times, just the two of us for our midnight run. No kids, no men."

"What's wrong with men?" Kee asked, stepping up to Rachel and putting his arm around her while he frowned at Willow. "We're very useful creatures."

"Aye," Duncan agreed, suddenly appearing beside Willow and putting his arm around her, also frowning. "We do all the heavy lifting."

"And you do it very well," Willow assured him, patting his chest with her once again soapy hand. "Thank you for picking up my new kayak in Ellsworth. I can't wait to try it tomorrow."

Duncan gave her a skeptical look. "Entering a race when ya've not paddled in two years is not the best idea you've had lately."

"I've been working out at an Augusta gym every evening for the last two weeks," Willow reminded him. "And paddling is like riding a bike. I'm going to reclaim my title tomorrow."

"Not without a fight," Jane said, sauntering over with Jason's arm wrapped around her shoulders.

"What is it with you guys?" Willow asked with a laugh, lifting a brow at Kee and Duncan and Jason, then nodding toward Luke across the room, who also had his arm draped around Molly. "Can't you stand up without a woman to lean on?"

"Ya're not holding us up, counselor," Duncan responded with a chuckle. "We're holding ya down, so ya can't wander off and get into trouble."

Willow snorted. "Like we're the problem," she said, rolling her eyes. She peeled Duncan off her and shooed him away, then shooed the other men after him. "Go away. We ladies are having a chat. Go save Ahab from Margaret. She's flirting with him again."

Duncan groaned, his gaze darting to the table, where he saw Margaret sitting beside Ahab and sliding another bowl of strawberries in front of him. Nick was now sitting on her lap, popping one of the plump strawberries in his mouth and wiping his sticky hand on Margaret's shirt-sleeve. The duchess didn't seem to notice. In fact, she didn't seem to notice much of anything other than Ahab.

"Will you tell me what she sees in that old goat?" Duncan muttered, looking back to glare at Willow. "This is your fault. She told me you asked her to stay until after the Fourth." He lowered his brows. "She won't tell me why, though. What are ya two concocting?"

Willow gave him an innocent smile. "Why, nothing, Dunky. I just wanted to get acquainted with your mom, that's all."

He obviously didn't believe her, but he obviously felt it more important to pull his mother away from Ahab than to argue. Duncan, Kee, and Jason, forming a wall of masculine support, rushed to Ahab's rescue.

Rachel covered her mouth to stifle a giggle. "And Duncan always thought his mother was a stuffed shirt. She's certainly been proving him wrong these last two weeks."

"He couldn't even stay in Augusta two nights with me," Willow said with a sigh. "Because he had to get back here and babysit his sister and mother, he told me, before they both ran off and got married."

"What about Ben Zane?" Willow asked Rachel. "How come he's still here, and how come he's not courting Molly?"

Rachel smiled and shook her head. "Luke, that devious devil, convinced Ben that he was too young to be thinking about settling down with a wife. He told Ben that Matt and Peter were looking for a new partner in their salvage business, and that a bright young man like him should be out seeing the world and going on adventures."

"And Ben actually bought that line?"

Rachel nodded. "Not only did he buy it, he's been waiting around to meet Matt and Peter. Apparently, coming here was the first time he'd ever traveled outside his hometown. And now he's decided there's a lot more to life than dipping sheep and getting kicked in the shins by cattle."

"What about his ranch?" Willow asked.

"He talked with his brother, James, back in New Zealand, and apparently James is already married and has two kids, and is more than happy to take over Ben's share of the ranch. James told Ben to go for it."

Willow looked out the kitchen window at Ben Zane, seeing him deep into conversation with Matt and Peter. The young man's face was shining with excitement. "Good," Willow said with a nod. "I think it's a great idea."

"That's not the only news," Rachel said, drawing Willow's attention again. "Luke is moving to Scotland. He and Molly are going to manage the Rosach Distillery."

"But what about Camden?"

"Camden's going to open a new distillery here in

Maine. It seems Duncan and Camden have been talking about it for the last six months. There's a problem with the spring that supplies the water to the distillery over in Scotland. It's drying up. Camden thinks there's only enough water left to produce a smaller, more specialized line of Scotch."

"But it won't be 'Scotch' if it's distilled here," Willow pointed out.

Rachel shrugged. "I'm just telling you what Kee told me that Duncan told him. I guess it will be *whiskey*, spelled with an *e*, and that Camden will try to market it as 'brewed in the tradition of Scotch whisky,' but with the distinctive flavor of Maine peat. We do have plenty of peat bogs here," Rachel pointed out. "And pristine water. And the farmers up north can grow barley if Camden sets up contracts with them. And Kee said Duncan told him this is the perfect climate. Maine has all the ingredients for a master distillery, and Camden has the old family recipe that he wants to try adapting. He's tying up loose ends in Scotland, and is due to come here this fall and look for some land to buy."

"Wow!" was all Willow could say.

"Ah, I have some news," Jane said softly, her cheeks tinging pink when both Rachel and Willow looked over at her expectantly. "Jason got a job at the University of Maine," she told them. "He's going to be working in the computer labs."

"Jason in a desk job?" Willow asked in disbelief.

"He's going to be in charge of field research computers," Jane said. "He'll be going to research sites and making sure the programs work for the type of data that needs to be input."

"You mean, like when a marine biologist has to collect data in the field, or, should I say, in the ocean?" Willow asked, raising one brow.

Jane's cheeks darkened even more. "Our labs requested the computer department to supply us with a data input specialist several months ago, long before I ever met Jason. He'll also be going to archaeological digs and forestry management sites."

Willow held up her hands in supplication. "Hey, I wasn't implying anything." She gave Jane a brilliant smile, darted a quick look around, and then hauled both Jane and Rachel into the living room and up the stairs to her old bedroom. "Now, about my little plan for when we attend tomorrow's celebration in the town square," she said, closing the door behind them. "Are we all on the same page?"

Jane nodded, though she looked uncertain.

Rachel also nodded, but she looked utterly worried. "This could backfire on you, Willy," Rachel whispered. "You could actually start a town riot."

"Or be publicly stoned with rotten fruit," Jane interjected.

"Or," Willow said, throwing her arms out and flopping back on her bed, smiling up at the ceiling. "I just might get elected mayor of Puffin Harbor."

Both Rachel and Jane broke into peals of laughter at that unlikely prophecy.

Chapter Twenty-two

❖

Willow did not reclaim her Crane Island Kayak Race title, but she did have a respectable sixth-place showing in a field of seven. The number seven guy, though, had been seventy-three years old, and Willow had been beat by three women in their fifties and a fourteen-year-old boy. Jane did indeed claim first place, but then, she'd been white-water kayaking all spring, and had the muscles to prove it.

Willow just knew she was going to pay for today's herculean effort for at least the next week. Every muscle in her body ached, but it was nothing compared to what she knew she'd feel tomorrow morning when she tried to get out of bed.

She was sleeping in her old room at Rachel and Kee's house, because Duncan just couldn't bring himself to let her sleep with him—not with his mother still in residence. Willow had told him they were going to have to practice doing it quietly some more, but she admired his respect for his mother's sensibilities.

Molly, however, didn't seem as concerned, and was spending her nights at Luke Skywalker's not-so-lovely house, which showed that Lady Molly Ross was adaptable. Either that or love really was blind.

Just about everyone from Puffin Harbor was gathered in the town square for the evening festivities, spending their time waiting for the fireworks to start by consuming plenty of lobster rolls, french fries, and cotton candy. There was a band playing on the flatbed of a tractor-trailer truck set up at one end of the park, and game booths set up at the other end, including a dunking tank with Deputy Sheriff Larry Jenkins as the latest victim.

Mikaela had come in a respectable third in the peewee race, just beating out Jane's niece by inches. Now the seven-year-old was walking with Margaret through the crowd, proud as all get-out, still wearing her red ribbon around her neck and eating a cone of cotton candy that was bigger than her head. Margaret was pushing Nick in his stroller, and Nick had a bowl of french fries in his lap, dropping more of the fries on the ground than he was getting in his mouth. Mickey was following closely, apparently ready to clean up any and all food spills. Willow was just now realizing that Mickey and Nick were a perfect match for each other.

Kee and Rachel and Duncan and Willow were strolling through the crowd while discussing this afternoon's lobster boat races. *The Corncobb Lady* had placed first in show and first in the five-mile race. Gramps was going around claiming they'd won because he'd been

standing right beside Ray, telling the young pup how to
outmaneuver the other boats.

The music stopped and Frank Porter stepped up to the
mike on the flatbed, calling for everyone's attention.
"Gather 'round, folks," he said into the microphone,
wincing when it squealed back at him. "The fireworks are
set to start in ten minutes, but first we have someone
who wants to make an announcement. Willow?" he said,
pointing the mike at her.

Willow took a deep breath, smiled at an obviously
confused Duncan, and stretched up and kissed him on
the cheek. "Don't go away. I think you'll want to hear
this," she said, turning and rushing through the crowd.

She ran up the stairs made from stacked crates, took
the microphone from Frank, and leaned up and gave him
a quick kiss on the cheek. Then she turned to the crowd
of people looking up at her, smiled, and took another
deep breath.

"First, I'd like for all of us to give a big round of ap-
plause for Frank Porter, Ray Cobb, and Cecil Fox. Because of them, our local lobster industry is safe and some
very bad people are facing many, many years in jail.
These three brave men are the true definition of *heroes*,"
she finished, tucking the mike under her arm and clapping as she faced Frank, who was blushing redder than a
cooked lobster.

Ray was pushed forward in the crowd, and he made
sure he was dragging Gramps along with him. The townspeople went nuts for a good five minutes, clapping and
whistling and shouting cheers of appreciation. Frank finally couldn't handle it anymore, and went running
down the stairs to hide behind his wife. Gramps and Ray

also disappeared into the crowd until the clapping finally died down and all eyes turned back to Willow.

"Okay. That was my first item of business. My second item is to let you all hear it directly from me rather than from the gossip mill that I'm moving back to Puffin Harbor in September and opening up a private law practice here in town."

"What about your AG job?" someone in the crowd shouted. "We thought you wanted to run for governor in a few years."

"Well, I thought I did, too," Willow admitted. "But I've decided I'd rather help people individually. And maybe I'll try running for mayor of Puffin Harbor instead." She shot them a brilliant smile. "I promise, if you elect me mayor, that I will once and for all get to the bottom of whoever is replacing people's mailboxes. It's a federal crime to mess with someone's mailbox, and they should be brought to justice. And that puffin statue," she said, pointing at the eight-foot colorful puffin standing in the middle of the park. "That is blatant disregard for town property. And so, as your mayor, I would promise to solve the mystery of the 'Mailbox Santa Claus.'"

A murmur rose through the crowd, and it didn't at all sound friendly. "We don't want to know who's doing it," someone shouted. "I ain't got a new mailbox yet. If you catch them, then it stops. We like the *Mailbox Santa Claus.*"

The murmur rose in volume as well as in agreement.

"He struck again last night," someone else hollered. "Heard Duncan Ross got himself a new mailbox that looks like a castle."

"Why a castle?" someone else asked just as loudly, all eyes turning to Duncan.

" 'Cause he's a Scot," another voice answered. "They got lots of castles over there."

"We don't care if it is a federal crime. We won't vote for a mayor who's going to get the 'Mailbox Santa Claus' arrested," someone deep in the crowd hollered.

"Okay. Okay," Willow said into the mike, nodding behind her smile. "Then as your mayor I'll start a fundraiser instead, to get a granite base made for Puffy. If you all like him so much, how come you haven't gotten him a real base?"

"Because we don't want to offend the Santa Claus," someone else hollered. "We like Puffy just the way he is. Someone gold-leafed his name in the wood base, though. Didn't you notice?"

Willow nodded again. "Okay. We can keep the base. Then how about we get a granite monument for our fishermen?"

"That sounds better," someone said. Everyone nodded.

"Okay. Now I have something else I want to take up with you good folks," Willow said into the mike. "It's about this betting pool that's been going on around here."

The crowd went utterly silent.

Willow rolled her eyes. "Yes, I know about it. And you should all be ashamed of yourselves. Betting pools are illegal."

Someone snorted. "Heard you placed your own bet, missy."

Willow grinned sheepishly. "Okay, I did," she admitted. "But only because I was hoping to teach you all a lesson."

She had to signal them to be quiet and listen, though it took her a good two minutes to get them to stop laughing.

"Listen up. The pool is now officially closed. As of—"

"You can't do that! It ain't been decided who won!" another voice shouted from the back of the crowd.

Willow held up her hand. "I am about to announce who won," she told them, not even bothering to speak into the mike but yelling instead. "And those of you who bet on the wrong person had better not be sore losers," she continued to shout. "Someone always has to lose when you gamble."

"Well, who won!" Cecil Fox shouted. "A good chunk of my retirement fund is at stake here."

"What!" Willow yelped, gaping at him. "Cecil, are you crazy?"

He suddenly smiled up at her. "Crazy like a fox, girlie. Come on, spit it out. Are you going to marry the guy or not?"

Willow felt her face flush with heat as she sought out Duncan in the crowd. She held the mike back up to her mouth and spoke quietly.

"I've been told that to have a wedding, someone's got to propose," she said softly. She took a deep breath and held out her hand beseechingly. "So, Duncan Ross, would you do me the honor of marrying me?"

There was utter and total silence for a full minute, as everyone turned to look at Duncan, their collective breaths held in their chests and their purse strings held in his answer.

It was the longest minute of Willow's life.

"Aye," came Duncan's softly spoken but definitely heard reply. "I'll marry ya, counselor."

There were several more heartbeats of silence, then as one the crowd roared into boisterous cheer. People actually started jumping in place and hugging each other, and several began urging Duncan toward the flatbed, slapping his back and wishing him congratulations. He took the crate stairs two at a time, swept Willow into his arms, and kissed her—quite passionately—right there in front of God, the townspeople, and his mother.

The crowd went wild, catcalling and whistling and egging him on, clapping so loud it sounded like thunder.

Willow suddenly broke away, turned to the crowd, and held up the mike. "Hey! Wait a minute!" she shouted, wincing when the mike screeched back. She held it a bit farther away. "How come you're all cheering?" she asked, glaring at them. "Most of you lost your money."

They stopped clapping, went silent, and just stared up at her. A few of their faces got red. Some of them scuffed their feet and looked everywhere but at her.

Willow gasped, the sound carrying through the mike and getting amplified by the speakers. "Did any of you bet on me!" she asked in a growl. She thumped her chest. "I'm your town daughter, and you bet against me?"

"But us winning means you win, too, Willy," someone she didn't recognize said. "You get Duncan."

"We'll still vote for you if you run for mayor," someone else piped up. "You can't be mad just because we all know a sure thing when we see it."

"Yeah," someone else said. "And we seen two people who ought to be together. We knew it was just a matter of time before you realized that."

Someone else snickered. "Only them fools over to Trunk Harbor bet on you. It's their money we're taking."

Willow was struck speechless. There wasn't one loser in the crowd. Not one person in Puffin Harbor had placed their money on her. She didn't know whether that was an insult or a sign that they truly cared for her.

Duncan slowly pulled the mike out of her limp hand, let it slide to the floor, and took her back into his arms. He shot the crowd a purely masculine, tigerlike grin, and then leaned down and covered her mouth in a kiss that set the crowd roaring again, this time to the backdrop of fireworks going off over the Puffin Harbor breakwater.

Plan Leap of Faith was certainly concluding with a bang, Willow decided. And with the approval of some very happy, newly wealthy townspeople.

Pocket Star Books
Proudly Presents

Only with a Highlander

Janet Chapman

Available in Paperback
October 2005

Turn the page for a preview of
Only with a Highlander. . . .

Winter MacKeage lost the thread of the conversation the moment the large male figure stepped into view. Rose continued talking, however, oblivious to the fact that the most gorgeous man ever to set foot in Pine Creek had just stopped to look at the painting hanging in the front window of Winter's art gallery.

"Tell her I'm right," Rose demanded, nudging Winter's arm. "Tell Megan that no one is whispering behind her back. Hey," Rose said more loudly, grabbing Winter's sleeve to draw her back into the conversation. "Your sister thinks everyone in town pities her."

Winter looked away from the divine apparition in the window and blinked at Rose, trying to remember what they had been talking about.

Rose sighed. "Darn it, Winter, help me out here. Tell Megan she's not the center of town gossip."

Winter finally looked into her sister's tear-washed eyes. "Oh, but everyone is talking about ya, Meg," she said, nodding. "But only because ya walk down the street looking like a rag doll that's been left out in the rain all summer."

"That's not helping," Rose snapped, using her grip on Winter's sleeve to nudge her.

Winter stepped away, crossed her arms under her breasts, and ignored Rose in favor of glaring at Megan. "Ya always have such a long face, it's a wonder ya don't trip on your own chin. And your eyes are sunken in your head, you're as pale as snow, and ya scuffle along like a beaten puppy." Winter reached out and touched her sister's hunched shoulder. "Pregnancy is not a disease, Meg," she continued more gently. "Nor is it the end of the world. The only one pitying ya around here is you. And if ya don't soon quit, your bairn will be born with a permanent pout."

Megan MacKeage swiped at her flushed face and met Winter's tender smile with a fierce glare. "You can say that when *your* heart gets broken," Megan hissed, "and you come running home because the love of your life walked out when you told him you're having his baby."

Winter took hold of Megan's shoulders and leaned close. "I love ya, Meg. Mama and Papa love ya. Rose loves ya. Everyone here in Pine Creek loves ya. That one stupid jerk in a thousand loving people *doesn't*, is not worth what you're putting yourself through. Wayne Ferris is a conniving weasel who's too stupid to appreciate what a wonderful woman ya are. Ya have to let him go, Meg, and focus on your child. Being depressed and crying all the time will make your unborn bairn think ya don't want it."

Megan moved her gaze past Winter's shoulder, looking at nothing, her lower lip quivering and her eyes misting again. "I thought he loved me," she whispered, looking back at Winter through eyes filled with despair. "He said he loved me."

"He loved what ya could do for his career," Winter told her just as softly, gently squeezing her shoulders. "But careers that have ya camping out on the tundra for months at a time do not mix well with babies. That Wayne chose—"

The tiny bell on the gallery door tinkled, drawing everyone's attention. Just as Winter began to turn, she noticed that Rose was staring at the door in utter disbelief.

Megan's eyes had gone equally as wide and her jaw had gone slack.

Winter spun fully around and actually took a step back. Who wouldn't feel a punch in the gut when finding herself in the presence of such incredibly virile . . . maleness? The man was just too stunning for words.

Which seemed to be an immediate problem for Winter, as she couldn't even respond when the tall, handsome stranger nodded at her—though she did hear Rose sigh, and she did feel Megan poke her in the back.

"Ah, may I help ya," Winter finally said.

Enigmatic, tiger-gold eyes met hers, and it took all of Winter's willpower not to take another step back. The man was standing just inside her spacious gallery, yet he seemed to fill up the entire space.

"Is the painting in the window by a local artist?" he asked.

The deep, rich timbre of his voice sent a shudder coursing through Winter, and another sharp poke in her back started her breathing again. "Ah, yes," she said. "She lives right here in Pine Creek." Winter waved a hand at the east wall of her gallery. "Most of the paintings are hers. Everything we sell is by local artists," she finished in a near whisper, unable to stop staring at his beautifully rugged, tanned face.

He simply stared back, his eyes crinkled in amusement.

"Feel free to look around," she added with another half-hearted wave, thankful that her voice sounded normal this time. "I can answer any questions ya have."

"Thank you," he said with a slight nod before turning to the wall of paintings.

As soon as he looked away, Winter spun around to face Megan and Rose. Neither woman noticed her warning glare, however, as they were too busy gawking at the man. Worried that he'd turn around and catch them, Winter grabbed them both by an arm and hustled them ahead of her into the back room.

"Cut it out," she quietly hissed. "You're being rude."

"Did you see how broad his shoulders are?" Rose whispered, craning around to look back at the gallery.

Winter moved the three of them farther away from the door. "Rose Dolan Brewer, you're a happily married woman with two kids. Ya shouldn't be noticing other men's shoulders."

Rose smiled. "I can still look, as long as I don't touch."

"Did you see his hair?" Megan whispered, her eyes still wide, not a trace of a tear anywhere in sight. "He's wearing a suit that probably cost more than my entire wardrobe, but he's got a ponytail. What sort of businessman has long hair?"

"And those eyes," Rose interjected before Winter could respond. "They're as rich as gold bullion. My knees went weak when he looked at you, Winter."

"That does it. Out," Winter said, crowding them toward the door that connected the back office of her gallery with Dolan's Outfitter Store. "You're going to scare off my most promising customer today."

Rose snorted and stepped into her store, combing her fingers through her short brown hair. "I doubt anything could scare that man," she muttered, smoothing down her blouse as she turned to Winter. "Send him over to my store after," she said with a cheeky grin. "I'll, ah . . . fit him into more suitable clothes for around here."

"Do you suppose he came in on that plane that flew over?" Megan asked. "We saw it bank for a landing at the airport. It looked like a private jet." Megan sighed. "My God, he's handsome. Maybe I should stay and help you set out the figures Talking Tom brought in this afternoon."

Winter didn't have the heart to remind Megan that she had sworn off men—handsome or otherwise—when she'd ome home from her field work in Canada last month, bandoned and two months pregnant. It was rather nice to e her sister's face flushed from something other than ears.

"Thanks," Winter said with a tender smile, "but I think ll wait and put out Tom's carvings tomorrow."

Megan took one last look toward the gallery door, ghed, then followed Rose down the aisle of camping quipment. Winter softly closed the connecting door, ran er fingers through her own mass of long red curls, raightened to her full five-foot-six height with a calming reath, and headed back into the gallery.

Mr. Tiger Eyes was still facing the wall. He had worked is way down the wall to a painting hanging toward the ont of the store, his arms folded over his broad chest and is chin resting on one of his large, tanned fists. The pose ulled the material of his expensive suit tightly across a set f impressively wide shoulders. He glanced only casually at Vinter when she stepped up to the counter, then went ack to studying the painting.

He was looking at a large watercolor she had painted st spring, that she had titled Moon Watchers. It was a ighttime scene set deep in a mountain forest awash with oonlight. Three young bear cubs were gathered around a ick old rotting stump, their harried mother catching a uick nap as they played in the shadows. One of the cubs as perched precariously on top of the stump, its tiny out raised skyward as it brayed at the large silver disk in e star-studded sky, its siblings watching with enchanted xpressions on their moon-bathed faces. And if one stud- d the painting long enough, he or she would eventually otice all of the other nocturnal creatures hidden in the adows, curiously watching the young bears watching the oon.

It was a painting that usually drew the attention of

women more than men, what with its endearingly familial subject and somewhat playful and mystical mood.

Winter slid her gaze to the man standing in front of it.

He was at least as tall as her cousin Robbie MacBain, and Robbie was six-foot-seven in his stocking feet. This man's shoulders were equally as broad, his legs as long and muscled beneath that perfectly tailored suit, his hands just as large and blunt and powerful looking. He had the body of an athlete, which said that whoever he was, he didn't spend all of his time sitting in board rooms or merely shuffling papers around.

Like Megan, Winter found herself questioning his choice of hairstyle, if he truly was the successful businessman he appeared to be. His hair was thick and smooth and soft, neatly brushed off his face and tied at the nape of his neck with a thin piece of leather. It wasn't overlong; Winter guessed that when loose, it would fall just past his shoulders.

She suddenly realized she was staring just as rudely as Megan and Rose had been. With a silent sigh, Winter dropped her gaze to the small piece of paper on the counter that Tom had tossed down when he'd brought in his latest batch of wooden figures. It was a short list, Winter realized as she tried to focus on something other than her customer. Only five carvings this time, written in very neat, tiny black letters.

The first figure on the list was a chipmunk, and Tom had written one hundred and fifty dollars beside it. Next was a fox, which he'd priced at two hundred. Then swimming trout—four hundred dollars. Snowy owl—two hundred.

Winter smiled at the last figure listed—crow tending young in nest, priced at twelve hundred dollars.

Tom, or Talking Tom as he was affectionately known to the locals, carved a lot of crows. And he always demanded a higher, if not sometimes ridiculous, price for them. The amazing thing was, Winter had sold quite a few of Tom's crows in her gallery over the last two years. It seemed the more expensive something was, the more desperately the tourists wanted it.

Talking Tom. He was at least seventy years old, had simply appeared in Pine Creek one bright April morning three years ago, and kept mostly to himself. Not much was known about him, other than the fact that he could be heard talking to himself when he walked the woods—thus the nickname Talking Tom. He was also quite good at tending sick animals, and the townsfolk had gotten in the habit of bringing their ailing pets to him rather than traveling the forty miles to the nearest veterinarian.

As far as Winter knew, Tom had never mentioned his last name to anyone. He had appeared seemingly from nowhere and taken up residence in an old, abandoned cabin just east of town, on Bear Mountain, which rose above the eastern shore of Pine Lake.

Winter had immediately taken to Tom, having recognized a kindred spirit. Like her, Tom endowed the forest and its creatures with a sense of magic and mystery, and his carefully carved wooden figures, like her paintings, were often more mystical than realistic.

It had taken Winter nearly a year to persuade Tom to let her sell his delicate figures in her gallery. His wants and needs seemed to be minimal, and a good deal of the money he did earn from his carvings was often spent on others. When he was in town, Tom could usually be found in Dolan's Outfitter Store, and every female—from birth to ninety-nine years old, married or single—would leave the store with a box of chocolates. Rose had started ordering chocolate by the caseload, once she realized Tom's penchant for spoiling the ladies always kept her in short supply.

"Does she do commissions?"

Winter looked up on an indrawn breath. How could she have forgotten she had a customer in the store? Especially this customer. "Excuse me?" she asked.

"The artist," he said, nodding toward the wall of paintings. "Does she take commissions?"

"Ah, yes. Yes, I'll take commissions."

One of his dark, masculine brows arched. "These are your paintings," he clarified softly, more to himself than her as he looked back at the wall. He studied the large watercolor for another moment in silence, then turned fully to face her, his deep golden gaze locking on hers. "I'll take *Moon Watchers*," he said. "But I would like to leave it here until I have a wall to hang it on."

Winter drew her own brows together in confusion. "A wall to hang it on?" she repeated.

He took several steps toward her, then stopped, his mouth lifting in a crooked smile that slammed into Winter like another punch in her gut. It was the smile of a cajoling little boy, and it didn't belong on a face that . . . that . . . *masculine*.

"I'm building here in Pine Creek," he explained, "and I would like to leave the painting with you until my home is finished." He nodded toward the wall without taking his gaze off hers. "You can keep it on display if you wish. That way I can come in and look at it whenever I want. Just put a sold sign in place of the price. Would that be okay?"

She had to stop staring into his eyes! She couldn't think, much less keep up with the conversation. Well, curses. She was acting sillier than Megan and Rose. Winter tore her gaze from his and searched the counter until she found her sales book under Tom's list. Then she found a pen.

Then she found her wits, and then her voice again. "I don't have a problem with ya leaving it here. Tell me, what is it that drew ya to Moon Watchers, Mr. . . . Mr. . . ." she trailed off, her pen poised to write his name at the top of the slip.

She looked up when he didn't immediately answer, and found him standing just two feet away, his golden eyes once again locking on hers. "It's Gregor," he said softly, his deep voice sending another shiver down her spine. "Matt Gregor. And I've always had a fondness for bears."

Okay, this was bordering on the ridiculous. He was only a guy. Granted, he was a stunningly gorgeous guy, but she was acting like she'd never even spoken with a man, much less been attracted to one. Winter again forced her gaze from his and wrote his name on the slip. She wrote the title of the painting, and then started to write the price beside it.

One large, unbelievably warm hand covered hers, and Winter stopped breathing. She looked up to find Matt Gregor smiling that little-boy smile again, and she could only helplessly smile back.

"Twenty percent discount if I take a second painting," he said, his beautiful, golden eyes sparkling with challenge. "I also want to buy that small watercolor of the panther."

Winter very slowly—trying very hard not to let him see how disconcerted his touch made her—slipped her hand from under his. "I'm sorry, but the panther's not for sale," she told him. "It's part of my personal collection. It's only on display because I had an empty space on the wall I wanted to fill."

Matt Gregor's expression instantly turned from that of a little boy to a fully engaged hunter. His eyes stopped smiling, their penetrating stare sending Winter's heart racing in alarm. "I'll pay as much for the panther as for Moon Watchers," he said with quiet force. "No discount on either."

Double curses! When he looked at her like that, she

wanted to *give* him every painting in the gallery—*especially* the panther. Winter just barely caught herself from snorting out loud. It was obvious Matt Gregor was used to getting what he wanted.

But then, so was she. "*Gesader* is not for sale," she told him, shaking her head to strengthen her words. "Choose something else that ya like, and I'll give ya a discount on it."

He leaned his weight back on his hips, crossed his arms over his chest, and studied her much the same way he had studied her paintings. Winter felt a warmth creep into her cheeks, but she stubbornly held his stare, determined not to let him see her discomfort. And she decided then that this would be a lesson to her—stunningly gorgeous didn't automatically mean nice. In fact, it could sometimes be downright rude.

Then again, it could also be exhilarating. Winter couldn't remember the last time she had felt this provoked by a man. Or this warm and fuzzy inside. Or this challenged.

She set down the pen and stepped from behind the counter, walking past Matt Gregor to the east wall of her gallery. She stopped in front of a tiny pastel drawing and crossed her arms under her breasts. "If ya like cats, I have this drawing of a Maine lynx."

She sensed him moving to stand beside her, but she continued to look at the drawing of a confounded lynx that was searching for the hare it had been chasing. In the background, its head just slightly showing above a snowdrift, was a perfectly camouflaged snowshoe hare watching the lynx. "If you're building a house here, Mr. Gregor, ya might consider works depicting local wildlife. We don't have panthers in Maine, but we do have lynx and bobcat and bear."

"Where did you come up with the name *Gesader?*" he asked, not addressing her suggestion.

Winter looked down the wall until her gaze fell on the small watercolor of the black leopard napping on a large tree limb, and she smiled affectionately. "It's Gaelic for 'Enchanter.'"

"Gaelic," Matt Gregor repeated, stepping around to face her. "I thought I detected a slight accent. Are you Irish?"

"Nay, Scots," she said in an exaggerated brogue. She nodded toward the information card pinned next to the drawing, and held out her hand. "Winter MacKeage."

His own hand swallowed hers up, his grip warm and firm but not overpowering. "My pleasure, Miss MacKeage." He lifted one brow again. "Or is it Mrs.?"

"Miss. But it's 'Winter' to my patrons."

His grip tightened only perceptibly. "I'm not a patron yet, Miss MacKeage. We haven't concluded our negotiations."

Winter forced herself to leave her hand in his. "Full price for *Moon Watchers*, and you can have *By a Hare's Breadth* for half price," she offered, nodding toward the lynx drawing.

Matt Gregor, still holding her hand, let out a soft sigh. "Nothing I offer you will get me that panther, will it?"

She finally slipped her hand free, tucked it behind her back, and rubbed her fingers together as she slowly shook her head. "I'm sorry, but he's not for sale. Do we have a deal?"

"Deal," he said, turning to look at the lynx drawing more closely. He pulled the tag from the wall, then moved over to *Moon Watchers* and pulled its tag. He walked back to the counter and set them down next to the sales slip she had started to fill out. Winter walked around to the back of the counter and picked up her pen.

"About that commission," he said when she started to write.

She stopped and looked up. "What is it ya want? I must warn ya, I don't do paintings of mechanical things."

He shifted back on his hips again, and folded his arms back over his chest. "It's not a painting I want from you, Winter MacKeage, but your vision."

Winter set down her pen. "Excuse me?"

"Your artist's eye," he said just as cryptically. "I want to commission you to pick the spot where I should build my home."

Winter could only stare at him.

"And then I want you to do a large watercolor of what that home should look like," he added.

She was thoroughly confused now. "What it should look like?" she repeated. "Ya mean, from the architectural drawings? But they usually give ya a model to look at."

He shook his head. "There are no drawings as yet. I intend to take your watercolor to the architects and have them design the house you envision, sitting on the spot you choose."

More than being confused, Winter was utterly speechless.

Matt Gregor let out another soft sigh, set both hands on the counter, and leaned toward her. "It's a simple request, Winter. I want your input into what I should build for a home, and where I should build it. I purchased Bear Mountain last month, and I want you to pick the best view of Pine Lake, as well as the best type of home for the land, because I've decided I like what you see and feel for the forest."

"But a home is a very personal thing."

"Yes," he readily agreed, straightening up and crossing his arms again. "But after spending a few days with me hiking my land, you'll get to know me well enough to come up with something I'll like."

Winter was no longer confused, she was back to being

alarmed. A sudden thought struck her. "Shouldn't your wife have some say in what ya build for a house?"

"I'm not married."

"Oh. Ah . . . well . . . I will have to think about your request. I'm an artist, Mr. Gregor, not an architect."

"It's Matt," he said softly, reaching inside his suit jacket and pulling out a slim, black leather wallet. "And I've explained that I'm not asking you to design my home, but to envision it and choose where it should sit." He pulled out a credit card and set it down on the counter next to the still incomplete sales slip. "I've taken a suite at The TarStone Ski Resort," he continued, pulling out a business card and setting it beside the credit card. "You can call my cell phone tomorrow morning at ten and give me your answer."

He then picked up the pen she'd been using, wrote SOLD in bold black letters on the back of the tag, and walked over and pinned it on the wall beside *Moon Watchers*. He came back, did the same to the tag for *By a Hare's Breadth*, and walked over and pinned it beside the drawing.

Winter finally finished writing out the sales slip, ran his card through her authorization machine, watched the credit slip print out, tore it off, and handed it to him to sign.

He scrawled his signature in bold letters, then took the credit card and receipt and slipped them in his wallet. "You have no problem with my leaving my paintings here?" he asked.

"No problem," she agreed. "So ya bought Bear Mountain, did ya? Are ya moving to Pine Creek, or just building a vacation retreat?"

"I'm building a home, but I haven't decided yet when I'll be moving here," he told her, tucking his wallet back inside his suit jacket. "That depends on my brother."

"Your brother?"

Matt Gregor smiled benignly, nodded, and turned and headed toward the door. He stopped and looked back. "I'll expect your call at ten in the morning, to tell me you've accepted the commission. Don't disappoint me, Winter. I don't take rejection well."

That said, he opened the door, walked out to the tinkle of the overhead bell, and disappeared down the street as quickly and mysteriously as he'd appeared.

Winter picked up the business card he'd set on the counter. Matheson Gregor, it read in solid green letters, with a New York City address but no mention of what type of business he was in. She looked over at *Moon Watchers*.

He had a fondness for bears, he'd told her.

And he'd just purchased Bear Mountain.

Another shiver ran down Winter's spine, but this time there was nothing warm and fuzzy about it. It hadn't been a tiger's eyes that had captured her attention this afternoon, but those of an equally impressive creature.

Matheson was Gaelic for "son of the bear."